OUT OF SIGHT

OUT OF SIGHT

T. J. MacGregor

PINNACLE BOOKS
Kensington Publishing Corp.

PINNACLE BOOKS are published by

Kensington Publishing Corp.
850 Third Avenue
New York, NY 10022

ISBN 0-7394-2868-3

Printed in the United States of America

DEDICATION

With much love to Rob, who helped shape it;
to Megan, who thought the idea was cool
and wanted to know what happens to the kid;
and to Phyllis Vega, who listened to every idea.

My deepest thanks to
Al Zuckerman and Kate Duffy,
the best agent and editor in the business.
Thanks also to Diego & the rest of the staff
at the Haciende Manteles in Ecuador.

PROLOGUE

October 10, 1998
Broward County, Florida

The hangar doors clattered shut with a finality that unsettled Logan Griffin. She fidgeted with the end of the silk scarf that held her blond hair in a ponytail and swallowed the remnants of the tiny pill that had been dissolving under her tongue. It left a bitter taste in her mouth, like limes mixed with cloves. It was the third dose she and Tyler had taken in the last twelve hours and was supposedly a necessity. No one had told them what it was. Such questions weren't allowed. That was in the contract.

She glanced over at Tyler. He seemed calm and probably looked that way to others. But the tension in her husband's jaw and the pinched wariness at the corners of his dark eyes told her that he felt uneasy. Not that he would ever admit it to himself or to her.

They were seated in the middle of the old hangar, in comfortable canvas chairs on a raised platform, their suitcases at their feet. They also wore backpacks stuffed with various items that George Nash had insisted they bring with them. It seemed excessive, but hey, she wasn't paying the bills. If Nash wanted them to bring mousetraps and birth control pills, she would do it. The project was his baby and he had paid her and Tyler thirty grand to be the first human guinea pigs.

That money would pay off some of their graduate school debt, allow them to update their car and move to a larger, more comfortable apartment. It would give them a cushion until they found jobs. They couldn't depend on Tyler's family for help and she had no family. They needed the money.

They had been told what the project involved and it had sounded exciting and cutting edge at the time. But now Logan was having serious second thoughts. Even though Nash had assured them repeatedly that they could back out at any time and keep half the money, she knew from the start that it really wasn't an option. They had signed too many legal documents with fine small print about liability issues. For thirty grand, they basically had signed away their rights to sue if something went wrong.

Nash and his assistant, Colleen Roth, had also assured them the process was reversible and that nothing would go wrong. And in private, Colleen had told Logan that if she really thought there was even a remote possibility that the procedure was risky, she wouldn't be involved. This little confidence had soothed Logan's misgivings at the time, but did nothing for her now.

Even though the temperature in the hangar stayed at a comfortable sixty-five degrees, her palms were damp, her shirt stuck to her back. She wished she and Tyler were inside the open cockpit bi-wing plane parked some fifty feet away, taxiing toward that the hangar door, about to soar through the blue skies above the South Florida peninsula. It was December and the thought of all that cool, sweet-smelling air held infinite appeal at the moment.

"You two know the routine," Nash said over the PA, his voice crisp and efficient despite the ridiculously early hour. "You'll hear a humming, the air may crackle, as if with static electricity, then there'll be a flash of light. At that point, you may feel some disorientation. Just breathe normally, stay seated, hold hands, do whatever roots you in the here and now. Any questions?"

Tyler took her hand, their fingers lacing together. "Not from us," he replied.

She envied the confidence in his voice, the apparent certainty. He brought her hand to his mouth and kissed one of her knuckles. With his other hand, he covered the mike attached to the collar of the shirt she had bought him for his birthday last month.

"An adventure," Tyler whispered. "Right?"

"Right." Logan looked over at him, Tyler with his big smile, his square jaw, and those dark eyes that looked rich enough to eat. "But, Tyler, if anything goes wrong . . ."

"I know, I know." He sounded exasperated. "We've been over this five million times, Logan."

She jerked her hand away from his. "We need a few minutes here, George." She spoke loudly into the mike attached to her jacket, then pinched the thing open and set it on top of her bulging suitcase so the people in the control room wouldn't overhear them.

"Sure, no problem," Nash replied.

Tyler also removed his mike and set it down. "What did you do *that* for?"

"I feel uneasy. There are *risks,* Tyler."

"Well, shit, we knew that four months ago. If we walk out, we lose the other fifteen grand."

"And if they turn on their gizmos, we may be zapped into never-never land."

He rolled his dark, beautiful eyes toward the ceiling, making it clear that he thought she was having eleventh-hour jitters, nothing more. "Look, they have all kinds of stringent rules and safeguards in place for this kind of research."

"Maybe so, but we're the *first,* so they really don't know." She gestured toward the side of the platform, where several Tesla coils were attached. "We don't know for sure what happens with those things."

"We've seen what happens, Logan. We've watched the experiments dozens of times."

Ha. They had watched experiments with *objects*—pens and pencils, gum, tools of all shapes and sizes, books, bottles of water, every conceivable type of inanimate object. But the only living thing they had seen undergo this process was a cockroach and that had happened accidentally. The bug was in the wrong place at the wrong time, and as the process had reversed itself, the cockroach had died.

Not exactly a rave review.

"They haven't even told us what's in these pills we've taken."

"They're probably just to take the edge off."

"But we don't know for *sure.* We don't know anything for *sure.* Suppose the process doesn't reverse itself?"

"Of course it will reverse itself." He sounded irritated now. "We've seen it happen over and over again. You're thinking about the roach, that what happened to it might happen to us."

"It could."

"There's nothing remotely similar between a roach and human beings, Logan."

"Are we ready, people?" Colleen's voice rang out in the cavernous hangar.

"Just about," Tyler called back. Then, to Logan: "If you're uneasy with this whole thing, then don't do it. I'll do it. The contract says we get paid as long as one of us participates."

Before Logan could say anything, George Nash limped out into the hangar from the control room. He was using his cane today, leaning heavily on it so that he could move more quickly. Colleen hugged his left side and to his right and slightly behind him stood a small man with hunched shoulders, a rich, olive complexion, and the features of a South American Indian. He had thick, black hair, long hair pulled into a ponytail. He continued to hang back as Nash and Colleen stopped just short of the platform. Logan knew she had seen the Indian before at the compound in northern Florida where she and Tyler had trained. But she'd thought he was just a *campesino,* one of the many migrant workers who tended the grounds. If that were the case, though, he certainly wouldn't be here, now.

"Well?" said George Nash. He fixed his hands to his hips.

He was an eccentric-looking man, Logan thought, very tall and lanky, with a wild, untamed beard streaked with gray. His right leg was apparently shorter than his left because he wore a special shoe with a stacked heel. Even with the shoe on, though, his limp was pronounced. His wire-rim glasses reflected twin points of light.

"Are we ready?" he asked.

"I am," said Tyler.

Nash stared at Logan, just daring her to back out. Tyler watched her, too, the weight of his gaze as heavy as a hand against her shoulder. "I'm ready," she finally said.

Nash smiled. "Excellent. The transponders attached to your shirts are already emitting a noise our radar will pick up, so don't worry about our losing you." He turned to the Indian. *"Luis? Tienes algo que decir?"*

The Indian gazed at Logan with dark eyes as ancient as the blood that rushed through his veins. She held his gaze, aware that something inexplicable and strange passed between them. *"Solamente una cosa. Esto no debe pasar."*

Logan's Spanish was basic, but she caught the gist of what the Indian said: *This shouldn't be allowed to happen.* It wasn't what she wanted to hear and it certainly wasn't what Nash wanted anyone to say in front of her and Tyler. He looked miffed and gave the Indian a dirty look. "Okay, let's start the sixty-second countdown now." Nash raised his arm and sliced it down through the air, signaling the control room to start the countdown. "Good luck," he added, and moved swiftly back toward the control room, Colleen hurrying alongside him.

The Indian remained still for a moment, watching them, watching her. "Who is that guy?" Tyler whispered.

"I don't know," she whispered back.

The Indian smiled slightly, then pulled something from the pocket of his baggy, faded cotton slacks and hissed, "*Chica, guardelo,*" and tossed something at her.

Logan caught it, her fingers closed over it. Then he turned away and she opened her fist and stared down at a small, flat rock with some sort of fossil embedded in it. She looked up quickly, but the Indian was already gone.

What's that? Tyler mouthed.

A stone, she mouthed back, and pocketed it before Nash or anyone else in the control room could see her holding something that hadn't been authorized.

Colleen, her voice calm and businesslike, had already started the countdown. "Twenty-one, twenty . . ."

Tyler reached for Logan's hand again and gave it a squeeze. "I'm glad you stayed," he whispered.

"It'd be worse sitting inside the control room."

He laughed. "Love you, Logan."

"Ditto," she replied, an echo of the line from their favorite movie, *Ghost.*

Those were the last words they spoke to each other before a piercing hum filled the air and the platform began to vibrate. She felt the vibrations through the soles of her feet and tightened her grasp on Tyler's hand. The hum escalated in pitch until it felt as if hot needles were being driven into her skull. She gritted her teeth and squeezed her eyes shut, but the noise got worse and she screamed and doubled over at the waist, hands pressed to her ears to block out the horrible noise.

The air exploded with light and for long, terrible moments she felt as if her body were being torn in opposite directions, the skin flaying, muscles ripping open, bones snapping like dry twigs. Her blood boiled, froze, then melted and froze again. Her brain screamed at her to leap up, to run, to flee, but her body paid no attention to her brain. It refused to move, couldn't move. She felt welded to the chair. She knew that she screamed, that she struggled to free herself from the paralysis that gripped her, but she didn't know if any sound came out.

Just as suddenly as the paralysis had seized her, it released her and she jumped up so fast that the mike and the transponder were torn away from her clothes. *"You lied,"* she shrieked. *"You lied about everything!"*

Logan stumbled over her suitcase, fell off the platform, and landed hard on her knees. As she heaved herself up, she spun around and grabbed her suitcase, dimly aware of voices shouting over the PA system, of people running toward her, of the strangeness of the light. Yes, that more than anything. Everything beyond her looked as though it were enveloped in a thick haze. But when she glanced back at Tyler, who stood unsteadily in front of his chair, his features seized up with puzzlement, the light seemed normal.

"Tyler, fast, we have to get outta here!" She shouted the words, but he didn't seem to hear them.

Logan ran toward the hangar door, dodging the technicians who dived for her, her panic so extreme that she never looked back, never slowed. Voices blasted over the PA, locks clattered into place on the hangar door, employees poured out of the control room area. She barreled toward an EXIT sign to her right and slammed through it, setting off alarms, bells, whistles.

She raced outside, into bright morning light that pierced her eyes like shards of glass. *Hide, fast, but where?* Fields of vegetables to her right, a wall of pines to her left, the road to nowhere straight in front of her. But on that road to nowhere was a Florida Power and Light truck, its two technicians staring toward the hangar.

Logan, still moving, glanced back. Nash, Colleen, and a dozen other people spilled from the hangar door as though the building were spitting them out. She forced herself to run faster, faster. Air burst from her mouth, blood pounded in her veins. The FP&L guys would help her. She couldn't scream, she didn't have the breath, so she waved her arms frantically to attract their attention, waved until her pack slid off her shoulder and down her arm and she nearly lost it. She kept racing toward them.

They didn't seem to see her. Or maybe they thought she was part of Nash's group. She didn't know, couldn't tell. She almost had reached the truck when she tripped and fell gracelessly forward and rolled down the soft grass, into a shallow gully, her suitcase tumbling down after her.

She rolled into weeds, rocks, discarded bottles and cans, a roadside dumping ground. Dazed, her side aching, her eyes burning from the light, she sat up and saw the FP&L workmen not three feet from her. They were looking straight at her, but neither of them moved.

"Hey," she wheezed. "Hey . . ."

The men looked at each other. "You hear something?" the taller one asked.

"Uh, yeah. Must be those wackos from the hangar."

"Sounded closer than that."

JesusGod. No wonder I got away.

Logan shot to her feet, hoisted her bag to one shoulder and her pack to the other, and moved quickly toward the road, the waiting truck. She put her bags inside as quietly as she could, then climbed in, settling among the cables, the ropes, the tools. She gazed toward the hangar, across what now seemed like a vast distance separating her from Nash and his people and from Tyler.

Tyler, forgive me, I'm sorry, sweet Christ, I'm so sorry. But I can't go back in there.

The shrouding had worked.

Something broke inside her then, something huge and irreparable, and she sank down against her bags, hands covering her eyes, and wept for what Nash had done to her, to Tyler, to their marriage. She wept for her own stupidity, for trusting someone she didn't know.

She could feel pain. She could cry. She could feel discomfort, hunger, anguish, fear. None of that had changed. What had changed, she thought, was the most obvious thing.

She was completely invisible.

PART ONE

INTO THE BELLY
OF THE BEAST

JUNE 8-9, 2001

". . . consciousness thinks it's running the shop.
But it's a secondary organ of a total human
being, and it must not put itself in control. It must
submit and serve the humanity of the body."
—Joseph Campbell

1
THE TOWNSENDS

Fort Lauderdale, Florida

Renie Townsend believed in signs—not the road variety, but those that seemed to rise unbidden from some place within the hidden order of things. And on June 8, all the signs seemed to be pointing to the same thing, that she should stay home and let her husband and daughter head out together on their camping trip to the Everglades.

Ordinarily, this wouldn't be a difficult choice. Renie hated camping. The bugs, the hard ground, the sleeping bags that stank of mothballs, the flimsy tent, the absence of lights and air-conditioning and a decent bathroom: it spelled disaster in her book. Youth hostels were fine when you were eighteen, but she was forty-four and liked her creature comforts. It seemed, though, that for the last six months, she and Andy and Katie had been running in opposite directions from morning till night. Now that school was finally out, Andy had gotten some time off from the ER and they had a chance to spend a long weekend together.

She had been hoping for a resort somewhere and, if not that, then at least a motel on the beach up the coast. But Katie had informed her in that blithe, offhanded way endemic to young teens that she and her dad were going camping in the Everglades. And they hadn't asked her if she wanted to come. That was what had prompted her to say she was going, too.

You'll hate it, Mom, Katie had said. *Bugs, humidity, snakes, the hard ground . . .*

I'm going.

As it turned out, the camping trip wasn't just a critical turning point in their lives. It was the worst decision they ever made.

2

The first sign happened shortly after eight that morning.

Andy was outside, loading the Jeep, and Renie was standing in front of the fridge, wondering what else she could jam in the cooler. Did she have time to run up to Publix to buy a new, larger cooler? Would there be room in the canoe for three people, two coolers, and all their camping gear? Probably not. But Christ, she had to have cold water, lots of it. Never mind that the ice would be melted by tomorrow morning. As long as it lasted, cold water would go a long way toward mitigating other physical discomforts.

She flipped open the lid on the cooler, wondering how the hell they were going to lug this thing through the Everglades. But she couldn't remove anything. Tonight they would have the cold chicken she'd baked and the potato salad she'd made and a can of baked beans. Camping food, for sure. She had grapefruits and cereal with milk and fresh strawberries for herself and Andy for breakfast and the usual coffee yogurt for Katie. She had bread for tuna fish sandwiches tomorrow for lunch. That left canned shit for dinner tomorrow night because by then the ice would be melted. No point in packing anything for tomorrow night, she thought, and removed the hot dogs and veggie burgers.

I'm going to be an insane woman by Sunday morning.

No, no, no. It would be fine. She would do okay on this little jaunt into the wilderness. She would slather herself in insect repellent and turn on the little reading light that clipped right on to the book, and make sure that she was having a *good time.*

And that was when Katie started screaming.

Until just then, Renie never had understood the phrase *bloodcurdling scream.* But that's what this was, a sound so primal that she felt it in her cells, her blood, at the very core of her being. As she slammed open the French doors to the back porch, she had visions of Katie lying on the ground next to her trampoline, her spine broken, her body paralyzed from the neck down. She had visions of Katie lying at the bottom of the swimming pool, her hair drifting like pale seaweed around her.

She exploded through the porch door and the humidity struck her instantly, air of a texture like cotton. The screaming collapsed into shrieks.

In the morning light, the pool looked tranquil, inviting, not even a ripple on the surface. She knew even before she could see the bottom that Katie hadn't fallen in. The surface was too still, too perfect. She rounded the corner of the house, where the trampoline was, and spotted her daughter. Katie wasn't on the ground. She was standing at the fence, her back to Renie. *Not dead, not injured, she's okay . . .*

So why the hell was she screaming like that?

"My God, Katie, what's going on?"

Katie's head whipped around, horror frozen in her eyes, one hand stabbing at something Renie couldn't see, the other plastered against her mouth. She was trying to stifle her cries and they sounded like great, heaving hiccups.

Renie stopped beside her, struggling to catch her breath, to stem the assault of adrenaline that now raced through her body. She followed her daughter's fingers to the grass, where a tiny bird lay on its back, chest moving up and down so fast that Renie knew it was dying. She knew it before she saw the foam caked at its beak, knew it before she slid her hands up under it and felt its heartbeat faltering.

"It's . . . it's dying, oh God, Mom, it's dying," Katie wailed. "Do something. It's in pain."

Give her something to do, get her out of here. "A shoe box, get me a shoe box from my closet and an old towel, a soft towel. Quick, go, go . . ."

Katie took off and Renie, with the bird now lying in her cupped hands, rocked back onto her heels. She raised her hands to the light, so she could see the bird better. It was such a little thing, a baby mockingbird, and it probably had fallen out of its nest somewhere at the top of the tall ficus tree to her left. Or perhaps the mother had pushed it out of the nest because it was sick. She knew from experience that wild birds rarely survived such injuries.

Over the years, she and Katie had rescued injured doves, ducks, crows, and all but the ducks had died. Baby birds often took a long time to die, hours of excruciating writhing and wheezing while their organs shut down. She didn't want to bring this little mockingbird along in their canoe, on their camping trip, not in a shoe box or any other kind of container. It was already suffering more than she could bear. So she did for the bird what she had done for her father. She moved her hand in small, tight circles over its little head, opening the energy center, making it easier for its spirit to depart. Then she pressed her thumb and index fingers over the slits that served as its nostrils and, with her other hand, gently closed its little beak.

It was over in seconds, the suffering done, the life gone.

She started to cry, she couldn't help it. She cried and

closed her hand over the little bird and waited for her daughter to return with the shoe box.

3

She and Katie buried the little bird in the backyard, in among the marigolds, the violet Mexican heather, the flaming vines. Other pets they had lost over the years were also buried here, the Townsend pet cemetery.

Katie patted the dirt with her hands and made a cross out of twigs. "At least it died fast," she said. "I . . . I just couldn't stand seeing it suffer like that."

"When we get back from this camping trip, we'll buy a new plant for the grave."

"Something blue."

"Perfect."

"Did you talk to Dad yet about getting a dog?"

"I'm planning to do it on this camping trip."

Pets were a touchy subject. During her and Andy's sixteen years together, they'd had all sorts of animals, from hamsters, guinea pigs, and mice to cats and birds. But each adoption was preceded by ranting and raving from Andy, who invariably listed all the rational reasons why they shouldn't have this pet or that pet. He eventually came around, but Renie had learned that half the battle was timing. Andy seemed to believe that *someone* had to object, to present an opposing viewpoint, so once he'd done it, then it was okay to join the tribe. She figured this trip would be the perfect opportunity. Right now, they were without animal companions and as Katie entered her teen years, pets might mitigate some of the problems she and Andy were anticipating. That would be her argument, anyway.

"C'mon, we'd better get our stuff. Your dad's probably wondering where that cooler is going to fit in the Jeep."

The screen door slammed open then and Andy called, "Hey, Renie, where's this cooler supposed to fit?"

Renie and Katie glanced at each other and laughed as they stood up. "It can go under my feet, Dad."

"What's so funny?" he asked, eyeing them both suspiciously as they strode toward him.

"Mom was just saying that you were probably wondering where the cooler would fit."

He smiled at that, a quick smile that lit up his blue eyes and reminded her of all the reasons she loved him. At nearly six and a half feet tall, Andy was more than half a foot taller than Renie. Like many very tall people, he had a slight stoop to his shoulders, a dead giveaway that he'd gone through his early school years feeling self-conscious about his height. He was the tallest doctor on the hospital staff, the tallest person among their friends. Katie apparently had inherited the tall gene, as they referred to it, because she was already five feet six inches. But she enjoyed her height, enjoyed the edge she thought it gave her, and never hunkered over to make herself less noticeable.

"So what was going on over there by the pet cemetery?" Andy asked once they were in the kitchen.

Katie told him about the baby bird. Andy slung one of his long arms around his daughter's shoulders and planted a kiss in the middle of her forehead. "If you really decide to become a vet, kiddo, you're going to have to develop a thicker skin."

"Maybe I'll just be an animal documentary filmmaker. Jeez, I'll be right back. I forgot my video camera."

"And her *I Ching for Kids*," Renie murmured.

"So what's the Ching say about this trip?"

Renie shrugged. "Beats me." She rarely had any idea what the *I Ching* hexagrams meant. Hell, she couldn't even interpret the simplified Ching for kids. Her mind simply couldn't wrap itself around archaic Chinese thought.

Besides, she didn't have to use the Ching to know she would be happier staying home.

"My God," Andy groaned as he picked up the cooler. "This feels like it has bricks in it."

"I even took out some stuff."

"We won't need all this, Ren."

"Ha. You'll see. I'm going to bring the little cooler, too. Just for more bottled water," she added quickly.

Andy just shook his head, as if to say she was a hopeless case, and headed for the garage door, struggling with the cooler.

When they finally hit the road, Andy handed Renie his pocket notepad and asked her to jot down the time and mileage. Mr. Organized, she thought with a touch of envy.

"It's a good idea if we keep track of all our stuff, just so we don't forget anything at the campsite," Andy said.

"I'll call out the stuff, you make the list, Mom."

This routine happened at the beginning of every vacation. Andy simply had to take inventory. Renie didn't know if the roots of this habit lay in medical school or in Andy's childhood, but either way, it drove her crazy at times. She was the most *dis*-organized person she knew. Leave her alone in a tidy room for about five minutes and when she walked out, there would be clutter everywhere. Her desk at work was constantly strewn with folders and papers and notes to herself. Yet, she usually was able to find what she needed when she needed it, and in her seventeen years in real estate, had never blown a deal because she had lost a file or papers.

Renie suddenly couldn't remember if she'd packed her toothbrush and toothpaste. There was nothing worse than going through a day with your teeth feeling as if they had moss growing on them. As soon as the list was done, Renie handed Andy his notebook and searched her purse, then her backpack for the toothbrush. Not there. She asked Katie to look through her bag, but she didn't find a toothbrush, either.

"We have to stop somewhere so I can buy a toothbrush and toothpaste, Andy."

Andy glanced at the clock on the dashboard and shook his head. "No time. We left an hour late, it's a two-hour drive to the park, and it'll take us another three hours of paddling to get to the campsite, depending on the wind. You can use mine."

"Gross, Dad."

"I don't want to use yours. I want my own."

"Okay, okay. As soon as we see someplace, I'll stop."

Yeah? Which exit? They were already speeding west and the farther west they went, the less of everything there was. Out here, she would be lucky if anyone even knew what the hell a toothbrush was. And what was the deal with the three hours of paddling once they put the canoe in the water? That meant Andy had some specific spot in mind, probably a place where he and Katie had gone on one of their frequent camping trips together, some hidden nook no one else knew about.

Thirty minutes later, they pulled into a place called Last Stop Quik Stop with a single rusted pump. Potholes riddled the parking lot and the window of the store looked to be covered with several years' worth of grime and dirt.

"This place doesn't inspire my confidence in the human race," Renie muttered as she and Katie got out.

Katie wrinkled up her nose. "I'm not using the rest room *here*."

Inside, an old geezer with an unshaven jaw sat behind the counter, paging through a tabloid. "Mornin'," he said. "Help you ladies wit' something?"

"Do you carry toothbrushes?" Renie asked.

"Ayuh, sure, over there." He gestured off to the right.

A scrawny cat came out from behind the counter and rubbed up against Katie's legs. "What's your cat's name?"

"Stray."

"What?"

"Stray. She lives out yonder, in the fields. Comes in here to cool down."

Shit, Renie thought, and wandered over to the right side of the store to look for a toothbrush. First the bird, now this. The universe seemed to be trying to tell her something.

She looked through rows of motor oil mixed with canned goods, camping supplies, and paper products. Then, on the very bottom shelf, she found the toiletry supplies: a box of tampons, two tubes of toothpaste, and a toothbrush in a container so dusty that she figured it had been in this same spot for as long as the Last Stop had existed. But it was better than brushing her teeth with her finger. She grabbed the toothbrush and a tube of toothpaste and hurried to the counter, where Katie and the scrawny cat already had bonded.

"Girl's a nat'ral with animals," the geezer remarked.

"Yes, she is. I'll take these."

"That's eight-fifty."

"For *this?*"

"Yes, ma'am."

Thief, she thought, and handed him a ten.

Less than twenty-four hours later, when their lives had veered into the unthinkable, Renie would be deeply grateful for that toothbrush and toothpaste. In fact, she would consider the eight bucks and change to be one of the best last-minute purchases she had ever made. She also would recognize the toothbrush episode, as it came to be known in the family history, as the second sign that she ignored.

4

When she and Katie exited the store, the Jeep was nowhere in sight. It was one of those surreal moments, when Renie felt as if she had stumbled off the track of her own life and into some other place. Then she spotted the Jeep parked at the side of the building, the rear hatch open, Andy digging around inside, some of their stuff lying on the ground.

"Uh-oh." Katie rolled her eyes. "This looks—"

"Like another sign that I should've stayed home," Renie finished.

The left rear tire on the Jeep was flat.

2
THE TESLA PROJECT

Throughout the brief chopper flight to the Everglades village, Dog whined and howled and threw herself against the sides of her cage. *She knows,* thought George Nash. *She knows what the chopper means.*

"Dog's in a fierce mood." The voice of Wayne Dobson, the pilot and Nash's right-hand man, came through loud and clear on the headphones.

"Can't blame her. This will be trip number twelve into the zone."

"Actually, boss, I think it's trip thirteen."

He was probably right. Dobson was a numbers man. For years, he had been keeping track of the project's minutia, all the stuff that slipped through the cracks in Nash's world. When things went wrong, Dobson cleaned up the mess. None of this was part of his job description, he simply did it because he was good at it. He didn't write anything down, either. He had one of those steel-trap minds that captured information that interested him.

In fact, Dobson knew nearly as much about the Tesla

Project as Nash did and never had given Nash cause not to trust him. Yes, he was paid very well for what he did. But money wasn't what motivated Dobson. He was here because he was as intrigued by shrouding as Nash was.

"Hey, Colleen," Nash said into his mike. "I thought you gave Dog some Dramamine."

"I did. I don't think the stuff works on her anymore."

"Then you'd better find something else that works." He sounded exactly like he felt, cross and irritable.

"I'm working on it," she snapped back.

Nash rubbed his aching leg and wished he'd worn the brace today. Lately, his leg had been giving him a lot of trouble and he knew it was due to stress, not to any change in the weather. The cane helped him balance when he walked, but he couldn't use the cane out in the Glades, not without looking like the cripple he was.

He had contracted polio when he was three years old and although his case was considered to be relatively mild at the time, it had left his right leg several inches shorter than his left. Sometimes at night when the leg ached, it woke him from a sound sleep and he spent hours soaking in a hot bath and talking to his leg, talking to it as though it were a separate entity with a life and will of its own. He often bargained with his leg—*if you stop hurting, I'll treat you to a Swedish massage*—and when bargaining didn't work, he got mad. He just kept moving and moving and moving, shutting himself away from the discomfort and the pain until it finally crashed over him, forcing him into bed. He hated his leg. But at the moment, he couldn't afford to have it fail him, not out here. So he massaged it and spoke to it in his head, assuring his leg that it would have some time off later this evening.

When the ache subsided, Nash shifted around in the passenger seat to look at Colleen. She sat in the backseat, an arm flung over the edge of it so she could grasp the cage's handles to keep it from sliding around in the well behind her. She glared at him, her pale green eyes like those of a cat, her lovely face now eaten up with annoyance. After all, he had pulled rank in front of someone else. Unforgivable in her book. Later, when this test run was over and they had time to be alone again, he would pay for his outburst. She might wrench away from him when he started to draw his fingers through the cascade of her luxurious black hair. Or if he suggested they get together, she might say she was busy. Or, even worse, she might be more blatant about it and turn away from him in bed.

Then again, she might not do any of those things. She was hard to figure at times. She had ambition, but she could be lazy. She had a profound sexual appetite, but sex didn't rule her life. She was bright and innovative, but not arrogant. No question that he loved her more than he had ever loved his wife. She didn't seem to notice his bum leg, his limp. His wife did, but Colleen never had. Love wasn't the issue. But sometimes, like right now, he didn't like her very much.

As his assistant, one of her jobs was the dog. She was supposed to keep Dog comfortable, fed, exercised, and she was responsible for drawing the animal's blood, spinal fluid, and everything else they needed for the lab tests. When they brought Dog out here and then transported her back to Homestead again, Colleen was supposed to sedate the animal enough so that she would remain tranquil.

At forty, Colleen was ten years younger than Nash, a looker by anyone's standards. She'd worked for him for six years, and for the last three, they had been lovers. Dobson knew it, of course, and although he'd never offered his opinion, Nash knew he didn't approve. At the moment, Nash wasn't so sure that he approved of the relationship, either.

Lately, the personal part of this equation had become a problem because *she* took advantage of it. She had dentist appointments, doctor appointments, hair appointments. In the past few months, it seemed she had been absent from

work more than she had been present, which had added to
his already considerable workload.

"Do you have any other tranks with you?" he asked.

"Yeah. I've got a couple of other things I can try. But
not until we're in the village. I can't do it in here or on the
airboat."

Dog's whimpers stopped, almost as if she were listening
to them, Nash thought. *Almost likes she understands every
goddamn word we say.* He didn't like the dog, never had.
He didn't like dogs, period. They slobbered, they drooled,
they could turn feral any second. But they made better test
subjects than cats, which were too unpredictable, too inde-
pendent. In the three years since the Logan and Tyler fiasco,
the project's use of live animals had been confined to reptiles,
rodents, birds, and a couple of cats. Dog was the first animal
to be used repeatedly in the shrouding tests.

She was a two-year-old black Lab that Colleen had picked
up at the pound about a year ago. She was smart, well
trained, and back then, eager for human companionship, an
ideal animal for experimentation. The first time she had gone
into the zone, out there in the village, everything had gone
without a hitch. The shrouding had held for three days before
she began to materialize again.

As she became progressively more solid, however, she'd
gotten sick. The blood tests had revealed some sort of anom-
aly, a virus that had lain dormant until the shrouding had
triggered it. Before her second trip into the zone, they had
bolstered her immune system with all sorts of antibiotics.
She still had gotten sick afterward, but not as badly.

After the fourth shrouding, she had gotten loose at the
project's Ponce compound and had been found in a field,
eating grass. The grass turned out to be wheat grass and it
had cured her of the *shrouding sickness,* as Luis had called
it. Nash always had detested that name, perhaps because he
wanted to believe that shrouding had no detrimental side

effects. But the name had stuck and they continued to refer to the side effects as such even though Luis was long gone, back to the Ecuadorian Andes where he belonged.

After half a dozen shroudings, the process had changed Dog in complex ways. She was no longer eager for human companionship. Her behavior was unpredictable. Sometimes she materialized in a matter of hours, other times it took days. They never knew which it would be and didn't have a clue why it happened. Nash suspected that Luis might know, but pride had prevented him from getting in touch with the old man. After all, Luis had left the project because he'd believed that Nash was meddling with ''forces and powers best left to God.''

God. Right. Like God had anything to do with it.

And the brass at the NSB sure wasn't thinking about God. They didn't give a shit about God. They had seen the dog videos, Dog fading, Dog materializing, and a couple of them had witnessed the actual process. They were impressed enough to keep the funding flowing. But they also were pressuring him for more. They wanted human subjects. They wanted concrete results and applications. They were chafing at their collective bit to cash in on the research and use it for their own agendas.

Invisible aircraft, invisible battleships, invisible spies. The future had not only arrived, it lay in the sweaty, grubby paws of the bastards who ran the country. Nash could hold them off awhile longer, but ultimately they would win. *You can't fight city hall,* his mother used to say. Like her other well-worn aphorisms, this one had gotten old quickly. Unfortunately, it also happened to be true. Nash's city hall, though, was more than he had bargained for ten years ago, when he desperately needed funding and Ross Farris had approached him with a deal.

He rubbed his eyes and wished he were in Europe with his wife.

2

The chopper came in low over the mangroves, mile after mile of greens checkered with blues, browns, tans. The drought had hit the Everglades hard, that was evident from the air. The peninsula was down sixty inches in rainfall for the year. Lake Okeechobee, which fed water into the Everglades, was so low that it had wide beaches. The sparse flow of water into the Glades had reduced many channels to mud and made them impassable by any kind of water vessel. Wildlife acted erratically. The delicate ecological balance on which South Florida depended had tipped in a dangerous direction.

In the lagoon where the village was located, however, the water level remained relatively high. It was fed by a small lake, and tributaries from the Wilderness Waterway ran into it. The chopper was able to land in the center of the lagoon, well clear of the mangroves. He felt immensely relieved when Dobson finally killed the engine and that relentless *whup whup whup* of the rotors ceased.

"I'll be waiting right here till you're done, boss," said Dobson. "You two need help with Dog's cage?"

"We can handle it, Wayne," Colleen told him. "Thanks."

For moments after Nash stood up, he was terrified his right knee would buckle, that his leg would betray him, and Dobson would have to help Colleen get the cage off the chopper. But his leg cooperated and they made the transfer to the waiting airboat.

The dog made no sounds at all. She cowered in a corner of her cage, her snout tucked into her tail. *She knows.* The airboat pilot kept the powerful engines at a fraction of their speed and noise, and within minutes the village came into sight. Built entirely on stilts, it consisted of interlocking chickees or wooden platforms with thatched roofs. Dobson had found the site, Nash and Colleen had come up with the concept, then Dobson had overseen its construction, and tax dollars had paid for it.

The half dozen huts in the center of the village weren't habitable, but they looked great on video. The NSB brass loved those goddamned huts, loved watching them fade—and appear again. In his darker moments—and there were plenty of such moments these days—Nash imagined the brass sitting around the Pentagon, bullshitting about how they had the capability of rendering an entire village and all its inhabitants invisible. Except there had been no inhabitants shrouded in this village. Only Dog.

NSB stood for National Security Bureau. It was one of what Nash had come to believe were many such shadow agencies, all of them enfolded in secrecy. This year, the bureau's budget surpassed the net worth of Bill Gates. In the bureaucracy's financial scheme of things, he thought, the Tesla Project comprised merely a slice of the bureau's interests. A drop in the old proverbial bucket.

So why was Ross Farris, the bureau's chief financial officer and Nash's immediate boss, waiting on the village's dock? *Guess what, guy,* whispered an insidious little voice in his head. *City hall has arrived.*

Nash leaned in close to Colleen, close enough to catch the scent of soap on her skin. "What's Farris doing here?"

"Beats me."

"You didn't call him?"

She looked at Nash as if he'd lost his mind. "Why would *I* call him, George?"

Farris was a muscular hunk of a man, an ex-marine with a large, bony head that looked even larger and bonier than it actually was because of his military buzz cut. He wore battle fatigues and combat boots, definite overkill for the Everglades, and his usual reflective sunglasses. The shades completed his resemblance to a redneck playing war games.

"Ahoy," Farris called as the airboat stopped next to the dock.

Ahoy? Nash felt like gagging. "And what brings you here, Ross?" *Old buddy, ole pal.*

"Just minding the store, George. I got your e-mail about the test run today and thought I should be here to observe from beginning to end."

"We don't observe from here." But Farris already knew that. "How'd you get out here, Ross?"

"I rented a skiff." Farris's phony cheerfulness dried up in a flash. When he spoke again, it was in his official don't-fuck-with-me voice. "I'm here to watch the entire process, from beginning to end—preparations, redundancy plans, the works."

Ha, Nash thought. Farris never showed up just to watch. He always had an agenda. And the three times in the past that he'd shown up to watch, he'd done so from their Homestead headquarters, within the safety of the bunker. Now he was in the field, dressed like a military commando on a security mission, such a radical departure from his past pattern that Nash knew today's agenda would not be music to *his* ears.

"You're here for the show, in other words."

"Something like that." Then Farris gave an inkling about what he was really doing here. "For some time now, I've felt this project is ready for the quantum leap."

Ahoy, minding the store, quantum leaps. Farris was supposed to be a bright man, but he often talked like a character in a badly written sitcom. And just which quantum leap was he was referring to, anyway? The human quantum leap? Good, let *him* volunteer. "Excuse me, Ross, we've got to haul the cage off the boat."

Farris stepped to one side as Nash grabbed hold of the ladder and prayed that his leg could stand the climb. The climb wasn't difficult for someone with two normal legs. But with his one leg shorter than the other, the climb might as well have been Everest. His right hip began to hurt before he reached the top and it was everything he could do to step on to the dock instead of collapse on it. Even when he knelt at the edge to grab on to the cage as Colleen and the airboat pilot lifted it, his joints cracked and creaked. He felt Farris watching him, measuring his physical performance, and hated him for it.

Even Colleen scrutinized him in that way sometimes. He knew her leg didn't repulse him, but sometimes he wondered if she pitied him. *A pity fuck, George.* Hell, maybe that was why his wife had married him. Maybe men with handicaps stirred some atavistic compassion in women like Colleen and his wife. In fact, as far back as Nash could remember— and that was *very* far, there was nothing at all wrong with his mind—the girls and, later on, the women he'd attracted were damaged somehow themselves. Not in obvious ways, as he was, but in deeper ways—psychologically, emotionally, spiritually.

"So this is the famous canine," Farris murmured once the cage was on the deck. He crouched down. "Hey, doggie, you have any idea how famous you are?"

He spoke to Dog in what Nash had come to think of as a "doggie voice," the same kind of voice that many adults also used with young children.

"She's in a bad mood, Ross," said Colleen. "Don't get much closer."

But Farris, a been there and done that sort of guy, either didn't hear or pretended that he hadn't, and stuck his fingers through the bars of the cage. Before either Nash or Colleen could say anything, Dog emitted a low, fierce growl and lunged for him.

Farris wrenched back so fast he fell on his ass—but saved his fingers. Dog chomped down on empty air, then snapped at the bars and kept on growling, her lips furled back from her teeth.

"My God," Farris spat, scooting back on his butt, farther from the cage. "What the hell is *wrong* with that animal?"

Colleen's expression was one of pure disgust. "What's wrong with the dog, Ross, is the same thing that would be wrong with *you* if someone put you in a cage, subjected you to an excruciating scientific experiment, and stuck you with needles. Just back off. Both of you. Get outta here so I can calm her down enough to get her out of the cage."

Farris scrambled to his feet. Nash touched his elbow and they moved away from the edge of the dock. Nash limped, he couldn't help it, and he hated his leg for that, hated its rebellion in the few moments it took him and Farris to get out of hearing range of the others.

The summer air here beneath the overhang of mangroves was thick and still, like a sauna, and Nash could tell that the heat and humidity bothered Farris. *Wait till August and September, pal.*

"Goddamn mutt's a liability," Farris said, brushing off his fatigues, wiping his arm across his sweaty face. "It's time for you to find another mammal, preferably of the human variety."

"Great, so why don't you volunteer, Ross? Talk about redefining the word *spook.*" Nash laughed.

Farris didn't look amused. His face was red from the stifling heat and droplets of sweat stood out on his forehead and between the prickly hairs of his buzz cut. "The committee wants things speeded up."

"The kinks aren't worked out of the process yet."

"We know that." Sunlight glanced off his reflective shades as if off chrome. "But unless the human element is reintroduced into the shrouding process, we'll never get the kinks worked out."

"We could end up with another Logan and Tyler fiasco on our hands."

"The committee's willing to take that risk."

But am I?

Nash stared at the twin miniatures of his own face in the lenses of Farris's sunglasses. He looked like shit. The hairs of his gray-streaked beard clumped together with sweat, his eyes had gotten smaller, darker, his face was flushed from the heat. His head ached, the inside of his mouth tasted the way the air here smelled, of something incomparably rich and fertile and excessively *wet.*

Farris apparently mistook his silence for reluctance and immediately said what he thought Nash wanted to hear. "Look, I can't force you to do this. The project has always been your baby."

It had started out that way, Nash thought. But once he had accepted Farris's offer of financial help, his *baby* had ceased to be his alone and gradually had become a communal child, subject to the rules and restrictions imposed by a number of surrogate parents. Yes, it was true that he had more money for research now, the one thing the project had lacked before, but at what price?

Now Farris really sweetened the pot. "The committee is willing to release a big chunk of change if the project is taken to the next level, George."

He felt a sharp stab of pain in his leg, almost as though it were a warning. "How big a chunk?"

His thin lips stretched like Silly Putty into a conspiratorial smile. "Huge." He named a figure.

Nash's incredulity quickly collapsed into suspicion. "What prompted this sudden change of heart? The last I heard, they were threatening to cut the budget."

"Let's just say that the committee took the videos to their contacts at the Pentagon and suddenly the Tesla Project is very hot."

A snake coiled in the pit of Nash's stomach. "*Which* videos?"

"Of, uh . . ."

"Of Tyler," Nash finished with a whisper.

"Yeah."

The snake uncoiled and struck. It felt like needles piercing the walls of his gut. "Jesus, Ross. What the hell did you do that for?"

Farris rubbed his jaw. "Look, I had to give them something. They were threatening to kill the entire project."

The hushed urgency in the man's voice led Nash to believe that Farris's ass had been on the line. He could just see it, the committee—six to eight men, of whom Nash had met only two in ten years—informed Farris that he would be out of a job and collecting a pension unless he produced something major in the Tesla Project. The committee was pressuring him for a new defense weapon, one that would make sense. Well, Tyler Griffin was major, all right. But until Farris had shown the committee videos of Tyler, they'd believed that he and Logan were dead. Knowledge of Tyler's existence had been confined to Nash's employees.

Farris rushed on. "When they realized we've had a snake in the grass for the last thee years, they were, shall we say, ecstatic."

A *snake in the grass.* That had been Farris's phrase for Invisibles since the first experiment they'd done with anything living—a black racer, one of Florida's common and harmless snakes. Nash hated the phrase. But it sure fit Farris. *He* was the snake in the grass.

"They want to see him for themselves," Farris continued, "and will be at the Ponce facility on the afternoon of the tenth."

Nash's head snapped up. *"What?* But . . ."

"No buts. It's set. It can't be changed now." He tapped the face of his watch. "I'll meet you back at Homestead at eighteen hundred hours."

With that, Farris strode to the back of the village, disappeared over the side, and moments later chugged off in the skiff he had rented. Nash just stood there in a kind of shock, his leg screaming in pain.

3
THE OLD GEEZER

The pathetic truth was that Andy Townsend didn't know how to change a tire. He could set a broken limb, provide emergency care for a gunshot victim, remove an appendix or a gall bladder, and could set up a camp anywhere and eke out an existence. But he couldn't change a stupid tire because he never learned how and never had a reason to learn how to do it.

He'd grown up in a family where nearly everything was done for him. The cook cooked his meals, the maids made his bed, cleaned his room, and ironed his clothes, the chauffer took him and his brother to and from school. When they got sick, the housekeeper had whisked them off to the pediatrician. Their lives had hummed along on automatic, all of it paid for by their parents' lucrative law practice.

During the summers, they were shipped off to Europe or to South America or some other far-flung spot to spend several months with their maternal grandparents, aging bohemians with strange passions and eccentric friends. They had given Andy and his brother enormous freedom, but in return he and Jim had to soak up some of the culture of whatever country they happened to be in. That meant museums, archaeological sights, coffee houses, odd villages with even odder mythologies. During Christmas and spring breaks, they'd gone camping with their grandparents, into the Everglades, out to the Rockies, into the back hills of Appalachia.

As a result, by the time Andy was sent off to boarding school, he knew he would not be going home again and that he would not be going to law school, as was expected of both him and Jim. He wanted to be a doctor. His old man was disappointed, but not for long. After all, being a physician was certainly as *respectable* as being an attorney and besides, he knew he couldn't force Andy to go to law school by threatening not to pay for med school, because the grandparents would pay for it.

But when he'd announced that he intended to go to the University of Florida medical school, which had an excellent emergency medicine program, his father had balked. ER medicine? Was he crazy? And at the U of F? Why not Harvard, where he'd been accepted? Why not neurology? Or dermatology? In South Florida, both specialties were incredibly lucrative. He hadn't bothered to argue. Where his old man saw dollar signs, Andy saw an opportunity to make a difference in the world. His grandparents had paid for college and med school and his fragile ties with his parents had snapped completely.

Jim, two years younger than Andy, had followed him to the University of Florida and majored in computer science. They had lived together, celebrated holidays together, and had created the sort of family for themselves that they'd never had, except during those long, magical summers and holidays. Then they'd both gotten involved in serious relationships, found their own places, and set up housekeeping.

Jim turned out to be fickle with women. Every time one of his relationships fell apart, he sold his house and bought another one. He was making incredible money by then and could afford to buy and sell homes. Good thing, too, because otherwise he might not have met Renie, who was Jim's Realtor on all those house deals. Jim had introduced them when Andy had been looking for a home. During their first hour together, while she was driving Andy around and showing him houses, her Buick had a flat. Instead of expecting him to change it or calling AAA, she'd changed the tire herself. He could still see her in his mind's eye, her dark hair wild and unruly, her deft fingers doing what had to be done.

But damned if he would ask for her help now. He would get this tire changed even if it took him the rest of the day.

Now and then he glanced at his wife and daughter, sitting on the curb in front of the rest rooms, in the shade, talking too quietly for him to hear what they were saying. Girl talk, probably. Katie was at that age where her favorite topics were animals and, well, what else? *Boys.*

Just as frequently, though, Renie and Katie were at each other's throats, and he and his daughter were able to bond in ways that had escaped him completely in his relationship with his parents. They hiked and fished together, played basketball, rode roller coasters, had insane adventures. This camping trip was supposed to have been one of those adventures. But when Renie had insisted on coming along, the old math had clicked in. Women against men, mom and daughter against dad, *two against one.*

He finally got the tire off the axle. By then, sweat rolled into his eyes, the summer heat pounded against his back, and his stomach shrieked for food. He rolled the spare into place and saw that it was flat, too. "Shit. Fuck." He stood up, his back and knees creaking like rusted hinges, and barely stifled the urge to kick the crap out of the tires. Both of them.

He caught Renie's glance at he headed toward the store and knew what she was thinking, that if *she* were changing the tire, it would be done by now. "Need a break," he muttered.

"Whatever," she replied, and he hurried into the store.

2

Water, a bag of trail mix, a cluster of bananas, a fresh bag of ice for the cooler. As the guy behind the counter rang up the purchases, Andy said, "You have any idea where the nearest triple A station is?"

"Sure thing. Right here."

Not exactly encouraging news. "Can you fix a flat tire?"

"Reckon I can."

"Here's my card." He dropped his AAA card on the counter.

"Good 'nuff. That'll be fifteen twenty-nine for yore stuff. Lemme get my pad so's I can jot down the triple A number."

Fifteen twenty-nine for *this?* "Excuse me, but a bottle of water this size usually costs about seventy-nine cents, several bananas are a buck tops, the ice is another buck, and the bag of trail mix is about a buck fifty. That's a little over four bucks. I think you made a mistake."

The man, frowning, leaned toward the register window. "Oops, reckon I did. That's five twenty-nine. Sorry 'bout that."

Andy doubted it was a mistake, but dropped six bucks on the counter and endured at least two full minutes of the man's hacking cough before he got his change. In between coughs, the man wheezed. Allergies? Andy wondered. The aftermath of bronchitis? Or was it what it sounded like, full-blown emphysema? "Better give up the cigarettes."

"Done it," the guy said. "Got me a patch." He rolled up the sleeve of his shirt and showed Andy the patch. "My body just ain't used to no butts yet." The man finished scribbling the number of Andy's AAA card. "Let's go look at that tire."

They walked outside and headed over to the car. "You goin' into the Glades?" the old guy asked.

"Yeah, camping trip."

"Strange shit goin' on out there. Best keep your eyes open."

"What kind of strange?"

"Lemme me put it t'ya this way. Me and my store's been here twenty-two years. Seen droughts, floods, po-leese chases, gator attacks, rats on the march. Yes, siree, seen plenty out here."

"So it's an animal strangeness?"

"Ayuh, that's how it starts. One day last month, reckon it was midweek, when things are slow, I opened the front door to hundreds of water moccasins out in that there parking lot. There was so many snakes I couldn't even git to my truck. I called the park rangers and they sent some snake people out here to scoop 'em up. Later that day, right around sunset, I was fishin' down the road a piece, right close to the park, and suddenly the sky fills with birds and the fish are jumpin' clean outta the water and the gators are scrambling to git away from *something*. Spooked me."

"What was it?"

The old guy shook his head and rubbed his unshaven jaw. "Dunno. But a while later, I'm puttin' back through the mangroves and the most god-awful sound takes hold of the air and sorta . . . I dunno, shakes it. Noise got so bad I nearly passed out. Then . . . then I see this . . . this explosion of light." The old man threw open his arms. "I got outta there real fast."

Andy wondered how much rotgut wine the old guy had been drinking that evening. "Did you ever find out what it was?"

"Nope. But six, maybe eight hours later, it was late, real late, the moon done gone down, I hear choppers. They's comin' in real low, too, *whup whup,* like they're gonna land in my parkin' lot. I poke my head outside and I see 'em, six big mothers headin' west into the Glades.''

Fascinating story, Andy thought. But alcoholics always had fascinating stories.

''And that's how it goes every two, three weeks.''

''That often?''

''Ayuh. Been keeping a record for eight months now. The longest time between is maybe a month. The shortest time's 'bout fifteen days.''

The geezer's story no longer sounded like that of an alcoholic. ''So it's a pattern.''

''That's exactly right.'' His head bobbed up and down. ''A pattern.''

''Have you reported it to the cops or the park service?''

He laughed then, a wheezing laugh that quickly exploded into that terrible hacking Andy had heard earlier. When the coughing fit passed, the geezer said, ''When people like you call the cops, they come. When people like me call, they laugh and maybe they show up the next day, maybe they don't show up at all. You hear what I'm sayin'?''

Loud and clear.

''Reckon I knew I should say something when your wife and kid come into the store lookin' for toothbrushes. Figured you three for campers. See, there's been a chopper out there already today. And jus' 'fore you folks pulled up, I go outside with a bag of trash and find an army of fire ants, marchin' fast and steady, headed right for the store. So I grab a bag of fire ant killer and lay it down in a thick trail around the store.'' He paused, glanced off to his right, squinted, then pointed. ''There. You can still see 'em.''

Andy followed the old man's finger. Trees bordered the old guy's property, pines and ficus and, beyond them, the ubiquitous mangroves. The ample shade the trees cast and the bright light out here slicing into his eyes made it difficult to distinguish much of anything at first. But the longer Andy looked, the greater clarity that shadowland took on. And then he saw them, two impossibly dark, long, and undulating lines that ran parallel to each other. Ants on the move, just like the old geezer had said.

"Jesus," Andy breathed, and inadvertently stepped back to put more distance between himself and those ants. Even a healthy man with no allergies risked anaphylactic shock if he were bitten by that many fire ants. By even a fraction of those fire ants. Hell, if a man with an allergy who was otherwise healthy was bitten by a dozen fire ants, all at once, a *collective* effort, and didn't get a dose of epinephrine within minutes, he was dead. And that's what this looked like, a *collective* effort, the entire colony of Everglades fire ants on the move.

"Won't even notice us," the geezer said. "They're on the run." Then he tapped Andy's arm with the back of his bony hand and grinned. "I put down a double roadblock of the shit that kills 'em. I made the great wall of China, so they're gonna have to follow the wall." Now he pointed. "It goes back yonder, back of the garage, 'round it, and leads right across the road to the other side. They won't be botherin' us none here. They're too busy collectin' the poison, which they'll take back to the nest and give to the queen. Then . . ." He slapped his hands once, very loudly. "She's a goner."

He wheezed and started coughing again. They picked up the two flats and walked on back toward the garage. The old man clutched a dirty hanky that he held to his mouth as he hacked and hacked. Andy reached into his back pocket for his wallet, opened it, and removed a page from his prescription pad, one of several that he always carried on him.

His instincts told him the old guy was well into emphysema and that if he happened through here next year, he would find the Last Stop boarded up and the geezer on oxygen. He couldn't do much for the old man's emphysema, but the prescription he wrote would lick what Andy believed to be an underlying secondary infection in the guy's respiratory system.

"Get this filled." He handed the geezer the prescription. "It'll ease that cough. And start doing exercises that make you breathe deeply."

They had stopped in front of the garage doors and the geezer glanced down at the piece of paper in his hand, then looked up at Andy, one eye winked shut against the light. "You really a doc?"

"Yeah."

"Goddamn," the old man breathed. "Thanks."

Andy stuck out his hand and introduced himself. "Andy Townsend."

"Fisher, Sam Fisher. Friends call me Sammy." He slipped the paper in his shirt pocket, patted it, and slid open the garage doors.

It took Andy's eyes a few moments to adjust to the dim, murky light inside. The air stank of oil and gasoline, but at least it was cool. A row of large, dirty windows lined the walls near the ceiling, above what appeared to be a loft. Sam flipped several switches and overhead lights flared, revealing a strawberry-red '57 Thunderbird and an antique Mercedes on concrete blocks, both of them in various stages of refurbishment. Stacked tires hugged the right side of the garage, cardboard boxes lined the left side, and the entire back wall of the garage was a workbench with what looked to be thousands of bucks' worth of tools and car parts.

"Reckon this won't take long."

They went over to a workbench cluttered with *stuff*, Sam picked up a pair of pliers and pulled a nail from the regular tire, put in a plug, and filled it with air. He also filled the spare with air, then rolled it over to Andy.

"How's that look?"

"About perfect, Sam. What do I owe you?"

"Reckon we'll call it even, Doc. The . . ." He suddenly

stopped and cocked his head, listening to something that Andy couldn't hear. "What the . . ." He loped toward the garage doors and slid them open partway.

Andy picked up the spare and glanced up through the narrow opening in the garage door and saw birds, hundreds of birds winging across the blue morning sky, squawking and cawing, crying and shrieking, a cacophony that rose and fell on currents of air. "Shit buckets," Sam breathed. "The ants, now the birds." He groped in the back pocket of his baggy jeans and pulled out a worn pocket calendar. He paged through it. "June eighth, right? Today's the eighth?"

"Yeah."

He made a mark in the calendar, slapped it shut. "Eighteenth day. Whatever's goin' on out there is coming this way again. And soon, six to twelve hours from now, that's what I reckon. If I was you, Doc, I'd pack the missus and kid into the Jeep and head home."

Renie would love it, he thought, but he and Katie had waited months for this camping trip. No, forget canceling the trip based on nothing more than birds taking flight. Hunters probably had spooked them.

And what spooked those fire ants, Andy? Hunters?

"We're not camping in this area," Andy replied. "We'll be farther south. But thanks for the advice, Sam."

"Sure thing, Doc. But reckon the missus won't be pissed if you change your mind."

Andy laughed at that, a quick, nervous laugh, and he and Sam hurried out of the garage and up the gravel driveway. To Andy's right, the fire ants continued their relentless march toward wherever they were going. He spotted his wife and daughter standing on a parking curb, both of them watching the fire ants.

"You got enough supplies for a couple days out there?" Sam asked.

"Absolutely."

"Stuff for mosquitoes? Plenty of batteries? At least one lantern? Food that don't need no cookin'?"

"Maybe I need to take a quick look around the store."

"Good, good, you do that and I'll change the tire."

"Thanks, Sam."

He patted his shirt pocket, the prescription inside, and grinned, exposing a lifetime of major dental problems. "Reckon that'll put us even steven, Doc."

3

While Katie trotted off toward the store to check on Andy, Renie stood near the Jeep, watching the geezer as he proceeded to change the flat tire. Although this old guy and her father were separated by education and quality of life, something about him reminded her of Buddha, as she used to call him. Maybe it was the shape of his head or the thinning hair or the sun spots on the backs of his hands. Maybe it was just that he was about the same age Buddha had been when Parkinson's had seized him.

"You live out here alone?" she asked, unable to fully shake the image of her father in his final months, his body frozen in a fetal position, hands hooked like claws.

"Ayuh. Missus died five years ago. Got a son down in the Keys, don't see 'im much. Bizness gits slow in the summer. Sell mostly to campers, tourists, the occasional oddball, and military fellas doin' whatever they're doin' down in Flamingo."

"Military in Flamingo? I thought there was just a marina there."

"They don't wear uniforms, nothin' like that, but they smell like military. Ten, twelve months ago, they started showin' up, haulin' airboats into the park. Got a friend down at the marina who says these fellas rent a coupla slips for airboats and a houseboat. Anyhow, that's when the wildlife 'round here started actin' up.''

"Acting up," Renie repeated. "You mean, like those birds and the ants?''

"Uh-huh.''

"What kind of oddballs?'' Renie wondered what *this* oddball considered oddball.

The old geezer rubbed his unshaven jaw. "Well, for a while some months back, I used t'see this guy come into the store. He never said nothin', jus' bought up all my bottled water and a couple cigars and went on his way. I figured him for a field worker, one of them migrant fellas from Mexico or someplace down south pickin' tomatoes or fruit or something. Then one afternoon when he was in the store, I fell flat on my face. Passed out.

"Woke up with this fella crouched over me, blowin' cigar smoke in my face and mutterin' incantations. He had . . . I dunno . . . these big ole sad eyes and I kept looking in those eyes and couldn't move. Didn't want to move. Hurt bad all over. So I jus' laid there, half chokin' on the cigar smoke, and after a while, I felt a whole lot better and he helped me sit up. He said I oughta move into town 'cause things were goin' to get weird out here in the Glades. I could feel blood on my head. . . .'' The geezer touched his right temple, where a tiny scar snaked inward toward his brow. "He touched it and then one of them military types comes into the store and says, 'Hey, Luis, let's getta move on. No time for your *brujeria* shit.''

"*Brujeria.* That's witchcraft, isn't it?''

"Ayuh. Anyway, he paid for the water and the smokes and they left. When I looked in the mirror, there was a shit load of blood all dried on my head, then I washed the blood away and all I saw was this scar.'' He touched his temple again and shrugged. "Go figure, huh? When I thought 'bout it later, I decided this guy didn't look like no Mexican. He looked like one of them Indian fellows from South America.''

''Which Indian fellows?''

''Y'know, those ancients Indians. The ones who built Picchu.''

''Machu Pichu?''

''Yeah, that's it. Machu Pichu.''

''An Incan.''

''Right.''

''That's quite a story.'' An AA story, she thought.

''And you don't believe a word,'' he replied, and laughed.

Then his laughter collapsed into a hacking cough, a wrenching sound. Renie moved quickly to his side and for a brief instant, she was twelve years in the past, stooping over next to Buddha's bed in a nursing home to retrieve the key he had dropped. He couldn't do it because his body was frozen.

Renie blinked the memory away and crouched next to the geezer, who now held a handkerchief to his mouth. ''You take a break, I'll finish up,'' she said, and immediately felt grounded again.

Ancient Incans, instantaneous healings. Yeah, right.

She changed the tire, grateful that her father had taught her to do many practical things, from changing tires and oil in her car to fixing plumbing and electrical problems. Good thing, too, since she'd married a man who couldn't do any of those things and had shown absolutely zero interest in learning.

In all fairness to Andy, though, he was an avid out-doorsman who could navigate his way through virtually any wilderness, had an impeccable sense of direction, and was a fantastic cook—which she was not—and everything related to their domestic lives was pretty evenly split. Andy did so much of the cooking, in fact, that when Katie had realized this wasn't the norm in the families of her friends, she'd announced that any guy she married would have to know how to cook.

"You change a tire like a pro." The old guy was now seated on the flat tire to her left.

"Thanks. So tell me more about these military types." *And the Incan.* "And the other oddballs."

"Not much to tell. And like I said, don't know for sure they's military. Now and then, though, these water choppers come flyin' in—"

"Water choppers?"

"Yeah, you know, with the pontoons on them."

"And they land in the Glades?"

"Reckon so. They go in low over the mangroves and then come out the same spot."

Renie considered this story to be just one more sign that they should turn around and head home. Military shit in the glades, ancient Incan medicine men, armies of ants on the march, hundreds of birds fleeing the mangroves . . . Even if she dropped her husband and daughter off and went home, she would spend the next three or four days worrying about them. Either they all went home or they all stayed. The challenge would be convincing the two of them that her way was the better way.

Once again, it all came down to the same old math. *Two against one.*

Twenty minutes later, they pulled out of the Last Stop parking lot, with the old man waving and calling after them, "Y'all come back now, heah?"

4
LOGAN

The Land Rover eased off Coral Sea Boulevard, onto the gravel shoulder of the road, and came to a slow stop about three hundred yards from the entrance to Homestead Air Force Base. One of the two women inside glanced around, pleased to see that the "boulevard"—a misnomer, for sure—was as deserted as it had been every other time she'd cruised through here. Not a moving car anywhere in sight.

On the other side of the rusted fence, in a parking lot pitted with potholes that suggested the base was barely used, she spotted maybe half a dozen cars, ordinary vehicles, Buicks and Fords, Oldsmobiles and Cherokees. Past the lot stood the ruined remnants of several hangars that hadn't been rebuilt since Hurricane Andrew had destroyed the base in 1992 and, beyond them, the concrete building that was her destination.

During Logan's numerous visits to this facility in the last two months, she had learned the layout of the base. In addition to the ruined hangars and the relatively new concrete bunker, the heart and soul of this place, there was another, smaller bunker and a new hangar that housed military jeeps, a couple of Humvees, choppers, boats and hitches, and military transport vehicles. As far as she'd been able to determine, there were only two guards on each shift for perimeter security. That was in keeping with Nash's policy that the best security lay in an appearance of no security. Besides the guards, there were sensors and hidden cameras, but nothing else outside that could detect her presence. Inside, though, she suspected it would be a different story. But maybe not, if Nash believed that she was dead, if he was arrogant enough to believe that an Invisible alone could not survive in a world of Visibles for three years.

Abigail Sparks turned off the engine. "You ready, Logan?"

Logan realized that even though Abby couldn't see her, her walnut-colored eyes always seemed to pinpoint her location. "Now or never." That had become her mantra in the last three years. She shrugged on her backpack, the original pack that she'd had with her the day her life and Tyler's had collapsed into the twilight zone, the pack that was as invisible as she was. Inside it were items she'd had with her that day three years ago, which were still invisible: her antique laptop, tools, odds and ends that might prove useful today.

"What time do you have?" Abby asked.

"Four fifty-eight."

"Me, too."

"Hey, Ab. Just curious. How do you always know where to look when we're talking?"

"C'mon, girl." Abby's smile had lit up the hearts of a lot of men in her time. She was Jamaican by birth, a forty-five-year-old grandmother who looked ten years younger, with a body to boot. "Just practice. Guess my hearing's improved since I came to work for you. So let's go over it real quick."

She went through the drill they had created during the

test runs these last six weeks. Logan knew it by heart and knew that Abby did, too. But it seemed important to hear it aloud right here, right now.

When she finished their checklist, Abby opened her door and Logan scrambled over the front seat, moving in right behind her. She wore shorts and a haltar top, clothes that had been inside her suitcase way back when that had never materialized. Although she had several pairs of shoes that had been in her suitcase three years ago, today she was barefoot. Even invisible shoes could squeak against floors.

Abby went around to the front of the Land Rover, lifted the hood. While she fiddled around, loosening wires that would make her story real, Logan kept surveying the area. Part of her expected to see George Nash himself striding out of the bunker, faithful Colleen at his side. Another part of her, though, knew that if she saw Nash right now, right this second, she might kill him. Three years of invisibility was three years too long.

But she didn't see Nash, Colleen, or anyone else. She saw waves of heat rising from the pitted black asphalt, heat that she could feel, heat that made her sweat. But her sweat, like all of her body fluids, was invisible. Heat from the sun made her sweat but sunlight didn't burn her. It touched her, yes, and seemed to provide her with sufficient vitamin D, but its damaging ultraviolet rays didn't affect her. Because of it, she didn't think she looked any older than she had three years ago. She couldn't see herself to confirm that, but her fingers felt only smoothness when she touched the corners of her eyes, the curves of her throat. She could see herself when she was wet, actually *see herself in a mirror,* but not in detail. That kind of detail, she thought, came from touch.

"Okay, we're done here," Abby said. "Let's do it. Once you're in, I'll be in the grove across the street till I hear from you. You'll have to call my cell number from inside the building."

Logan nodded. "What's the temperature reading out here?"

Abby looked at the watch on her wrist that gave readouts on temperature, wind speed, humidity. "Right here, ninety-four. Out there, with all that concrete and asphalt, probably a degree or two higher. Either way, you're safe."

Another side effect of prolonged invisibility was a body temperature about three degrees lower than what was normal for Visibles. It meant that if the facility had thermal detectors outside, she probably wouldn't register. But inside, where she guessed the temp was kept around sixty-five, that would not be the case. Inside, though, the detectors also would be picking up the body temperatures of everyone who worked there. In a sense, then, she actually might have camouflage inside the building.

"Ready now?" Abby asked.

"Ready."

Abby turned. In the event security cameras were trained on Abby, she wouldn't be able to speak now because the cameras would pick up the movement of her lips.

As they started walking, Logan realized she had waited for this day for three years, waited and hoped that once she located Nash, she would find Tyler. Now and then Logan glanced behind them. She didn't see a shadow or footprints. They got through the front gate, which was a real joke, just rusted metal that scraped noisily against the asphalt as Abby and Logan pushed it open. It hadn't been intended to keep anyone out, typical for Nash, Logan thought. *Don't draw attention to the facility with guards, alarms, barbed-wire fences.*

And especially don't do it, she thought, at bases that were officially shut down, dead, kaput. But inside, under the roofs, within the walls, security would be considerable. One way or another, her first goal was to create a diversion so she could get into Nash's computers.

2

During the first year of her life as an Invisible, she had scrounged for food, slept in bookstores, furniture stores, clothing stores, any place that had couches, a shower— and a computer. On-line, she learned that she and Tyler supposedly had died in a boating accident, that their memorial services had been held on campus, and that Tyler's family had launched an investigation into his alleged death. She hadn't held out much hope about the investigation, but it was good to know that someone cared enough to be suspicious.

As she became more adept at living as an Invisible, she eventually realized that she needed a single place to call home where she could stash money and food that she stole. She found a trailer in the Florida Keys that was used maybe two weeks out of fifty-two by a family from New York, and for the better part of a year the arrangement worked fine. She stole food and money late at night, when people were less likely to be out and about, an important criterion because the money and food were visible. She ate a single large meal early in the morning, so that the food was digested—and therefore not visible—by midafternoon, when she often stole rides in the backs of trucks to Key West.

Her main problem during that time was that she didn't have an identity. That meant no Social Security number, no bank account, no credit. Her search for an identity began in the Key West cemetery. For several days, she walked through it, studying the names and dates on the aboveground graves until she discovered the graves of three children whose dates of birth were close to her own.

The next afternoon, she began to use her invisibility to her advantage. Shortly before three, she walked into the Bureau of Vital Statistics and waited until the last employee had left for the day. Then she searched the bureau's records for the three names she had selected. Only one had a Social Security number when she'd died. Logan memorized it.

The next day, she went to the Social Security Administration Office and, once again, waited until the last employee had left. She entered the dead child's Social Security number in the computer, made the necessary adjustments, and proceeded to make a card for herself. It took her most of the night to figure out how to do it so that it looked authentic.

Two days after that, she used a bank's computer to create a credit history for herself and submitted a credit card request, using the name Rebecca G. Ayers. She'd always loved Tyler's last name and when they'd gotten married, had been proud to call herself a Griffin. So the G in her pseudonym honored the name. As Rebecca G. Ayers, she listed her address as that of a rental place two blocks from the trailer. Ten days later, the credit card arrived. There were definitely advantages to being an Invisible.

Although her laptop computer was invisible, it was also old, clunky, and outdated, so she had stolen a new one. No small feat, this, not when the laptop was visible as she scurried down the street. She used the credit card to sign up for an on-line service and over the next two months proceeded to set up three bank accounts on-line. Things probably would have continued indefinitely like this if the place she'd been using for an address hadn't been rented by a black woman named Abby Sparks.

Abby, refugee of a bad marriage, had gone to the Keys because her daughter lived there and it was as far away from Manhattan and her ex as she could get. Like Logan, she was looking for a new life, as though a life were something you could find, like a comfortable pair of shoes. When she'd walked into the house that day and discovered that someone else was obviously living in the place, she hadn't run off to the Realtor to complain. She had calmly unpacked her things, then waited in the living room for the tenant to return. Waited for hours. And while Abby had waited, Logan had waited, standing silently on one side of the room, watching this curious and astonishingly patient woman.

It was Logan who had broken the silence, broken it with a whisper, hoping to frighten Abby away, hoping she would think the place was haunted. But Abby just laughed. *You think some ole ghost scares the shit outta me?* she'd said aloud—and laughed.

So Logan had gone right over to her and leaned into her face and said, *I'm invisible.*

Abby had pressed back into her chair, shocked but not scared. There was a definite difference, Logan had realized, and everything between them had unfolded from that point on. It had taken Logan several hours to explain her story to Abby because Abby kept interrupting, grilling her for details about Tyler and Nash and the shrouding program and then about how Logan had managed to negotiate ordinary life as an Invisible. At some point, Abby had told Logan that she needed someone to help her manage her life, and right now she was looking for a job and how about if they tried it for six months? Six months turned into three years and here they were, both of them wealthier than Logan had thought possible.

Yes, she was three years older and still invisible. But she'd learned a thing or two during these years and she was betting that she knew a hell of a lot more than Nash and Farris and the rest of them about what it was like to be invisible. She was also ready to learn what had happened to Tyler and that answer, she believed, lay somewhere in the Tesla Project computers, which she believed were inside the main bunker.

All her instincts told her that he was alive, that after she'd fled that day, Tyler had been put away under lock and key somewhere, Nash's human guinea pig. She doubted that he was here at Homestead; that wouldn't be Nash's style. He would be somewhere else, at an isolated place, and she suspected that the security there would be extreme and risky to an Invisible.

They walked between two of the damaged hangars, past piles of wood and glass that had been swept into tidy piles. "Hello," Abby called. "Hey, anyone here? I could use some help."

"Here comes a guard," Logan whispered.

He was a husky black guy in jeans and a blue work shirt, with an automatic rifle slung over one shoulder and a radio hooked to his belt. Logan hoped the appearance of an attractive woman with curves in all the right places would make the guard careless enough to leave his post.

"You're trespassing, ma'am," the guard said.

"My car broke down out on the road and I don't have my cell phone with me. Is there a phone around here that I can use? I need to call a garage or something."

"No garage around here, ma'am. What'd the car do?"

"Stopped, just stopped dead."

"I'll take a look at it for you. Maybe it's something simple."

"Oh, thank you so much," she gushed. "I headed into that orange grove back there, hoping to find a house, people, something, but the whole area was deserted."

"Not much to be picked in those fields during the summer. Where's your car parked, ma'am?"

"At the side of the road." She extended her hand. "By the way, I'm Abby."

The guard smiled and took her hand. "I'm Jeff."

And I'm Mutt, Logan thought, standing very still and watching as they walked off together. She noticed that the guard didn't touch his radio, didn't alert anyone that he was leaving his post. Either there wasn't anyone around to report to or he was so taken with Abby that his obligations got away from him. Either way, Logan thought, this was good news for her.

Logan hurried toward the main bunker, moving quickly

because the concrete burned her bare feet. Since Andrew had devastated the base, the wooden electrical poles that had once lined the road were gone, the electrical cables now underground. They probably converged in several transformers somewhere on the base. During her previous visits here, she hadn't seen anything even remotely resembling a transformer, so she figured each building had its own transformer and had decided to tackle the hangar first.

Now or never, babe, ain't that how it goes?

As she picked up her pace, she noticed the dark clouds rolling in from the Everglades. Rain wasn't forecast—hadn't fallen for months now—but the clouds worried her nonetheless. Water—whether rainfall, sprinklers, even condensation—would make her and everything she carried visible. She was beginning to feel the first, early pangs of hunger, too, which added to her concern. She hadn't eaten anything in seven hours, couldn't even afford to think about food. A single bite or drink of anything would be instantly visible to other people as it made its way down her throat and through her digestive system. As an Invisible, her body used energy more efficiently, but by tonight, she would be craving food the way a cannibal craves flesh.

As Logan neared the hangar, she thought she heard a chopper. She paused, head cocked to one side, listening for what she couldn't yet see. *From which direction?* She turned slowly in place and stopped when she heard the distinctive *whup whup* most clearly. Southwest, she thought, from the Everglades. And definitely headed this way.

If it was one of the project choppers, the people inside or even the chopper itself might be equipped with thermal sensors. Was Abby right about the temp out here? Probably, she thought, but some habits died hard and she felt vulnerable out in the open. Logan hurried over to the side of the hangar and backed up to the wall, under the overhang, watching the chopper as it came in low over the base. The irony, she thought. Invisible and yet afraid of being detected.

The chopper was a Bell 430, a twin-engine with a spacious cabin that could accommodate up to ten people and reach speeds of up to 160 miles an hour. From where she stood, it looked as though it could set down on either land or water. *Your tax buckaroos at work.* Yes siree, only the best for the Tesla Project, and this little baby probably had set the budget back around six or seven hundred grand, maybe more, depending on how luxurious the interior was and how technologically advanced the instruments were.

It swept in over the bunker, the hangar, and touched down on a helipad behind the second, smaller bunker. Its touchdown was as graceful and precise as that of anything in nature—a dragonfly landing on a fence, a butterfly's wings folding down over a flower, a bee zoning in on a source of nectar. With the Bell, you got what you paid for. Accuracy, precision, speed, safety.

Logan watched as Colleen Roth got out, followed by Nash, who was using his cane. That meant he was really in pain. Good. She wished him an infinite depth of pain. She wished his goddamn bum leg would fall off from the hip down. He didn't deserve that leg, didn't deserve to have it. What Nash needed, she decided, was a couple of months as an Invisible. His bum leg was telling him something, but he wasn't listening. You didn't have that luxury as an Invisible. When your body spoke, you paid very close attention. You engaged in a dialogue with your body, asking why it hurt, how you could help, pleading for its wisdom. You had to pay attention because you couldn't run off to ER or check in with your family doctor. Even if your doctor, she thought, accepted that you were invisible, how could a Visible possibly treat an Invisible? The physiology of an Invisible was radically changed. Even Nash didn't understand the extent of those changes. No Visible could understand.

Just the sight of Nash, even from this distance, sent her heartbeat into double time. A kind of flutter started up in her stomach, fear or rage or both, she wasn't sure. But either one could cause her to take unnecessary risks. She quickly slammed a door shut on her emotions and a strange clarity filled her.

She noticed, for instance, that Nash had aged since she'd last seen him in that Broward County hangar three years ago. It was there in his downcast eyes, the slight hump to his shoulders, but mostly, she saw it in the way he moved, with such obvious discomfort and difficulty. If Nash were listening to what his bum leg was telling him, he wouldn't be here. He would be desperately seeking to discover his humanity, to finding the exact point in his life when his humanity, if he'd ever possessed it, had fled. He'd be dealing, as the pop psychologists said these days, *with his issues* and trying to *heal* them. Buzz words, yes, but they happened to fit Nash.

Logan studied Colleen carefully. She was only ten years younger than Nash, but everything about her had a spring to it, a certain restless impatience. In contrast, Nash seemed overly circumspect and pessimistic, as though he believed that any minute now, the worst would happen.

And hey, guess what, fucker. You're right. Your worst nightmare is right here, watching you.

She moved toward Nash and Colleen, eager to eavesdrop, but didn't have to get dangerously close to hear them. Her hearing had improved greatly over the years and Logan didn't know whether it was due to the invisibility or simply to some heightened survival mechanism. She and Abby had tested its parameters and, most of the time, she could hear whispered words at about 150 feet. When she was in the best of shape, that distance extended even farther.

Nash was speaking, his voice crisp, businesslike, urgent. "Get in touch with Panther. I want him on call during the test run."

"I've already done it. He'll be at the Flamingo marina, on the houseboat."

"And find a way to keep Farris out of the control room tonight."

"Should I find a way to keep God out, too, George?"

He looked over at her, a sharp, accusatory look that sent a chill snaking down Logan's spine. "He was at the village because he got an e-mail. I didn't send him a goddamn e-mail, Colleen."

Nash stopped. Colleen stopped. She said, "Hey, I sent him an e-mail. The weekly report. I didn't think he ever read them."

"From now on, you send those weekly reports to me first."

Colleen's lovely mouth twitched with annoyance. "Stop talking to me like I'm your lackey."

Nash squeezed the bridge of his long, bony nose, a gesture that Logan remembered well from those months she and Tyler had been in training. He paused briefly, leaning heavily on his cane. "The committee is pressing for human test subjects. They'll increase our funding substantially."

Colleen looked as if someone had punched her in the stomach. Her eyes widened, air hissed from her mouth. "Jesus, George. This is *great*. This is what we've been hoping for."

"Yeah, but the price may be too great. Some of Farris's Pentagon buddies want to meet Tyler."

For moments, everything suddenly stopped. Sound rushed out of Logan's world. She stood there, paralyzed, not entirely certain that her legs would continue to hold her up.

He's alive. Tyler's alive.

3

"Tyler's too unstable," Colleen said.

Nash nodded and started walking again, hating that he

had to depend so heavily on the cane. He felt ancient next to Colleen, who had to slow her pace considerably to match his. *C'mon, leg, not now.*

His head pounded from the heat, the humidity, summer in South Florida. "We know that, but we can't afford to let them know it."

Colleen touched his arm. "I don't think they're going to give a shit, George. And if they question us about it, we just point out the guy's been invisible for three years. Invisible. Trapped. Imprisoned. No freedom fucks your head. We'll give them psych reports, they'll believe it."

"If we use more human subjects, we're just going to have more Tylers. We need . . . I don't know, a place for Invisibles. Where they can live in relative normalcy."

"Like a village of Invisibles."

"Yes."

"Sort of like *The Truman Show.*"

Nash didn't like the comparison but, in some odd way, it fit. *If* more humans were used, they needed to believe they were living somewhat normal lives so that they would do what humans had always done—work, contribute, fall in love, and have babies. Especially those last two things. They needed to know if or how the effects of shrouding were passed on genetically. They needed to know if or how it affected the onset of puberty and menopause. They needed to know *everything* that one isolated Invisible could not teach them.

Yet, Tyler had taught them a great deal. He was unique. As Tyler the Invisible, he was Nash's greatest creation— and his most heinous. But there were limits to what they could learn from him.

Colleen went on: "I mean, we don't know at this point whether the shrouding, as it exists now, is dangerous to humans or not."

"Yeah? So you're ready to volunteer?"

"*Me?*" She laughed. "Yeah, right."

"Then we're not ready for human test subjects." Nash glanced over at her, at the sheen to her black hair, the perfection of her profile. "Colleen, what do you get out of this project?"

"What kind of question is that?"

"An honest one."

She hooked her arm through his, matched her pace to his. At that moment, she was the woman he had fallen in love with. "It thrills me to be a part of something that no one else is doing."

"Even though that means holding an innocent man prisoner?"

Colleen's response, when it came, was measured, something she obviously had thought about a lot. "Look, George, I don't like seeing anyone living in a cage. When I was a kid, my mother loved birds. She had dozens of canaries. And every single one of them lived in a cage and one night I liberated all of them."

"I've never heard this story."

She gave a small, quick smile. "Hey, don't go thinking I'm a security risk, okay? But sometimes, I feel that way with Tyler. Like we should just open the door and let him fly away. But then I think about how unique he is and . . . I don't know." She shook her head as if to say it was all one big fat conundrum to her. "I just can't do it. He's protected with us. And even if we told him to leave, I don't think he would. He knows that if he's going to regain his visibility, we're the ones who are going to find the way to do it. I feel . . . well, responsible for him."

Interesting, Nash thought, and suddenly slipped his arm around her shoulders. He could feel the sharpness of her bones against his palm, the softness of her skin.

As they rounded the corner of the hangar, Nash wondered where the guard was. Taking a leak, he thought. Or an early dinner break, if he was smart. He used his ID card to get them into the building and they immediately went into the air-conditioned office, deserted for right now. Colleen unlocked the supply closet and they replaced the equipment they'd taken out to the Glades with the already loaded packs they would need in the aftermath of tonight's test run.

His head buzzed with dozens of details. He made intricate mental lists of everything that had to happen between now and this evening. And every item on those mental lists triggered some other item that he'd overlooked.

You're headed for Armageddon, Georgie. This little ditty, along with his mother's favorite saying about city hall, kept running through his mind as if on an endless loop. Old tapes, he thought. These were the old tapes playing, the very old tapes that had been playing since he was a kid in coveralls, the kid who limped, the kid whom the neighborhood bullies picked on. Hell, these tapes played all the goddamned time, even when things were going right, even when he slept. They were still playing when he hoisted his pack over his shoulder and turned to see Colleen sitting at the edge of the couch, pulling her top off over her head. Then she rolled her jeans down over the blades of her hips and down her perfect legs. The tapes stopped playing when she was completely naked and lifted her eyes to his face.

''While there's time,'' she whispered, and extended her arms like a child begging to be hugged, a gesture as seductive and inviting as the sight of her lovely skin.

Nash hesitated, but not because of any mental lists. He worried that someone might come in. And he worried, as he always did, about Colleen seeing his leg. He preferred making love in the dark, where he could imagine that his leg was a normal leg. ''Close the blinds,'' he said, and sidled like a crab to the open door, suddenly and unexpectedly eager for the taste of her. But when he reached out to shut the door, he *felt* something. He couldn't say what, exactly, that *something* was—a breeze that seemed out of place, a weird sense that they weren't alone. He froze, his right hand gripping the edge of the door, left hand clutching the strap of the backpack.

He swung the pack and it crashed into the door—*a door, not a person, not an Invisible.*

"What the *hell* are you doing?" Colleen exclaimed.

"Shutting the door," he said, as the door swung shut, and then he laughed at his own paranoia and dropped the bag to the floor and turned the dead bolt.

4

Logan barely got past Nash and through the door before he slammed the backpack against it. She stood very still in the hallway, struggling to keep her breathing inaudible, terrified that he would hear the rustling of her clothes or the shifting of the backpack against her body. She didn't move until she heard the distinctive *click* of the dead bolt sliding into place; then she backpedaled down the hall and around the corner. There, she doubled over, eyes squeezed shut against a tidal wave of pain, sobs pulsing up her throat. And right behind it surged rage that Nash had stolen three years from her and Tyler.

No, don't make a sound, straighten up, go do what you came here to do. . . .

She pressed her hand to her mouth, swallowing the sobs before they struck the air, fists clenched against the rage.

Now or never. Get moving.

Logan moved quickly up the hall. To her right, through a line of windows, the inside of the hangar was visible, several people working on a jeep, three more working on a chopper. She passed several empty offices, a staff room where three employees chatted and laughed over coffee. At the end of the hall, she saw the doors to the rest rooms and another door with a plaque on it that read ELECTRICAL, PERSONNEL ONLY.

That's me. Personnel on leave for the last three years.

She glanced through the window, into the hangar, checking to make sure no one was close enough to see the door open. The hall behind her was also clear. She touched the knob, her hands slick with sweat, and turned it. Just then, the door to the men's rest room opened and a man in coveralls strode out, brushing within inches of Logan. He came so close, in fact, that he looked at her, frowning slightly, sensing something, just as Nash had. Then he hurried on and she, unmoving, watched him until he rounded the corner.

Go. Now. Fast.

A heartbeat later, she was inside the room, moving slowly through the shadows. No security cameras in here, either, just one more piece of evidence to support her theory that the hangar wasn't all that important in Nash's scheme of things. But in *her* scheme of things, this room proved to be a treasure trove. Next to the main circuit box for the hangar, she found diagrams of the buildings on the base that indicated the locations of the transformers, main circuit boxes, backup generators, and every motion and thermal sensor.

She studied the diagrams, then walked around the room, inspecting everything, nodding to herself. *Diversion,* she thought. *Create a diversion.*

What would cause enough chaos? A fire, certainly, but a fire in here would mean that the sprinklers would come on, which would make her instantly visible.

A power shutdown might do it. Main bunker plus backup generators. Nash, of course, would have that base covered with battery packs for the computers, but that was fine. The ensuing chaos from the blackout would give her the few minutes she needed alone with the main computer, enough time to remove its hard disk. It would be visible, but if she waited until twilight to kill the power, then she would be running in the dark, making the disk drive more difficult to see.

She glanced at her watch. It was ten after six. She would kill the power around seven and be on the run by a quarter after. *Sounds like a plan,* she decided, and shrugged off her pack, unzipped it, and brought out her tools.

5
LOST

The problem with being an only child, Katie thought, was that you saw more than you wanted to of what went on between your parents. It was hard to hide your feelings in a family of three and at times like this, she wished she had a couple of obnoxious brothers or sisters to distract everyone.

At the moment, with the three of them in the canoe, her parents weren't speaking directly to each other. They spoke to each other through her. *Katie, tell your father we seem to be lost.* Or: *Katie, tell your mother we're headed west by southwest to the next campsite.*

She could take only so much of this and finally put on her headphones and popped an 'N Synch tape into her CD player and turned the volume up loud. There. Let them talk to each other. But, no surprise, they didn't.

Katie's mother, seated at the front of the canoe, paddled with a savage intensity, her shoulders hunched against the low-slung branches of the mangroves. Her misery radiated from her like a smell. Now and then she slapped at her cheek or neck or her leg, chasing mosquitoes or no-see-ums, the hungry little gnats that descended on south Florida every summer. Katie didn't have to look at her father to know his expression was grim and dark, the way it got whenever her parents were in one of their silent arguments. She could feel him behind her, his presence like some massive weight.

They were lost and they all knew it, but no one had come right out and said it yet. She sure wasn't going to be the first to say it. For her, it was part of the adventure and she knew her father would have seen it that way, too, if it had been just the two of them. Besides, it wasn't like being lost in a foreign country or anything, in the Amazon or the wilds of Borneo. This was just the Everglades in the US of A and all of the channels eventually led somewhere, right? People didn't die in the Everglades, didn't wander around in here for weeks or months or anything.

Last night, she had thrown an *I Ching* on the camping trip. She'd gotten the hexagram called *Waiting*, no changing lines. This hexagram was all about holding back, not something she'd wanted to hear about last night. But here they were, lost after wasted hours at the Quik Stop, light leaking out of the sky. Of course, her parents wouldn't have listened to *her* if she'd suggested they wait another day. Her father would have demanded to know why and if she'd told him about the hexagram, he and her mother would have exchanged one of those secretive parental looks. Even though her parents *respected* her right to personal interests, at least intellectually, neither of them placed much value in the *I Ching*.

They navigated a narrow channel in the mangroves, a spot where the trees grew so closely together their branches braided overhead, forming a dense green canopy that blocked out most of the sky. Not that she needed to see the sky to know it was just around dinnertime. Her stomach told her that much. Her stomach, in fact, craved one of those fat tuna sandwiches in the cooler, some Pringles chips, a handful of Skittles, and a chilled Coke to wash it all down. Unfortunately, the cooler didn't have any Pringles, Skittles, or Cokes. Her parents ate chicken and fish, with the emphasis on the latter, and a lot of salads and fruits. They rarely ate desserts, so she practically had to beg for candy and cookies, and forget soft drinks. Neither of her parents drank the stuff, so they just didn't buy it.

In the world according to Renie and Andrew Townsend, Gatorade was okay, water was better, and distilled or spring water was the best yet. Oh, she also got plenty of milk and cheese, those were always available in her refrigerator because she needed calcium, her father said. *I need Pringles, I need Cokes and salt, I need McDonald's, I need junk food.* But if she couldn't have any of that, the tuna sandwich on whole wheat would do just fine.

She lifted the lid of the cooler wedged between her legs and brought out three neatly wrapped tuna sandwiches. She handed one back to her father without turning to look at him and passed one forward to her mother, who didn't glance around. She passed out bottles of cold water, individually wrapped slices of Swiss cheese, drumsticks.

Her father tapped her on the shoulder and she moved the headphones off her ears and let them fall around her neck. "Tell your mother there's a campsite about a mile from here."

Katie rolled her eyes. "Tell her yourself, Dad," she said, and put her headphones back on and finished the rest of her tuna sandwich.

She knew things were going to be tense when, at the entrance to the trail, her mother had tried to convince her father that they should just turn around and go home. She hadn't been included in *that* conversation. Democracy had gone straight out the window. Her father, naturally, had refused—what sane person wouldn't?—and her mother had been faced with an immediate choice. She could drop them off, go home, and wait for their call in three or four days—or she could join them. She had joined them.

Big mistake.

They had reached a campsite within an hour, but it was an ugly spot, a spit of sand with some scraggly trees, no bathroom facilities, no grill, as primitive as primitive got. Her mother had refused to get out of the canoe and insisted they find a chickee for the night. It would be safer, she argued. No bugs, no creepy crawlers, no gators, no surprises, yada yada, hallelujah and amen.

A chickee was a wooden platform raised seven or eight feet out of the water or the saw grass. The Seminole Indians used to build them way back when and the park service had copied the design for campsites. The park chickees had Jiffy Johns, grills, thatched roofs, about as good as it got out here. In fact, in her mother's mind, a chickee was the Everglades equivalent of the Hilton. But her father wanted the raw outdoors. Katie just wanted to get somewhere, anywhere at all, before it got dark.

They'd gotten lost after they'd left the beach campsite, lost despite the compass and her father's usually terrific sense of direction. They were looking for a particular "loop," a prescribed route that wound through the ten thousand islands along the hundred-mile trip along the Wilderness Waterway. This loop went from Flamingo, to Middle Cape, Carl Ross, and back to Flamingo. The problem, she knew, was that her father had put in at a spot that was supposed to be a shortcut because he wanted to cut down on the paddle time so that her mother wouldn't complain. Her father had been so sure about his ability to navigate this loop, he hadn't brought along a map. He'd tried hooking his Pocket PC to the cell phone so he could download a map, but the cell phone didn't work in here.

Technology, she thought, could be a pain in the ass when you needed something you could touch, hold, grip in your sweaty little palm.

They'd found one choked, narrow channel after another. Sometimes, the channel was impassable even for a canoe because the drought was sucking the Everglades dry. Other times, the channel was impassable because of fallen trees. In either case, they always turned around and looked for yet another channel and another. In fact, if there was a system for getting lost, this was it.

She finished her sandwich and realized the light was going and so were the batteries in her CD player. Just as she unzipped her pack to dig around for more batteries, the channel widened, emptying into a lagoon, and the sky opened up. Way on the other side of the lagoon stood a village on stilts—not a lone chickee, not even two chickees connected by a bridge, but a *village*.

"What the hell is *that?*" her mother exclaimed.

"There're no villages out here," her father said.

"Yeah? So what would you call that *arrangement*, Andy?"

They were finally speaking to each other again, Katie thought, and brought the video camera out of her pack. "Awesome." She zoomed in on the village, but because they were still so far from it, she couldn't tell much about it. "I think it's a bunch of chickees. Let's camp there. I bet they have a Jiffy John and a grill." And hey, maybe even vending machines crammed with junk food!

Her mother raised her arms toward the sky. "Oh, God, make it so. Please make it so. And let them have a hot shower, too, and maybe a Jacuzzi?"

Katie's dad actually *laughed* and her mother glanced around, smiling at that, at the fact that she'd made him laugh, and suddenly, just like that, everything between them was okay again. Katie just shook her head and turned the camera first on her father, and then on her mother, capturing their expressions, that *point of transition*, as her communication teacher had called it. Even though her teacher had been referring to writing and speaking, Katie knew it applied to her parents' marriage as well.

"We'll go take a look," her father said.

"If we're going all that way just for a look, Andy, then

I think we'd better call it home for the night. We've got maybe half an hour of daylight left.''

"More than that, Mom.''

"Not much more.''

"Okay, so we'll call it home for the night,'' her father said. "I'm as anxious to get somewhere as everyone else. But how come this spot isn't on any of the park maps as a designated campsite?''

"I thought you didn't bring any maps,'' Katie said.

"I brought a *general* map,'' he replied.

"Maybe this area is new, Dad.''

"Or maybe it's intended for group camping,'' her mother remarked. "Although I really can't imagine a whole lot of groups out here in the summer.''

Once they were out in the lagoon, a slight breeze kicked up, licking the sweat from Katie's skin. She zoomed in on the village again and this time she could see details—interlocking wooden bridges, five or six wooden huts with thatched roofs, a wooden dock, all of it built under the shelter of mangrove branches, so that it probably wasn't visible from the air. No boats, though. But then, they hadn't seen another boat since they'd put the canoe in the water.

What struck her as a bit weird was that there wasn't a bird in sight. In a lagoon like this, she expected to see a lot of wading birds—blue herons, egrets, wood storks. She expected to see vultures hiding in the mangrove branches. And where were the gators? The snapping turtles? She hadn't even seen a jumping fish since they'd entered the lagoon.

"Hey,'' she said. "Stop paddling for a second. Listen.''

They pulled their paddles up out of the water. Except for the gentle noise of water against the sides of the canoe, a tight, eerie silence permeated the lagoon. Katie thought of that dark cloud of birds they'd seen at the Last Stop, of the army of ants on the move. And suddenly, this camping trip didn't seem like such a great adventure. Suddenly, she wished she had sided with her mother and convinced her father that they should have turned around and gone home.

2

Ross Farris had shown up right on schedule, at eighteen hundred hours. Now he moved restlessly around the control room, studying each of the monitors, questioning Nash's employees to clarify details he supposedly didn't understand. His presence here was a goddamn distraction, Nash thought, and signaled Colleen to stick to him like Velcro.

Each of the monitors provided a different view of the Tesla village, from the dock to the bridges to the inside of the huts. Everything looked about as perfect as perfect gets. The area was still and uninhabited, except for Dog in hut four, who was agitated at the moment, pacing back and forth as far as her chain would allow. She was quite alone in the hut, not even a lizard in sight.

It worried him that the wildlife had been getting the hell out of Dodge long before the process began. It was the sort of pattern someone on the outside might notice. It also meant they didn't catch too many animal specimens, except for ants and spiders and an occasional fish that were usually killed by the shrouding. Farris, of course, had some questions about that, about why he'd seen so many birds fleeing the Everglades earlier today.

"Colleen implied that the animals know when the shrouding is going to take place, George. You have any explanation for that?"

Nash was standing at one of the computers, his fingers flying over the keyboard, locking in the automatic countdown. "Nope, no explanation, Ross. I'm not a biologist."

"Interesting. It's how animals act in an earthquake zone days before an earthquake hits."

Nash just nodded. Let him think what he wanted. The truth was actually stranger. The first few times the Tesla village had been shrouded, they had caught all sorts of wildlife—birds, gators, fish, reptiles. By the third or fourth shrouding, wildlife started leaving the area long before the shrouding happened. Nash believed this was the hundredth monkey shit in action, but he wasn't about to say that to Farris.

"Ross, take a look at this."

Colleen appeared at Farris's side, rescuing Nash. But the way she touched Farris's arm bothered Nash, a touch that was too familiar, almost too intimate. She led him across the room to yet another monitor, another computer, and Nash, distracted, watched them for a moment.

She was animated now as she explained something to Farris. And Farris listened carefully, nodding, taking it all in, his eyes never leaving Colleen's face. Then he leaned toward Colleen, whispering something, and her soft, seductive laugh made Nash's blood boil. He knew that laugh, all right, knew it as intimately as he knew her body. He had heard it only a few hours ago, in the hangar.

You're imagining things, pal.

Maybe. But when he compared himself physically to Farris, it was certainly easy to see why Colleen was attracted to him. Farris didn't have any disabilities. His legs were perfect, strong and muscular. He walked without limping, without using a cane. *Jesus, leg, I hate you.*

As if in response to the thought, his leg felt suddenly weak and he had to grab on to the edge of a desk to steady himself.

The weakness passed and Nash forced himself to focus on the computer, on the monitors, on the automatic lock for the countdown. No time now to think about Colleen, about Farris. No time for anything except the immediate task.

3

Now that they were closer to the village, Renie thought that it resembled a movie set. The huts, clustered together in the center, weren't really huts, she could see that now. Most of them lacked something—four walls, a roof, doors, windows. Any second now, the crew would appear and a director would saunter out, shouting, *Cut, cut.* Given how large an industry filmmaking had become in South Florida in the last fifteen years, it was a great theory. But it didn't hold up. If the village were a set for a movie—or even for a commercial—there would be other people around in canoes and Zodiac rafts. There would be lights, cameras, action! But the village looked to be as deserted as the lagoon itself.

That made her uneasy.

The village backed up to saw grass, a vast field of the stuff already suffused with twilight and shadows. Beyond the saw grass stood another mangrove. Rope ladders hung from the dock and in the screen on Katie's video camera, Renie thought she spotted a grill, a Jiffy John, semblances of civilization, thank God.

But no people, no boats, and definitely no crew, no directors, no movie set. *Forget that theory.*

Moments later, the canoe bumped up against the sides of the village dock and Katie grabbed the rope ladder, steadying the canoe as she and Andy tied it up. "Before we unload all our gear," Andy said, "let's have a quick look."

"Yeah, good idea," Renie said. *And then we'll head back to town and find a Hilton.* Except that by then it would be dark.

They grabbed their packs and Katie went up the ladder first, not scrambling, but moving with uncharacteristic caution, as if she, too, were disturbed by the eerie silence of the place. Renie followed her and when she stepped foot on the wooden platform, she felt the silence in the pit of her stomach. Andy came up last and stopped next to Renie.

"I don't think this is a campsite," he whispered.

"Good. Let's go home."

She started to turn, but he grabbed her hand. "C'mon, Ren. We're here, we should at least look around."

Renie stabbed her finger at the sky and in a low, urgent voice, said, "Take a look, babe. We've got about ten minutes of light left. I, for one, do *not* want to be paddling around in the Everglades in the goddamn dark."

"We've got at least half an hour of light," he argued.

"Ten minutes, thirty minutes. The point is that we're either camping here or we're sleeping in the goddamn canoe. And that isn't even an option, as far as I'm concerned. I'm going to start unloading the gear."

He rolled his eyes and shook his head, a clear sign that he thought she was making a big deal out of nothing, and walked on, hurrying after Katie.

"Yeah, great." *And fuck you, too.*

Renie stood there, glaring at him, at his receding back, at father catching up to daughter, and once again felt the familiar mathematical axiom clicking in. *Two against one.* And in the next moment, her anger gave way to outright fear that everything about this place was *wrong,* and the smartest thing they could do would be to get out of here now.

4

"Uh, George?" Colleen came up alongside him, her voice an urgent whisper. "Take a look at monitor three. We have a problem."

Nash glanced to his right and everything inside him went

dead. People in the village. A man, a woman, and a kid. "Who the hell are *they?* Where'd they come from?"

"I . . . I don't know," she stammered. "I was checking the monitors and there they were."

Like they'd dropped in from outer space. "You're supposed to keep tabs on the monitors." *And if you hadn't been flirting with Farris, you would have caught this sooner.* "Get Panther on the radio. *Fast.*" Nash played the computer keys and zoomed in on their faces, as if their features would tell him who they were and why they were in the village and why Panther and his crew had missed them.

"Looks like a rather interesting situation, George." Farris paused beside him, watching the intruders on the monitor. He sounded calm, even pleased with this turn of events. "Let's proceed as planned and pick them up along with the dog."

"That's insane," Nash hissed. "They're tourists, for Chrissakes. They haven't been trained, they—"

"Training didn't help Logan and Tyler, now, did it?" He leaned into Nash's face, whispering, "We need human subjects."

"Jesus. The countdown." The countdown had already started. "*Abort,*" Nash shouted, and lunged toward the main computer. "*Abort the countdown!*"

Then the lights blinked off, on, off again, the screens went blank, and the entire control room shut down. The silence, the utterly complete silence, shocked Nash so deeply that for a moment or two he simply stood there, blinking against the dark. *Why haven't the generators come on?*

5

"Mom, Dad," Katie shouted, gesturing wildly from the doorway of one of the huts. "There's a dog in here. Come fast."

A dog? Here? How could that be good? It might be feral.

Or rabid. Renie lurched forward, driven by maternal instinct and something even deeper than that, something more primal, the reptilian brain shrieking at her to retrieve her daughter and husband and get out of the village.

The dock swayed and creaked beneath her feet, a noise that seemed out of place, somehow false, like a sound effect in a movie. Renie glanced around for boats, people, some sign of habitation. But there wasn't even a trash can in sight. Forget the movie theory, the sixty-second commercial theory. This village was as out of place here as human constructs on the moon.

Later, in the moments between Renie's first sight of the dog and the incipience of the humming, it would occur to her that it was already too late. It would feel like one of those fated moments when your life rushes toward you in all its grand splendor and pathetic squalor and you just stand there, knowing this is the point where everything diverges, knowing that if you don't do something, you're going to be mown down.

She didn't leap aside.

The dog was a young black Lab, tethered to a thick and nasty-looking chain in one of the huts. No water, no food, the heat beyond endurance. Like the little bird earlier today, the dog was suffering. But it wasn't mortally wounded like the bird. In fact, it got to its feet and wagged its tail when it saw Katie and Andy.

"You poor baby," Katie crooned, crouching in front of the Lab. "Let's get you off this chain. What jerk did this to you?"

"Katie, hon, you can't just take the dog off the chain," said Andy. "The dog belongs to someone."

"No food or water, it's hot, the chain's too tight . . . This owner doesn't deserve the dog. Besides, I'm not saying we should keep it. We should just take it out of here."

Andy glanced to Renie for help and support, but she happened to agree with Katie. "We're rescuing her, Andy, not keeping her. Get that chain off her, Katie. I'll give her some water. And then let's leave. I don't like this place."

"Minutes ago you were saying we should camp here." Andy sounded exasperated now. He always did when the family math went against *him.*

"There's something . . . I don't know . . . eerie about this place. I don't like it."

She dug a bottle of water and a paper cup from her pack, filled the cup, and held it on the floor in front of the dog as Katie unhooked the chain from the leather collar. A new leather collar, Renie noticed, and it was fastened so tightly around the dog's neck that she wondered how it—*she*— could swallow.

"This is theft," Andy muttered.

"It's animal cruelty," countered Katie.

Two against one, Renie thought. The dog lapped up the water, her tail wagging. She finally raised her head, water dripping from her mouth, barked, and alternately licked Katie, Renie, then looked up at Andy as if asking if he would like to be licked, too.

"Maybe she's hungry," Andy said, and handed the dog half of his tuna sandwich.

She wolfed it down as though she hadn't eaten in weeks. "Let's get going," Renie said. "We—"

Renie never finished her sentence. A humming filled the air, but not like any kind of humming she'd ever heard before. This was eerie, physically uncomfortable, and quickly escalated in pitch. The dog started howling and running around in mad, frenzied circles, as if chasing her tail. Renie slapped her hands over her ears, but it didn't help. The humming pierced her skull and drove her to her knees.

Suddenly, the air around her crackled. It sounded exactly the way Rice Krispies sound when milk first touches them, except that it seemed to be amplified a thousand times. *Snap, crackle, pop.* Then there was an explosion of light so brilliant, so blinding, that she threw her arms up to shield her eyes. The high-pitched, agonizing sound stabbed through her eardrums, deep into her skull, and she sank into blackness as if beneath some huge, inexorable tide.

6

Within two minutes of the power going down, the damage reports had begun pouring in by radio and cell phone. And with every report, Nash thought, the picture looked progressively bleaker.

The electricians wouldn't be able to bring the power back on-line for several hours—and that was an optimistic estimate. The backup generators in the bunker were dead, but the ones in the hangar and the other bunker were not. The backup batteries for the computers in this room were dead, but the battery-operated emergency lights throughout the bunker were working. Nash already had dispatched the special forces unit trained for the challenges of moving around in a shrouded space. Someone on that team would check with security at the entrance to the park to find out if the man, woman, and child they'd seen had registered when they'd entered. If they had, Nash's job would be somewhat easier.

But the more immediate problem was that neither the special forces unit nor Panther had the expertise to assess anything like this. Nash needed to be there. He limped over to Colleen, who was on the radio with one of the electricians. "We need to get out to the village. Get your things."

"But Ross said—"

"I don't give a shit what Ross said."

"You should." Farris came up behind Nash on feet made of silk, feet that didn't make a sound. "A chopper's waiting for us outside. I already alerted the Ponce facility that they should secure the area for three more Invisibles.''

''You did *what?*'' Nash exploded.

Farris's small dark eyes—*predatory eyes,* Nash thought—regarded him as though he were an annoying rodent. ''Let's get something straight, my friend. In the light of this major fuckup''—and he opened his arms wide, a gesture that embraced the entire nightmare—''I become the damage control and *you*''—he rocked forward on the balls of his feet and sank his index finger into Nash's chest—''take orders from *me.* Are we clear on that?''

Nash shoved Farris's hand away from his chest. Farris simply smiled, a thin, terrible smile that didn't touch those shark eyes, and turned. ''Let's get moving.''

Can't fight city hall, son, whispered his mother's voice.

Colleen touched his arm. ''C'mon, let's get our stuff. If we don't go out there with him, things will really get fucked up.''

She didn't get it. Farris wasn't just appointing himself head honcho of damage control. He was seizing control of the project. He was no different than some petty dictator. Never mind that Farris didn't know shit about science. Never mind that he didn't have a clue how the shrouding worked. He knew about politics and defense and spoke the same language as the committee members, the Pentagon assholes, the *money* people. He was their liaison, their voice, and when they applied pressure on *him,* he put the pressure on Nash. They wanted human guinea pigs—and now they would have not only Tyler, but three more.

No, Colleen didn't get it at all.

''Get these people out,'' Nash said, gesturing at the people around them. ''And lock the door. I don't want anyone in here.''

7

The lock clicked shut, a sharp, distinctive sound, and for several moments Logan stayed still, barely breathing, a part of her believing it was all some elaborate trick. She could hear the noise in the hallway, the chaos, radios crackling and cell phones pealing. She had one hand in the pocket of her shorts, where her fingers touched the cool stone with the embedded fossil that the Indian—Luis—had tossed her three years ago. Her good luck charm.

And those people, who were those people who stumbled into Nash's secret little village?

The door still hadn't opened. *You're safe, get moving.* She finally moved and God, it felt good, her leg muscles stretching, the kink in her shoulders loosening, her knees cracking—and no one around to hear. She made a beeline for what she believed to be the main computer, set her pack on the floor, unzipped it.

If it hadn't been for Nash's insistence three years ago that she and Tyler pack a variety of objects in their bags, she wouldn't have these tools. Granted, they were basic. But they would get her into the box of what appeared to be the main computer so that she could remove the hard drive. It took her longer than it should have. Her own thoughts sought to sabotage her, throwing up images of herself later on, extracting files from the hard drive and finding nothing on Tyler or his location. *The Ponce facility,* Farris had said. *Where is it?*

Logan got the damn thing out and zipped it into a small pocket of her pack. To a Visible, it would look strange, a little rectangular object floating in midair like some miniature UFO. But the emergency lights were dim, it was nearly dark outside by now, and she knew she would make it. She had to make it. If she were dead, she would be of absolutely no use to Tyler. And she would never get even with Nash.

Logan screwed the back of the case onto the computer, then punched one of the buttons on the phone. She hesitated before she picked up the receiver, weighing the risk, then decided the need was greater than the risk. She grabbed a piece of Kleenex from a box on the desk, wrapped it around her index finger, and rubbed it once across the button she had just pressed, smearing her fingerprint. Invisible, yes, but she still left fingerprints.

She punched out Abby's number—not her cell phone, but a number she used for call-forwarding. That number, in turn, would forward the call to yet another phone and finally, to her cell phone.

Click, click, click. Your call is being forwarded . . .

One ring. Someone picked up, but didn't speak. Logan said, "Delaney." The name of Abby's grandson.

"You ready, girl?"

"Be as close as you can."

"Right."

She disconnected and Logan set the receiver down, rubbed her prints off of it, and moved swiftly to the door. Ear pressed to the wood, she listened.

Noise, chaos, nothing had changed. *Now or never.*

One of the phones in the control room rang. She froze, listening as the answering machine picked up the call. "George, it's Panther. Your cell is turned off or dead. I contacted the guard at the park entrance. Only one family with a girl registered today. Their names are Andrew and Renie Townsend and their daughter, Katie. He supplied Social Security numbers, work numbers, everything we need. He's an ER doc in Fort Lauderdale, she's a Realtor. They won't get out of the Glades. I'll be in touch."

A family in deep shit because of me, she thought. If she hadn't killed the power, the experiment wouldn't have gone forward until the intruders had left the site. They were going to need help.

Using the Kleenex, she turned the dead bolt on the door, spun the knob. The door swung inward, Logan behind it, peering through the crack. People hurried past, the emergency lights continued to glow, and way back in the bunker somewhere, an alarm shrieked.

Move. Fast.

She moved like the wind, around the edge of the door, into the hall, her body aimed at the exit. The main door stood open now because the lack of power meant no AC and the windowless bunker had heated up rapidly. Even with the door open, the fresh air was practically nil.

Before she reached the open door, someone shouted, "Hey, what the hell's *that?*"

And then she ran, flat-out ran like she had never run as a Visible, her arms tucked tightly against her sides, her body straining. She burst into the outdoors, into the humid June evening, and that air, fresh as it was, felt like hot cotton when she inhaled it.

Her bare feet pounded the concrete and, behind her, someone gave chase, shoes hammering the pavement. Logan ran on, toward the fence, through the gate. It clattered as she swept through it, she didn't dare look back. She zigzagged across the old tarmac, plunged down a gentle slope into the darkening shadows along the side of the road. The Land Rover's headlights flashed once; then it raced toward her, pebbles and dirt flying up around it. As it slowed, the passenger door flew open and Logan dived inside.

Abby gunned the accelerator and spun in the middle of the road, a perfect one-eighty, and shouted, *"Hold on to your seat, girl, it's gonna get rough!"*

Behind them, two jeeps careened out of the hangar, but before they hit the road, Abby had left them gasping in the dust.

6
INTO THE DARK

His eyes. Something seemed to be wrong with his eyes.
That was the first thing Andy noticed when he opened them.
The lids felt heavy, weighted, as though a hot, sweaty hand
lay against them. They also felt gritty and dry and it occurred
to him that he probably should take out his contacts. Then
he realized that he was sprawled on his stomach, his right
cheek pressed against damp wood, and that he was staring
into the amber eyes of a dog.

It all rushed back to him then, the Everglades, the weird
village on stilts, the dog, the humming and crackling of the
air, and the blast of light. As he lifted up on his hands, the
dog blinked, whimpered softly, and struggled to its feet.
What happened? What the fuck just happened?

Andy rocked back onto his heels. His head spun. His
mouth tasted of deserts, dry heat, sand, and something bitter.
His cheek ached. He guessed that when he'd passed out—
is that what happened? We passed out? From what? Why?—
the right side of his face had struck the wooden platform
floor.

He turned his head to the right and saw his wife, struggling to a sitting position, her long dark hair wild, disheveled. She looked as confused as he felt. The dog was licking Katie's face, waking her.

"Everyone . . . okay?" Andy asked.

Katie knuckled her eyes. "I feel weird."

"I feel like I died," Renie groaned. "Maybe we *are* dead." Then, whispering, "Is that possible? Is it possible we're dead and don't know it?"

"I didn't see any tunnels or lights," Katie said.

Andy hadn't either, but just the same, he pinched himself. It hurt. Not dead, he thought. "We're not dead. I don't think you feel like this when you're dead."

"But we don't know for sure," Renie said.

"Mom, if you were dead, you'd be at a Holiday Inn."

"Forget the Holiday Inn. I'd be at a chateau in Tuscany. So if we're not dead, what the hell happened?"

"I don't know."

Andy rocked onto the balls of his feet, then stood. His entire body felt strange, loose, and rubbery, as if it didn't really belong to him. He went over to his wife, grasped her hand, helped her up, then went over to his daughter. Katie stood unsteadily, gripping his hand for a moment.

"Let's get back to the canoe," he said. "The light's nearly gone. Will the dog follow you, Katie?"

"Her name's Lucky."

"When did you decide that?"

"Just now. I think that's what she's going to be for us." Katie whistled for her. "C'mon, Lucky."

The dog needed no encouragement. She darted out ahead of them, then paused in the doorway, growling softly. "What's wrong with her?" Renie asked.

Katie shook her head. "I don't—"

And then Andy heard what the dog had heard: engines. A lot of boat engines. No, not boats. These engines sounded louder—*airboats*. A lot of them. He had a sudden and disturbing vision of drunken rednecks descending on the village, dangerous men with guns and a blood lust. He stepped out of the hut, looked quickly around the corner of it. What he saw didn't connect with anything he understood. His brain struggled to find a context into which the scene would fit.

Then something clicked and he realized he was seeing half a dozen airboats racing through the rapidly fading light that varnished the surface of the lagoon. The airboats carried armed soldiers in battle fatigues. Behind and to the sides of the battalion of airboats were more soldiers in small boats with outboard motors.

Not rednecks.

Renie, peering over his shoulder, stammered, "Jesus, what—"

"Stay back," Andy hissed, his arm shooting out to stop his wife and daughter.

The dog darted out of the hut and veered away from the approaching maelstrom. Katie shouted, *"Lucky, no!"*

The dog kept right on going and Katie, naturally, went after her. Andy and Renie raced after Katie and, seconds later, gunfire riddled the area where they all had been standing. *Lucky, for sure. The dog saved our butts.* The thought flitted through Andy's head as they ran into what appeared to be the back of the village, into deepening shadows and across a wooden bridge that swung wildly over saw grass and black water.

More gunfire exploded off to his left but instead of bullets, he saw darts embedded in the posts, dozens of darts. *What the hell's going on here?* A chopper appeared overhead. Moments later, a second chopper joined it, this one with bright searchlights that made sweeping arcs through the village. Hunkered over, the three of them dashed after the dog. Lucky ran in and out of shadowed places, working her way farther and farther from the gunfire. Now and then she glanced back, as if to make sure they were still behind her.

"I knew we should've gone to a motel," Renie shouted. "There's no way off this thing."

"Keep following the dog," Andy shouted back.

They pursued the dog. Then she stopped, barked, and ran back and forth along the edge of the platform until they reached her. Breathless, Andy stood there with his wife and daughter, peering down at a ladder and a canoe. It seemed too damned convenient, that canoe bobbing in the darkened waters with what looked like a supply container in the back of it. But what the hell. They couldn't get back to their own canoe. This was their only ticket off the chickee.

"Renie, you first. Then Katie. I'll pick up Lucky and hand her down."

His wife scrambled down the ladder, then Katie followed. Lucky moved restlessly along the edge of the platform, alternately barking and whimpering.

"C'mon, girl, you're going with us." Andy sat back on his heels at the edge of the platform. Lucky hurried right over and allowed him to pick her up. She didn't squirm, didn't try to break free. She seemed to understand what he intended to do. He handed her down to Renie, swung around, and scrambled down the ladder.

A chopper suddenly swept in over the back of the village, searchlights blazing. "Start paddling," Andy shouted at his wife, and pushed away from the dock with the edge of his paddle and steered them straight toward the field of saw grass.

Beyond the saw grass lay thickets of mangroves. If they could reach them in time, then they stood a ghost of a chance of getting out of here. It was nearly dark. He doubted the airboats would follow them into the narrow channels in the mangroves. The low water level wouldn't be a problem for the airboats, but the overhang of branches might deter them. The small boats, however, would make it through easily enough and Andy fully expected them to give chase. He didn't have any idea what the hell they had stumbled into.

They paddled hard and furiously toward the saw grass. The choppers kept circling, sporadic gunfire rang out behind them. Andy didn't understand why the choppers didn't pursue them. They hadn't reached the saw grass yet, the guys in the choppers had to have them in sight. The twilight, he thought, that had to be it. Here in the lagoon, so close to the mangroves, the light seemed especially murky, brooding, strange.

He switched to the right side of the canoe, Renie to the left. Andy steered around a tangle of branches, and a moment later they slid into the saw grass. It was tall stuff that grew in clusters of tough, slender stalks with serrated edges sharp enough to slice skin to the bone. The stalks clawed the sides of the canoe as it passed through the stuff.

Katie pulled her arms in close to her sides and wrapped them around the dog, which huddled between her legs. She dropped her head back, peering up at the sky. "It's dark. We're going to make it."

"*Make it?*" Renie exploded. "Make it where? We should've stayed home or gone to a motel."

Shut up, Andy thought. *Just shut up.* They paddled through the saw grass, the sound of the choppers moving farther and farther away from them. He finally heard swamp noises again—crickets, frogs, fish splashing in the dark waters.

"I've got to stop, Andy. My arms are killing me. We're pretty deep into this stuff. The choppers can't see us."

"Good idea."

As the canoe came to a standstill, Renie shifted around. "We need to . . . oh Jesus . . . What . . ."

Andy spun around so fast that the canoe rocked precariously to one side. Perhaps a hundred feet behind them, through the passage the canoe had cut in the saw grass, he had a clear line of sight of the brilliant lights that bathed the lagoon. Lights from the choppers, the airboats, lights so bright they were like a new sun. And through that light ran armed men, up and down bridges, the dock, into and out of the huts. But they looked as if they were running around in midair because the bridges, the dock, the huts, the entire goddamn village was no longer visible.

Right then, all of his training and habituation as an ER doc went south. Everything he'd assumed to be real about the world shriveled up and blew away like dust. An atavistic fear seized him. He thrust his paddle into the shallow water and paddled like a madman. Right side, left side, right again. *Get away, fast, fast . . .*

2

The lagoon was lit up like a stage, the powerful searchlights on the surrounding airboats all aimed at the village. But there was no village, at least none that the eye could detect. Only the people in the village were visible, the best of Nash's best, his special forces unit, a dozen men and women trained specifically to move through invisible locations.

They looked like large insects as they navigated the brightly lit space with eerie precision, their steps rarely faltering. All of them were armed with tranquilizing rifles, fully loaded weapons, and certain instruments that made their presence in the zone easier to deal with. They wore battle fatigues and boots and thermal-sensitive goggles.

Even so, Nash knew, some of them would be suffering from spatial disorientation by tomorrow. The reports from medical would trickle down—acute nausea, fevers, diarrhea, mental confusion, Christ knew what else. Training didn't offer automatic immunity from the effects. But put an *untrained* person in a situation like this and it would knock him out flat in seconds. The brain had trouble assimilating the movement of the physical body through a place that couldn't be perceived, that had no points of reference.

After all, it wasn't just the village that had been rendered invisible. Everything within a thirty-foot radius had also been zapped into the twilight zone. Trees, brush, saw grass. Everything except for the water. He could see the water. He could see the ripples on its surface, the way its dark face reflected all the lights.

"Stop here," he called to Dobson, who was piloting the airboat.

"No, go in farther," Farris snapped.

Dobson killed the engine and looked at Nash, at Farris, at Colleen, and then back at Nash again. In the spill of the lights, the stipples of sweat on Dobson's face stood out. Nash could see the cords of tendons in his neck. But his eyes looked calm, steady. "No offense, Mr. Farris," he said. "But it's not safe to take the airboat any farther. Too risky." He climbed down from the pilot's seat and went over to the Zodiac raft that lay facedown at the back of the airboat. "This won't damage the village dock if we bump into it."

A vein in Farris's temple pounded hard, furiously. For tense, terrible moments, the two men just stared at each other, Farris's hand in his jacket pocket, going for his weapon, Dobson's hand on his holstered Glock. Nash realized that although Farris believed he had seized control of the project—at least for the moment, Nash thought—a major part of the project involved people who were loyal to Nash. He also realized this possibility never had occurred to Farris, who simply had assumed that Nash's people would do whatever *he* told them to do.

"Goggles, Ross, you'll need goggles," said Colleen, touching Farris's arm in that strangely intimate way that made Nash's blood boil. "The goggles cut down on the spatial disorientation. We don't know why, they just do. They also enable us to see body heat." She thrust a pair of goggles into his hand, distracting him from his struggle of wills with Dobson, then she dropped the Zodiac over the side, holding on to the rope. "Let's go."

Her intervention dispelled the tension and, just that fast,

the balance of power shifted again. Farris didn't look too happy about any of it and Nash knew that somewhere down the line, Farris would get even with Dobson for his loyalty to Nash.

"How many cylinders do we want, Doctor Nash?" Dobson asked.

"Let's load them all."

The cylinders, half a dozen of them, were filled with pressurized water, which they would spray throughout the entire village. If the intruders were still there, the water would make them visible.

So far, though, the team in the village hadn't found any evidence of the intruders and Nash didn't expect they would. He was pretty sure the intruders had recovered before the team had arrived and had fled with the dog, in the supply canoe that had been tied at the back of the village. But he had to be sure.

In the village, a Special Ops man saw them and waved one of the thin, sturdy canes that everyone on the team carried. It was equipped with an electronic sensor that beeped when the tip of the cane got within several inches of something solid. The man swung the cane this way and that as he moved along the dock, then sliced the cane through the air, indicating that Dobson should cut the engine.

"It's really tricky in here," he shouted. "So make sure you keep the goggles on and use the canes."

"We'll do just fine, don't you worry," Farris called.

Jesus, Nash thought, and rolled his eyes at Colleen, who simply shook her head, as if to say that Farris was a hopeless case. But if he were so hopeless, why did she flirt with him? Why did she use that soft, seductive laugh on him? *Not now*, he thought. *Not while city hall is here.*

Dobson paddled closer, and then the Special Ops guy tossed them a rope and pulled them in. As they bumped up against the invisible dock, he crouched down. "Ladder should be right about here." He slid his hand along what

Nash assumed was the edge of the dock, then grasped something. "Give me your hand, Mr. Farris. And if I were you, I'd put on the goggles. Otherwise you may end up in the water. Spatial disorientation isn't a myth."

Farris slipped on the goggles that Colleen had given him, groped for the top rung of the ladder, and had to feel around with his foot before he found the bottom rung. He slipped before he got to the top and, for seconds, just hung there, his feet scrambling for purchase against the side of the invisible dock. Nash felt a smug satisfaction watching Farris struggle with the very thing Nash himself struggled with every time he climbed a ladder anywhere.

Then he clambered to the top and the Special Ops man grasped his forearms and pulled him onto the dock. "Just sit there for a few minutes, Mr. Farris. Get your bearings."

No bravado from Farris this time. He was breathing hard, sweat covered his face. He pushed the goggles back onto the top of his head, pulled his legs up against his chest, and sat there looking like he was going to throw up any second now. Nash managed to climb the ladder with more ease than he usually did when it was visible and silently thanked his leg for cooperating. Once he was on the dock, he helped Dobson and Colleen unload the cylinders, their packs, and the canes. Practice, he thought, made for certain advantages in the field.

"Please help Mr. Farris get acclimated up here," Nash said to the Special Ops man.

"You got it. So far, there's no sign of the intruders, Doctor Nash."

Hardly surprising. "What about Dog or the supply canoe?"

"No."

"Any word from Panther? He was supposed to be here."

"He was here briefly and left. You're supposed to call him."

Nash and Colleen moved away from Farris and the Special

Ops man with their packs and canes and cylinders of water slung over their shoulders. "Ross Farris doesn't belong out here," Colleen said.

"Maybe if you stopped coming on to him he would go away."

The words were out of his mouth before he even realized he'd blurted them. Her head whipped toward him and those cat eyes narrowed with a kind of terrifying fierceness, as though he had cornered her in a room without windows or doors. "You're married, George. I'm single. Until that changes, you don't have a pot to piss in on that score."

"How eloquent," Nash drolled.

They walked on, using their canes now, alternately tapping and swinging them. The *tap tap tap, tap tap, tap* sounded like some sort of Morse code, three taps, two, then one.

The team had already sprayed this part of the dock with water and had collected whatever they'd found here. Just the same, Nash turned on the cylinder and aimed the nozzle at the dock. A fine mist shot out and the damp wood materialized slowly, a plank here, a plank there. Nash hurried on, seeking to put some distance between himself and Colleen, and limped his way into Dog's hut.

The team had been in here already and parts of the floor and one wall were still moist and visible. He used the partially visible wall to his left as a reference point and moved cautiously forward, spraying the water from right to left about a foot in front of him, so that he could see where he was walking. The next spray made part of Dog's chain visible. Nash sprayed along it until he could see all of it, including part of the dog's collar that Colleen had bought only last week at PetSmart. Dog couldn't wiggle out of the collar on her own, it had been buckled too tightly. He sprayed until he could see the entire collar, unbuckled and discarded against the floor.

Kid saw the dog and freed it. And Dog, recognizing an

ally, had stuck to the kid and her parents and escaped with them on the supply canoe.

Nash began to feel dizzy and short of breath, effects of spatial disorientation, and sat down on the floor, his back to the lagoon and the airboats and all the brilliant lights. He slipped his cell phone out of his pack, dismayed to see that it was off. No wonder he hadn't heard from Panther. When he turned the phone on, he found five voice messages from Panther, all of them brief and exactly the same. *Call me pronto, boss.*

Panther answered on the first ring, his voice low and gruff, a troll's voice. "Can't stay in touch if your cell phone's not on, boss. I left a message on the control room answering machine. You get it?"

"No. Who the fuck are they?"

"Mr. And Mrs. Ordinary America and their kid," Panther said, and gave Nash the specifics. "They got a life, boss. Jobs, friends, coworkers . . . They've got to be reported missing."

"Family?"

"Yeah. Doc Townsend has a brother in the Keys. We're checking on the exact location now. The missus is an only child, parents dead."

Nash squeezed the bridge of his nose. His head pounded, the dizziness deepened, and he had to close his eyes to ground himself, to make the world stop spinning. "What about in-laws?"

"None that I could find, except for the brother."

"The brother has to be removed from the equation. But brought in alive."

"Got it. Two men are headed to Marathon as we speak. The brother won't be a problem. But the Townsends may have close friends who would help them out."

Shit, Nash thought. Close friends, coworkers . . . Risks, they were all risks. But he couldn't take in everyone within their circles of friends and coworkers without drawing undue attention to the Townsends' disappearance. "Where'd they park their car, do we know?"

"They left it in one of the lots at a hammock. We've got the car covered."

"If they get out of the park, we need someone covering their home, their workplaces . . ."

"I'm on top of it, boss. Trust me. This won't be a repeat of Logan."

"I want them alive, Panther."

Panther laughed. It was a chilling sound even to Nash, who had known Panther for twenty years, the laugh of a man who lived at the edge of sanity. His temper could erupt so suddenly and unexpectedly that he'd been kicked out of the FBI after beating up a fellow fed who probably had done nothing more than look at him the wrong way. But he could track anything, anywhere, human or animal, Visible or Invisible.

Yeah, anything and anyone except Logan.

"Boss?"

"Yeah?"

"Leave your goddamn cell on this time."

Before Nash could reply, Panther had disconnected.

7
TRUTHS

Andy came awake suddenly, listening hard to the fading drone of an airboat. *Not that close, but still too close.*

He sat forward in the canoe, his shoulders stiff, his legs like wood. He gently moved his wife's head off his thigh and onto the folded blanket Katie was using as a pillow. Neither of them stirred. Even the dog, snuggled against Katie's legs, didn't move.

Andy drew his legs up against his chest, swiveled around, and stretched his legs over the side of the canoe. His knees cracked. His leg muscles sighed as they stretched. He leaned forward and gripped on to the sides of the canoe to pull himself forward, up, and out.

His shoes sank into the soggy ground. Not quite quicksand, but not quite solid, either. For seconds, he just stood there, feeling unsteady, light-headed, as if he'd had a couple of beers on an empty stomach.

He peered into the surrounding darkness. The canoe was wedged between two trees in a mangrove where the low tide had left a spit of soggy land. Safe. *But for how long? An hour? Till daybreak?*

He felt a sudden urgency to get out of the Glades before dawn. But first he had to know where they were.

He rubbed his eyes. They still ached, but not like they had when he'd had his contacts on. He suddenly realized that his wire-rim glasses were folded inside his shirt pocket and that he could see just fine without them. How the hell could that be? He'd worn glasses or contacts since he was sixteen. Maybe the extreme darkness had something to do with it, the absence of any glare. Whatever it was, he had more pressing concerns at the moment, like how long they had been here and where they were going to go next.

His watch, however, proved useless. The hands were still frozen at seven twenty-five. Even the clock on his cell phone had stopped at that time. He figured it was about the time the village turned invisible.

Invisible.

He couldn't move beyond that fact, beyond its impossibility. His thoughts circled it, trying to view it from every conceivable angle as though it were a symptom of ill health, a clue to disease. He struggled to see it as the doctor he was and found nothing reasonable. The notion took him so far beyond reason that it exhausted him.

What'd we stumble into?

It was like a medical koan, one of those imponderable riddles that confronts every doctor at least once—the sudden remission from cancer, the patient who is given a week to live and goes on to live for another twenty years. The difference, of course, was that this time it was *personal.*

A terrible, suffocating panic surged in his chest and Andy doubled over at the waist, allowing blood to rush to his head. *Don't think about it now.*

A door slammed shut in his head, one of many doors that sealed off one of many internal rooms. So often in ER, the ability to divorce himself from his emotions had saved him and it saved him now. After a few moments, he was able to straighten up. He was still aware of an undercurrent of panic, but it didn't seem to belong to him. His thoughts were clearer. He needed a plan, a strategy, a *program of treatment,* as they called it in ER.

Andy plucked his backpack from the canoe, slung it over his shoulder, and flipped open the lid of the supply container at the rear of the canoe. It held useful supplies—freeze-dried food and plenty of bottled water, blankets, pillows, flashlights, sleeping bags, clothes, a first-aid kit, virtually anything an efficient camper might need. There was even a large bag of dried dog food in the container.

Yeah, so what the hell did *that* mean? Why had there been a fully loaded canoe tethered to the rear of the village? Obviously, the canoe and the dog had been part of the experiment. More imponderables. He couldn't afford imponderables right now. He needed *facts.*

And the facts were that Lucky had gobbled up the generous portion of dog food that Katie had given her. And he, Katie, and Renie had added water to some of the freeze-dried packets and Andy had discovered how delicious shit can taste when you're starved.

Now he dug out a plastic tarp and one of the flashlights from the supply container. A part of him feared turning on the flashlight. In this immense blackness, its glow might be visible. But another part of him, the more primitive part of him, craved light.

His thumb slid over the switch, turning the flashlight on. He kept the beam aimed at the ground, illuminating his muddy running shoes. New Reeboks, big mistake. He spread the tarp on the soggy ground, lowered himself to it, set his pack in front of him, unfastened it. He brought out his Pocket PC and cell phone, connected them, and prayed that the cell phone would work out here. He punched out his access number and, moments later, went on-line. Here. In the middle of the Everglades. Never had technology struck him as more miraculous.

He needed information and the only person he knew who might be on-line at this hour was his kid brother, an insomniac who spent half the night on the Internet.

jimbo, need info fast on any military activities in everglades national park between 7–9 pm this past evening. will stay on-line. we're in deep shit. andy

Next, he accessed a Web clipping service and requested a nautical map of the area where they'd put the canoe in the water and everything within five square miles of it. Andy and Katie had done this loop in the Everglades before— Flamingo-Middle Cape-Carl Ross-Flamingo. He used to do this loop with his grandfather years ago. The difference this time, however, was that they hadn't entered the loop at Flamingo, but at a point eight or nine miles north, where he'd believed they would connect with the loop and, later, with the Wilderness Waterway.

The waterway extended from Everglades City south a hundred miles to Flamingo. And in between it was as much as forty miles wide and held some ten thousand islands and innumerable channels. It twisted through some of the most primitive areas left in the southern U.S., and he was arrogant enough to believe his sense of direction was so flawless that he couldn't possibly become lost in here. Christ, up until now, he could be plopped down in the midst of a strange city and be able to get to wherever he was supposed to be. Years ago, he and Jim had visited Marrakech with their grandparents and Andy had managed to find his way back to the hotel through the Kasbah, a labyrinth of mythical proportions. But none of that helped them now.

He studied the nautical map he'd downloaded, following their route from the spot where they'd put the canoe into the water to the campsite that Renie had hated. He doubted they'd gone farther than three or four miles beyond that, but in which direction? The longer he studied the map, the more deeply he believed they had encountered the village somewhere between South Joe Chickee and Joe River Chickee campsites. He estimated their present position, then charted a course southeast to Flamingo. Their car wouldn't be there, but at least from Flamingo they could contact the authorities and report what had happened and perhaps bum a ride to their car.

Granted, it wasn't a very good plan. A thousand things could go wrong—and probably would, considering the way their luck had been running so far. But it was the best he could do at the moment.

He checked his e-mail and found a response from his brother.

> *Hey, amigo. You were short on details. I didn't find anything on military activities in the Glades last night or any time in the recent past. Nada on the wire services. Nearest military installation is Homestead and Hurricane Andrew wiped that out. Next nearest is in the Keys. What kinda deep shit you in, anyway? I'll stay on till I hear from you.*
> *Jimbo.*

Seized with paranoia, Andy didn't know whether to call his brother or continue the e-mail exchange. The people responsible for the disappearance of the village had been shooting because Andy and his family were witnesses to what had happened. It wouldn't be difficult for *them*—whoever they were—to find out who he was. Then he remembered the darts he'd seen and admitted the possibility that perhaps they had been shooting to *capture,* not to kill. *Darts, like we were animals.*

The Cherokee was parked in the lot across the road from where they'd put the canoe in the water. Whoever was after them would find that information easily enough because Andy had registered with the park service. In fact, he'd given a shit load of information at the park service—name, address, Social Security number, the names of the people he was with, the make and model of their Jeep, their license plate number. Once they had his name and Social Security number, the rest would be a cinch. He might be putting his brother in jeopardy.

Make it quick, he thought.

Will call from public phone at Flamingo Marina. May need help getting out of here. If you don't hear from me in 2 hrs. call my cell. It'll be on.

He waited to see if Jim was still on-line, and within two minutes had a response.

I get bad vibes on this, bro. I was on my way to Miami tomorrow, so I'll just leave earlier. Maybe we can stay up in Paradise? Will be in touch.

Bad vibes, Andy thought. *Shit.* In his brother's charmed life, he'd had *bad vibes* only once that Andy could remember, and that had happened during one of their summer trips. They'd gotten caught in the middle of a banana republic revolution, he and Jim and their grandparents and some of their eccentric friends. They'd escaped by the skin of their teeth. So if Jim was serious that the vibes were bad enough to shove him out of the house for the night, then Andy knew they were in very deep shit.

As for the Paradise route, he wasn't so sure. Paradise was an equestrian community west of West Palm Beach, way west, at the edge of the Everglades. Their grandmother had a winter place there and although she was in Massachusetts at this time of year, he didn't want to do anything that might jeopardize her. On the other hand, they couldn't go home.

Andy disconnected from e-mail, saved the nautical chart, then stood and reached down to pick up the tarp. The dog whimpered, stirred to life, and struggled to her feet. And it was a struggle. She reminded him of so many patients he had seen over the years, men and women who, through sheer strength of will, got up out of wheelchairs and *walked.* The dog got her footing and climbed out of the canoe. She nudged his leg with her nose, as if saying hello, then weaved a few feet away from him and sniffed around in the mud for a place to go to the bathroom.

He watched her because it was an easier thing to do than think his way out of this mess. She nibbled at something in the mud, a cluster of grass or some other growth, then squatted and did her business. Andy walked over to her, his new Reeboks sinking into the mud with every step, making soft, squishing sounds. Grass, she had eaten some sort of grass. He pulled a handful out of the ground, sniffed at it, but it didn't have much of a smell. "Upset stomach, Lucky?"

The dog came over to him, tail wagging, and offered her head for a pat. He stroked her behind the ears, wondering about her, about what she'd been doing in the village.

"Good dog, you're a good dog, Lucky. Someone obviously trained you. And they had dog food for you in the canoe, so the canoe was part of the experiment, right?"

You got it, Andy, ole pal. She understands every word you're saying. Uh-huh, sure. Talking to a dog in the middle of nowhere. Christ.

She licked his hand, then got back into the canoe and settled down next to Katie again, claiming her. She might not understand a word he'd said, but the certainty of her actions, her responses to him, her apparent acceptance of the situation: shit, it spooked him.

He slipped the Pocket PC in his shirt pocket, clipped the cell phone to the waistband of his shorts, and retrieved a compass from the container. He put it in the pocket of his shorts and tried to recall the last time he had needed a compass. His uncanny sense of direction had deserted him.

Andy wedged the flashlight between the edge of the container and his backpack, so he would have some light, then started pushing the canoe off the mud, toward the water. The difficulty of such a simple act shocked him. He hurried around to the front of the canoe, figuring it might be easier to pull it across the mud, but he didn't have the strength to do it. He realized he would have to wake his wife or daughter or both of them and have them get out of the canoe.

"Ren," he whispered, gently shaking her shoulder. "Ren, wake up."

She came to, her voice muffled with grogginess, and grasped the edges of the canoe to pull herself to a sitting position. She groaned. "What time is it?"

"I don't know. My watch stopped. You have to get out so I can push the canoe into the water."

"We're leaving? But it's not light yet."

"We need to get to the Flamingo marina before daybreak."

"How far is it?"

"I don't think it's far. We're not safe here."

He helped her out of the canoe and as soon as she stood, her knees buckled and she went down in the mud. "I'm okay," she said quickly, then repeated it as if to assure herself that she really was. "My body just feels . . . I don't know, weird."

Andy shone the flashlight on her knees, where the mud had seeped into the denim of her jeans. "The muddy areas look different than the rest of you," he remarked.

"What're you talking about? It looks the same to me."

"No. Watch." He dug the toe of his Reebok into the mud and shone the flashlight on his foot. "See?"

Renie studied his shoe, shook her head. "It's the flashlight, the darkness. It doesn't mean anything."

He had the uneasy feeling that there were many things

about the effects of whatever had happened to them that they hadn't discovered yet. And what they didn't know might get them killed. "We've just got to remain aware."

"We agree on what happened, right?" She sounded frightened, uncertain. "On what we saw? That the village became invisible?"

"Absolutely." It alarmed him that Renie was doubting the evidence of her own senses. His wife rarely doubted her own feelings, experiences, opinions, beliefs. It was one of the things that had attracted him so strongly when they'd met. "And we were shot at."

"They weren't just *shooting* at us. They were trying to *kill* us."

"No, they were using darts."

"Darts?" The word staggered off her tongue as though it were new to her vocabulary.

"Yeah. Like what they use for animals. Tranquilizing darts."

"I don't get it."

"Me either."

"They're going to be looking for us. I mean . . . *invisibility,* Andy. We're witnesses . . . You gave your name at the park entrance," she went on in that same whispered, urgent voice. "Christ, we're in the fucking phone book."

"A step at a time. That's all we can do." He brushed the excess mud off his shoe, then washed his hand in a nearby puddle. The part of his hand that was now damp looked different than the rest of his hand. Why? "You feel like you can get up now?"

"I think so."

She leaned into him and for moments there in the darkness, on this spit of land, they hugged each other. He drew immense comfort from her presence, her nearness, her energy. It had been like that since the first time they'd met, outside a real estate office in northern Florida.

His most vivid memory of that initial meeting was that

he'd been struck mute by her hair, the thickest, blackest, shiniest hair he had ever seen, a dark waterfall that spilled over her shoulders and halfway down her spine. Asian hair on a slender American woman with a generous, seductive mouth and magnetic blue eyes.

He had finished a twenty-hour shift and was light-headed from lack of sleep, coming off the adrenaline rush of ER and not quite coherent. Her exuberance, such a rarity in the world he inhabited, had nearly overpowered him.

But it was when she'd changed the tire on her minivan that he'd really fallen for her. And while she'd changed the tire, she had plied him with questions—about ER, about what kind of house he was looking for, why he'd chosen medicine as a profession, what kinds of books and movies he liked, what he did in his free time. Camping, windsurfing, rock climbing, adventure travel, he'd said. She'd glanced over at him, those brilliant eyes frowning. "Nope, nope, nope, and yes."

He'd laughed, delighted with her honesty, and two weeks later, she had moved into his new place with him. Five months after that, they had gotten married and left for two weeks in Peru.

In their years together, they had managed to work around their differences, some of them major, and had discovered mutual interests that compensated. But even those interests had barely sustained them during their toughest years together, when Renie's father had lived with them, his body already failing from Parkinson's. Buddha had been in a wheelchair then, his speech slurred, one of his arms nearly frozen, his legs useless. Yet, in all, Andy never had regretted any of their sixteen years together.

"A penny," she whispered.

He kissed her. It felt just fine, felt exactly as it always did, a kiss that moved his blood. "Kissing you still feels great. That's a good sign."

"You're just trying to shut me up," she replied.

He could tell she liked hearing it. He handed her the end of the long rope and the flashlight. "Hold on to these. Let the rope out as needed."

She stood there, the rope in one hand, the flashlight in the other, the beam shining across the mud, toward the water. The dog, who had gotten out of the canoe shortly after Renie had, now trotted alongside Andy as he pushed the canoe toward the water. Although the canoe was lighter, he still found the job difficult and realized that it wasn't just fatigue. Despite the time he'd slept—*how long?*—his body still felt strange, too. His worries escalated now about the possible physical affects of whatever had happened out there in the village.

He had to lean into the canoe for the last several yards and his glasses kept sliding down on the bridge of his nose. He finally whipped them off so they wouldn't fall into the muck, folded them, and slipped them into his shirt pocket. Once the canoe was in the water, the dog climbed back in and settled next to Katie, who was still fast asleep. Andy clasped the rope and made his way back toward his wife.

"Hop in," he said.

Renie climbed into the front of the canoe and he hurried to the rear. He pushed off, scrambled onto the top of the container, and thrust his paddle down through the shallow water, into the mud and silt, and pushed hard against the bottom. The canoe drifted away from the spit of land, into slightly deeper water. Renie fitted the flashlight under a strap on her backpack, which was beside her on the bench, and the beam shot out into the channel.

Andy got out the Pocket PC, brought up the nautical chart, and took a reading on the compass.

"Promise me something, Andy." Although Renie's voice was soft, it echoed strangely in the tunnel of trees.

"What?"

"The next time I volunteer for one of your adventures,

send me to a resort somewhere. But no more swamps, okay?''

He doubted that he would go within miles of a swamp anywhere, ever again. ''You got it.''

''So where're we going? What're we looking for?''

''A channel that leads left, toward the southeast.''

''And that will take us . . .''

''Eventually, it'll take us to the Flamingo marina. We'll call Jim from there.''

''What about your cell phone?''

''I'll call him from a phone at the marina. Or, if he hasn't heard from me in two hours, he'll call the cell. But frankly, that makes me nervous. If they know who we are, they may also know our cell phone numbers, place of employment . . . Hell, they may be looking for *us* in Flamingo.''

''Right.'' Her voice cracked slightly, a dead giveaway that her terror was like his own, lying in wait just beneath the surface of their words. ''But who the hell are *they?*''

''That's the next thing we find out. But first we need to get someplace safe.''

In response, Renie paddled harder, faster.

2

They managed to keep working their way to the southeast, but not on his navigational skills. The compass kept them moving in the right direction. Here and there, the canopy of branches parted enough to see the moon, a slivered thing no larger than the clipping of a fingernail.

For some reason, Andy thought of the ER, always a madhouse on weekends. Gunshot wounds, rapes, heart attacks, strokes, the whole gamut of human misery. The nutcases, though, didn't appear in significant numbers until the full moon. He used to think the full moon stories were bullshit, but his first month in ER had taught him differently. He used to think *X-File* stories were bullshit, too. Now he knew differently. So much for *his* version of reality.

"Andy," Renie whispered.

"Yeah?" he whispered back.

"Are you wearing your contacts?"

"I've wearing my gla—" He stopped. He had put his glasses into his shirt pocket, yet he could see as clearly as he could with his glasses or his contacts on. How? He'd been wearing glasses or contacts since he was sixteen years old. *What the hell's going on?* "Uh, no. No contacts."

"How can you see where we're going?"

"I don't know."

"Uh-huh."

They mulled this over in silence for a few minutes. Since there was no satisfactory answer to the question, they didn't pursue it. Andy had the feeling this was going to be the norm until they figured out what was going on.

"Andy, that nautical chart you downloaded. It had Coast Guard markers on it and I think I just saw one back there."

"How far back?"

"A couple of yards. And just ahead here, I can see moonlight on water."

"I'll take a compass reading."

They backtracked to the marker and Andy took a compass reading. Southeast. He turned into a new channel and kept the canoe hugging the trees in case they had to make a hasty retreat back into the mangroves. But the channel was so devoid of anything human that they could be on another planet, he thought.

A breeze rose, humid and thick, swollen with the fecund smell of earth and water. It pushed them out into the open part of the waterway. Moonlight spilled across the dark waters and cast the sporadic clusters of saw grass in a surreal light.

The simple beauty of it lulled him into a sort of complacency so that the farther they got from the village, the less real all of it seemed. He speculated that he, Renie, and Katie had suffered some kind of collective hallucination. He might have believed it, too, except for the dog.

The dog was real.

The canoe they were in was real.

"Let's stop for a second," Renie said. "I've got to splash some water on my face."

She slid her paddle along the inside wall of the canoe and Andy flipped open the lid of the cooler to get them a couple of bottles of drinking water.

"I feel dirty," Renie said, still whispering. "And . . ."

She didn't finish her sentence.

Andy glanced up from the cooler. Renie was leaning over the side of the canoe, one hand holding her hair at the back of her head. She looked frozen, a Narcissus paralyzed by the sight of her own beauty.

"Ren?"

"Fuck. I . . . aw, shit . . . Christ . . . I . . . Look down, Andy."

"What?"

"Look. Down."

He looked and saw only moonlight, painting the surface of the water. "Yeah? So?"

Renie grabbed her pack, dug out a compact, popped it open, and shoved a mirror into his face. "What do you see?" The words hissed out.

He stared into the mirror, then snatched it out of her hand and held it up close to his face. His heart beat wildly, erratically. He touched his fingers to his face, to his chin, feeling his unshaven jaw, his cheekbones, his eyelids. He leaned way over the side of the canoe, seeking his reflection in the moonlit water, then he looked in the mirror again.

Nothing. I'm not there.

He was as invisible as the village.

He dropped to his knees beside Katie and the dog and held the mirror up to them.

Nothing. Zip. *Nada*.

Andy held the mirror out over the side of the canoe, praying for a reflection. It wasn't there.

He held the mirror to his backpack, the supply container, the paddle, but nothing changed. The mirror remained empty.

Impossible, this isn't happening.

He looked into the mirror again. *Wrong*. It *was* happening. It *had* happened.

And suddenly his stomach heaved and he threw up over the side of the canoe. Dinner, lunch, everything he had eaten and drunk since they'd gotten here. Then he thrust his hands into the water, splashed water onto his face, and Renie gasped.

"My God. Andy. Look."

She had retrieved the mirror from the floor of the canoe, where he'd dropped it, and held it up to his face. He saw himself now, his face still dripping with water, his reflection a kind of truncated version of his own face. "I . . ."

"Watch."

She splashed water onto her own face and he held the mirror toward her and saw that she, too, was visible. When he looked at her without the mirror, he realized he could see her with greater clarity.

"When we're wet." A soft voice, barely audible. "That's when we're visible to others. Remember what you said about the mud? How it made our shoes and hands look different? That's why. Moisture."

He opened his mouth, but nothing came out. Language had deserted him, his brain had shut down. He ran his tongue over his lips, swallowed hard. Only with great effort was he able to say, "But . . . but I can see you when you're not wet. I can see Katie and the dog and the canoe. . . ."

"Yes. But it's different. We're clearer then."

No words for this, Andy thought. No words, no concept,

nothing that made sense. He struggled against the weight of this incomprehensible *thing,* and that's what it was, a fucking *thing,* too alien to assimilate, to understand, to verbalize.

But his wife verbalized it for both of them. "We can't see our own reflections, but we can see each other and our own bodies when we look down at ourselves. Maybe our brains are supplying what's missing out of habit or something. We see the canoe, the dog, the supply container, but they don't have reflections. We can see ourselves when we're wet . . ." She held out her hands, turning them over slowly, almost with a kind of wonder. "But we have no reflection . . . We couldn't see the village. . . ."

The weight of her words stacked up against him, palpable, heavier than a truck filled with slabs of concrete. But he couldn't offer an opinion, didn't have a *diagnosis,* because he didn't have enough facts. He might never have enough facts.

He started to say something, he didn't know what, but Katie sat up, yawning, stretching her arms over her head, a Rip Van Winkle awakening into some brave new world. "What's going on? Where are we?"

Andy and Renie just looked at each other there in the moonlight, and his wife stammered, "We've got a problem," and then she burst into hysterical laughter, her head thrown back, her hair wild. This left him holding the bag.

Well, hon, it's like this . . .

And because he couldn't find the right words, he thrust the compact at Katie, thrust it even as his wife's weird and terrible laughter echoed through the moonlight.

Katie glanced into the mirror, brought it closer to her face, looked at Andy, then into the mirror again. "No wonder they didn't catch us. They couldn't see us. *Awesome.*"

"*Awesome?*" Renie wasn't laughing now. "Christ almighty. There's nothing *awesome* about this. How the hell are we going to function? How're we going to drive cars? Shop for food? How're we going to work? How—"

"Shut up, Renie," he snapped. "Just calm down and shut up."

"Don't you dare tell *me* to *shut up*. This trip wasn't *my* idea. It wasn't *my* idea to take a look at the village, to—"

"*Stop it*," Katie shouted, her voice echoing across the water. "Just stop it. It's my fault, okay?"

The near hysteria in her voice shut them up.

Then Katie grabbed Renie's paddle and started paddling so hard the canoe veered sharply out into the waterway. Andy quickly picked up his own paddle and steered them toward the mangroves again, where it was safer.

Safer? They can't see you, guy. No one can. How much safer can you get?

Andy glanced back. The canoe was invisible, but it left a wake. The paddles made ripples in the water. Physical laws still applied. Gravity, weight, motion. *What else?*

When he had puked, he'd been able to see the contents of his stomach, just as he was able to see his wife, his daughter, the dog, the canoe, and everything else that had been zapped. In retrospect, though, the vomit had possessed the same clarity, so he had to assume the stuff wouldn't have been visible to anyone else. Did that mean all their body fluids would be invisible to others? If he had been eating food that hadn't been zapped, would his puke have been visible?

Just thinking about it made him nauseated again.

What would happen if they ate food that wasn't in the canoe? What would happen if they put on clothes that hadn't gotten zapped? What then? *What?* Why had the village been invisible to them? Given what he had learned so far, the village should have been visible in the same way that they were visible to each other.

His head ached with questions that begged for answers. But the good ole bottom line was quite simple: were the effects temporary or permanent?

8
FLAMINGO

The seaplane banked steeply through a wash of light the color of pearls, allowing Nash to get a good look at the Flamingo marina below. The place hardly qualified as a tourist mecca: two dozen slips, half a dozen boats anchored in the nearby cove, a small store and bait shop, and a snack bar joint that probably was just opening its doors for the early risers. Way off to the right was a small campground.

"We're in luck, boss," said Dobson. "There's one other seaplane down there. We won't draw undue attention by landing."

Dobson, who could fly anything, Nash thought. He wished he had a dozen Dobsons working for him. "You think Panther's right? That the Townsends are headed for Flamingo?"

"That's what I'd do. Put yourself in their shoes, boss. They saw a village go invisible, they were shot at, they're on the run. They're probably scared shitless to go near their car, so it makes sense they'd head for the nearest bastion of civilization. They know that because they registered at the park entrance, we've got all the information we need to track them down.''

Yes, it did make sense. But at the moment, with his body screaming for sleep, he needed to hear this from Dobson. ''Radio Colleen and tell her to keep Farris away from here.''

''He'll still be sleeping off that Demerol.''

After several hours in the village, Farris had gotten violently ill and Colleen had taken him to a small houseboat the project kept near the lagoon and given him a shot of Demerol. Nash had caught a couple of hours of sleep before Panther had called and suggested they meet at Flamingo. He had a hunch, he said.

Nash slipped on his thermal-sensitive sunglasses, a newer and more stylish variation of the goggles they'd worn in the village. The glasses wouldn't draw attention.

Moments later, the seaplane landed and pulled into a slip next to the other seaplane that Dobson had seen from the air. Panther waited on the pier, a short and muscular Micossukee Indian with a thick black ponytail. His hands were thrust in the pockets of his windbreaker, shoulders hunched against whatever threat he thought might lie behind him. The windbreaker, Nash knew, covered his holstered weapon or a gun that shot tranquilizer darts. The bag that hung over his right shoulder probably carried a rifle.

Over the many years of their association, Nash and Panther had disagreed on numerous issues and philosophies. His independence and renegade mind-set sometimes enraged Nash. But he couldn't fault Panther's preparation. Drop him into a crisis situation and he would get the job done. Nash knew that even now, Panther had backup here in the marina—men on the houseboat tied up in one of the slips, men who blended in. The big question in Nash's mind, however, was how had anyone slipped unnoticed into the village? Panther's men were supposed to be watching the entrances to the lagoon, particularly before a test run.

Nash limped across the dock, relying heavily on his cane.

The lack of sleep, stress, a new crisis every five minutes: everything had taken its toll on his leg. The pain, though moderate, was relentless, a constant ache that traveled in hot, pulsating waves from his foot to his hip. Nash knew that Panther noticed, but he didn't comment. He never did. He simply nodded hello and adjusted his pace to Nash's as they moved up the dock, out of Dobson's range of hearing. Nash wasn't worried about anything that Dobson heard. But Panther was. Panther was paranoid about most people.

"How the hell did they get into the lagoon without someone seeing them, Panther?"

"I don't know. I've got four men on a permanent watch out there. But four isn't enough to cover every channel that flows into the lagoon. By the time we saw them, they were pulling up to the village pier and I was trying to get you on the phone—any phone—and every line was tied up. I figured you had them on the monitors."

The power outage, Nash thought. When the power had gone down, everyone had been calling everyone else, trying to track down the problem or find out what, exactly, had happened. He had yet to see the reports on the outage, as to what had caused it. But forget the past. He needed to focus on the immediate future. "So where do we stand?"

"No sightings yet. Everything's covered—their car, their house. The doc's brother wasn't home, so we've still got his place under surveillance. He may be on his way up here, though, because very early this morning, the doc's cell phone was used to call an on-line service."

"Christ," Nash breathed.

Panther stopped and gazed at something just ahead, his eyes narrowed, his forehead furrowed. "I'm telling you, boss, they're headed this way. It's the closest spot to the village. They're invisible, they need wheels to get out of here, but they're probably scared to go back to their car, so they figure they'll come to the marina and the brother can pick them up here."

"You sound awfully certain of that."

"Hey, he's a doc. An ER doc. He's used to thinking in a crisis situation. And this is a crisis and what I just told you makes the most sense."

Makes sense. Just what Dobson had said. "Unless they headed north."

"The current flows south. He'll go with the current." He drew his eyes away from whatever had captured his attention and looked at Nash. "We need to become part of the scenery here. And fast. Ten, fifteen minutes, the sun'll be rising up over these trees and the boaters are going to be up and about. Let's blend and get some chow." He tilted his head toward the snack bar, which was just opening for breakfast business.

Nash glanced around quickly. Unfortunately, the thermal-sensitive sunglasses didn't distinguish a Visible from an Invisible. It simply registered physical heat—a dog, a cat, a grill, a human. Egalitarian glasses. The glasses would be useless once more people were up and around, but at the moment, Nash caught sight of two quick movements along the pier. He peered over the rim of the glasses and saw two dogs, sniffing their way toward breakfast. *Visible* dogs. Not *the dog.* Not the project's dog. And there, off toward the boats, shapes moving around on the deck of a catamaran. Visibles.

"Suppose you're wrong, Panther?"

Panther reached into his shirt pocket, pulled out the sunglasses, put them on. "Hey, man. You're with your wife and your kid. You stumble into some very weird shit and discover that not only did a village on stilts go invisible, but so did you, your family, the dog you picked up, the canoe you're in, the clothes you're wearing, the stuff that's in the canoe . . . After you get over your initial, *Aw, fuck, this isn't happening,* your only thought is to get home. It's *safe* at home, boss. And you know the Flamingo marina is closer—"

"How do you know?"

"Cell phone to call on-line service, remember? He's a doc, he can afford toys like a Pocket PC or a Palm Pilot and a wireless service. I figure he downloaded a nautical chart of the Glades and headed straight for Flamingo."

They had reached the front porch of the snack bar, a raised wooden platform with tables and chairs set up. Panther pulled out a chair for Nash. "Take a load off, boss. We've been on a fishing trip. We're staying on that houseboat over there." He gestured toward the slips. "We'll have some breakfast, keep our eyes peeled."

When Dobson joined them a few minutes later, the sun had risen about even with the tops of the trees. Boaters were up and about, some on their way to the bathrooms and showers, others moving slowly around deck. Now Nash had to rely more on his own perceptions than on the thermal glasses. He looked around slowly for the telltale signs: inexplicable ripples in the water, the sudden flight of birds, dogs barking for no apparent reason, objects that seemed to move of their own volition, noises that had no apparent source, and, of course, signs of heat where there was nothing visible. But he didn't see anything unusual.

Over near the public phone, two men were cleaning fish at an outdoor sink. One of them glanced up and Nash recognized him as Ocho, Panther's right hand. For some reason, he felt more hopeful then, hopeful despite the fact that surveillance at the lagoon had failed and that Invisibles were out there, loose cannons that could blow apart everything he had done for the last fifteen or twenty years. After all, if the Townsends managed to elude them and blew the whistle, it wouldn't be Farris and the committee who would take the fall. Nash would be the fall guy.

2

One of the great ironies of Nash's life was that he had stumbled into this research because of his father, a physicist who had worked with Nikola Tesla, John Alan Von Neumann, and Albert Einstein. Nash had known that his father was involved in classified research, but didn't know the extent of it until his old man had died suddenly in the mid-seventies.

It had fallen on him, as the only child, to go through his father's numerous papers. In the basement of the New Jersey home that his parents had shared for thirty some odd years, he had uncovered dozens of file drawers stuffed with his father's unpublished papers, notes, and correspondence with Tesla, Einstein, and Von Neumann concerning ''the Rainbow Project.'' He could still remember his incredulity when he had started reading the material—invisibility, for Christ's sake, science fiction shit. But the more he'd read, the more plausible it had become.

Then he'd run across the files on how the Rainbow Project had been applied to the USS *Eldridge* in what had become known as the Philadelphia Experiment. The shrouding of a naval ship, its teleportation to a shipyard, the insanity of the crew, a possible rift in the space-time continuum . . . Today, of course, he understood that the Philadelphia Experiment ultimately had led to stealth technology and to a host of other technological discoveries that the government had used for its own agenda.

One of the most dire examples of how the technology had been developed and used involved a navy experiment conducted two years ago on the island of Piper Key, on Florida's Gulf coast. Ostensibly, the experiment was supposed to have been part of the navy's mammal defense program, in which dolphins were trained to be defensive

weapons. But Steve Dylan, a military lifer in naval intelligence, had sculpted the project to fit his own research into
teleportation and the manipulation of space-time. Using technology that had grown out of the Philadelphia Experiment,
Dylan ultimately had caused what the military experts
referred to as a ''tear in the fabric of space-time.''

A heady conclusion, but apparently correct, from what
Nash had been able to determine. Thanks to Farris, he had
read the government's classified reports on the project and
had recognized the similarities to his own research. He also
had recognized the considerable differences. Dylan's focus
had been teleportation and the manipulation of space-time,
a far more ambitious goal than Nash's concentration on
invisibility. Dylan had been in pursuit of power; Nash didn't
give a shit about power. He just wanted to do what he loved,
what excited him, and shrouding ignited his passions in a
way nothing and no one else ever had.

He'd also found disturbing similarities between himself
and Dylan. Both of them were continuing research that their
fathers had begun. Dylan's old man, like Nash's, had been
involved with Einstein and Von Neumann as the assistant
to one of the researchers in the early days of the project.
Nash's father had been involved in a more direct and immediate sense, particularly in the light of his friendship with
Tesla. But the research community at that time had been
relatively small and it seemed likely that the two men had
known each other. Nash hadn't found any evidence to support this and never had the opportunity to seek out Dylan
because he had perished in the Piper Key incident. But the
possible connection continued to bug him.

About a year ago, he decided to look for Dylan's old
girlfriend to find out what, if anything, she knew about
Dylan's old man. If she could supply him with dates and
places where Dylan's old man had worked, then he might
be able to cross-reference dates and places in his own father's
life. So he'd flown to Piper Key, where Gail Fairfield, a

marine biologist, had worked. But when he'd arrived, he'd discovered that the dolphin research center where Fairfield had worked no longer existed. He was told it had been sold a couple of months after the incident up at old man Livingston's place and a time-share condo had been built on the site.

This was clearly impossible. The Piper Key incident had happened in early August of 1999. Fairfield had given numerous statements to investigators between September and November of 1999, while she was employed at Dolphins on the Gulf. Those dates were documented in the classified material. He'd ended up at the county offices, but that only deepened his confusion.

According to the county real estate records, the research center had been sold on September 6, 1999, construction on the condo had begun on October 1, 1999, and had been completed six months later. Either the classified documents or the real estate records were wrong. He'd never been able to prove anything one way or the other and, even more puzzling, hadn't been able to track down Gail Fairfield, either. He'd run inquiries through Social Security, the IRS, even naval intelligence, but nothing turned up. So Nash was left with a mystery far more puzzling than the question that had triggered his search.

He often wondered, though, if perhaps the answer was that Dylan had succeeded in what he was trying to do and reality had split off in some way. Maybe the dolphin research center still existed in one version of reality and Nash simply happened to be living in the version where the center had been replaced by a time-share resort. Sometimes at night when his leg ached and he couldn't sleep, he thought about those various shoots of reality, played with them, speculated about how they differed or were the same.

Perhaps, in one of those realities, his town for Invisibles was already a done deal and Tyler was living there along with Invisibles, living in a setting as free as it would get for him. He liked to fantasize about this town for Invisibles, a more humane place than where Tyler had lived for the last three years. But the fantasy usually collapsed when Farris and his goddamn committee entered the picture.

Had he really needed Farris? Had there been a point way back when *his* reality diverged?

Three days before Tesla had died, Nash's father had traveled to New York to visit the inventor at the Hotel New Yorker, one of the various hotels where he had lived during the last twenty years of his life. According to a journal entry, the two old friends had spent the day together and before Nash's father had left, Tesla had unlocked the safe in his room where he kept some of his valuable papers and had given Nash's old man the ones that pertained to their mutual interest in invisibility.

After Tesla's death, his safe was broken into and his papers were seized by the FBI and the Office of Alien Property. In fact, all of the boxes of papers that Tesla had left in various hotels as collateral for unpaid bills had been seized. But Tesla's documents and notes on invisibility had remained with Nash's old man, who had worked on the riddle until the end of his life. The meticulous notes left by his father and Tesla, combined with a stroke of luck, had enabled Nash to solve the riddle within four years of his father's death.

That stroke of luck had come in the form of an Ecuadorian shaman named Luis Diego Manteles, a complex man with profound knowledge and power. Manteles, part of a cultural exchange program at Yale when Nash had been teaching there, had known about *ghosting,* as he called it. Born to a wealthy Ecuadorian family with Spanish roots, Luis had gotten lost in the jungle when he was a young boy and had been raised by the tribe that had found him. Twelve years later, he had made his way out of the jungle and been reunited with his family. By then, he knew how to ghost and had begun his shamanic initiation.

Although he went on to college in the U.S., Luis's ties with the tribe that had rescued him remained unbroken. In the best sense, Nash thought, Luis was a man who straddled two worlds and was at home in both of them.

He had supplied the shrouding with its missing ingredient, a way to stabilize the object or person that went "out of phase" during the process. An ingredient, Nash thought, that had worked too well, trapping Tyler in the land of the unseen. Not long after the Tyler and Logan disaster, Luis had left suddenly, without a word to anyone.

Nash knew he'd gone back to Ecuador, to his beloved jungle, his rapidly shrinking adopted tribe, and that he had done so primarily because he had objected so vehemently to the use of humans in the Tesla Project. He knew it—and had never been able to prove it. There was no record of a Luis Manteles on any flight, anywhere, at that time.

Since they had moved the project to the Everglades, the shaman had been sighted twice by several of Nash's employees. Even though Nash hadn't seen him, he knew this was something that Luis might do—*hey, I'm here, watching you, keeping tabs*—and, frankly, it worried him. Luis was a wild card and wild cards always worried Nash.

Sometimes, Nash imagined that he went in search of Luis, that he traveled into the Ecuadorian jungle and brought him back to the States. He had the resources to do it without ever having to step foot himself in the goddamn jungle. But what purpose would it serve? Luis could not be cajoled, bought, or forced to do what he did not want to do. And if he would not help, then he would become a hindrance— rather like Tyler, Nash thought.

So here he was, years after he had rendered a pencil invisible for sixty-eight seconds, facing his greatest crisis— a man, woman, and child who had been at the wrong place, at the wrong time, invisible now for more than ten hours. Everything from here on in was nothing more than a crap shoot with miserable odds. But if he beat the odds and brought them in, then there was nothing the committee would deny him.

3

As the canoe cleared the edge of the mangroves, Renie saw the concrete seawall of the marina directly in front of them. Palm trees leaned out over the wall like eager children waving to whoever passed by. Light from the rising sun splashed across the tiny beach, turning it a pale yellow. Birds swooped through the humid air, singing as if their hearts could barely contain their joy. It looked deceptively tranquil.

Farther up the beach, a concrete pier led to the marina, where several dozen boats and houseboats were anchored, some in slips and others in the cove beyond the pier. Perpendicular to the boat-launch area lay the seaplane tie-down dock, two little planes bobbing in the water.

The longer she surveyed the marina, the stranger the light seemed. She rubbed her eyes several times, but the light remained hazy, as though she were looking at everything through a veil or through glasses with dirty lenses. But when she looked at Katie, Andy, the dog, even the container and the canoe, her vision seemed normal.

"What's wrong with the light?" Katie asked, squinting her eyes.

"It's not the light," Andy replied, his voice soft, cautious. It's connected to our, uh, physical condition."

"Our invisibility, you mean."

Katie, the realist, Renie thought.

"Yeah."

"Then why don't you just say that, Dad?"

"Because it sounds so . . . well, strange," Renie told her.

"C'mon, you guys." Katie sounded exasperated now.

"Let's say it like it is. The weird light is related to our invisibility, not our *physical conditions.*"

"She's right." Andy steered the canoe parallel to the concrete seawall, close to one of the overhanging palm trees, and tied the canoe to the trunk of the palm. "We can't pretend."

Ha, Renie thought. So far, her entire approach to this trip had been nothing *but* pretend. She had convinced herself that she could camp in the Everglades for several days with her husband and daughter, that she could do it despite living like a savage—no bed, no hot showers, peeing in the mangroves, coffee that tasted like warmed shit, starving while the fire for meals got hot, enduring bugs, snakes, gators . . . Jesus, she had to have been out of her mind when she had insisted on coming along.

"We have to remember that if we get our feet wet as we climb out, our feet are going to be visible to other people," Andy was saying. "When we're up there around people, we have to remember *they* can't see *us,* so we have to get out of their way. We can't talk above a whisper, otherwise they'll hear us."

Katie remarked, "It's like we're ghosts."

"Yeah, except that ghosts don't leave tracks." Renie pointed at the imprint that Andy's paddle had left in the sand where he'd tossed it. "And we do."

They climbed onto the wall. "We'd better take off our shoes," Andy said. "And put them in our packs. If our feet get wet, they'll dry fast in this heat. Or we can wipe them off with leaves or something."

"What about the sand?" Katie asked. "Our feet will get sandy and the sand will show."

"We brush them off before we walk onto the dock."

"Hey, Dad," said Katie. "How can you see without your glasses or contacts on?"

"I don't know."

Interesting, Renie mused, that Katie had asked Andy the

same question she had and Andy still didn't have an answer. That was atypical.

Katie and the dog hopped out first, onto dry sand. Lucky immediately picked up an interesting scent and wandered to the edge of the sand, then sat down, watching them, waiting for them, panting from the heat. "What about the dog's paws? We'll have to brush them off before we get to the dock," Renie said.

"I'll do it," Katie said.

"How's she know not to bark?" Andy asked.

"She's a smart dog," Katie said, as if she had the inside scoop on the whole thing. "And I think she's been invisible before."

"If that's true," remarked Andy, "then there's hope for us."

Renie steadied the canoe so that Andy could pick up the supply container and pass it to her. They had agreed to bring the container with them because it held food and shelter that they might need. But when Andy suggested they also bring the canoe, Renie balked.

"It's too heavy to cart through the marina," she said. "Besides, the bottom of it is wet."

"But if Jim doesn't show up, it's our only way out of here."

"He'll show up. Your brother has a lot of faults, but when he says he'll do something, he does it. Besides, even if he doesn't show up for some reason, we can always walk, Andy. According to that map on your Pocket PC, the road out there leads to the park entrance."

"It's at least thirty miles to the entrance," he exclaimed.

"My vote's with Mom," Katie said. "Forget the canoe."

Two against one. Andy didn't look too happy about the majority vote, but he couldn't ignore it, either, since he had used it innumerable times to get his way. He glanced once more at the canoe, shrugged. "I guess we can always come back to get it if we need it. But maybe we should take the rope. That could be useful.''

He quickly untied the rope from the tree and from the canoe, draped it around his neck, then pulled the canoe higher onto the sand. He and Renie lifted either end of the container and they started up the beach toward the dock and the marina, with Katie and Lucky in the lead.

Renie's spatial disorientation worsened with every step she took. It was one thing to be confined to a canoe with two people and a dog as invisible as she was. But now that they were walking among people who couldn't see them, she felt the way she imagined the dead must feel as they moved among the living, seeing them but unable to be seen by them. It *spooked* her. She kept pinching herself, a silly assurance that she was really alive, conscious, *here*.

Even worse was the haze that seemed to surround everything she looked at. She tried to keep her eyes on Katie and the dog to lessen her disorientation. But when she did that, the haze dominated her peripheral vision and disturbed her equilibrium. She stumbled once and nearly lost her hold on the container. Now and then, she felt seasick, her stomach churning, bile rising in her throat, and the only way she could cut off the feeling was to shut her eyes and pause to feel the earth's stillness under her feet.

At one point Lucky darted well ahead of them, maybe forty or fifty feet away, and just seemed to *fade* from view. It shocked her and she immediately drew Andy's and Katie's attention to it. As they watched, Lucky faded back into view as she trotted back toward them. "That's it," Andy whispered. "That's why we couldn't see the village. We were too far away."

"So if we're more than forty or fifty feet away, we won't be able to see each other," Katie said.

"This isn't the place to test it," Renie reminded them. "Let's stay close together once we're on the pier."

They paused at the end of the sand, brushed off their feet

and the dog's paws, then headed up the pier. More people were up and about now, boaters and campers crossing the pier, headed to the snack bar, bait shop, and rest rooms. She and Andy dodged this way and that to avoid colliding with anyone. It was already so humid that her shirt stuck like a Band-aid to her back, beads of sweat rolled down the sides of her face. She suddenly worried that sweat made them visible and, as soon as they were past the slips, signaled for Andy to stop.

He didn't argue. He looked completely beat and washed out, and just stood there wiping his arm across his face as Renie brought out her compact. It still shocked her to peer into a mirror and not see her reflection. But it didn't shock her as badly as the initial realization that she was invisible. Nothing could quite match that. At the moment, however, her mind had molded itself around the fact that she could not be seen. Intellectually, she was beginning to adapt to the reality, except that she needed to understand the details.

Did her sweat make her visible? If she bled, would that make her visible? Did invisibility change her blood chemistry? The way her body used energy? Did it alter the intrinsic function of her organs? She touched her fingers to her forehead, yet couldn't see it. She slid her fingertips through the sweat at the sides of her face, feeling the wetness, the grit, skin that screamed out for a hot shower. But the mirror remained as empty as a waiting coffin.

Apparently their body fluids were as invisible as the rest of them. Spit, sweat, blood: all invisible. Good to know in the event that her period came early. But then she thought of the repercussions of *that*—wearing a tampon that was visible to other people. Oh, yeah, this was going to be a barrel of laughs.

If it rained, she thought, they would be visible as long as they were wet. What about when they showered? Or went swimming? She was worrying so much about the variables that she didn't see the woman coming toward her until Andy wrenched sharply to the left, which jerked Renie in the same direction.

Too late.

The woman tripped over the corner of the container and sprawled gracelessly on the dock. She looked back for what had tripped her, her frown deepening. Renie and Andy quickly picked up the container and hurried to catch up with Katie. She had stopped just ahead of them and pointed frantically at something behind them.

Renie's head snapped around. In subsequent moments that seemed to unfold in a maddening slow motion, she saw two men on the deck in front of the snack bar—a Swartzenegger body type with a black ponytail and a taller, thinner man with a wild beard. A third, younger guy was turning away from the counter, holding a tray. All three wore identical glasses, which struck her as odd, since the sun was barely up. The man with the tray quickly set it down and the other two men now aimed identical guns at her and Katie. *"Guns, they have guns,"* Renie shrieked, and threw herself at Andy, knocking him to the ground.

Even though other people couldn't see them, her voice rang out. Just the word *guns* triggered a collective panic in the people around them. Pandemonium erupted on the docks, in the boat slips, at the snack bar, people running, screaming, diving for cover. The woman who had stumbled over the supply container had managed to sit up and was looking around in a daze when she suddenly grunted and toppled back. She landed less than a foot from where Renie and Andy lay, hugging the pier. Renie saw a dart sticking out of the woman's shoulder.

Dart, a tranquilizing dart meant for us. In the village, now again here. Think again, assholes.

Renie and Andy scrambled to their feet, grabbed the container, and took off, weaving their way through the chaotic crowd. At one point, she glanced back and saw that the three men had separated, each moving rapidly in different directions, none of them moving toward her and Andy. The glasses, she thought. Something about the glasses enabled them to detect her and Andy and Katie, except in a crowd. *Body heat?* Maybe. But what the hell did she know? She sold real estate, for Christ's sake. She tightened her hold on the container and moved faster, beyond the slips and the snack bar, to the strip of grass where Katie crouched, waiting.

"Those guys," Katie whispered. "They were . . . were shooting tranquilizer darts, like before, like . . . like we're *animals*."

"Ssshh," Andy hissed. "Let's get into the trees on the other side of the marina. Then I'll call Jim, see when he'll be here. You two grab the container, I'll get the—"

He stopped and stared down at one end of the rope draped around his shoulders. He whipped it off, hurled it away from him. The air around the rope quivered like a mirage. The quivering spread rapidly, here, there, one end and then the other. Parts of it became less clear, hazy, the way the world around her looked. Renie realized the rope had started to materialize, that the men would see it.

Katie scooped the dog up into her arms and Renie and Andy raced for the trees on the far side of the parking lot, their bare feet slapping the ground. Once or twice, Andy and Katie got too far ahead of her and faded from view, just as Lucky had. It terrified her not to be able to see them and she ran faster, crashing through pines, palmetto bushes, sea grape trees. Then she reached the edge of the water, the end of the line, and there they were.

Renie sank to her knees, chest heaving, Lucky leaped out of Katie's arms, and Andy collapsed against the container, his body folding over it. "Their glasses," Renie said when she caught her breath. "I think they detect body heat. Or something. That's how they knew where we were."

Andy raised his head, his face so worn, so weary, that it hurt her to look at him. "Shit."

Katie shrugged off her pack. She brought out a bottle of

water and studied it for a moment, frowning. "It was zapped, so it's safe to drink, right?"

"We think so," Renie replied. One more detail to remember. All the rules had changed. She had to keep reminding herself of that.

Katie chugged down some, passed it to Renie. "If the rope turned visible again, then so will the container. And the stuff inside. And . . . and us," Katie said.

"That's why we're not moving until Jim gets here," Andy replied. "I don't get it. We splash water on ourselves and turn visible. But the bottles of water in the container are still invisible and so are our body fluids—spit, vomit, urine, sweat, blood. We can see each other within a certain range, but we don't have reflections." He snatched a leaf from the nearest bush, stuck it in his mouth. "Does it look different, Renie?"

What the hell was that supposed to mean? Different from what? Different from his skin? From his eyes? Then she realized that she could see the leaf resting against the surface of his tongue even though his mouth was shut. She knuckled her eyes, looked again. He had bitten off a piece of the leaf, his tongue played with it.

"Spit it out," she said. "Jesus, just spit it out."

Andy leaned toward her, right smack in her face. "You can see it, right? Shit, I knew it. I just knew it. If we eat or drink anything that wasn't zapped, it's visible. It takes food six to eight hours to work its way through the digestive system."

"So if we eat unzapped food, three times a day," said Katie, "then our bodies will be digesting food around the clock and the goons will be able to find us because they'll see the food. I'm calling Uncle Jim. We need help. Where's your cell phone, Dad?"

"We can't use the cell phone. They might be tracing the signal."

"Well, we're not going out there to use the public phone."

Katie stabbed her thumb over her shoulder, indicating the marina. "They'd see it the second someone picks up the receiver."

Renie dug the cell phone out of Andy's backpack, punched out Jim's cell number, and passed him the phone. "She's right. Forget the public phone."

While Andy talked to his brother, Renie got up, her legs unsteady, rubbery, and made her way toward the edge of the trees. She continued to feel queasy, as if she'd eaten something that had disagreed with her and her body hadn't decided yet how to get rid of it.

At the edge of the trees, she peered out. Things looked more settled now—not quite calm, but not chaotic, either. A number of people continued to mill about, talking among themselves, perhaps trying to find out who had shouted. *Hey, guys, over here,* Renie thought, and waved. Over near the slips, three uniformed cops appeared to be questioning several employees. The three men were seated at a table outside the snack bar with two more cops.

None of them wore sunglasses now.

Renie considered going over to the cops and pleading with them to take her and her family into custody. But how, exactly, could she do that without creating a scene? The cops would hear her voice but not see her and as soon as they created a commotion, which they would surely do, the three men at the table would be alerted. From there, no telling what would happen.

Bad idea. She would wait for Jim.

Renie heard a noise behind her, spun around. Katie stepped carefully toward her. "Mom, Dad said to tell you that Uncle Jim is almost at the park entrance. Dad thinks we should start walking down the road . . ."

"I'll catch up with you."

"But . . ."

Renie pointed at the snack bar. "I'm going to eavesdrop."

Katie wrinkled her nose. "Bad idea. You'll have to keep

brushing dirt from the bottoms of your feet. So you won't
be visible.''

"We need information. We need to know what we're up
against.''

"I'll come with you.''

"Your dad needs help with that container. And Lucky
needs to stay here. She follows you.''

"We'll wait in the woods till you get back.''

Renie squeezed her daughter's shoulder and moved out
of the trees.

4

She ducked behind the snack bar building.

The tantalizing aromas from the kitchen drifted through
the open windows—eggs, bacon, toast. She was so hungry
for something substantial and it would be so easy just to
reach inside the window and grab a slice of bacon, a piece
of toast, a slug of freshly squeezed OJ. *And that food will
be visible for another six hours, making you a sitting duck.*

Renie hurried past the window and came around the side
of the building. From here, she could see the three men and
two cops. Since the men still weren't wearing the sunglasses,
she felt it was safe to get closer. As she stepped forward,
she nearly collided with a waitress who strode past with a
breakfast order. The waitress actually glanced back, frowning, as if she had felt something in that near collision, and
Renie stood there a moment, hand balled against her chest.

Relax, they can't see you. Right. Of course. All the rules
were different, she had to keep reminding herself of that.

Renie ducked under a railing and came up behind the
three men. They were all leaning forward, whispering. The
two cops now stood some distance away, cell phones pressed
to their ears. She got closer to the table.

The Schwartzenegger muscle man with the long ponytail looked Native American, perhaps Seminole or Miccosukee. He was leaning forward, saying, "Rednecks. A couple of redneck cops. Nothing worse. We shouldn't have fired on them in a public place."

Beard: "We didn't have any choice, Panther."

Younger guy: "They're on foot. They won't get far. Things already are starting to materialize—the rope, the canoe."

Panther: "Colleen should be here with the car before these assholes finish checking our IDs. Then we head for the park entrance."

Younger guy: "They could be right here, listening to every word we say."

Panther: "Trust me, they aren't. " He pushed the glasses toward the young guy. "Go on, Dobson. Take a look. You'll see dozens of reddish yellow blobs. Right now, the Townsends are heading up the road on foot."

They know our name.

Beard: "We need men and dogs. And we need at least one unit to stay here. Wayne, get Colleen on the phone."

"Right." The younger guy—Dobson—got up and walked off toward the slips, cell phone in hand.

One of the cops returned to the table. "Sorry for the delay, Doctor Nash, Mr. Ortega. Your credentials check out."

He dropped several plastic ID badges on the table that Renie definitely wanted to get a good look at. She moved close to the table, stepping ever so carefully, her bare feet not making a sound. She was acutely conscious of her breathing, that she couldn't breathe too hard, that she couldn't sneeze or cough or even swallow. She peered at the cards, at Baldie's photo. *National Security Bureau, Dr. George Nash, #34718905.* The second card, for the muscle man Nash had called Panther, had the same heading, with *William*

Ortega and a different series of numbers that also ended in 05.

"I'm supposed to help you folks in any way I can," the cop said. "I'll need a description of the suspects to distribute to my men here in the park."

"Thanks for the offer, Sergeant," said Nash. "But the NSB has plenty of agents on duty to handle the situation. Once again, we apologize for the confusion. . . ."

Renie didn't stick around to hear the rest. She backed away from the table, then spun around, and ran back toward the road to catch up with her husband and daughter and the dog.

9
THE CHASE

Men and dogs. How many men? Andy wondered, mulling over what his wife had told him. How many dogs? And just where would they hide when this small battalion of men and dogs descended on them?

At the moment, they waited for his brother in a picnic area off the road, next to a cypress swamp. They couldn't sit on the grass because if it stained their clothes, the stains would be visible. They couldn't sit at a picnic table, either, because they shared the area with dozens of tourists, any of whom might want to claim the table. But if what Renie said about the men's glasses was true, then other people were their best camouflage. So they remained within the crowd— and yet as far apart from other people as they dared.

Andy had fashioned a sort of leash out of a length of rope that had been in the container so that Lucky couldn't stray too far. But given what had happened with the other piece of rope, he worried this piece might materialize before his brother got here. His worry about their situation was so extreme now that he was surprised his ulcer hadn't started acting up. There was no sour lake in the pit of his stomach, no burning in the center of his chest. Weird. As weird, he thought, as the fact that he still could see perfectly without his glasses or his contacts.

His cell phone rang, a soft ring that was barely audible, but that still drew the attention of a Japanese man who stood about four feet away. Andy quickly answered the phone and moved away, toward the trees where he would be alone.

"Hey, man, it's me." His brother's voice boomed through the receiver. "I'm nearly there."

"Christ, what's taking you so long?" Andy whispered.

"Took a wrong turn. I'm about twenty miles into the park now, following the road toward Flamingo, just like you said. Where should I meet you?"

This would be touchy. His brother still didn't know the full truth, that Andy and his family were invisible. "You've got to be very careful, Jim. We've already been shot at, chased, and—"

"Hey, calm down, okay? I know you're in deep shit. I just got a call from one of my neighbors. He says my place is under surveillance. I ditched my car at the airport and rented another car just to get here. I've got my gun, too."

"Your *gun?* Since when do you own a gun? Is it registered? Jesus, Jim, I can't believe that you—"

"Chill, man. It's legal. Where should I meet you?"

Andy slid his fingers under his wire rims and pressed the tips against his dry, aching eyes. He gave Jim the landmarks, then blurted, "Listen, whatever we stumbled into had, uh, repercussions that are strange, Jim."

"Strange, okay, I can handle strange. How strange?"

Andy cleared his throat and walked farther down the path that took him into trees. "We're invisible." He could barely say the goddamn word.

"You're . . ." Jim exploded with laughter.

That went over well.

"Invisible?" Snicker, snicker. Ha-ha. "Right. Hey, I'm glad you still have a sense of humor, Andy."

"Yeah." *Let's hope you've still got yours five minutes from now.* "See you in a few minutes in the picnic area."

As he walked out of the trees, he didn't see Renie and Katie. He realized they were too far away. He stood there for a moment, struggling against his mounting panic. Then they came into view, the two of them frantically pushing and pulling the supply container across the grass and into tall weeds at the edge of the water. They left the container in the weeds and dashed for the boardwalk where the tourists were. Andy knew what this meant, knew it in his gut even before he saw the men in their identical glasses, and dropped to his knees behind a thick cluster of palmetto bushes. If the glasses detected body heat, would the plants protect him? He didn't know.

He flattened out against the ground and crawled deeper into the brush, his mind racing. If he could come around behind them, if he could . . .

Andy heard voices, people coming up the trail from the woods. How many people? Enough so that his body heat would simply meld with theirs? Was that how it worked?

He couldn't stay here on the ground. He was so fed up with being chased and shot at that as soon as the group of tourists drew even with where he was hidden, he sprang to his feet and fell into step behind them, close but not too close. Big problem, they were Japanese tourists and none of them was over five feet four or five. At six and a half feet tall, Andy towered over them.

He hunkered down, moving like a Neanderthal, trying to stay close enough to the group so that his body heat would be indistinguishable from theirs, yet far enough from them so their bodies didn't brush or collide.

As they emerged from the trees, he spotted two men moving toward the boardwalk, walking slowly side by side, their heads turning this way and that. A third man was in

the picnic area. *Come up behind them, slam them into . . .*
He was taller than the guy named Panther by eight inches
or so and taller than Beard—*Nash, your name's Nash*—by
at least half a foot. Andy would have the element of surprise
in his favor. On the down side, though, he didn't have the
physique that Panther did and if something went wrong and
it came down to a physical struggle, he would lose, no doubt
about it. He was no muscle man, no jock.

Andy hesitated, mustering his courage, then raced out
from behind the group of tourists, arms tucked in tightly at
his sides, the humid air biting his eyes. But he was moving
like the fucking wind and Christ, but it felt good, his legs
stretching, stretching . . . Then he leaped, his feet rising as
if climbing the very air in which he moved, and his aim
was so perfect, so right on target, that he struck them both
simultaneously. Even as they stumbled forward, arms pin-
wheeling for balance, Andy kept right on going, a human
missile.

He landed hard on his feet, a jarring violence that tore at
tendons and muscles, then toppled forward onto his hands.
For a moment or two, he remained on all fours like a jack-
rabbit, body tensed, as if ready to spring and flee. Then he
leaped up, whirled, and saw that neither Baldie nor Panther
wore his sunglasses. One pair lay on the ground just to
Andy's left. He stomped on them, breaking the lenses. He
scooped up the other pair, snapped them in half, and hurled
the pieces into the weeds.

Now that Panther and Nash were deprived of any way to
see him, Andy raced toward the weeds where his wife and
daughter had left the supply container. The third guy raced
their way, but a group of tourists stood between him and
Andy. He couldn't do anything about the third man. He
grabbed one end of the container while Renie lifted the other
end.

"Fast, Katie. Get out to the road and call Jim. Tell him
to stop just ahead of the boardwalk, on the shoulder of the

road, and to open the doors. You get in and make sure the doors stay open until your mother and I get the container inside.''

Katie dashed across the picnic area, her ponytail flying out behind her, and then she faded from his sight. Renie took hold of the container's other handle and she and Andy ran toward the road. It occurred to him that in the last twelve hours his tidy, orderly life had plunged into the unimagined and, worse, he didn't have a clue how to rectify or undo any of it. Right now, his main concern was losing the goons and getting out of here alive.

2

Nash lay on the ground, gasping for air, his fingers digging into the grass, his leg shrieking with pain, the muscles in the calf twitching, tightening, cramping. He knew that one of the Townsends, undoubtedly the man, had come up behind him and Panther and slammed into them and that a group of Japanese tourists had witnessed it.

As Nash raised his head, he saw the tourists' collective expression, puzzlement and astonishment, but realized that they really hadn't *seen* anything except two grown men catapult forward for no apparent reason. With luck, they would write it off to some oddity of American pop culture, a fad, a game, an arcane religious ritual.

The thermal-sensitive glasses lay on the ground next to his cane, about a yard from him. Before Nash could get close enough to retrieve them, the lenses shattered. He supposed some of the Japanese tourists saw that happen, too, but right about then, he didn't give a shit about the Japanese or the glasses. He struggled to his feet, waving at Dobson, who weaved his way through another group of people, trying to alert him to the situation, and limped his way toward the cane.

Panther was already on his feet, his massive body astonishingly agile and graceful, and lunged. At that same moment, about four feet from where Panther aimed his body, the other pair of glasses lifted into the air, snapped into two pieces, and sailed toward the trees, inscribing a steep arc in the air.

Then: the grass being trampled. The Townsends were on the run again.

Nash found his radio, pressed a button on the side. "Dobson, they're headed your way."

"Got it, boss."

He limped toward the road, hating his leg again, hating that it slowed him down, that it prevented him from getting to the road quickly. Panther exploded past him, with Dobson close behind, and here he was, *limping,* for Christ's sake. He cursed his leg, cursed the goddamn pain, cursed the polio that had rendered his leg so useless. And when he finally reached the road, a dark Ford Explorer was already peeling away from the shoulder, still close enough for him to see the license plate number. He took a mental snapshot of it and hobbled as fast as he could to Panther's Pontiac, and climbed into the passenger seat.

The Pontiac had gotten them from the marina to the park, a sleek, fast vehicle with enough horsepower under the hood to overtake the Explorer in seconds. But because Nash believed in backup plans, he called the ranger's station at the entrance to the park. He instructed the man who answered, a ranger whom Nash paid under the table, to stop a dark Explorer when it reached the gate, and ticked off the license plate number.

"How many people inside?" the guard asked.

"One." *That you can see.* "A man. Make sure that none of the doors are opened until we arrive."

Dobson, who was at the wheel, drew neck to neck with

the Explorer and Panther lowered his back window, aimed at the front left tire, and squeezed off two shots. The Explorer suddenly swerved, veered crazily from left to right, tires shrieking against the pavement. It spun into a one-eighty and stopped.

"We've got them!" Panther shouted and Dobson gunned the engine and slammed the Pontiac into reverse.

Seconds before they drew parallel with the Explorer, the passenger window came down. The only thing Nash saw was a gun, frozen in midair. A gun held by an Invisible. "They're armed," he shouted, and Dobson swerved sharply away from the Explorer.

Even so, the first shot punctured a rear tire—Nash heard the air hissing from it, felt the back of the car sinking down— and the other ricocheted off the roof. Then the Explorer lurched forward, engine racing, spun on a dime, and rushed back up the road, toward them, gathering speed. Before Panther or Nash could fire, the vehicle blurred past them.

Nash immediately put in another call to the ranger's station. "Armed and dangerous and headed your way," he said without preface.

"Got it, Doctor Nash. The gate's already down."

His next call was to the cop who had checked out their ID, who had said he had been instructed to help them in any way he could. He was delighted to be of service. Not to worry, Dr. Nash. This wouldn't be a problem.

It's already a problem, Nash thought, and hung up.

He flashed on that day three years ago when he and Panther and two dozen other men and women had chased Logan. Their thermal-sensitive glasses had allowed them to detect her until she had neared the electrical transformer box near the road, where the Florida Power and Light truck had been parked. Then they'd lost her completely. Only later had he realized that the transformer emitted an electromagnetic field that somehow had shielded her from detection.

From this single insight, he had realized that from that

point on, the actual experiments would have to be held well clear of electrical wire, transformers, underground cables, satellite towers, or anything else that generated an electromagnetic field. That was the main reason the Everglades had been chosen as a test site.

Now that he knew the committee was willing to up the ante, he realized that the Townsends could be his ticket to near autonomy. If they were brought in and placed as human guinea pigs in the project—perhaps brought in to begin populating his town for Invisibles—he would call the shots on every facet of this project, call them independently of Farris and the committee.

Instead of hiding the Townsends from the committee, as he had done with Tyler Griffin, he would use them to negotiate for funding, for power and control of the project, and the first thing he would do, he thought, was get rid of Farris. With three more Invisibles to study, including a girl at the brink of puberty and a woman who would be in menopause in eight or ten years, they would learn things about Invisibles that they hadn't been able to learn from Tyler. The NSB and the Department of Defense would find endless uses for the information the Tesla Project would generate on the effects of invisibility on a pubescent girl.

He had no data on how hormonal changes affected invisibility. In fact, if the woman was caught, then her eventual menopause and the ensuing hormonal changes could be as potentially useful to the project as the child's hormonal changes with the onset of menses. Both ends of the hormonal spectrum: the brass would love it. And Farris and funding would never be a problem again.

"Can we drive on a flat tire?" he asked Panther.

"Bet your ass," Panther replied.

"Step on it, Wayne," Nash said.

3

Shitdamnfuck . . . The roar of the engine, the shouts inside the car, the echo of gunfire, the hammering of her own heart: the din nearly deafened Renie. She slapped her hands over her ears and screamed at Katie to stay down and stared at the blur of light and sagging blue sky that rushed toward her through the Explorer's windshield.

Jim, Andy's brother, clutched the steering wheel with the fierceness of a kamikaze pilot on a death dive. Renie braced for a crash that would send all of them into the hereafter. Andy just kept shouting—about the gunshots, the Pontiac, the recklessness with which Jim drove, and Jim suddenly screamed, *"Shut the fuck up!"*

Silence. The only noise Renie heard just then was the whistling of the wind against the windows. Just ahead lay the entrance to the park—a ranger's station, a guardrail, and the rail was down.

They're on to us, they know.

But what, exactly, did they know? Did the rangers know the Explorer carried Invisibles? Probably not. Renie figured the rangers had been told to stop the Explorer, that they'd been told only what they needed to know. If they stopped, she and Andy and Katie wouldn't have any problem getting away, but what about Jim?

He apparently was thinking along the same lines because the Explorer shot forward at about ninety miles an hour and when it hit the guardrail, the thing snapped like a piece of dry pasta. Bits and pieces of wood flew away, the ranger leaped back, and the Explorer kept right on going. For a while after that, no one spoke. Renie heard Jim breathing, breathing hard, as if he'd been running. Andy muttered to himself and Katie lifted up from behind the seat and groped for Renie's hand.

Renie squeezed her daughter's hand and held on tightly. She wanted to say that everything was okay, but nothing was okay and Katie was too old to fool with platitudes. Jim glanced in the rearview mirror, his handsome features pinched, frowning, very worried. "Christ," he muttered. "This is too fucking weird. You're not there, really not there."

"We're here, Uncle Jim," Katie said. "And all the physical laws still apply to us. I mean, we think they do."

"Uh-huh." Jim's eyes darted again toward the rearview mirror. "And you said there's a dog with you?"

"Lucky," said Katie. "Her name's Lucky."

"Lucky," Jim repeated. "Yeah, well, we sure could use some of that." Then he swerved off the road, into a sugarcane field, onto a narrow footpath, and slammed on the brakes. The engine died, dust rose up around them. The tall stalks of cane and the jungle of long narrow leaves closed around the car. Jim twisted around in his seat, his face bloated with rage. "What the fuck is going on, Andy?"

Lucky whimpered. Renie winced. She had never seen Jim lose his temper. Not once in the eighteen years she'd known him.

Andy swallowed hard. Renie realized that although she could see the slight movement of his Adam's apple, Jim could not. Jim was looking at air. Jim probably didn't know that Andy was seated right behind him. Jim might have a general idea concerning his brother's location, but the specificity was missing. *You're at the edge of the middle seat. You're in the backseat.* Nope, for Jim, it was, *You're somewhere.*

"As soon as I know what the hell's going on," Andy said in a quiet, even voice, his ER voice, "I'll be sure to let you know."

"Uh, Jim," said Renie, "I think we'd better keep moving."

"Moving where?" A pulse beat hard and fast at his temple. "Just where the hell are we going?"

"You said something about using Nana's place," Andy said. "In Paradise."

"Yeah, great idea. Except she's there. Can't you just see it? Hey, Iris, we're here. But three-quarters of us are invisible. She's eighty-eight years old, for Chrissakes. She'd probably have a heart attack."

"That's a load of crap," Andy shot back. "She's healthier than we are. And she's lived through weirder stuff than this."

"Yeah? Like what, Andy? What the hell could be weirder than this? And suppose these assholes find us? Then she'd be charged with harboring fugitives or something."

No, Renie thought. Iris wouldn't be changed with a crime; she would be silenced. "He's right, Andy. We can't jeopardize her. Bad enough that we've put Jim at risk."

Silence. The brothers were like boxers who had retreated to their corners to lick their wounds and prepare themselves for the next round. Jim was the first to speak. "There's an apartment in the barn. You could use that. Iris wouldn't even have to know you're there."

Andy glanced at Renie, brows lifting, asking her what she thought. She nodded and Andy said, "Let's do that until we can make other plans. For right now, let's just get outta here."

Jim cranked up the engine and sped down the narrow road, leaves slapping the sides of the car.

4

Renie had known Jim before she'd met Andy. She had sold him his first house, a great little bungalow where he had lived with a woman he was seeing at the time, a geologist,

Renie remembered. She also had sold him his second house, which he'd moved into with an English lit professor. By the time he was on his third house, into which he moved with yet another woman, he had given her name to Andy and told her his brother would be getting in touch with her.

This was not welcome news. She figured Andy was a clone of his brother and only insane women invited men like that into their lives. But Andy in the flesh had been a complete surprise. Unlike Jim, he didn't look like a male model. His face was beautifully flawed, a chin that was a bit too square, eyes set a shade too far apart. He didn't talk too much, either. When he had something to say, he said it. Otherwise, he kept quiet. Maybe it was the adage about still waters running deep. Maybe it was just that she was at the right time and place in her life. Whatever it was, she fell for Andy within the first five minutes that she'd met him.

But that didn't mean she had to like his family. It didn't mean she had to put up with Jim. So it was a relief when Andy got a job in South Florida, way at the other end of the state from his brother. But about five years into Katie's life, Uncle Jim decided it was time to get to know his niece better and moved to the Keys. Moved alone this time.

It didn't take him long in the Keys to meet women. He was making tons of money in computers, doing whatever it was he did, and men who looked like he did and had bucks to boot were rarely alone for very long. For the last eighteen months, he'd been dating a red-haired honey with the energy of a hummingbird, breaking the usual Jim ceiling of between ten and twelve months. Renie liked the woman well enough, but was grateful Jim hadn't brought her along. She felt bad enough about getting Jim involved. But they might not have gotten out of the park without him and he would get them to Paradise, a place to hide. The irony. They were invisible, yet needed a place to hide. A grotesque irony.

"I think we have a major problem," said Katie.

Jim laughed. "Hon, we've got a shitload of problems."

"No, I mean the problem is the car. I'm sure they got the license plate number for this car, the make, the model, everything."

"Iris has a car we can use." Jim glanced in the rearview mirror again, then shook his head. "This is going to take some getting used to."

"You oughta try it from this end," Renie remarked.

"If these people know who we are," Andy said, "then chances are they know who you are, Jim, and they may even known that Iris is still alive, that she has a place in Paradise."

"Her last name's different than ours," Jim said.

"I hear something." Katie pressed her face to the side window. "I think it's a chopper."

"I don't hear anything," Jim said.

Renie listened. What she heard was not sound so much as vibration. Then she saw it, a tiny stain against the blue sky to the south. "It's a chopper. Get off the road. *Fast.*"

Jim swerved abruptly off the narrow road. The Explorer bounced down a shallow incline, into another sugarcane field, and stopped. The stalks scraped against the sides, the long slender leaves cut off much of the light. A kind of claustrophobia clamped down over Renie and she threw open the side door and stumbled out into the sugarcane. She sucked at the humid air and backed toward the car, leaning back into it to steady herself. *There. Okay. It's better. It's passing now.*

"Mom? You okay?" Katie touched her arm and Renie raised her head and realized she was gazing across the roof of the Explorer. The leaves and the stalks didn't cover the goddamn roof. The chopper would see them.

"Katie, get on the roof and lie down flat on your stomach. *Go, do it now.*"

Katie scrambled onto the roof and sprawled out on her stomach. Renie pushed a sugarcane stalk toward Katie. "Hold on tight." She ran around to the other side of the car and did the same thing. By then, Andy had climbed onto the roof with Katie and was stretched out beside her on his stomach, but in the opposite direction. Renie pushed leaves and stalks toward him and he grabbed on, holding them over himself and the roof of the car.

Renie ran to the back of the Explorer and Jim hurried to the front. They each pulled at the stalks, bending them like straws, inward toward the Explorer, and pretty soon green closed over the top of it, hiding it. Renie didn't realize she was holding her breath until it *whooshed* out of her. The chopper was nearly on top of them and she dropped her head back and peered up, up through the green leaves, the stalks. *You can't see me, but I see you, fucker.* The chopper flew past, about five hundred feet above the edge of the field, flying parallel to the main road. It circled the field twice, then lifted and flew off. As soon as it was out of sight, they piled back into the car.

"There are horse trails that go all the way from northern Dade County to Paradise," Jim said. "If we keep following these little roads north, we'll eventually run into the trails."

"That's great," Andy said. "But can you drive on these trails?"

"Sure."

"Let's just get somewhere," Katie groaned. "I'm not feeling too well."

Moments later, the Explorer nosed out of the field and onto the dirt road.

TWO

GHOSTING

JUNE 12-28

"The superior person stands firm without losing his aim"

—the *I Ching*

10
LUIS

Baños, Ecuador

The old man carried a heavy backpack the color of charcoal. He stood on the curb outside a vegetarian restaurant where the food was cheap but not very good. The "vegetarian" in the restaurant's name attracted the health-conscious tourists, the gringos and the Europeans who stopped in Baños for the medicinal thermal baths before they headed into the Oriente, the jungle that Luis called home.

Even at this early hour, there were plenty of tourists in Baños. They wandered past him, awed by the majesty of the mountains that rose sharply at the edge of town, green so green it surpassed the hue of the most precious emeralds. Sunrise spilled down the seventy-degree slopes, where the land was plowed with oxen and the geometric green shapes were crops. The tourists were captivated by the numerous shops that sold native art, everything from tapestries and handwoven rugs to the exquisite animal figures carved from the seed of the tagua fruit, a hard whiteness that resembled ivory.

Luis watched a pale-colored SUV, a Toyota, circle the plaza. As it passed him, he caught sight of the young woman at the wheel and smiled. His own daughter didn't see him. Luis bowed his head, shut his eyes, and felt the shift deep within himself. When he opened his eyes again, the Toyota was approaching the corner, slowing down, then pulling over to the curb. The window went down and his beautiful daughter leaned out, her smile flashing. *"Epa, hombre. Cómo andas?"*

"Con los dos pies, hija."

This had been their traditional greeting for each other since Elena was just a small child, a sort of inside joke. *Cómo andas* was one of those idiomatic Spanish phrases that meant: *How's it going?* But the verb *andar* literally meant "to walk" and his response meant he was walking with both feet. As always, Elena laughed as if hearing the joke for the first time, then she opened the passenger door and Luis climbed in. She hugged him hello, a quick but fierce hug that told him she sensed something unusual was going on and she wasn't sure she was going to like whatever it was. "When I went around the block the first time, I didn't see you. Were you in one of the shops, Papi?"

"I was on the corner the whole time."

She gave him a *look,* but didn't comment.

They headed out of town and onto a narrow dirt road that twisted like a pretzel up the mountain. Early morning clouds huddled against the steep slopes and hid the top of the Tungurahua volcano in the distance. The clouds would be gone by midday and back again by late afternoon, accompanied by a fine mist that would fall until twilight. Even though it was winter here, just south of the equator, the weather at this altitude was fairly predictable.

Luis glanced over at his daughter, struck by how much she resembled her mother—that same black, thick hair, the high cheekbones of her Incan ancestors, the black, piercing eyes. The Incan blood came from her maternal lineage; Luis's wife had been a member of the tribe that had rescued him as a young boy. Elena was the eldest of his three children, thirty this month, and like his two sons, she was completely Westernized and had no interest in the world he inhabited. She had been educated in the States, majored in business administration and, for the last five years, had been running the hacienda that had been in the family for nearly four centuries.

"I didn't expect you until July or August, Papi."

"A change in plans." Luis rubbed his right hand against his jeans, a feeble attempt to stem the burning sensation in the center of his palm. He knew that Elena noticed it and that even if she didn't understand the significance, she would make an intuitive connection between the movement of his hand and his unexpected visit. "I need some herbs that aren't grown in the Oriente."

"Herbs," she repeated.

Luis heard the tremor of fear in her voice and understood it. To his daughter, herbs spelled illness. All of the herbs and magic in the *curandero's* arsenal hadn't saved her mother.

"Are you ill?"

Luis heard the anxiety in her voice, the dread.

"No, no, nothing like that. No one is ill."

Her dark eyes quickly searched his face for answers. "Is this about that, uh, business in the States?"

"I believe so, yes."

"Aw, Papi, I thought you were finished with all that three years ago."

"It won't be finished until it ends. I didn't understand that then. But I understand it now."

The road got steeper, rockier, and narrowed to a ribbon of dirt and pitted holes. Just beyond the edge, the side of the mountain plunged down six thousand feet, into a vast valley, a paradise of green. He couldn't stare down too long, the heights dizzied him. But in his dreams, he often soared through this valley, a sorcerer with wings.

To his daughter, everything about his life smacked of sorcery. Elena wanted no part of it. Yet, the power he possessed ran through her veins as well. She simply refused to acknowledge it.

Elena downshifted as they approached a sharp turn and honked twice, warning whoever might be coming down the mountain on the other side of the curve. "Are you going back to the States, Papi?"

"I don't know yet."

"*Tía* Consuelo says you are."

"Ah, then it must be so, no?" He smiled as he said it. "I understand she's staying at the hacienda full-time now."

"We moved her into the apartment we built on the property. I think she misses the Oriente, but she claims the climate here in the mountains suits her better. Anyway, she reads for clients from time to time. Our Web site has been bringing in many European and American tourists who are interested in the indigenous culture and beliefs."

A part of Luis—the Westernized part of him—desperately wanted to believe this interest was a good thing. But the part of him who had been raised in the jungle knew that the interest of outsiders could be deadly to a culture like his own. His adopted tribe had existed since Atahualpa had ruled most of South America and was the only tribe on the continent that had mastered ghosting. But the tribe had been driven deeper and deeper into the jungle by the assault of civilization. Apparently *Tía* Consuelo had learned to accept this—but he had not. He found it most interesting, though, that his daughter could accept the fact that Consuelo was "doing readings" for the tourists even though she dismissed its veracity. Anything to improve business, he thought.

As they negotiated the final stretch of rocky road, two golden retrievers raced alongside the road, barking at the Toyota. Max and Shadow, the hacienda mascots. The dogs

followed the car along the final stretch, past the field where
the hacienda horses grazed, past the sheep, the pens that
held hogs. Sacred ground. In all of Ecuador, there were only
two other spots as sacred to him and this spot was the most
sacred of all.

Behind the hacienda, the mountains angled toward the
heavens, a carpet of green ascending into the clouds. In the
distance, clouds rolled away from the volcano, revealing the
spill of white around the top of it, snow that rarely melted.
For several hours, the entire valley would be visible, sunlight
sweeping across the greens, the strips of dirt roads, the
grazing cattle and sheep and horses, the humble huts, everything exposed, raw, and achingly beautiful. Then, in late
afternoon, the clouds would move in again and a fine mist
would fall. Once more, the mountains would be filled with
shadows and secrecy, and the kind of magic that one could
feel but not explain.

Elena parked between a van and another SUV and as soon
as Luis's feet touched this sacred ground, the retrievers were
all over him, sniffing, licking, whining, remembering him
even though they hadn't seen him for a very long time. The
youngest dog, Shadow, sensed the strangeness in his hand
and tried to lick it. Luis's fingers clenched shut, he dropped
into a crouch, and met the dog's yellow eyes. "No," he
whispered, and Shadow cocked her head to one side, then
barked, just once, and sat back, watching him, waiting.

She understood.

When Luis stood again, his daughter was watching him.
Her hair, now falling loosely around her shoulders, glistened.
"Food is ready whenever you're hungry, Papi. I think Con-
suelo is expecting you. Do you want me to take your pack?"

Luis shook his head. Already, his eyes were moving in
the direction his daughter had pointed, toward the small,
new building off to his right. The apartment, Elena called
it. Consuelo's place. It seemed to tug at him, that building,
an energy so palpable that he couldn't ignore it even if he

wanted to, an energy that represented the past and perhaps the future as well.

Consuelo was his first teacher, a *curandera*—a healer—whose ability at ghosting surpassed his own. She was born to it the way the condor is born to the skies. Although his daughter called her *tía*—aunt—she wasn't related to any of them by blood. His connection to her went deeper than blood, into soul, spirit, and the ghosting itself.

He moved cautiously through the wet grass, down several earthen steps, Shadow hugging his heels. The center of his right palm burned fiercely now, burned and itched so terribly that he kept rubbing it against his jeans. He thrust his hand in the pocket of his jacket, hiding it, demanding that it behave. He hadn't looked at his hand since the burning began last night, in the jungle, and he didn't dare look at it now.

He paused at the front door of the small yellow building and rapped his knuckles against the wood. He waited, rapped again, and finally turned the knob and opened the door. A fire burned in the hearth and its warmth welcomed him, its warmth and the fragrant scent of smoke. A cat slept curled up in a nearby chair. Relics covered the walls and filled the display cases, pre-Columbian artifacts dug up from this sacred ground. A huge bookcase dominated the wall directly opposite where he stood. And the air . . . the air smelled of something familiar—not wood smoke, not food, but something more fundamental. The air, he thought, smelled of antiquity.

"Some greeting, Consuelo," he said aloud, squinting as he looked slowly around the room. "C'mon, *Vieja*, show yourself. I don't have all day."

A log crackled in the fireplace. The cat sighed in its deep sleep. Shadow waited at his side. Silence punctuated each small noise in the apartment. Then her voice, coming from nowhere and everywhere: "Hold out your hand."

Luis extended his left hand.

"Not that hand." She sounded annoyed.

He let the backpack slide off his arm, to the floor, and walked over to the couch in front of the fireplace. He settled into it and worked off one shoe, the other. He unbuttoned his jacket, shrugged it off. "Show yourself."

"With the Sight, I am easy to see, Luis."

He traveled all night through the Oriente to Baños to get here and wasn't in the mood for hide-and-seek. But he understood that Consuelo was testing him, so he allowed his eyes to roll upward, under the lids, until only the whites of his eyes were showing. He moved his head from side to side, looking for her.

"To the right of the fireplace," he said finally, and let his eyes roll back into place.

Consuelo laughed, a low, almost rumbling sound, then unfolded herself from the wall to the right of the fireplace. She reminded him of a slender tree with a gnarled trunk and twisted branches. No one knew exactly how old she was, not even Consuelo herself. Somewhere between eighty and a hundred, that was what she told people. Regardless of her age, she looked remarkably fit.

"So," she said, shaking out her arms, then each of her legs. "It hasn't ended."

Luis shook his head. "But I knew that when I left."

"Then what has changed?"

Luis rubbed his burning, itching palm against his jeans. "The day of the ghosting, the young woman was frightened. I told you that, remember?"

Consuelo pulled a cigar from her voluminous clothes, lit it, and sat in the chair closest to the fire. "Yes, of course I remember. I am old, Luis, but I am not addled."

"I gave her an object of power."

"*Dios mío*. How foolish." She unfastened the clip at the back of her head and her long, gray hair fell loose, spilling over her shoulders. "Why give her an object of power if you knew you were going to leave?"

"At the time, I didn't know that I was going to leave."

"Then why give her anything, Luis?"

"I thought . . ." What? What had he thought? That the object would give her courage? A lie. An object couldn't impart courage. The object that he'd given her, however, had helped to maintain a connection between them.

"You thought . . . ?" Consuelo leaned forward, scrutinizing him with her ancient eyes.

"I wanted to maintain a connection between us. So that even if I left the project, I would be able to keep track of her."

"So you are only getting what you wanted." A small smile altered the shape of her wrinkled mouth. "And there has been contact since you gave her this object?"

"From time to time. In dreams, in visions. She has been living as a Ghosted One for three years, Consuelo. *Three years.* And her husband . . . he, too, has been living as a Ghosted One. But not as a free person. Who among our tribe can do such a thing?"

"It's not the same. They aren't ghosting as we do it, Luis. They use technology and the bitter herbs that you gave them."

"It doesn't matter what they use to attain the ghosting. My point is that this young woman has lived as a Ghosted One—and free—for many years now and you and I know how that changes the spirit, Consuelo. And now, something has happened. . . ." Even as he spoke the words, heat exploded in the center of his palm. It was as if he were clutching a hot coal. He winced and pressed his palm against his thigh.

Consuelo saw it; nothing escaped her. She reached out and gently touched his hand, turning it over so the palm was exposed. There, in the center of his palm, the skin was red and raised, as if blistered. The raised area resembled the fossil embedded in the stone he'd tossed to Logan three years ago. As he stared at it, both repulsed and fascinated, the area pulsed, the red deepened to scarlet. Consuelo blew cigar smoke over his palm and stroked it gently with her thumb. Almost instantly, the burning ceased and the red began to pale. In moments, his palm looked almost normal again.

"Shake it," she said. "Shake your hand."

He shook his hand, thumb and forefinger snapping together.

"I can take away the discomfort, Luis, but I cannot break the connection. Only you can do that."

"Can you see what has happened?" He hated the eager desperation in his own voice, hated the fact that he had to ask the question at all. To ask was to admit that his Sight was limited.

"Perhaps. Has this happened before with your hand?"

"Several times, yes. But not this badly."

"And what did you do when it happened before?"

The first time, when they were transferring Tyler to the Ponce facility, he was with Nash and didn't do anything except hide his hand. The second time happened during the first year after Logan's escape. In a vision, he saw that she had met someone who would help her, who was with her still, a black woman. The most recent episode began shortly after dark last night, while he was still in his village in the Oriente, and it got steadily worse for several hours, bad enough so that he caught the first ride out of the jungle.

Consuelo listened carefully, saying nothing until he had finished. In a slow, quiet voice, she said, "Luis, Luis. There are no shortcuts, *me entiendes?* You and I have always known that, but we keep looking for shortcuts. This has always been our failing. Only you can see the truth of the situation." She stood and went over to the mantel, where she dug around inside a large earthen bowl. She returned holding an exquisitely colored stone that was the clearest, deepest green that Luis had ever seen. "Right now, you are tired and need sleep. Keep this in your hand as you sleep.

It heals and gives clarity in dreams and visions. Later, when you are rested, we will seek the answers.''

"I can't sleep," he said crossly.

"You will sleep right here. By the fire. With the dog, the cat. I will get bedding.''

She left the room and Luis kept turning the stone over and over again in his hand. Not a stone, but a crystal of some kind, raw, unpolished, and oddly formed, with tiny, sharp angles and multiple surfaces. He gazed into the clearest surface and saw his own eyes, reflected back to him. And within those eyes, he glimpsed other faces, swirls within swirls, man, woman, child, dog.

He didn't understand. His eyes felt dry, his heart beat hard, his body wasn't accustomed yet to the altitude. Consuelo brought back a thick quilt, pillows, and a cup of steaming herbal tea. "Drink that and sleep, my friend. It will take me a while to prepare something that will help us find the answers.''

"What kind of something?"

"I'm not sure.''

"Liar.''

She laughed at that, laughed because neither of them could lie to the other. "I have been preparing the Demon Drink for nearly two days. It will be ready by tomorrow.''

Ayahuasca, the vine of death, and the most powerful of helpers.

"But I don't know if you're ready for the demon.''

Her smile now was a challenge and the smile triggered a memory of the earlier days, the two of them in the jungle. She was squatting by a cauldron that simmered over an open fire, and inside the cauldron was the vine, the hallucinogenic vine that would mark his initiation as a shaman. The jungle sounds surrounded them as completely as the darkness. And she asked if he was ready and he remembered what he said.

"I would drink lava, if lava could provide the answers."

Firelight danced in Consuelo's eyes. "You remembered, Luis. Very good. Now sleep," she said, and touched his forehead with her fingertips.

And just like that, he was gone.

11
THE UNEXPECTED

A persistent tapping woke Logan and she sat straight up in bed, blinking away sleep, and looked slowly through the gloom, trying to determine the source of the noise. Her vision seemed hazy, clouded, and it was difficult to make out anything clearly. Then, at the window, she caught sight of something, but couldn't say exactly what that something was. In seconds, she was out of bed, her feet seeming to glide across the floor, not quite touching it, and she threw open the window and leaned out into light so strange, so eerie, that she drew back, inexplicably uneasy, wary.

"Over here," a voice whispered.

She peered through the strange light and saw Luis, the Ecuadorian who, three years ago, had tossed her the stone with the fossil embedded inside it. "You," she said softly. "Luis."

"You must keep the stone with you. It's a bridge between us. Remember *Manteles.*"

The light faded slowly into darkness and Logan backed away from the window, confused, puzzled by what had happened. And suddenly she bolted forward in bed, fingers clenching sheets, her body covered in a thin film of sweat. Her eyes darted about wildly, trying to fix on something familiar, something that made sense. Pale yellow walls. Pale yellow blinds. Light fell through the blinds, creating patterns on the wooden floor. The bathroom door stood ajar. Her cat slept in a slant of sunlight. She was home.

A lucid dream, she thought, and immediately reached for the bedside journal where she recorded her dreams.

During her years as an Invisible, her dreams often had provided her with invaluable information about her situation. Through dreams, she had gotten hints about which foods to eat, which foods to avoid, how to bolster her changed immune system, and what she should do and not do to enable her body to use energy more efficiently. Dreams had been her first hint that invisibility had altered her physiology in ways other than what was obvious, that perhaps her brain was now wired very differently. Dreams also had provided the first inkling that Tyler was alive, but she hadn't known for sure until she'd broken into the Homestead control room.

Logan knuckled her eyes and struggled back into the dream. She could see Luis in the strange light, see his face, his ancient eyes, and heard him saying something about the stone, about keeping the stone with her. She always kept the stone with her. At the moment, it was in the pocket of the gym shorts she'd worn to bed, *visible* shorts that held a stone as invisible as she was. She slipped it from the pocket of her shorts, turned it over in her hand, ran her thumb over the fossil embedded in the stone. Then she scribbled in her journal, recounting what she could recall of the dream.

This wasn't the first time she'd dreamed of Luis, but the dreams never had been this vivid or real. *The stone.* She knew that referred to the stone he'd tossed her that day. *A bridge.* What bridge? From where to where? Perhaps Luis meant that the stone was a power object of some kind that created a deep connection between them.

Way back when she and Tyler were being trained for the shrouding, she'd heard rumors that Nash had an Ecuadorian on the payroll. Some people had referred to him as a professor, others had called him a shaman. It seemed ludicrous at the time that a man of Nash's scientific background would have anything to do with a shaman. There had been other rumors, too, she remembered, that the shaman had provided an essential ingredient in the shrouding and that he disapproved of human experimentation. Until that day in the hangar, however, neither she nor Tyler had ever seen the man.

Remember mantle. Or was it *mantles?* Either way, in the singular or the plural, she had no idea what it meant. She went through the usual dream-association techniques—fireplace mantel, a mantle as a cloak, a mantle as something that covers, enfolds, or envelopes, but nothing resonated for her. Maybe that wasn't the right word.

She sat up and swung her legs over the side of the bed. She was dismayed to see that all the food she'd eaten since the break-in was still digesting. She had engorged herself for several days, eating like some medieval glutton, and this was her equivalent of gout. The sight of it revolted her and she quickly looked away.

Her cat, Jazzy, lifted her head, yawned, and came over to Logan, rubbing up against her. Even when her food wasn't digesting and she was completely invisible, the cat was able to locate her. Logan didn't know if she did it by scent or if the animal actually could see her. The same was true for most dogs. Once, she had gone to the zoo to find out how or even *if* other animals could sense her. They didn't pay any more or less attention to her than they did to other people—to the Visibles—until she got to the area where two Florida panthers were kept.

Both cats went nuts, leaping at the walls of their cage, hissing and spitting and howling. The larger of the two cats, the male, made such a racket that it agitated the other animals. Or perhaps they were communicating something to the other animals, she didn't know for sure. But pretty soon, a cacophony of shrieks and howls and birdcalls echoed throughout the zoo, a ripple effect. Alarmed, Logan got out of there fast and never went back.

From this experience, she'd learned that her presence rarely alarmed domesticated animals, perhaps because to them, an Invisible wasn't much different than a Visible. Wild animals tended to spook, probably for the same reason they spooked when Visibles were around. Of the variety of wildlife that visited the two acres on which her house was built, birds and certain reptiles seemed to be the most sensitive to her presence.

She got up and showered, then stood dripping wet in front of the mirror, the only time she could see herself in a mirror. That aspect of invisibility hadn't changed in three years. She still stood about five eight in her bare feet. Invisibility hadn't robbed her of her height. Since her body used energy more efficiently now, her weight had dropped about ten pounds, to 120, and she liked the flatness of her stomach, the solidness of her thighs, the tight spareness of her body. Her hair, once long and very blond, was now short and several shades darker. Or perhaps it only looked darker because it was wet. She didn't care one way or another.

Logan could tell that her skin had turned so pale that the tan lines she'd had three years ago had faded completely. As far as she could tell, her face still looked pretty much the way she remembered, mouth too generous, dark eyes set too far apart, nose too long, but the overall effect pretty good. Not that it mattered now. Since invisibility protected her from the worst effects of ultraviolet light, she didn't think she had aged much in three years. Invisibility had repercussions and advantages that even George Nash probably hadn't anticipated.

As she began to dry off, she watched for the glow or shimmer that she sometimes saw in the mirror. She didn't know what it was or what it meant. It had started a year ago and she saw it only when she was dry, a shimmer where her body should be. From her research, she thought it might be her body's natural electromagnetic field. But in her heart, she was hoping for a miracle, that the shimmer meant the invisibility was wearing off. Speculation, she thought. It was all speculation. She felt a vague disappointment that she didn't see the shimmer today.

But perhaps that was due to all the food she'd eaten, to the sluggishness that still afflicted her. Whenever she went so long without food or liquid, she pigged out and suffered the consequences.

She dried off a limb at a time and, in the mirror, watched her reflection fade away—an arm, a leg, a foot, her face. Well, not fade away, exactly, since she could still see herself. But it wasn't the same. Her brain, habituated for so many years to seeing her body, filled in what her eyes couldn't perceive and the fill-ins, she thought, weren't the same as the real thing. The digesting food remained clearly visible.

She quickly dressed in visible clothes, jeans and a T-shirt that would hide the digesting food from Abby and from herself. She was barefoot and didn't wear gloves or a hood to fill in the missing parts of her body for Abby's sake. Abby was used to it. She was used to the sight of digesting food, too, but it seemed uncivilized or something to subject her to it when it wasn't necessary.

Jazzy followed her downstairs, where Logan heard the tap of computer keys in the library. Abby was already at work, tracking the stock reports from last week, searching for information on the Townsends, checking her long list of Internet sites. Logan's first stop when she woke was usually the gym at the other end of the house or the jogging path that wound through her two acres. Sometimes, she did both. But this afternoon, she was eager to get to the Tyler files, something she had avoided for the last several days. Hell, she'd been too busy eating.

She poured herself a cup of coffee from the pot in the kitchen and went into her office—her refuge, haven, hub, her connection to the visible world. Light streamed in through the picture windows to the east and north, which overlooked fields, pines, a vegetable garden, a pond. The spill of bougainvilleas, their blossoms like bright spots of menstrual blood, covered the electrified fence that surrounded the property.

Yes, she was paranoid.

The electrified fence that surrounded her little compound not only discouraged trespassers, but also rendered Nash's thermal detectors impotent. Video cameras were mounted at strategic spots. The house itself had a security system with all the bells and whistles. Did she feel safe here? Absolutely. Did she feel isolated? Yes. But she figured that was the price of her survival.

Three computers were already booted up, humming away. One of them was her invisible laptop, with three days' worth of e-mail and snail mail stacked beside it. Logan often wondered how Abby managed to place an invisible object in exactly the right spot. Practice, she supposed.

The first thing she did was to transfer the Tyler files into her desktop PC. One of the many mysteries to which she hadn't found a suitable answer was why the files she had downloaded onto her invisible laptop remained invisible to others as long as they were on the laptop, but became visible on the PC. Data occasionally got lost in the transfer, but not enough to make a significant difference. One more question, she thought, to pose to George Nash when she got the opportunity.

"Hey, girl," Abby said from the doorway. "I thought I heard you. How're you feeling?"

"Fat and sluggish, but otherwise okay. How'd our stocks do last week?"

"We lost about two G's, but made about six."

Logan laughed at the irony. It wasn't until she'd become

invisible—and met Abby—that money had ceased to be a problem. "Well, goddamn. It was a good week. Any information yet on the Townsends?"

"I've got home and work addresses and found an address in the Keys for Andy Townsend's brother. They've been reported missing. Just in case you're thinking about paying them a visit at home, I think we should wait on that score. Nash probably has the house under surveillance."

"How about e-mail?"

Abby shook her head. "Not now. The local cops are probably involved in the search and even their e-mail at work won't be secure. But I can put together something and send it, if you want to."

"I feel like I owe them something, Abby. If I hadn't shut down the power, the monitors in that control room would have picked them up and—"

"Hey, I know all about guilt, okay? We'll give it a shot. They're going to need help and maybe, in return, they'd be willing to help us spring Tyler. We could use three more Invisibles on our team."

Abby plopped herself in a chair near the desk. As usual, she was impeccably but casually dressed—plaid shirt tucked into the slender waist of her khaki shorts, expensive sandals the color of beach sand, toenails and nails painted a deep red, short, curly hair with just the faintest blush of gray. Logan sometimes missed nail polish and lipstick, makeup and jewelry, especially when she looked at Abby, who wore everything well.

In that first year, Logan remembered, once she had her little trailer, she used to do herself up, all the makeup and nail polish and jewelry she could steal. An adult playing dress-up. After a while, it lost its appeal. Nail polish and lipstick and mascara were tough to get off completely. Some itty-bitty speck usually remained and that itty-bitty speck made her visible to others. It gave her away.

"You have a chance yet to look at Tyler's files?" Abby asked.

"I'm just getting them on the PC."

"Well, before you start, I've got something to show you." Abby pulled a gold and blue scarf out of a pocket in her shorts. "Remember this?"

Of course she remembered it. The scarf was silk, a gift from Tyler that she'd been wearing that day in the hangar. She had used it to tie her hair behind her head and it, like everything else that she'd worn or carried, had been rendered invisible. "What about it?"

Abby held it in front of her, like an offering, the silk draped over her palms. "Look closely."

Logan looked. She leaned forward and studied the scarf, as if for imperfections. She stroked her fingers over the fabric. It was only when she pulled back somewhat that she saw it. "It's *visible*," she breathed.

"You got it, girl. I pulled it out of the dryer with some regular clothes this morning and it wasn't till I saw those gold hummingbirds that I realized what had happened. I mean, c'mon, *gold hummingbirds?* You told me humming-birds, but you didn't say anything about them being *gold*."

Logan ran the scarf through her fingers, stroked her cheek with it, and laughed, laughed until tears streamed down her face. She knew what this meant. They both did. If an object could turn visible after three years, then so could she.

As soon as the Tyler files were on her PC, Logan backed them up, then began printing them out. She wanted Nash's three years of notes in hard copy, in chronological order, before she read them. A part of her dreaded reading them, but another part of her knew that to free Tyler, she had to locate him and then she had to know as much as she could about what she would be up against.

As the files printed, she put the scarf around her neck and moved to one of the other computers. She kept touching the scarf, loving its luxurious softness. She always had loved the softness of it, but now it thrilled her because the scarf was *visible*. It symbolized hope.

She went on-line, to the Google search engine, thought a moment, then typed in the words *Mantle, Ecuador.* It was a long shot, but she had to start somewhere. Dozens of sites came up on Ecuador, Mickey Mantle, mantle cell lymphoma, mantle family genealogy, companies with mantle in the name. She started clicking on the Ecuador sites, scanning each one for anything related to mantle. Forty minutes later, she hit one possibility: *Manteles Yachts & Tourism,* a company that specialized in boat trips around the Galapagos. That word, *manteles,* seemed familiar, but probably because it sounded close to mantle. Just the same, Logan clicked om the link.

A wonderful Web site came up filled with photos of the Galapagos—the tortoises, the iguanas, the birds that existed nowhere else on the planet, the clear azure waters.

> *Manteles Yachts & Tourism operates the largest tourist company in The Galapagos. We have 12 yachts and many different kinds of tours through our magnificent islands. Diving, bird-watching, photo cruises: whatever your interest, we offer it. Whatever your budget or your time and the size of your group, we have something you'll love.*
>
> *We have been cruising the Galapagos for two decades and the Manteles family has been living in Ecuador since the Spanish came here looking for gold. We specialize in you finding YOUR gold.*
>
> *• Our yachts take you through our beautiful islands.*
> *• Our mountain hacienda provides an exquisite setting for peace and quiet, with 17 species of hummingbirds, horseback riding through breathtaking terrain, and some of the best indigenous food in the country.*
> *• Our bed-and-breakfast in Quito is right in the*

middle of the new town, close to cybernet cafés, book-
stores, museums, restaurants.
    • *Ali Shungu, our hotel in Otavalo, is four blocks*
from the world-famous Otavalo Indian market.
    JOIN US FOR THE ADVENTURE THAT IS
ECUADOR.
    Antonio Luis Manteles

Coincidence? How many Manteles could there be in Ecuador? She quickly scrolled through the page until she found
an e-mail address. She composed her thoughts, then wrote:

    Hi. I'm looking for Luis Manteles. Please tell Mr.
Manteles that I still have the fossilized stone he gave
me. I would appreciate it if he would get in touch with
me through the above e-mail address. You might also
tell him that shrouding isn't all it's cracked up to be.
    Best wishes, Logan

She wondered about signing her name, about whether it
would mean anything to Luis. Had he even known her name?
Well, he would recognize ''shrouding'' and figure it out,
she decided, and sent the e-mail.
    Logan heard something outside, something other than the
usual daytime sounds, and went utterly still, listening hard.
She heard it again, a car approaching the house. Abby
wouldn't hear it for another fifteen or twenty seconds, she
thought, and shot up from her chair. She ran to the door of
her den and whistled twice, signaling Abby that someone
was coming, then shut the door again.
    Off came the visible clothes, on went the invisible clothes.
She looked down at herself, dismayed to see that some of
her coffee was still making its way through her system. But
that would be gone soon and the important thing was that
the food had been digested. She shut down her PC, gathered

up the printed pages from the Tyler files, and stashed the pages and her visible clothes in the closet safe.

Outside, fast.

She opened the door a crack and Jazzy slipped out. Logan quickly followed and moved silently into the front room and stopped at the window, next to Abby. An unmarked police car appeared at the end of the driveway. "Shit," Logan whispered. "Someone must've phoned in a description of the Rover."

"Goddamn helpful guard," Abby muttered. "Girl, some of your coffee is still visible. But just barely. I'll buy you a couple of minutes before I open the door."

"Make sure they leave the front door open slightly so I can snoop around their cruiser."

"I know the drill."

They waited away from the windows while the men rang the doorbell. Abby didn't answer it for a full sixty seconds, until the coffee was completely gone, and this elicited a second ring of the bell. She turned her head away from the door and called out, "Hold on, I'm coming, just hold on."

When she finally opened the door to a pair of men, Logan immediately sensed they were FBI agents. One was short and squat, the other tall and thin. Logan wondered if they intentionally paired up cops to look like Abbot and Costello. "Afternoon, ma'am," said the skinny one, and held up his badge, and introduced himself and his partner. "We're looking for Abby Sparks."

"I'm Abby. What can I do for you gentlemen?"

"Where were you the afternoon of June ninth, around four P.M., Ms. Sparks?" asked Chubs.

"The ninth," she repeated, frowning. "What day was that?"

"This past Saturday, ma'am," said Chubs.

"Oh, sure, I remember. I was on my way to the Keys when I took a wrong turn, ended up near Homestead Air

Force Base, and my car died. A very nice guy named Jeff helped me out. He's a guard at the base. Why?''

They ignored her question. Chubs went through a notepad. ''And about what time would you say you left the area?''

''Less than an hour later. I don't know the exact time. I got to Marathon around seven or seven-hirty, I guess it was. Why?''

Again, they ignored her question. The skinny guy, Bones, took up the questioning now. ''Is there anyone in Marathon who can verify your whereabouts at that time?''

''Excuse me, but I'd like to know what this is about.''

''There was a disturbance at the base and a dark Land Rover was reported in the vicinity.''

''I was definitely in the vicinity. My car was dead. The guard fixed the problem and I was on my way less than an hour later.''

''On your way where, ma'am?'' asked Chubs.

''I just told you. To Marathon. To visit my daughter and grandson. I got there around seven or seven-thirty, I guess it was. If you'd like to verify my whereabouts, gentlemen, I'll give you her number.''

''We'd like to see the car, ma'am,'' said Bones.

''Sure.''

Logan stepped silently to the side as Abby led the two men through the utility room to the garage. As soon as they were out of sight, Logan hurried through the open front door, to the cruiser parked in the driveway.

The windows were down, no police dogs were in the backseat. She leaned through the open window, searching for a clipboard, but found a Pocket PC instead. Wireless high tech for the feds. *Your tax dollars at work.* It rested in a cup holder and was still connected to a cell phone. Too tempting, she thought, and climbed through the open window.

Once she was settled in the passenger seat, she picked up the PC, flipped open the lid. The device was on, with the most recently accessed folder on the screen. This consisted of a list of names and addresses, each one followed by a vehicle model and year, and then a license plate number. All the vehicles, she noticed, were dark Land Rovers, and all of the addresses were located between Key West and the northern reach of Palm Beach County.

It didn't take a genius to figure out the information had come from the Motor Vehicle Department, generated by a search for the owners of dark Land Rovers. With the stylus, she touched various folders until she found the original report that had generated the search.

Colleen Roth, Operations Manager, Homestead Air Force Base, National Security Bureau.

Logan quickly scanned the report, noting that Colleen had called in a break-in and theft to the NSB control room well after Logan had been there and gone—at four-thirty that morning. She claimed that the stolen computer items were "vital to national security"—but didn't spell out what they were. She apparently hadn't mentioned that several employees had chased the suspect through a field, either. And, of course, there was no mention of the object that had been seen moving out of the building and across the old tarmac.

Even if Colleen had heard that story and connected it to an Invisible—i.e., to either Logan or Tyler—it made sense that she would have the feds do the grunt work first and locate the right address. Only then would she and Nash move in with their detectors, their dogs, their technology. *But we'll be long gone by the time you figure it all out.*

Logan glanced toward the house. No sign of the agents yet. *Shit, give it a shot,* she thought, and went into the phone directory. She touched the number for the FBI computer, waited impatiently as it dialed, then she was on-line, the cursor blinking. Using the stylus again, she tapped in *Townsend, Andrew.*

When the name finally came up, it was accompanied by a Social Security number, work and home addresses, and the words *Reported missing by Everglades Park Service 6/10/01. Contact liaison agent.* Already reported missing. Nash's information machine didn't waste any time, she thought, and without a second thought, tapped in Tyler's full name.

Case # 325671296, Missing Person, 12/12/96. Pending. Contact liaison agent for more information. Or enter password.

In other words, it was classified, she thought. Okay, so who was this liaison agent? Liaison to what? Covert federal agencies?

Logan thought a moment, then tapped *George Nash* into the search engine. She didn't know what she expected— nothing, bells and whistles, another note to contact the liaison agent, a shutdown to the system. Instead, a single word came up: *Farris.*

That was it. Farris. She had met Ross Farris exactly once, the day she and Tyler had gone into the twilight zone. She started to tap in something else, but heard voices and saw that Chubs and Bones had nearly reached the car. She tapped the screen, bringing the image back to the folder that had been visible when she'd flipped open the lid, turned it off, dropped it back in the cup holder. She started to vault out of the passenger window, but Chubs was too close.

Drivers' window.

Nope, not unless she was the size of a dime. Now Bones was opening the door, closing off any other options. Logan quickly slid over the back of the seat and went as still as a suckling mosquito. Moments later, the car moved down the driveway.

"So," said Bones. "What do you think?"

"Shit, man, this whole deal stinks. We get half-assed information from the Roth woman, we still don't know what the hell was stolen, then the boss gets a visit from some honcho at the NSB and suddenly, this is high priority and I spend three hours running down lists on dark Rovers in

South Florida. And for what? To pacify some turkey from
NSB?''

Shit, got it. Now let me outta this car fast. . . . Christ, aw
Christ . . . windows going up . . . gonna roast back here . . .
The door, throw open the back door . . .

But the car turned onto the road and immediately picked
up speed. Blocks whizzed past. Neighborhoods blurred.
Adrenaline rushed through Logan. She fought back waves
of panic and barely resisted the impulse to hurl open the
door and leap out. One hand clutched her thigh, the other
gripped the door handle, pressing down, holding the door
shut until the car braked for a light. Then she threw it open,
leaped out, and ran. She ran with her arms tucked in tightly
at her sides, her bare feet slapping the hot pavement.

When she reached the curb on the other side, she nearly
collided with a woman pushing a baby stroller. Logan veered
around her and the baby immediately began to scream. She
looked back to see the men standing outside their car, glancing around, everything about them suggesting puzzlement
about what the hell had just happened. Logan ran on, damn-
ing herself for such a stupid stunt. It would take just one
remark to Farris, Colleen, or Nash for them to piece together
what actually had happened back there and that would be
it.

She dug her hand into the pocket of her shorts, hoping
she still had loose change she'd been carrying three years
ago. Invisible change. She unzipped an inner pocket, but all
she had was a penny. She walked for a while, headed back
toward the house, watching the cars that sped past her. At
the end of the block, she followed a woman into a convenience store. She ducked behind the counter and waited until
the clerk turned his back on the register and then she helped
herself to a quarter.

Since it was visible, she had to get rid of it quickly. So,
before the clerk turned again, Logan flipped the quarter into
the air and it sailed over the counter and landed on top of

the stack of newspapers, barely making a sound. She slipped out from behind the counter and, when the clerk wasn't looking in her direction, plucked the quarter off the stack and pushed through the doors.

A car was pulling up outside, teenagers inside. Loud music pounded from the radio as three teenage boys got out, all of them laughing, swearing. One of them noticed the quarter moving through the air and stopped, staring at it, his expression frozen in astonishment, incredulity, puzzlement. Logan stopped close to him and whispered, "You got a problem, kid?"

He wrenched back, spun around to see who had spoken to him, then lunged for the doors of the store as if the devil himself were nipping at his heels. Logan hurried around the corner to the public phone. *Make it fast,* she thought, and fed the quarter into the slot. She punched out her home number.

One ring and Abby picked up. "Where the hell are you?" she asked before Logan had said a word.

"About a mile from the house. Did they come back?"

"Nope. But I'm getting the RV out of storage. It's time to hit the road, Logan. I feel unsettled."

Hit the road? She'd been thinking they should move to their cottage up the coast, a little two-bedroom place in Sebastian, just north of Vero Beach. It was as fully equipped as the house for anything they might need. The RV, on the other hand, hadn't been used in a year and a half. They would have to move stuff into it from the house and that could take hours. She wasn't so sure they had hours.

"I was thinking Sebastian, Ab."

"Why the hell would we go there? They've got the license plate number for the Rover. The RV makes us mobile without that worry. We can head to the Keys, to one of the campgrounds. It won't take more than a few hours to get the RV in shape."

Logan tried to think it through. But before she got very

far, she heard the teenage boys coming out of the store. The kid who had seen the quarter was still trying to convince his buddies about what he'd seen, about the voice he'd heard. If he came around the corner of the building, he would see the phone receiver floating in midair.

"Okay, the RV it is."

She hung up, praying this was the right choice. It galled her, though, that Nash had her on the run again.

12
THE GLASS HOUSE

Ponce, Florida: it was just a pit stop for small planes that flew across the state. Its year-round population was impossible to measure, Nash thought, because so many Mexican transients worked the surrounding fields, picking strawberries and tomatoes, papayas and mangos. In the afternoon light, the tiny town a thousand feet below him looked to be made of papier-mâché, like some kid's science project. The actual downtown consisted of little more than an antiquated movie theater, a grocery store, and shops of one kind or another.

Just beyond the town lay the airstrip that Dobson now circled. It was used mostly by crop dusters, student pilots practicing touch-and-go landings, and by the choppers and small planes that catered to the facility. The residents believed the complex was connected to the University of Florida and never questioned anything that went on. After all, the project bought food and supplies from the local merchants, infusing the miserable economy with a little hope.

As soon as the plane touched down, Nash saw a waiting Jeep, with Colleen at the wheel. Dobson frowned and gave voice to exactly what Nash was thinking. "Since she's here, that must mean the honchos from Washington have arrived, boss. Otherwise Farris himself would be here to pick you up."

"I'll ride up with Colleen. You tie down the plane and drive one of the cars to the compound. Go meet these assholes. Pass out copies of the report we've prepared on Tyler. Keep them busy while I talk to Tyler."

"Hey, boss," Dobson called after him as he got out.

"Yeah?"

"Don't let the bastards take over."

"I'll do my best."

"You and I can run this entire operation with blindfolds on. They'll just screw it up."

Yes, he and Dobson could run it just fine. Dobson knew as much about the operation as Nash did. But neither of them had the funds it took to run this operation and, at the moment, Nash's best wouldn't be good enough. Without the Townsends, he had little leverage. Since the Townsends' escape from the park, they had eluded Panther and his men completely. Yet, the situation could shift at any moment. No one in this day and age lived in a vacuum. They had ties to family, friends, clients, coworkers, neighbors. Panther would find them. But until he did, Nash had to stall the committee.

His leg ached as he made his way toward the Jeep. It seemed to have been aching steadily since this whole fiasco had started, a dull, steady ache that traveled up and down his leg and often settled in his hip. Yesterday, he'd refilled his codeine prescription and was now eating the shit like candy, two every six hours. Sometimes the codeine helped, sometimes it didn't. Right now, he was approaching the five-hour mark and didn't think he would be able to make it to six hours. He reached into his pocket for one of the pills, popped it in his mouth, and chewed it up. In the next few hours, he would need whatever relief it might provide.

He leaned on his cane and saw Colleen watching him. *Cripple:* was that how she saw him? Last night, he'd lain awake for hours, massaging his leg, seriously considering the prospect of amputation. But where, exactly, would they amputate? At the knee? Not high enough. At the hip? Too high. He needed his goddamn hip. Just below the hip, perhaps, low enough so that he could be fitted with a prosthesis, but high enough to end the pain. He'd even imagined himself with a hollow leg, imagined walking without pain, without the cane, and then he'd imagined making love to Colleen without his prosthesis and the idea disgusted him so deeply that he canceled the notion altogether.

He put his gear in the back of the Jeep and climbed into the passenger seat. Colleen smiled hesitantly, obviously unable to gauge his present mood. "Hey, any news on the Townsends?"

"Not yet." He rested the cane against the edge of the seat. "I expected Ross to pick me up."

"He's with the committee members." She put the Jeep in gear and started up the dusty road. "Four of them are already here. I put them in the conference room, where they can observe Tyler on the computers."

Nash snickered. "Watching an invisible man. I hope he's dressed, so there's something to see."

"Dressed and busy at his computer. They're waiting for you and Dobson and the report."

"Well, you can send them all back to D.C. We're not ready for them to scrutinize Tyler."

She peered at him over the rims of her sunglasses as though he'd lost his mind. "Why the hell should we do *that?* All we have to do is get through thirty or forty minutes of their observing Tyler and asking him some questions, and our funding goes through the roof tomorrow. We'll have all the money we need for this research, George."

"Yeah? In exchange for what? The Pentagon as our over-seers?"

"You're exaggerating."

"You're naive."

"They're here. We have to deal with them."

"No, we don't. They aren't going into Tyler's quarters. He's not some goddamn lab rat, Colleen." He hadn't meant to say that, but now that he had, he realized how protective he felt toward the man whom he had rendered invisible. "And I won't have him treated like one."

She swerved to the side of the road, slammed on the brakes. Dust rose up around them, drifted through the open windows. "Let me spell it out for you, George. Either they see him today or we're shut down by tomorrow *and* we lose Tyler. They'll take him and they'll take the Townsends, too, when they catch them."

Her passion at moments like this always struck Nash as grossly misdirected. After all, invisibility wasn't *her* baby, it was his. But Colleen was an opportunist who would rise quickly in the NSB scheme of things. It had occurred to him on more than one occasion that her ambition might be one of the reasons they had become lovers. On her résumé, *assistant to the creator of the shrouding process* could just as easily be interpreted as: *I was fucking him. I've got his secrets.*

As soon as he thought this, though, he felt guilty. Colleen wasn't like that.

"We've tested nearly every goddamn object known to man, George, from hairpins and microchips to clothing and cars." She pushed her sunglasses back onto the top of her head, anger rolling off her in waves that he could smell. "We've rendered these things invisible innumerable times, have run countless tests on them, and we know pretty much everything there is to know about how the shrouding affects them. Thanks to Tyler, we even know the long-term effects of shrouding on human beings. We need to move forward and that means escalating human experimentation under conditions so stringent there won't be any repeats of Logan. No rogues, no renegades.''

What arrogance, he thought wearily. They would never know *everything* about shrouding. And they would never know everything about how shrouding affected human beings. Despite the fact that they'd been observing and studying Tyler for his three years as an Invisible, mysteries remained that medicine and psychology couldn't explain. Forget the blood and spinal fluid samples, the tissue and bone marrow samples. Forget the IQ tests, the stupid ink blot tests, the Jungian dream analyses. The bottom line was that they'd known Tyler as a Visible only during the six months they had trained him, and six months amounted to piss in a bucket when you were talking about the years of a man's life, his emotional and spiritual history. And on numerous occasions, he had felt that even though Tyler played along with the tests and the bullshit, he withheld the fundamental truths of life as an Invisible.

If the NSB and the committee ignored what they didn't know—which they would surely do—and went ahead with their ambitious plans to introduce more human beings into the Tesla Project, then they would be opening a Pandora's box. On a more personal level, he and his employees would be phased out gradually while the Pentagon, the CIA, the NSB, and a dozen other agencies with acronyms would be panting in the bureaucratic wings over this potentially perfect weapon.

Imagine the uses. From the invisible spy to the invisible terrorist, the possibilities of how shrouding might be used stretched on to infinity. Invisible bombs. Invisible planes to drop those invisible bombs. Invisible military installations. The idea of it sickened him, but the concept was hardly new.

He said none of this to Colleen. ''You've made your point. Start the Jeep.''

But she didn't. She just sat there, looking at him, beads of perspiration glistening on her forehead. ''Don't blow this for all of us, George,'' she said softly. ''We'll still maintain control. But we need more money. Tyler is costing us close to three million a year, this search for the Townsends is going to cost hundreds of thousands, and right now, we've got another major expense.''

''Yeah? What? Farris's plane fare down here and his expenses?''

She ignored his sarcasm. ''It looks as if Logan has surfaced.''

Of all the things she might have said, this possibility hadn't even occurred to him. Before he could say a word, she proceeded to explain in a voice that seemed eerily calm, considering the possible repercussions. Nash rubbed his temples, trying to ease the hard, persistent aching in his head. When he shut his eyes, he could see what Colleen was describing, see it as if he'd been there: an object moving through the air and across the tarmac as if of its own volition. And that object, of course, was undoubtedly the hard drive of one of the control-room computers.

''Which hard drive is missing?'' His voice sounded high and squeaky and riddled with dread.

''From the main computer.''

Sweet Christ. ''Then she knows Tyler's alive.'' In the moments that followed, Nash became intensely aware of the heat here in the shade of the tree where she'd slammed on the brakes, an intense, penetrating heat. ''But not where we're keeping him.''

''In the event that she figures it out, we'll be ready for her. Tyler, Logan, the Townsends. Five human subjects, George. The committee will eat it up. We'll be able to write our own ticket.''

''To where? To what? Just what the hell do you envision here, Colleen? Peer recognition? Articles in academic and scientific journals? *Oprah*? A Nobel?'' He laughed. ''Get real.''

''I'm interested in the research end of it, just like you are,'' she snapped. ''I don't give a shit about peer reviews and scientific journals. We're on the cutting edge here, working at *molecular* levels, busting old paradigms.''

''And in six months, they'll be busting our asses with severance packages.''

''That's cynical. Really cynical.''

''It also happens to be true.''

''How can it be? You're the only person who knows the essential ingredient in the shrouding, George. Without you, there's no Tesla Project.''

Her idealism appalled him. ''It's naive to think that Farris's people haven't been working on the technology on their own. They don't need me.''

''I'm not talking about the technology. I'm talking about the knowledge that Luis gave you.''

Was she fishing? Was that it? *No comment*, Nash thought.

''Sure, I think they can shroud. For *seconds*, George, just for seconds. Their process is unstable. Yours isn't. Your process lasts for days, weeks . . . hell, with Tyler and Logan, it's lasted *three fucking years*. They can't match that and they know it.''

She spoke with authority, as if she knew precisely what Farris's people were doing and how they were doing it.

''How would you know?''

''Ross confided in me.''

He refused to touch *that* one. She already had pointed out that she was single and he was not and until that situation changed, he had no right to question what she did or with whom or when. On the other hand, he had known Farris and his kind longer than she had and recognized a line of crap when he heard it.

''Ross told you what you wanted to hear, Colleen.''

She shook her head and strands of her hair fell loose from

her ponytail. For moments there in the shade and the terrible heat, she seemed either very old or very young, he couldn't decide which. He knew, suddenly, that his inability to decide such a small thing might prove, ultimately, to be his nemesis.

"C'mon, George," she said softly, and looked up, at him. "I play to Ross for information, that's it."

Play to him how? Have you fucked him, Colleen?

She started the Jeep again and he glanced off toward the fields that surrounded the facility. *You can't fight city hall,* whispered his long-dead mother.

Maybe not. But he might be able to outwit them.

"Does Ross know about Logan?"

"Not from us. Officially, she's been dead for three years and that's what he believes. He and I called the FBI about the break-in and they sent somebody out to Homestead, but the people who witnessed this *thing* moving through the air talked to me privately about it. I also spoke to the two men who pursued a dark-colored Land Rover with a woman inside."

"How much funding is Farris really talking about? In dollars, Colleen. Not in abstracts."

"One hundred million for the first two years. The contract would be renewable after that."

One hundred million? For seconds, it rendered Nash speechless. "And aside from selling our souls, what do we have to do for that money?"

"We have to figure out how to reverse the process on humans."

Nash exploded with laughter. "Fat chance. What else?"

"We have to train four people for shrouding—two they select, two we select. The process has to be reversible for these people. In other words, we can't just wait for the process to reverse itself. That has to be accomplished by the end of the first year."

Nash suddenly realized something that should have been obvious since she'd started laying out the terms. Farris had sent her to pick him up for precisely this reason, to lay the foundation, to prepare him for the terms he would hear from the committee. "What else?"

"Half of our staff will be replaced by people they choose."

Nix that one, he thought. "What else?"

"You would answer directly to Ross."

"In other words, he would be in charge."

"No, you maintain control, but Ross has to be informed about what's going on."

"And what would your job be in this brave new world?"

"I'll be the liaison between the project and Farris and the committee."

"Like you're doing now," Nash remarked.

This brought a quick, furtive glance from Colleen. "Ross asked me to discuss it with you first, before you saw the committee."

Uh-huh, he thought, and looked away from her.

And if you're stupid enough to fight city hall, son, his mother had said once upon a time, *then the only way to do it is to be prepared to walk away from what's at stake.*

Was he prepared?

The road led through three acres of woods and farmland that surrounded the facility. On either end of the facility stood concrete walls that fortified the most important areas— Tyler's apartment and research and medical. The complex's three concrete buildings were impervious to just about anything short of a nuclear blast.

The bulk of Nash's employees worked there, between thirty and thirty-five individuals with the highest security ratings. They were engineers and computer wizards, biologists and chemists, psychologists, physicians, lab techs, blood and tissue specialists, and research scientists like himself. He had handpicked all but two of them, Farris's lackeys.

As Colleen ran her ID card through the slot at the main gate, Nash brought a pad of paper and a pen from the glove compartment. He quickly jotted down six items and handed her the sheet. ''Here's your second job as the liaison. I don't care how you negotiate this, but this list is my absolute bottom line, Colleen. Unless they agree to every single item, they can do whatever they want with this project. I'll be gone and the element that makes shrouding stable goes with me.''

''You'd *leave?* Now? When we're so close?''

The shock in her voice thrilled him. It meant that Farris and the goddamn committee hadn't considered that he might be willing to walk away from something that had consumed most of his adult life. It meant his mother was right. But before he walked, if it came to that, he would free Tyler. They didn't deserve to benefit from Tyler's imprisonment.

''As a very wise woman once told me, Colleen, if you're going to be stupid enough to fight city hall, then you have to be prepared to walk away from what's at stake. And I am. Dobson will pass out the reports we've prepared and I'll let him know when Tyler's ready to see the committee.''

With that, he got out of the Jeep, gathered up his belongings, and headed into the building.

2

At a thousand square feet, his office was large enough to accommodate the equipment that fed him continual information on Tyler Griffin—his physiology, his daily routine, with whom he spoke and for how long, the content of the conversation. When he was seen by the shrink or by a doctor, this was also noted. The dreams that he recorded on his computer or shared with his shrink were studied, analyzed, picked apart for possible insights into his psyche.

Nash could find out what movies Tyler had watched, what books he had read, when he showered, jogged, and used the computer. Although his computer didn't have e-mail access and he couldn't post messages on the Internet, he could surf to his heart's delight. Every night after Tyler had gone to sleep, one of the computer techs accessed his computer remotely. Any new cookies on the computer were noted and checked out. Any new files were transferred. Practically every facet of Tyler's life was public knowledge within the project. In a sense, he was the real-life equivalent of *The Truman Show,* but far smarter than the character Jim Carrey had played and invisible to boot.

The surveillance equipment in the apartment didn't rely on closed-circuit TV, which used expensive coaxial cabling, industrial VCRs for recording, and an individual wire for every camera. The security in Tyler's apartment and through-out much of the complex was accomplished through digital surveillance. This network-based product enabled access from anywhere in the world using the Internet. The number of live images that could be viewed at any second depended on the speed of the Internet connection and all images were stored in a network-accessible computer database for later viewing.

The three cameras in Tyler's apartment could be calibrated to switch angles at specified intervals and could be zoomed at the touch of a button. Only two of the cameras were equipped for thermal sensing, thus giving Tyler privacy in his bedroom. Nash controlled the settings, the archives, and the remote access to the surveillance of the apartment. He decided he needed privacy to speak to Tyler, so he cut off the conference room access. The committee, he thought, had seen enough for the moment.

He tapped in the password that allowed him to speak directly to Tyler though the apartment's audio equipment, without anyone else hearing the conversation. Even the guard in the control booth outside the apartment wouldn't be able to hear them. He changed the angle of the camera until he found Tyler in the computer room.

Just as Colleen had said, he was wearing clothes that made him visible, which meant his food was still digesting. Tyler disliked people watching his food digest. Nash couldn't blame him. It was a grotesque sight. He even wore a jacket with a hood, so that from the back he looked like a Visible.

"Hey, George, I hear you spying on me." Tyler's voice came through the intercom, then he spun around in the chair, the space inside the hood as empty as an old shoe. "Spooky shit, isn't it, George?"

Extraordinary hearing, Nash thought. That was one of the effects that they had noticed in prolonged visibility—and that Tyler had never mentioned directly. Withholding: Tyler did that very well.

"Got your books, Tyler."

"Great. Thanks." The sarcasm vanished. "You were able to find all those titles?"

"Got them all. I'll be over shortly."

He clicked off the two-way intercom and Tyler turned back to the computer. Surfing the Web? Reading an e-book? Nash pressed a button and the camera turned slightly, then zoomed in on the screen. Tyler suddenly threw out his arms and leaned forward, his body blocking the screen.

"That's not nice, George."

He could hear the smallest *click*. Nash turned the two-way intercom back on. "Sorry about that, Tyler. I was just curious."

"So ask your tech wizard to check it out like he does when I'm sleeping.' "

"Everything you do and think is of interest to us."

"Too bad the feeling isn't mutual."

Nash let the remark pass. "I'll bring those books over."

"Fine. Whatever."

Nash opened his briefcase and removed four paperback novels, early Asimov, a book on government conspiracies, and a scientific tome on molecular biology. Most of Tyler's

Web surfing involved science. Not too surprising, given his physical condition. And what harm could it do? Tyler was a bright man with a unique perspective and it was possible he might see things that Nash and his team had overlooked.

He put half a dozen mangos, Tyler's favorite fruit, into the bag with the books and walked down the hall to where the golf carts were kept. Because of the size of the complex, electric golf carts were the preferred method of transportation.

From one end to the other, the complex covered about three city blocks. This particular building, one of four, was shaped like a rectangle with corridors shooting off from each corner that led to other smaller buildings—labs, a gym, the research area, medical. Tyler's apartment lay at the north end. It wasn't an apartment in the usual sense. It was a glass house with no front door—only double electronic doors made of unbreakable glass. The main room accommodated the living area and kitchen and was where Tyler spent most of his time. The small bedroom wasn't useful for much of anything except sleeping. Only the bathroom was truly private—no camera at all, a detail Farris had objected to. *He's invisible, for Chrissakes. What's he need privacy for in the bathroom?*

Because he spent twenty-nine years of his life as a visible person and is psychologically habituated to privacy in the john. If memory served him, those had been his exact words to Farris.

And Tyler had gotten a private bathroom.

When the weather was good, Tyler spent a lot of time on the patio just off the living room with his easel, his canvasses and paints, the works. Over his years here, he had become quite an accomplished painter. He had a unique perspective as a man whom others couldn't see, a profound sense of isolation that was evident in his paintings. Whether it was a landscape, an animal, or a person, or even an abstract, each painting possessed a stark, terrible loneliness about it.

The guard in the control booth buzzed Nash through the first door. He stood for a moment in the space between it and the next door, while the guard jotted down his name, the time he visited Tyler, what he'd brought with him.

"So how's it going, Doctor Nash?" asked the guard.

Old buddy, old friend. I hear you had major problemas out there in the Tesla village the other day. That was what the guard didn't say.

"Fine. How's that son of yours doing?"

"Good, really good. He was seven months old yesterday. What've you got in the bag?"

Back to business. "Books and mangos." Nash went over to the control room window and tilted the bag so the lieutenant could see into it. He held up two books and pressed them to the glass so the lieutenant could read the titles. "How've his spirits been today?"

"About normal."

Which explained nothing at all. When you were invisible and captive, there was no such creature as *normal.*

A click, a buzz, the door slid open. Nash hesitated, he always did, he couldn't help it. He invariably felt as if he were entering an alien world where none of the familiar rules applied. It was one thing to watch a wooden village in the middle of nowhere fade away and later materialize. It was something else to speak and interact with a human being you couldn't see.

He swallowed hard and limped into the apartment. The codeine had kicked in, so the pain in his leg was manageable now and he didn't need to lean so heavily on the cane.

Despite the lack of privacy, the place was luxuriously comfortable, furnished in the best of the best. Nash himself had signed the vouchers for nearly every object in here, from the couches and ottomans to the large-screen TV with the DVD and VCR to the computer and the fancy electronics. Total cost? Not much, until you added in all the security and surveillance extras. Then it tipped into seven figures.

With maintenance, research, and Tyler's upkeep factored in, Tyler Griffin was a very expensive guinea pig. And if Nash included employee salaries and benefits, airplanes and choppers, and supplies, the figure soared.

Valuable? Oh, please. *Valuable* barely covered it.

Nash set the bag on the coffee table and went over to the panel on the wall that controlled the audio feed to the control booth. He turned it off. It was one of the small privileges Tyler had. "I've got some mangos," Nash said, setting everything on the coffee table.

"Thanks, George."

Tyler got up from the chair and strode toward Nash. He wasn't wearing shoes or socks, so his legs ended where his jeans did, at the ankles. It looked as if he were walking on air. Then Nash's eyes moved up Tyler's body—visible, but only because of the clothes he wore—to where his head should have been. Nada. Zip. Gone. *I'll never get used to that.*

Tyler laughed again. "Still a bit of a shockeroo even after three years, isn't it, George?"

"Somewhat. Yes."

"I heard about the snafu out there in the Glades. I don't suppose Farris is too happy with you at the moment."

How'd you find out? "He hasn't been happy with me since I fought for a private bathroom for you. How'd you hear about the Everglades, anyway?"

He tried to make the question sound casual, but knew he hadn't succeeded when Tyler laughed, a low, sly sound that made Nash uneasy. "I've got news for you, George. You have—what? Forty people working here? Then there are the people who work at Homestead, the people at the NSB . . . say, a hundred people or so who know about this project. That may be a conservative estimate. The bottom line is this: can a hundred people keep a secret?" He laughed again. "I don't think so. It's on the Web."

"The *Web?* Where?"

"I'll show you."

They settled in front of the computer. Since Nash couldn't see Tyler's hands, all he saw were the keys pressed down at lightning speed. Just one more eerie effect that made him feel slightly unbalanced. He raised his eyes to the screen.

"The weird and the strange dot-com," Tyler said. "It's got all kinds of fascinating shit on it." Tyler scrolled down the screen. "A UFO sighting in Nebraska. A Loch Ness monster report from Inverness. Chem trails over southern Georgia. An update on Roswell. The real scoop on the government's psychic spies." Tyler paused. "I don't suppose you know anything about that stuff, huh, George?"

"Out of my area. I told you, Tyler, I'm a scientist. So where is the Everglades mentioned?"

"Right here."

He scrolled past another half dozen entry titles and clicked one called *The Village*.

"On June 8, 2001, I was fishing in the Everglades. Most of the time in the evenings out there, I see birds, hundreds of birds and other wildlife. But not yesterday evening. There wasn't one bird, not a single alligator, not so much as a snail or fish in sight. That was weird enough. Then a while later, the air went still. I mean really still, okay? No frogs, no crickets, nothing. It was as still as a cemetery in the middle of the night.

"Then there was this high-pitched humming, a noise so terrible that I thought I was going to pass out. Then it ended. I got so spooked I canceled the rest of my fishing trip. I was near the North Joe Chickee when this happened."

—Anonymous by request

For months, there have been reports rolling in about strange doings in the Florida Everglades. The events described in this e-mail fit the pattern of the other reports.

*My sources, in fact, tell me the government is testing
invisibility out there in the Everglades. What an ideal
spot, right? The perfect camouflage, an isolated location . . . You get the idea here.*

*From what I understand, this site is actually a sort
of village made of interconnected chickees and wooden
platforms and, at regular intervals, it fades from sight.
Interesting, no?*

*I refer readers to the following sites, documents,
and books on invisibility that*

Nash rubbed his eyes and struggled against an almost
crushing incredulity. How the fuck had this happened? The
techs in the computer department were supposed to monitor
the Internet for shit like this. They were supposed to know
about the odd message boards, the eccentric Web sites, the
fringe groups.

But as soon as Nash had thought this, he knew what had
happened. The Tesla Project was manned by people, not by
robots, not by automatons. People weren't perfect. People
had problems, families, issues, crowded lives.

He took note of the domain name—*weird&strange.com*,
who could forget *that?*—then insinuated his own hands over
the keyboard and went to the domain registry.

Weird&strange.com was registered to INOU Industries.
Nash had never heard of them.

"I'll save you some time, George," said Tyler. "The
corporation supposedly makes computer chips. It's registered in the Netherlands, to an address in Amsterdam. And
even with all your NSB contacts, you won't ever find out
who owns the site or who's posting. I mean, Holland is
leagues ahead of the world in their attitude toward the rights
of the individual. Prostitution is legal. The use of marijuana
is legal. People have the right to die. And hey, guess what.
To track down who owns this site, you'll have to call on

Interpol and I bet you don't want to do that because it would draw too much attention to you and the project.''

True, it was all true, Nash thought. But just because a company was registered in the Netherlands didn't mean the message had been posted from there. A Web site had to have a server. A server billed a credit card. The credit card would have a name and number. Even if the name was of a business or a corporation name, he could track the credit card number to see where purchases had been made. There were ways. Information could be bought.

On the other hand, why bother? To take action on this would be to admit there was veracity to the rumor. Besides, he had other concerns right now.

''Hey, George. Did you notice that the acronym for that company spells out *I know you?* Isn't that a hoot? You think it's a coincidence?''

Nash didn't dignify the question with an answer. He got up, relying on his cane, and limped over to the sliding glass door. He stepped out onto the patio, into the blistering heat. The ''yard'' where Tyler exercised was large, with a half-mile jogging path lined with plants and shrubs that hid the twenty-foot concrete wall that enclosed it. The screen over the top allowed him access to sunlight, but kept him securely within the yard. The porch table and four chairs were bolted to the concrete patio, so they could never be used as weapons. Like everything in the apartment, the yard had been designed for comfort but with security in mind.

Tyler followed him outside. Here, they could talk without being observed and recorded. Out here, in fact, was where he and Tyler had their most honest and stimulating conversations.

''Hey, Tyler, take a look at this,'' Nash called. ''A fox.''

''I don't see a fox.''

''You're going to see four of them in a few minutes.'' Nash spoke softly and moved farther away from the porch, out onto the grass. "And they're going to ask you a lot of questions."

"Talking foxes," Tyler drolled. "How different. And I suppose these questions will revolve around what it's like to be invisible for three years."

"Among other things."

"And you want me to behave." He sounded bemused. "No nose picking, no belches, no tantrums, no madness."

"Something like that."

"And why should I cooperate with you, George? Or with them?"

Tyler stopped. Nash stopped. The afternoon heat made Nash slightly dizzy. "Because if you don't, the program will be shut down and you'll be taken to D.C. There, I imagine you'll be treated like a fascinating lab animal, poked and prodded and subjected to grotesque experimentation."

"So what else is new?"

"There won't be anything humane about it, Tyler. You'll be kept under such tight security that all of this"—he threw out his arms, a gesture that took in the grounds, his porch, his living quarters, the special privileges—"will seem like paradise."

"I get the idea, George."

"I don't think you do." Nash stared at where Tyler's face should be. "These men, part of a committee that oversees this project, represent acronyms, Tyler. CIA, NSA, NSB, the Pentagon . . ."

"That's not an acronym." Tyler jammed his invisible hands into the pockets of his visible jeans. "But you made your point."

They walked for a while without speaking. Or, rather, Tyler walked and Nash limped along. Nash's cell phone rang; he glanced at the caller ID and saw Colleen's cell number. He turned off his phone. "And if I cooperate, George, what do *you* get?"

Nash took a deep breath, then spelled it out.

Tyler whistled softly. "That's probably as much as a stealth bomber costs."

"True invisibility is worth more than a stealth bomber."

"And what do *I* get in return for cooperating?"

"A continuation of what you already have." He quickly added, "As opposed to a dungeon in D.C."

"Uh-huh."

More silence. More walking and limping. Nash knew Tyler was turning this all over in his mind and didn't press the issue. They finally settled in a couple of Adirondack chairs in the far corner of the grassy area, near the wall.

"Sometimes, I sit out here and think about making a break for it. I can almost see myself doing it, invisible to everyone, but free. I can smell earth, pine, crops. Then I hit I-95 and the stink of exhaust fumes nearly overwhelms me. The sight of all the cars paralyzes me. The sight of an endless tide of humanity terrifies me. And . . . and I realize that I'm really not very adventurous. I'm *intellectually* adventurous . . . that's what got Logan and me into this mess . . . but when it comes right down to it . . . nope. I don't want to be hunted and terrified and scrounging for food and safety out in the real world, George. I can't even imagine what it would be to like to try to function as an Invisible. Every time I ate, I'd be visible. If I put on clothes that hadn't been zapped, I'd be visible. Logan could do it, she has that kind of spirit, but not me. Besides, I figure that sooner or later you're going to come up with the answer about how to reverse the shrouding and I intend to be the first volunteer."

Over the years, he and Tyler had formed a tenuous friendship that had moments of complete honesty. But Tyler had never talked as openly as this. "One of the provisions of this funding is to find a reversal within the first year." And train four other unfortunates, Nash thought, but didn't say it.

"Can you do it?"

"I don't know."

"What happens if you don't succeed?"

"Then the project probably closes down and you end up in the D.C. dungeon."

"I know you make my life as comfortable as possible. I know you don't have to get me books and mangos. I know that the Internet connection was your doing. And I deeply appreciate all of it, George, don't get me wrong. Because of you, I haven't gone stark raving wacko. But quite frankly, if I'm going to cooperate with you, I need something more."

"Like what?"

"Some private time each day—no cameras, blinds I can lower, that kind of thing. Sex and companionship would be great, although I can understand how that might present several touchy problems. I want to be able to buy books on-line. It'd be great to be able to trade e-mail with people. Ordinary stuff. That's what I crave, George. *Contact.* And if I can't have that, then shit, it doesn't matter to me if they poke and prod me and cut open my skull and attach electrodes to my fucking brain."

Of course, Nash thought. They all had bottom lines, the absolute minimum they needed to avoid feeling compromised. *What can you live with, Georgie?* his mother used to ask him when he was very young.

And he would spell it out for her, just as Tyler was spelling it out for him now. "I've got bottom lines, too, Tyler. But I'll do what I can."

One of Tyler's invisible hands touched Nash's arm. The touch didn't startle him, but the fact that he couldn't see the other man's hand spooked him badly. He barely resisted the powerful urge to wrench his arm away. Now Tyler leaned in close to Nash, so close he felt the heat of the man's breath, smelled the garlic he had used on his salad at lunch.

"I figure it this way, George," he said softly. "Without us, they don't have a goddamn pot to pee in."

Without us.

Us against Them.

It had come down to that.

Nash squeezed the bridge of his nose, a nervous habit, one he needed to break. When a man was obviously nervous, it put him at a distinct disadvantage with his enemies. "But to gain what you want, you sometimes have to be willing to walk away from it completely."

"I'm willing. I'm ready. What about you, George?"

He didn't hesitate. "Yes."

"One request, George."

"Only one?"

"For the moment. What's the date today?"

"June twelfth."

"Tell the bozos I'll answer their questions when I'm ready. And right now, I'm not ready. I'll give them twenty-four hours' notice."

Nash laughed, laughed because he knew the committee would balk. They would complain. They would protest. But in the end, they would comply. "Tell them I'm not feeling well, tell them I'm crazed, tell them whatever you want. But I refuse to even talk to them until I'm ready. And then I'll answer all their questions."

"Done."

"And, George?"

Something in Tyler's voice gave away what he was about to say, a question about Logan, and Nash squeezed the bridge of his nose again. "Yes, the answer's yes."

"*Alive?*" Tyler breathed. "She's alive?"

"And apparently still invisible."

"Jesus," Tyler whispered.

"I'd better go inform the committee that you aren't feeling well," Nash said, and pushed up from the chair.

"Wait. There's something you need to know. Just you, George, not the others."

"What's that?"

"Your word. I need your word that it stays between us."

"You trust my word?"

"You've been as straight with me as you can be, all things considered."

"All right. It stays between us."

"Before Logan and I applied for the program I had some health problems."

"What bullshit, Tyler. Any health problems you had would have shown up in the medical tests we ran during training."

"Other than some preliminary vision tests, you didn't check our eyes."

True, Nash thought, and wondered where this conversation was headed. "So you had eye problems?"

"The sight in my right eye was intermittent. It so happens that the day you did the vision test, I could see well enough to pass the test. I saw a doc in Georgia about it before Logan and I got married. He attributed the problem to a virus I'd picked up overseas that had settled in my eye. By the time the actual shrouding rolled around, I was completely blind in that eye and had been for about two months."

He's lying, he has to be lying, we wouldn't have missed something like that. "And you're still blind in that eye?"

"That's the interesting part, George. I regained my sight within ten days and my vision has been better than twenty-twenty ever since."

Nash suddenly understood what Tyler was really saying. "A fluke," he countered.

"I don't think so, George. There have been some other dramatic improvements. I used to have migraines once or twice a month. Since the shrouding, I haven't had even a hint of a headache. I used to get four or five colds a year, but except for the shrouding sickness, I haven't been sick at all."

"That could be due to your isolation from other people."

"True. But this isn't. Take my hand, George."

Nash took his hand.

"With your pocketknife, cut into my palm."

"No way," Nash said.

"I'm not saying slash it open, George, just cut lightly across it."

Nash was too curious to refuse. He brought out his Swiss Army knife and pressed the tip deeply into Tyler's palm, but not so deeply that it would require stitches. Then he drew the tip across his palm. He couldn't see the blood, but he felt the sticky warmth when he ran his thumb over Tyler's palm.

"Now dab at it with a Kleenex so you can see the blood," Tyler said.

He brought a clean handkerchief from his shirt pocket and wiped it across Tyler's palm, soaking up the blood that was now visible. "So what's your point, Tyler?"

"Wipe off all the blood, George. You'll see what I'm talking about."

"Okay." He wiped the hanky across Tyler's palm once more. "Now what?"

"How deep would you say the cut is?"

"How the hell should I know? I can't see your hand. *You* tell me."

"Well, the only thing I can tell you is that to me it looks pretty deep, maybe half an inch. But remember, I don't see myself in a normal way, okay? My brain fills in the missing pieces. Anyway, it's deep enough to keep bleeding for a few minutes unless pressure is applied against it, right?"

"Yes."

"Notice that I'm not touching it." He held his arm out in front of him. Nash could see his arms only because he was wearing a jacket and his arms didn't move for a full minute. "Now wipe your handkerchief across my palm again."

Nash brought his hand up under Tyler's invisible hand, cupping it, then with his other hand wiped the hanky across the palm again. Not a speck of blood appeared. "Maybe the cut wasn't that deep."

Tyler laughed. "Maybe this, maybe that, maybe anything except the truth, my friend. Shrouding not only accelerates healing, but can also reverse long-standing health problems." He leaned close to Nash and whispered, "Just think about it, George. No limp, no pain in your leg." He rocked back. "Tempting, isn't it? The price is high, of course. Prolonged invisibility. But maybe it's worth it, right?"

Then he laughed, a low, rumbling, crazy laugh, the laugh of Satan after Adam had bitten into the apple. Blood rushed into Nash's face and he looked quickly at his watch. "I need to get going. Talk to you later, Tyler."

And he hurried back inside the apartment, the echo of Tyler's crazy laughter echoing inside him.

13
PARADISE

Renie lay very still, her eyes shut, and listened to the vast, eerie silence. It was like that of an empty cathedral, so profound that it seemed to echo in the darkness behind her lids.

She knew where she was, in the garage apartment behind the house that belonged to Andy's and Jim's grandmother. She remembered how she had gotten here and everything that had preceded it. She also remembered that she had become violently ill while they were unloading Jim's Explorer and had vomited in the flowers that lined the driveway. Beyond that, she couldn't remember much of anything at all.

Her memories seemed to be spliced together, as jumpy and out of sequence as some old family movie. Here: Jim lifting her head, coaxing her to drink a little of this, to nibble a little of that. There: Jim carrying her into a room, setting her carefully on a bed, as though her bones were fragile. And over here, Andy's voice, Katie's voice, and the dog licking her face and hands. As long as she didn't move or open her eyes, as long as she barely breathed, her head didn't spin, she didn't feel sick. But her fatigue didn't lessen. It was as if she were weighted down, impaled against the mattress by excessive gravity.

She turned slowly onto her right side and her stomach instantly heaved. She groped for the pail at the side of the bed that someone had brought her. Who? Andy? Jim? Katie? No, not Katie. Her daughter, she realized, had been just as ill as Renie herself.

Her stomach was so empty that nothing came up but bile. Renie wiped her arm across her mouth, her stomach rumbled. She was starving, but the mere thought of food brought on another wave of nausea. But she could do with a sip of cold water. Cold anything.

She struggled to a sitting position, her entire body rebelling against the movement. Her vision immediately blurred, edges running together, floor with ceiling, windows with corners, the whole room tilting. Only once in her life had she felt this bad, when she'd come down with a flu that had kept her flat on her back for ten days. Aches. Nausea. Vomiting.

Then something took shape within the blur, her father, it was her father, looking young and fit. *Buddha*, she whispered, and rubbed her eyes. When she looked again, her vision focused, and she saw the dog. Lucky was sitting directly in front of her, watching her. "What the hell're you looking at?" she said hoarsely. Lucky wagged her tail, barked, and trotted toward a door on the other side of the room. When Renie didn't follow, the dog turned back and barked again. "You're a smart dog. Let yourself out. I can barely move."

But the damn dog was persistent. She grabbed the foot of Renie's blanket and pulled it off the bed. Cool air from the AC vents spilled over her sweating body and she started to shiver. Where were Andy and Katie? The dog had to pee and she could barely move.

Lucky ran toward the door again and vanished through a swinging pet door at the bottom of it. Renie remained as she was for a moment, perched at the side of the bed, arms wrapped around her body, shivers tearing through her. Heat. Sunlight. Summer. That was what she needed, she thought, and weaved down the hall after the dog.

Then suddenly she was outside on a stoop. The flight of stairs that led down to the grass and the wide open spaces below began to blur. The stairs tilted, her stomach heaved, her knees buckled, and she went down, her stomach heaving again. She finally rocked back on her heels and pressed her cool hands to her burning face. After a few minutes, the nausea ebbed and she dropped her hands to her thighs.

Lucky sat at the bottom of the stairs, watching her, waiting. Renie didn't think she could stand, she still felt too unsteady, no more familiar with the upright world than a baby learning to walk. She brought her legs out from under her, dropped them over the first step, and proceeded to bump down the steps on her butt.

It seemed to take a long time just to bump down a few steps. On the fifth step, a crippling dizziness seized her and she had to stop. She knew she had a fever—hell, she was burning up. Her skin felt scorched, as if she'd spent a day roasting at the beach. Her hands dropped to her sides and she peered below.

Lucky sat at the foot of the stairs, watching her, waiting. "I'm coming, I'm coming," she murmured, and continued bumping down the steps, shuddering from the fever, her teeth chattering.

When she reached the last step, Lucky barked and licked her face. Renie pushed herself to a standing position and clutched the railing so she wouldn't topple forward. Once she felt balanced enough to let go of the railing, she weaved her way across the grass, following Lucky. At one point, Lucky got more than fifty feet away from her and just faded away.

Renie whistled for her. "Come closer, girl. I can't see you."

Lucky faded back into view a few moments later and this time stuck pretty close to Renie. All the day's warmth pressed against her, embraced her, and she stopped shivering. She felt weak and used up, but at least the terrible shaking had stopped and the ground felt solid and fine under her bare feet.

Lucky never got more than twenty or thirty feet away from her and finally stopped about three hundred yards from the house, at a thick cluster of grass. She glanced back at Renie, barked, then proceeded to eat from the cluster. When Renie reached her, her legs felt rubbery, weak. She could barely lower herself to the ground beside the dog. She sat there for several moments, arms clutched around her legs.

Beyond her lay paddocks and fields where horses grazed in the warm light. A dirt road passed in front of the house. Directly across the street stood a rambling two-story place with a concrete barn to one side that looked to be as large as many homes.

Welcome to Paradise, country living as good as it gets. Wasn't that how the real estate ditty for this town went?

She pressed her face against her thighs, the light against the back of her neck as warm as a hand. She began to feel dizzy and nauseated again. A crushing fatigue clamped down over her and it helped to keep her eyes shut, her face pressed to her thighs. The light caressed her spine, warming her through the T-shirt she wore.

Eat the grass, Ren.

She raised her head at the sound of the voice and saw her father again. He stood next to Lucky and pointed at the grass the dog was eating. *Eat that.*

"You're dead, Buddha." *You're dead, I know you are. Andy refused to give you the extra morphine and I . . .* "You're dead."

And you'll wish you were if you don't eat the grass.

She blinked and Buddha vanished and there was only the dog, nibbling away at the grass. Renie closed her fingers around the grass and pulled out a handful. She pressed it to her face, breathing in the scent of it. Grass, but not just grass. An herbal richness. *The dog isn't sick.* Why not? A spliced, jumpy memory surfaced of the dog eating grass as soon as they had arrived here. She was sure this was a real memory, yes, of course it was. In her mind's eye, she could see Lucky bounding out of the car as soon as the doors had opened and sniffing her way to a patch of grass near the corner of the house. Grass that had looked like this?

Renie nibbled at the grass like a squirrel. It tasted bitter, but no worse than the seaweed sold in the gourmet food section at Publix. She stuffed some into her mouth and chewed, chewed until saliva ran out of the corners of her mouth. She wiped her hand across her mouth, smearing green spit on the back of her hand. She swallowed once, then again, then waited. Did she feel any different? It seemed that she did, but she might be imagining it. She stretched out on her stomach on the ground, in the cool grass, and kept chewing and swallowing, chewing and swallowing. Then she could barely keep her eyes open and rested her head on her arms. Just a few minutes, she thought, until she felt strong enough to go back inside the house.

She woke suddenly. Long, narrow shadows lay against the grass, the sun huddled low in the sky, and Lucky was nowhere around. She guessed she had slept several hours. Except for a terrible thirst and an acute hunger, she felt shockingly good. She rolled onto her back, her T-shirt rising, and saw that the grass she'd eaten was still making its way through her digestive system. It resembled pea soup. It wasn't especially pleasant to look at, but Renie found the digestive process itself fascinating—not just anyone's digestive system, she thought, but her own.

It reminded her of a series of articles that *Readers' Digest* had run some years back. "I am Joe's Pancreas." "I am

Joe's Stomach.'' Well, here it was in living color—''I am Renie's Stomach and Intestines and Colon.''

If the grass or whatever it was had mitigated whatever had ailed her, then it would help Andy and Katie, too. She plucked handfuls of the stuff, jammed it into the pockets of her shorts, and hurried back up the stairs to the apartment. She found Katie in the second bedroom, with Andy sacked out in a recliner near the window. Between them was a bucket half filled with vomit and, on the nightstand, mugs of cold tea and cups of cold chicken noodle soup, a bottle of Advil, and Andy's prescription pad. Next to the pad was a note from Jim: *Went to fill the prescriptions you wrote. Be back in jiffy.*

A prescription for antibiotics, she guessed, that would be made out to Iris, whose last name was different from theirs. Well, forget the drugs. She would steep the grass and have them drink it. But first, she washed out the bucket, put in a clean garbage bag, put it next to the bed again. She brushed her mouth against Katie's forehead. Her skin felt cool, clammy, the way it felt when a fever had broken. Renie stripped the blanket off her body so that only a sheet covered her, and went over to Andy.

He looked uncomfortable, his head at an odd angle, a quilt tucked under his chin. As soon as she leaned over him, she felt the heat radiating from his body. He was burning up. Alarmed, she shook two Advils from the bottle, broke them into small pieces, and coaxed Andy to swallow them with sips of the cold tea. He muttered, moaned, thrashed about in the recliner, then fell asleep again. She wondered how high his fever was and whether the invisibility had caused it and how long ago Jim had left to get the prescription filled.

The prescription, she thought, and stepped over to the nightstand again. She stared at the pad and noticed that it looked slightly hazy, like the mugs of tea and the bowl of soup and the bottle of Advil. *It's visible.* He'd been carrying it when they were zapped and now it was visible. The rope, the canoe, and the prescription pad.

She rushed into the adjoining bathroom and looked into the mirror.

Nothing.

She looked down at herself. Yes, she could still make out her body, that strange, fill-in-the-dots sort of image that her brain supplied in the absence of actual perception. So if she could see that, why couldn't she see her reflection? She looked into the mirror again, squinting her eyes in the hopes that might help. It didn't.

A sharp, terrible sound escaped her, equal parts anguish, rage, terror. *Suppose it's permanent?*

No, she refused to think like that. If the canoe, the rope, and the prescription pad had regained visibility, then so could she and Andy and Katie. The dog had been invisible before and had regained her visibility, right? So there was hope for them. She needed answers, information, specifics about just the simplest things. What, for instance, was the date today? How long had they been here? Had there been anything at all about their disappearance on the local news?

But first she needed to tackle the invisibility sickness.

In the kitchen, she washed off the grass and heated water in the microwave. While the grass was steeping, she made herself a Swiss cheese sandwich with lettuce and tomatoes, gulped down three bottles of ice-cold water, and helped herself to an apple, a plum, a banana. She would be visible for hours now, while all this food digested, but she felt it was more important to restore her energy with real food than with the freeze-dried shit that was in the supply container.

As soon as the water turned a little green, she removed the softened grass and tossed it into the blender with a banana, chunks of papaya, fresh strawberries and blueberries, honey, milk, and ice. She poured the green water into the blender, then went into the pantry, searching for vitamins, herbs, anything that might be useful. Judging by the vast quantities of herbs and vitamins, Grandma Iris was apparently into alternative medicine.

She added antioxidants to the blender, C and E, CoQ10 and Pycnogenol. She added echinacea and goldenseal, colloidal silver and some fish oils, lecithin and a bunch of B vitamins. The only vitamin Andy believed in was C and even that was stretching the parameters of the existing paradigm in which he practiced emergency medicine. But he didn't have to be a believer for the stuff to help him. The grass, she thought, would cure him and Katie of the invisibility sickness and the vitamins and herbs would bolster their immune systems.

As she poured the shake into three glasses, Lucky trotted into the kitchen from somewhere. Renie poured the rest of the shake into a bowl for the dog and she lapped it up. "I wish you could talk," she said to the dog.

Lucky lifted her head from the bowl and barked.

"Yeah, yeah, okay, so you talk. But I can't understand what you're saying."

Another bark and she followed Renie into the bedroom where Andy and Katie were.

She fed the concoction to her husband and her daughter, a time-consuming task that required enormous patience. *C'mon, baby, sip this. Please, Andy, take a little more.* It reminded her of the months before she and Andy had moved Buddha into a nursing home, when she pretty much surrendered herself to a role as full-time caretaker. He was in diapers by then, bedridden and nearly immobilized, and when he was conscious, he knew precisely what was happening to him.

I want to die, he would tell her. *Please help me die, Ren. Please help me. Please . . .* And he would be clutching the key that opened the floor safe, where he kept memorabilia about his life before Parkinson's.

One morning she walked into his room and found him with a plastic bag over his head and his stiff fingers fumbling to hold the bag at his throat so that no oxygen got in. She ripped it away from his head and screamed at him, screamed that she couldn't allow him to do this in a place where Katie might find him. *I don't care about Katie,* he shouted back. *I care about dying. Help me die, please help me die. . . .* And that night, as she and Andy lay in bed, talking softly, she begged him to give Buddha a dose of morphine large enough to kill him.

He refused.

There were no shouts, no arguments. He simply said no, he couldn't do that, and turned onto his side and fell asleep as she lay awake in the dark, weeping for her father's pain and despair. A short time later, they moved him into a nursing home. Three weeks after that, when her father could no longer swallow and the doctors had put in a permanent feeding tube, she granted his wish. While Buddha slept in a frozen fetal position, hands curled into claws, she pinched his nostrils shut and pressed her hand over his mouth. Within moments, he was dead.

And when it was over, she got up and walked outside. She began to shake, to sob, and begged for a sign that she had done the right and merciful thing. Just then, a hummingbird fluttered past her in the dusk, and hovered at a hibiscus bud in a nearby hedge. She stared at it, struck through with awe. In all her years in Florida, she had never seen a hummingbird. She had seen them in the tropics, where she and her family had gone for vacations, so Buddha could observe them, but never here.

Right then, she knew she had done the compassionate thing.

There was never an investigation into how Buddha had died. Only in nursing homes could Americans die in peace, without suspicion or intervention, without violation. She never had told Andy the truth, but wondered if he suspected.

Around dusk, headlights flashed against the windows. Renie went over to the window and peered out through the blinds. Jim pulled into the driveway below, stopped in front of the garage, and got out. He glanced around furtively, his body language screaming that paranoia gripped him. And since when did it take so long to fill a goddamn prescription?

He heaved the garage door upward, but before he could drive inside, Grandma Iris stepped out the side door of the house and called his name. In the backwash of the headlights, she looked like a little old woman in a housecoat. Jim hurried over to her.

Renie felt a sudden urge to eavesdrop and slipped quickly out of the apartment, making sure that Lucky didn't follow her. She didn't dare venture too far beyond the deep shadows in the garage; the food she'd eaten would be visible. But it turned out that she didn't have to move beyond the garage to hear them.

"You okay, hon?" Iris asked.

"Sure. I hope I didn't wake you."

"No, I mean, are you okay in general?"

"Well, yeah. I'm fine. Why?"

"Ever since you got here, you've been acting so strangely. Five days, Jim, but I hardly see you. You just hole up in that apartment."

Jim laughed quickly, nervously, and jammed his hands in the pockets of his shorts. "I've been trying to finish up some computer projects, Iris. That's all."

"You're also worried about your brother and Renie and Katie."

"Of course I'm worried. They're missing."

"You're such a bad liar."

"What the hell's that supposed to mean?"

"It means, Jim, that you know what's going on and you're not saying."

Shit, Renie thought.

"I'm old, hon, but I'm not stupid. How can I help?"

Shit and double shit. Don't do it, Jim. Please don't.

Jim reached out and ran his hands over his grandmother's arms, then hugged her. "It's okay. Really."

Iris jerked back from him. "If you're not going to tell me the truth, then I'll just find it for myself." And she strode toward the open garage with such determination that Jim just stood there, rubbing a hand over his face, his shoulders slumped, as if the burden that he carried were simply too much for him to endure alone. Then he hurried after her and caught up with her before she reached the open garage.

"Wait, Iris."

She stopped. Jim stopped. They faced each other and neither of them said a word. Renie pressed back farther into the shadows in the garage and heard Jim blurt, "They're sick."

"Who's sick?"

"Andy, Renie, Katie. And . . . and the dog. There's a dog with them."

"They're *here?*"

"Here and invisible."

Damnshitfuck. . . .

It wasn't supposed to happen like this. Iris wasn't supposed to be put in jeopardy. Jim had promised that Iris wouldn't know anything, that she wouldn't find out. Jim had . . . Fuck Jim.

"Invisible?" The word rolled off Iris's tongue, then she laughed. "What do you mean they're *invisible?*"

"It's a long story, Iris."

"We're okay," Renie said quietly, stepping out of the garage.

Iris glanced toward Renie's voice and saw just a blob of digesting food. Her hand flew to her mouth, her eyes widened as she wrenched back. "Oh my God."

Jim quickly slipped his arms around his grandmother's shoulders, as if to hold her up, to support her. "Jesus, that was stupid, Renie."

"You shouldn't have told her anything," Renie snapped.

"Just what the hell were you going to do, Jim? Bring her inside? Show her the freaks?"

"She—"

"Hey." Iris waved her hand between them. "Don't refer to me in the third person. I'm fine, okay? I'm not going to have a heart attack or anything. Let's go inside." And she disengaged herself from Jim and moved quickly into the garage.

Jim cast a dirty look Renie's way and followed his grandmother through the garage and into the apartment.

Renie took the antibiotics that Jim thrust toward her and went into the bedroom to give them to Andy and Katie. Then she rooted through the closet, looking for visible clothes that would fit her. She found a pair of shorts and a T-shirt, slipped them on. It was one thing for *her* to watch food digesting in her own body, but she didn't like the idea of Jim and Iris watching. It seemed too intrusive, too bizarre.

As soon as she entered the kitchen, though, she realized it was equally bizarre for Jim and Iris to see her as only half visible—clothes but no head, no arms, no legs. "Oh my," Iris said softly. "How . . . how unsettling."

"Better than watching my food digest, Iris."

She gave a small laugh that brought light and mischief back to her soft blue eyes. Although she was pushing ninety now, she didn't look her age and moved with the grace and agility of a much younger woman. There wasn't much that shocked Iris. "Jim told me what happened, Ren. What can I do to help?"

"Forget that we were here. We'll leave as soon as Katie and Andy are feeling better."

"And go where?"

"My office maintains a list of unoccupied houses that are for sale. We'll pick one of those."

Iris frowned and shook her head. "You won't have food or anything you need in one of those houses. I insist that you stay here."

"Look, Iris. We've been chased and shot at. We don't know what these people are capable of doing and I don't want to put you at continued risk."

"Then I'll leave. I'll get on a plane tomorrow morning and go back to Massachusetts. That's not a problem. But in the meantime, I want you to stay here. Tomorrow, Jimmy, we'll both drive to the airport. You leave your car in long-term parking and use my Mercedes. It's got a Mass plate on it. They won't be looking for out-of-state license plates. Do you need money, Renie? I've got plenty of cash on hand."

"That'd be great. I'm hesitant about using the ATM. I can write you a check . . . No, forget that. The checkbook is invisible."

"Forget the check. As soon as Andy and Katie can travel, Jim will drive you to the house on the cape. You'll be safe there."

"The cape?" Jim balked. "Iris, I've got deadlines. I can't just take off indefinitely and go live on Cape Cod."

Her mouth pursed with disapproval. "I'm asking you to drive your brother and his family to Cape Cod, Jim. I'm not asking you to live there indefinitely. Besides, I thought you told me your place was under surveillance."

"Well, yes, but—"

"Don't worry about it. I'll send my driver. He can pick up the—"

"Never mind. I'll do it. I can drive them. I'm just real uneasy about this situation. You're probably going to get a call from the pharmacy tomorrow, Iris. The prescription I filled was for you and the pharmacist knows you and was concerned and—"

"I'll take care of it before I leave."

Iris left a little while later to make her reservation and pack. As soon as she was gone, Jim turned on Renie with utter fury in his expression. "This is so fucking typical of you and Andy. Everything is *me me* with you two. I mean,

Andy calls me in the middle of the goddamn night and now my house is under surveillance, the feds are talking to my neighbors and my clients . . . Christ, I'll be lucky if I even have a business when this is over.''

Renie had known him long enough to realize that he was trying to get a rise out of her, that he was itching for a fight. Hell, who could blame him? When Andy had asked for his help, he had put Jim at risk. Never mind that if the situation had been reversed, she and Andy would have answered Jim's call for help. Never mind that it was what you did for family. Jim was Jim and there were certain fine points that would escape him forever.

''I understand how you feel, Jim. And you're right. We involved you. So why don't you just hop into your Explorer and be on your way? We'll take care of ourselves.''

''Yeah? And just how the fuck are you going to do that, Renie? You going to drive the Mercedes yourselves?'' He laughed. ''There'll be three invisible people in a car. Can you just imagine pulling up to another car at the light and the driver looks over and doesn't see anyone at the wheel? Shit, that'll be it. A call to nine-one-one and curtains.''

''Like I said, Jim. No one's holding you here.''

''You're not getting it,'' he said. ''You three have been reported missing in the Glades, okay? There hasn't been any mention of the chase, the shooting, none of what happened in Flamingo. Whoever is behind this has the resources to engineer a massive cover-up.''

''This seems to come as some big surprise to you, Jim. Whoever has the power to render people and objects invisible *obviously* has the power to engineer cover-ups.''

''You've been here five days, Renie. Sicker than dogs for *five* days. . . .''

He was still running at the mouth, but Renie no longer heard him. She was stuck on the time element—*five days*. How long would it take for these people to uncover the fact that Jim and Andy had grandparents who owned a home in Palm Beach County?

''We'll be out of here as soon as Andy and Katie are well enough to travel.''

That said, she walked out of the kitchen, anxiety tying her stomach in knots.

14
STRATEGY

Andy knew he was sick. His torn and fragmented memories coughed up numerous bits of scenes, but they weren't in a sequential order. They were like fragments of a thousand-piece jigsaw puzzle scattered across the floor of his mind. The longer he attempted to order them, the less sense they made.

It seemed that he slept fitfully and woke frequently. Sometimes the room was dark and sometimes it was sunlit, but other than that he had no inkling about the passage of time. He didn't know what day it was. His watch still showed the time it had been when they'd gotten zapped in the village. Now and then he woke to find Renie at his bedside, coaxing him to drink this or swallow that.

He gradually realized the constant nausea and vomiting had stopped. He felt weak, but no longer feverish, yet when he struggled to a sitting position the room spun. He squeezed his eyes shut and fell back against the pillows, then lay there for a while, forcing himself to breathe deeply. Sweat streamed from his pores, his clothes and the sheets were damp. His high fever was still breaking.

While he waited for the nausea to subside, he touched his index and third fingers to the underside of his wrist and took his pulse. Fifty-three, the lowest it had ever been. Was that good or bad? And what did the vast improvement in his eyesight mean? He still wasn't wearing contacts or his glasses and his sight was at least twenty-twenty. In terms of life the way it was before they were zapped, all of this was great news. Now he couldn't say with any certainty what was good or bad, normal or abnormal.

He sensed his illness was related to what had happened in the village, but without a lab he didn't know what that might mean. He couldn't even say for sure that the prescription Jim had filled had resulted in his apparent improvement. For all he knew, the illness had simply run its course. At the moment, his medical skills were useless.

Andy finally opened his eyes and sat up. No dizziness, no gripping nausea. *So far, so good.* He swung his legs over the side of the bed and was struck by the design that the light from the bedside lamp made against the rug. In fact, as he glanced slowly around the bedroom, memories rushed over him of the many times he and Jim had stayed in this very room while their parents were involved in some high-profile legal case and had dumped him and Jim here for a week or two because they didn't have time to be parents. That usually had happened during the winter months, when their grandparents were down here for the season and the family was in between housekeepers.

Andy finally stood and although his legs felt weird, he managed to get into the bathroom and relieve his aching bladder. By the time he returned to the bedroom, Renie had come in with soup and toast and another tumbler of whatever she'd whipped up in the blender and put the tray on a small table near the window.

"I bring chicken soup for the soul and the bod," she said. "It sure is great to see you up and about. How do you feel?"

"Warm shit on toast."

"Yeah, that's how I felt yesterday."

"How long have we been here, Ren?"

"We're nearing the end of the sixth day."

"Six days," he repeated. "Jesus. And Katie?"

"She started coming around early this morning. She's good." She pulled out a chair for him. "Here, sit down. You'll still have to take it easy for a few hours."

"When did you—"

"Yesterday."

She filled him in as he ate and before he'd finished, Katie joined them, Lucky trotting along behind her. She hugged Andy, then plopped down on the bed, with the dog settling on the floor at her feet. Katie listened to everything that was said, then offered her own insights on the "invisibility sickness," as she called it, and the plan to move to one of the unoccupied homes listed for sale by Renie's company.

"I know you guys don't think much of the *I Ching*, but I asked it what we should do. I got hexagram sixty, changing to sixty-one."

"Which means?" Andy asked.

"Limitation changing to Inner Truth. My interpretation is that if we go to one of these unoccupied houses, we're restricting ourselves because we'll be hiding out—cowering—instead of trying to uncover what happened, who did it, and how we can reverse the invisibility. The *I Ching* refers to this excessive restriction as causing pain and misfortune."

"Great," Renie muttered. "So what's this oracle of yours advise?"

"Well, the Inner Truth hexagram talks a lot about sincerity and trust."

The physician part of Andy was appalled that he was even considering advice from an oracle where everything was couched in terms of Chinese life five thousand years ago. Even though neither he nor Renie had done anything to discourage their daughter's fascination with the *I Ching*, they hadn't done anything to encourage it, either. When she talked about it, they listened with the same courtesy she exhibited when they discussed stocks or international politics or their respective professions. But invisibility seemed to have changed the basic rules, Andy realized, and the invisible part of him listened with great interest to what she said.

"Who're we supposed to trust?" he asked. "With whom are we supposed to be sincere?"

"Ourselves. That hexagram is about trusting our intuition."

"I was hoping for a strategy," Renie remarked. "A plan, you know? My intuition is in short supply at the moment."

Katie shrugged. "I'm just telling you what the hexagrams say, Mom. And I don't think your intuition is in short supply, either. I mean, you had a feeling that you should eat the same grass that Lucky was eating and a couple of hours later you felt almost normal again. You didn't even have to take any antibiotics."

"I think we'd better have a supply of that grass," Andy said.

"Mom and I have already collected some."

Jim's footsteps echoed loudly in the hall and Andy frowned, trying to determine what seemed wrong about the sound. Renie noticed his expression. "I think you'll find that your hearing is incredibly acute now. I first noticed it when we were in that sugarcane field. It's gotten stronger and better ever since."

"My hearing, too," Katie said.

"Good to know you're on the mend, bro," Jim said from the doorway.

He glanced at the table, then looked around, as if trying to determine where Renie, Katie, and the dog were. A Visible among Invisibles, Andy thought. How strange it must seem to his brother. "I appreciate all your help. I know this hasn't been easy for you."

Jim didn't comment on that, a sure sign, Andy thought, that his brother felt put out. He pointed at the TV on the bureau. "Katie, hon, can you turn that on? There's some news you guys need to see."

"Sure. What channel?"

"Four."

She plucked the TV clicker from the nightstand. To Jim, of course, the clicker looked as if it were floating through the air. The sight obviously disturbed him. He seemed to recoil from the three of them, shoulders drawing in, his body tightening as he leaned back against the doorjamb.

"And in local news tonight, we have some additional information about the Townsends, the Palm Beach County family that has been reported missing. What's known is that the Townsends left their home on Friday, June ninth, for a camping trip into the Florida Everglades. We know that they definitely entered the park because they signed in at the gate, a practice recommended by park officials for anyone camping in the park. We know that their vehicle was found in a lot inside the park on Monday, June twelfth.

"Local police are still treating their disappearance as a missing persons case. But there's some speculation in the department that Andy, his wife, Renie, and their fourteen-year-old daughter, Katie, may have met with foul play. Police are requesting that anyone with any information about their whereabouts to contact the sheriff's department in their respective county. In other news today . . ."

Katie turned the TV off.

In the subsequent silence, Andy heard the ticking of Jim's watch, a maddeningly rhythmic sound that reminded him they might well be running out of time. Farther away, he heard noises outside the apartment, night sounds from the surrounding fields.

"We could go to the police," Renie said finally. "Tell them what happened."

"Bad idea," Jim said. "Any authority right now is a bad idea."

Andy agreed. "Even if they got over the fact that we're invisible, we'd still be considered freaks. They'd call in the public health department, the CDC, the FBI . . . Forget it. We'd be kept in protective custody. For right now, we have to handle this on our own."

"But where do we start?" Katie asked.

"We start by doing exactly what you do with the *I Ching*. We ask the right questions. Who's behind this? Has anyone else been zapped? What are these people really up to?"

"I've been poking around on the Internet," Jim said. "There's a site called the weird and the strange dot-com where there're reports about invisibility experiments in the Everglades. Katie and I e-mailed them, but haven't gotten anything back."

"Look, I agree with asking the right questions." Renie now paced restlessly around the room. "But right now, we've got more immediate concerns—like safety. We've been here nearly a week. I think we need to move around so we're not sitting ducks."

"We can't move around very freely as Invisibles," Katie said. "We need Uncle Jim to drive us. And he doesn't want to be here."

Jim folded his arms across his chest and stared at the floor. Andy knew his brother well enough to realize that his body language indicated that Katie had hit very close to the truth. "I don't blame him," Andy said. "If I were him, I wouldn't want to be here, either."

"It's not that I don't want to be here," Jim said, raising his head. "It's just that . . . well, quite frankly, I'm scared shitless. We've seen what these people can do, the kind of resources they have at their disposal. The last thing Iris said to me this morning when I dropped her at the airport was to promise her I'd drive you all to the cape. I don't have a problem with that. I'd rather get the hell out of Florida.''

Of course, Andy thought. Cape Cod. The house on the dunes. Sure. What a convenient escape for all of them. He and his family could hide out indefinitely on the cape, Jim could drop the problem in their grandparents' lap, and then he would flee back to his life. They could all run away and hope the invisibility would reverse itself. Hey, that was a great solution.

"We're not running away."

"How noble," Jim spat. "What the hell am I supposed to do?"

"Whatever you want, Jim. If you decide to leave, fine, no hard feelings. We understand. If you choose to stay, you have our appreciation.''

Jim rubbed his jaw, jammed his hands in the pockets of his shorts, rubbed his jaw again. "I'll drive you to wherever you want to go tomorrow. Beyond that, I don't know. I have to think about this.''

"Fair enough," Andy replied.

2

Nash woke to Colleen leaning over him, shaking him gently by the shoulders, the scent of her skin and hair touching him all over. "George, the phone's ringing. You'd better get it.''

"What time is it?''

"Nearly one-thirty in the morning. It's probably midday in Tibet.''

This vague reference to his wife, that the call might be from her, annoyed him. He grabbed the receiver. "Hello?''

"It's Panther. We found them.''

Nash bolted upright in bed, turned on the bedside lamp,

and swung his legs over the side. His right leg immediately started screaming. "Where?"

"Paradise, an equestrian community in western Palm Beach County. Traced them through a prescription the doc wrote for Iris Townsend, an elderly woman who just happens to be Andy Townsend's grandmother. She owns a home in Paradise."

"A prescription for what?"

"Augmentin."

Good try, Nash thought, massaging his leg as he held the receiver between his ear and his shoulder. But Augmentin wouldn't do shit for the shrouding sickness. "Describe the neighborhood, Panther."

As Panther spoke, Nash limped across the room, pulled on his jeans. He popped a couple of codeines in his mouth and chewed them as Panther spoke. He tried to visualize what Panther described, the dirt roads, the sprawling equestrian estates, the fields and paddocks.

"How do you want us to proceed, boss?"

"Very carefully, with full thermal gear." Nash explained precisely how he wanted everything to unfold. "Be ready, but wait for us to arrive. Clear?"

"You got it, boss."

"My cell phone will be on. Stay in touch."

He hung up and immediately called Dobson. By then, Colleen had figured out what was going on and hurried around the room, getting ready. "Should I call the Ponce facility?" she asked as soon as he finished talking to Dobson. "And tell them to get things ready?"

"Let's make sure we have them first."

If Farris knew about this, he would insist on being present, dressed in his full riot gear or his stupid fatigues, and would butt in, snapping orders and generally screwing things up. Besides, if he knew and the Townsends got away again, Nash would never hear the end of it and his position would be weakened even more than it already was. Right now, the only thing that stood between him and a complete takeover by Farris and his committee was Tyler Griffin. *I'll answer their questions when I'm ready.* And so far, he hadn't been ready.

Twenty minutes after they left his house, they pulled into a private airfield in western Broward County where Dobson kept his Cessna. The plane was ready to taxi and Dobson, of course, had come prepared.

"There's gear in the back for each of us. Trank guns, thermal glasses, the works. I'm going to land at the western end of the Aero Club, which will bring us to within a mile of the address that Panther gave you."

"What's the Aero Club?" Colleen asked.

"An aeronautical community. Has a private airfield and hangars. Buddy of mine lives there. The three bikes in the cargo area will take us the last mile quietly. How many people will Panther have?"

"Four."

"We can do this," Dobson said.

Mr. Clean-it-up and Fix-it-up, Nash thought. Thank God for Dobson.

Dobson shut the doors, taxied down the grass strip, and moments later, the Cessna lifted into the moonlit air, as graceful as a dragonfly.

15
CHAOS

A hot shower, Andy thought, was like comfort food, no less soothing than a plate of mashed potatoes or a bowl of chocolate ice cream or, yes, a bowl of Renie's chicken soup. The difference was that he had eaten the chicken soup with his eyes open and he had yet to open his eyes since he'd stepped under the spray.

Andy kept his left arm out of the spray, completely dry, hand propped against the wall, and thrust his right arm under the spray. Then he opened his eyes to see the difference. His left arm looked the same, but incomplete somehow, as though a child had sketched an arm and then colored it in too lightly, without much detail. His right arm, saturated now from the water, looked like a *real* arm with *real* hair, *real* freckles, *real* curves and slopes and creases. He suddenly realized how much he had taken for granted all these years.

Every time a patient had come into ER with an illness as opposed to a wound—gunshot, stabbing, something obvious—he'd felt annoyed that it would take time to get to the source of it. Blood tests, urine tests, ultrasounds, MRIs, dozens of *tests* that were supposed to pinpoint whatever had gone haywire and that often failed to do so. These kinds of cases invariably struck him as a mockery of medicine and technology. It was as if nature were reminding him that medicine was an imperfect science, that all the answers would never be in because they were looking in the wrong places, with the wrong frame of mind. Never had this concept been so real as when Buddha had come to live with them.

At the time, he'd had Parkinson's for six years. It didn't afflict him with tremors in his hands; it affected his speech and his ability to walk. He was using a walker back then and was just beginning to lose control of the muscles in his mouth. He was on Sinemet, of course, the only treatment for the disease, which merely mitigated the symptoms but didn't cure it. His dosage then was moderate. Within a year, he had nearly maxed out on the dosage and got around in an electric wheelchair. Although he could still feed and bathe and clothe himself, the Sinemet was clearly beginning to falter. The episodes of paralysis were more frequent and his depression didn't help his condition.

Andy had tried several other drugs to help prolong the effects of the Sinemet, but nothing helped. Because of his age, Buddha wasn't a candidate for the brain surgery that temporarily stilled Michael J. Fox's tremors. Although Buddha tried to get into the pool every day, although he ate healthily and continued to take his vitamins, Andy knew that he was on that one-way road that led inevitably to the complete shutdown of muscles, his ability to swallow, and eventual death. Buddha had known it, too.

Two years after he'd moved in with them, Buddha had become incontinent and needed help doing everything. They hired help, a wonderful woman who had come in ten hours a day to tend to his needs. Less than six months later, Renie was his full-time caregiver and Buddha was begging Andy to put him to sleep. *We do it for our pets, Andy.*

Andy suddenly couldn't follow this train of thought anymore. Emotion welled up in his throat and his memory tossed
him back to the many months he and the old man had played
chess at night. Buddha had been playing for eighty years
and Christ, he loved those chess games. And toward the
end, he could barely play because he couldn't think that
far ahead, the Parkinson's was slowly killing the neuronal
connections in his brain.

Andy turned his face into the spray and opened his mouth,
letting the hot, cleansing water wash down his throat. That
time with Buddha, those heartbreaking years of his steep
decline, had taught him that the only way to live with chaos
was by embracing it. Only then could you see the underlying
order. He did it daily in ER, but always with the knowledge
that when the patient was transferred elsewhere, the chaos
would end. With Buddha, the chaos ended only with his
death.

Their present situation wasn't so different. Through unexpected circumstances, their lives had plunged into chaos. So
far, they'd resisted it, run from it, hidden from it. And
because of it, they were no closer to answers than they'd
been the night it had happened. If they could somehow
embrace the chaos of their invisibility, perhaps they would
be able to see the underlying order, the *pattern*. That might
enable them to recognize the pattern at other, deeper levels
and perhaps find a way to reverse the process—or to live
with it.

One plus one no longer equaled two, he thought. It was
like Mandelbroit's fractals. By using nonlinear equations
that plugged an answer back into the equation, Mandelbroit
discovered that what appears to be based on discontinuity
and chaos actually possesses a pattern, an order. He, Renie,
and Katie had stumbled into a nonlinear system and unless
they applied nonlinear thinking to their situation, nothing
would change.

He heard sounds on the other side of the bathroom door,

a cough, and then the door opened. "You couldn't sleep either?" he asked.

"I'm slept out. Or maybe my body doesn't need the kind of sleep it used to need. I have a feeling we're just discovering the physiological changes, Andy. At least Katie's sleeping."

"I've been thinking about fractals."

"The only thing I'm thinking about right now," she said, opening the shower door, "is having sex in the shower."

Andy laughed and Renie ducked under the spray. Instantly, the deep blackness of her hair sprang into vividness. The seductive curve of her shoulders, the swells of her breasts, the hard tautness of her thighs: all of these details now possessed the color and brightness of *visibility*. She snapped into such utter and complete clarity that for a moment he was certain it wasn't just the water that made her that way, but that she—they—were actually *visible* again, ordinary again, and now their lives would return to what they had been before they'd gone into the Everglades.

This illusion shattered when she turned to him and touched her finger to his mouth and shook her head. "We're the fractals?"

"Not exactly," he replied, and explained as he soaped her back and arms, rendering her body even more visible.

"I don't want to embrace this experience," she said when he'd finished. "I want my life back." Then she slid her hand behind his head, against the nape of his neck, and drew his mouth toward hers.

They made awkward love in the shower, but the familiarity of marriage rescued them from the strangeness of their physical conditions. After all, they were still solid. They were still creatures of skin and muscle and bone, of soft curves and smooth planes, a geometry of desire.

And afterward, with her face pressed to his chest and her wet, beautiful hair tangled in his fingers, she cried and whispered, "What the hell are we going to do?"

She didn't understand a word of what he'd explained to her earlier. He held his hand against the small of her back, his spine was crushed to the wall, and the endless assault of water poured over them. That was when he heard it, a sound so clear, so distinct, and so *wrong* that it seemed preternatural. "What was that?" He turned the faucet, shutting off the water. "I heard something."

She dropped her head back, rolling her lower lip against her teeth, and listened. "I heard a toilet flush."

"Something else." There was a leak in the shower head and the constant *drip drip* punctuated the immense silence.

Head cocked, he listened. Listened hard.

"What?" she whispered.

"I don't know." He broke away from her. "Maybe nothing." He stepped out of the shower, grabbed a towel, and rubbed himself dry as he hurried into the bedroom, Renie right behind him.

At the window, he peered out the side of the blind. Starlight spilled across the dark dirt road, offering up the shape of the house across the street, the fences that enclosed paddocks and fields. But when he moved to the other side of the window, so he could check out the opposite direction, he saw three people on bikes headed this way.

Bikes didn't make enough noise for him to have heard them in the shower. Even more to the point, why would anyone be riding a bike in the middle of the night? "Wake Katie and get out of here. I'll wake Jim. Head into the fields behind the house. I'll meet you out there." He tossed her one of the invisible packs.

She caught it and raced into the hall. Andy finished pulling on his clothes and slung the other pack over his shoulder. He looked down at himself and was relieved that his food had digested. His hair was still damp, but the darkness would cover that.

He checked the window once more. The bicyclists had stopped about a quarter of a mile past the house, next to a truck, maybe a U-Haul or a small moving van, it was difficult to tell. Andy ran down the hall and shook his brother awake. "Trouble, man, wake up."

Jim came instantly awake, almost as if he slept in a state of hyperalertness, and bolted out of bed. He scooped up his clothes, lurched for the window.

"Shit, a moving van," Jim whispered. "Forget the car in the garage. Five houses south, Andy, on the opposite side of the road, is a place that's vacant for the summer. Iris moved her car behind the barn so we could park the Explorer in the garage here. That's where we'll meet. When it's safe."

Safe? What a foreign concept. "Renie and Katie are heading into the field. I'll be with them until—"

An explosion of glass cut his sentence short. The room immediately filled with smoke and his eyes began to burn and he realized it wasn't smoke but tear gas. Andy dived for the floor to stay beneath the gas and scrambled for the door on his hands and knees. His eyes burned fiercely now, he could barely keep them open. Behind him, he heard Jim shouting, then another explosion of glass. He sprang to his feet and lurched into the hall, coughing hard to clear his lungs. Nearly robbed of his sight, he had to lean into the wall to keep from falling over.

Back door, got to get to the back door.

Just then, two men in gas masks appeared at the end of the hall, their rifles sighted on him. Andy didn't know if they wore thermal glasses under those masks or if the lenses of the masks were thermally sensitive or if the rifles had thermally sensitive sights on them. And he didn't have time to think about it or take any defensive action before he heard a soft *pop*, felt a hot stinging in his thigh and another in his chest. *Tranks, Christ.* He pulled out the darts and ran blindly in the other direction, toward the room where Katie had slept. If he could get inside and lock the door, if he could get out the window, if . . .

He weaved another two steps, felt his knees buckle, and

knew he hadn't gotten the darts out in time. He passed out before he struck the floor.

2

Katie stumbled through the starlit field behind the house, her pack banging against her spine, her hand clutching her mother's, her throat sour with fear. Lucky, who had been outside when she and her mother had fled, raced alongside them, tail tucked between her legs.

Behind them, Katie heard the shattering of glass, shouts. Her fear collapsed into terror and she ran faster, faster, until she and her mother were neck to neck. She glanced back, hoping to see her father tearing toward them. Instead, she saw two people race around the side of the garage and into the backyard. Her mother saw them, too, and dived into the tall weeds, yanking Katie to the ground with her. Lucky stopped, whimpering, and dropped to her stomach beside them. Katie slung her arm over the dog, holding her against her.

"We can't stay here," Katie whispered.

"We're going to run for that woods just ahead. The trees should make it tougher for them to detect us with their thermal equipment. Let's put Lucky on the rope, so she doesn't stray, then make a break for it."

"What do you think that shattering glass meant?"

"I don't know."

Katie knew from the tone of her mother's voice that she didn't want to think too closely about what the shattering glass meant.

"But they aren't going to catch us, hon. Ready?"

"Ready."

And they ran, hunkered over, for the woods, Lucky racing slightly ahead of them, the rope stretched almost to the limit.

They plunged into the trees and night noises exploded around them, frogs, owls, insects. They hurried on, working their way steadily away from the house and the garage and deeper into the woods.

The woods consisted of tall, scrawny Florida pines and bushy melaleucas, nature's version of Big Foot. The melaleucas were native to Australia and had been planted all over the South Florida peninsula to soak up water. Their pale, peeling bark seemed almost luminous in the starlight. Thanks to the drought, the ground was dry, but the weeds were high, often reaching to Katie's waist. Mosquitoes swarmed around them, but didn't bite either of them. Katie wondered if the invisibility had altered their blood chemistry in a way that repelled the mosquitoes or if the invisibility prevented the insects from detecting them.

The trees began to thin and Katie and her mother paused at the edge, not quite ready to step out into the starlight again. "This isn't a woods," her mother whispered. "It's just a couple of wooded acres."

"We're safer in here than we are in the open."

"We might be tougher to detect in here, but I don't think we're any safer." She wiped her arm across her sweating face. "Once it gets light and they can see where they're going, it won't take them long to find us. We need to get someplace where there's heat, a lot of heat, so they can't distinguish our body heat from other heat."

"Like a sauna. Or a fireplace. Fat chance."

"Yeah." She took Katie's hand again. "But maybe that barn will do for now. C'mon, I don't want to stop here too long."

As they ran across an open field, the distinctive *whup whup* of a chopper echoed through the night air. Katie didn't see it, but her hearing was sharp enough to determine that it was coming from behind them, from the south.

"It's close," her mother whispered. "Too close."

They raced toward a paddock and ducked under a railing.

They lost precious moments because Lucky's rope got tangled on one of the wooden beams. The sound of the helicopter seemed so close now that Katie felt its vibrations in her bones. But she couldn't see it. "Hurry, Mom, hurry, we don't have much time."

"Shitshitshit," her mother muttered, fumbling with the rope. She finally slipped it off over Lucky's head, scooped the dog up in her arms, and they ran on toward the barn.

Even in the pale light of the stars, Katie could see that the barn was huge, larger than many homes. It was built of concrete rather than wood, probably to withstand hurricanes. They ducked inside just as the helicopter appeared above the treetops of the woods, and moved deeper into the structure, away from the arched doorways at either end. Empty stalls stood on either side of them and the air smelled faintly of horses, manure, hay.

"Can their thermal equipment detect heat through concrete?" she asked.

"No. Maybe. Christ, I don't know."

They moved into a windowless tack room and her mother set Lucky down. "Stay, Lucky. You have to stay."

Lucky, panting hard from the heat, flattened out against the concrete floor, not interested in going anywhere. Katie and her mother collapsed on the wooden bench, sweaty hands clasped tightly together, the *whup whup* sound almost on top of them now.

Katie glanced from one end of the barn to the other, a part of her expecting to see lights at any moment as the chopper landed. She squeezed her eyes shut, her mouth so dry with fear that she couldn't even swallow. "If the chopper lands," her mother whispered, "I want you to take off. I'll distract them. We'll meet back here tomorrow at noon. You've got enough zapped food in your pack so that you'll be able to remain invisible."

Katie looked up at her mother and tightened her grip on her hand. "Forget it. I'm not going anywhere without you."

"Don't be difficult, Katie."

"I'm staying with you," she said again.

Her mother suddenly closed her arms around Katie, hugging her close, then they sat huddled together as the chopper passed overhead. They both looked up, as if they could see through the roof, listening to it. It went on, the sounds becoming more and more faint until they vanished altogether.

"Stay here," her mother said. "I'm going to check outside."

Katie remained on the bench in the tack room, stroking Lucky. Beads of sweat rolled down the sides of her face and she wiped them away with the hem of her T-shirt and tried not to worry about her father. She pulled out a bag of Lucky's zapped dry dog food, and poured some on the ground.

Her mother returned to the tack room. "It's clear. For now. Let's have a snack and move on."

Katie unzipped her pack and brought out bottles of water and some dried fruit. Everything had been zapped, so they wouldn't be visible if they ate and drank. The water was warm but it was better than nothing. She passed one bottle to her mother, poured some water from a second bottle into a cup for Lucky, and chugged down the rest. The dog lapped it up and pawed at her leg for more water and then for a bite of the dried fruit, too. They ate and drank in silence and every few seconds her mother glanced at one of the doorways.

"Let's get moving."

"To where?"

"I don't know. A vacant house, if we can find one. A lot of these places are seasonal and the people have left for the summer. There's one on Iris's street, where she put her car. We have to stay around here because your dad's going to meet us in the field when he can."

If he can, Katie thought, but didn't say it.

3

Renie didn't know how far they walked. Miles, her feet said it was miles. She and Katie talked about everything that had happened since they'd left for the camping trip and exchanged theories about why they were invisible and how the process might reverse itself. Her daughter, like Renie herself, knew that if you talked about what you feared, it began to lose some of its power over you. But conquering fear was something entirely different than embracing chaos, as Andy seemed to think they should do.

It's our way out of this mess, Ren. She should embrace chaos, surrender to the experience, go with the fucking flow. That was Andy's way of telling her she should look at it all as another adventure. Well, she had news for him. She had gone with the flow back there in the village, done it despite her strong instincts to run in the other direction, and here they were. She had no intention of surrendering to anything or anyone. In her book, surrender was just a synonym for defeat.

And where the hell's Andy? She didn't want to think too closely about that, not now.

Every so often, they ducked into another vacant barn or made their way along the edge of another wooded area. Once, they heard the chopper again, but it swept past them by several miles, its lights flickering in the darkness. The irony, she thought. Here they were, invisible, and yet she worried constantly about being *seen.*

Thanks to her lousy sense of direction, she wasn't sure where they were now in relation to Iris's place. Maybe that was just as well. Maybe they were far enough away to be safe and she should just choose one of the many houses that appeared to be vacant and settle in for what remained of the night. The more she thought about it, the more reasonable this seemed.

"There," Renie said, and pointed at the house that was closest to them. "It looks vacant." The hurricane shutters were up, the paddocks were empty, no cars were in sight.

"How're we going to get in with the shutters on the windows?"

"I don't know. Let's check it out." Renie took her hand and they crossed the road, Lucky sniffing along just ahead of them, their intrepid companion.

The shutters would be a challenge. But as long as she had a challenge that her mind could chew at, she wouldn't speculate about what might have happened to Andy and Jim. As long as she focused on this moment and the next, there was no room to think about what the hell she and Katie would do when the sun came up.

The house was large, a sprawling one-story concrete block with a fenced backyard and extensive landscaping. Even though she'd never sold a house in Paradise's equestrian community, she knew what land and homes went for up here and this one was expensive. With about 5,000 square feet under air on two or three acres of land, a barn and paddocks and probably a swimming pool in that backyard, she estimated a listing price of close to a million. And homes like these, she thought, always had a weakness, even with the hurricane shutters up.

The front of the house had twelve windows—large windows—and each one had a hurricane shutter, electric shutters, top of the line. At the press of a button, your window was sealed. No sweat, no toil, no endless hours in the brutal heat trying to fit bolts into holes, panels into slots. They opened the gate to the backyard and slipped inside, Lucky now in the lead, her nose to the grass.

No security lights came on: that was good. No alarms went off: that was even better. But best yet, no vicious dogs, no snoopy neighbors.

They passed a door to the garage. If all else failed, locks could be jimmied and once they were inside the garage, she could pick the lock on the door that led to the house. It was nearly as easy as changing a tire. Thank you, Buddha, she thought, and walked on, following Katie and the dog.

The backyard was lush and thick with trees until they came around the side to the back. Here, a tremendous screened area covered the pool and patio. The screened door wasn't locked, which worried her a little until she realized that the owners were still paying for a pool service. Of course. Four or five months of no chlorine and no pump to keep the water circulating would produce a green swamp. The pump was electric, so that meant the electricity was still on. People with this much money, she thought, didn't worry about the monthly electricity bill. As if to confirm her conclusion, an outside AC unit clicked on.

The windows on the porch all had shutters and do did the sliding glass doors. Her hope began to sag. Maybe this place had no weaknesses.

"We'll never get in," Katie whispered.

"Ha," she replied with false bravado. "Light a couple of matches, hon."

As soon as she had light, Renie took a closer look at the shutters. They weren't electric. They were accordion shutters that had to be pulled shut, less expensive than the shutters on the front of the house. Once the shutters were closed, they were locked—and a lock could be rendered useless.

She fumbled around in her backpack until she found her first-aid kit. She fished out her longest sewing needle, stuck it inside a tube of antibiotic ointment to lubricate it, and slid it into the lock. She wiggled the needle and listened. She wiggled the needle some more, working it more deeply into the mechanism. Then she heard a sharp little click, and turned the handle.

The shutters creaked and moaned, betraying a period of neglect that probably dated back to the end of the horse show season in early March. Once she pulled the shutters open, her hope surged again. The easiest kind of window. She popped out the screen, set it on the ground, pressed her fingers to the glass, and lifted upward. The window slid open and a breath of cool air struck her face. The air felt to be about sixty-five. These folks definitely weren't worried about electric bills. The best news yet was that no alarm went off.

Renie stuck her head inside, listening to the silence for any noise that indicated a human presence. She heard nothing.

"You ready?" she asked Katie.

"I don't want to sleep out *here,* that's for sure."

So they climbed through the opening, a pair of Alices and their loyal dog, sliding down the rabbit's hole.

They emerged in a lavish, sunken living room with lavish, expensive furniture, the kind of stuff no one ever sat in. Collections of figurines filled several display cases. Horse show trophies filled another display case, and a third case held China dishes and crystal drinking glasses.

They made a quick circuit of the house. There wasn't a computer in sight, but the phones and appliances worked. They made their way down the massive hall to a large bedroom that faced the pool. The shutters were in place on the sliding glass doors and windows, so Renie figured it was safe to turn on a lamp. The soft, buttery circles of light revealed a huge walk-in closet, with clothes still inside, women's clothes, and a king-size bed.

Katie fell back onto the bed and sighed. "Oh God, this feels good." Lucky jumped onto the bed with her and settled at the foot of it. Katie immediately bounced up again and went into the adjoining bathroom and started a bath. "You think we can do a wash, Mom? My clothes are really dirty and smelly."

"My thoughts exactly." Renie removed two bathrobes from hangers in the closet and went into the bathroom and tossed one to Katie. "Strip off those clothes and I'll dig out the dirty clothes from our packs."

"Is it safe to turn on the light in here? And the TV?"

The bathroom, like the bedroom, faced the back of the house and was shuttered. "Sure."

She gathered up Katie's dirty clothes, then went over to her pack and unzipped it and realized that Andy had tossed her his pack. "Christ." Instead of her own carefully selected toiletries, she had Andy's—a razor that had seen better days, drugstore shampoo that would make her hair dry and frizzy, a bar of Dial soap that would leave her skin as dry as a reptile's, and no face or hand cream at all. No makeup or perfume, either. But she had the cell phone, its charger, the Pocket PC, and a number of other items that might prove more useful to her now than makeup and perfume. She plugged in the cell phone so that it could charge and turned it on.

She stripped off her own clothes, shrugged on the robe, and checked through Katie's pack. Dirty clothes, clean clothes, toiletries they could both use, bottles of water, and Tupperware containers from the zapped supplies that held people food and dog food. Thank God. They wouldn't endanger themselves by eating visible food and they wouldn't starve.

Renie gathered up Katie's laundry and walked to the other end of the house, where the utility room was. Detergent on the shelf. How considerate of these people, whoever they were. And how considerate of them to leave the electricity and phones on. These expenses were obviously pocket change to them, whoever they were.

As she loaded the washer, she realized how comforting this small act was. It was familiar, something she did at least three times a week in her ordinary life. It also kept her busy and if she kept busy until she dropped, she wouldn't think too closely about what had happened back there. Her imagination wouldn't conjure dire what-if scenarios about

Andy. And she wouldn't have to wonder about fractals and chaos theory and surrender.

After she put in the wash, she checked out the fridge, the freezer, the pantry. She was hungry for real food, *visible* food, and there was plenty in the freezer and the pantry. It was now nearly four in the morning. If she and Katie snacked on visible food, they would be visible until at least ten or eleven. They would have to stay in the house.

But was that so bad? She could pull the hurricane shutters closed and who would know? Once her food had digested, she could head into the field to look for Andy. Then the three of them could lie low in the house for a day or so. They could monitor the news and surf the Web for information and then make a well-informed decision that wouldn't involve Jim.

But even as she thought all of these reasonable things, she knew—*knew* deep in her heart—that Andy wouldn't be meeting her in the field, that whoever had shattered the windows in the garage apartment had gotten him. A crippling wave of fear swept over her, dizziness gripped her, and she grabbed on to the edge of the refrigerator to steady herself, to hold herself up. The dizziness passed, but her fear did not.

And when she was afraid, deeply afraid as she was now, she got hungry. She was suddenly famished and began to remove items from the fridge, the freezer. They needed a meal, she and Katie. They needed *real* food.

While Renie whipped up a meal, Katie came out into the kitchen wrapped up in one of the robes, her hair combed and wet from her bath. She was carrying the cell phone and Andy's Pocket PC. "Mom, is it okay to go on-line using the phone here? I'm going to check Uncle Jim's e-mail. Maybe someone responded from that Web site."

Renie thought a moment, wondering if it would be safer to use the cell phone. She decided against it. "Yeah, use the phone here. Do you know his password?"

"Yeah. *Katie Iris,* one word, no caps."

Renie smiled. Jim's two favorite girls, his niece and his grandmother. "You know how to use that thing?"

"Dad showed me."

"Food will be ready in a jiffy."

By the time Katie was on-line, Renie's frozen food bonanza was done. She scoffed down her food as she stood behind her daughter, watching the tiny screen.

Katie's ease with this puzzling bit of technology called a Pocket PC astonished Renie. And yet, Katie always was the one to adapt first to whatever newness came their way. She had learned to read from computer games, comic books, and TV. The world of *Rug Rats* had been as real to her as her flesh-and-blood friends. Thanks to the remote control and channel surfing, she was able to watch two or three TV shows at the same time, without losing track of any of the story lines. She loved science fiction of any type, books or movies, but preferred the kind of sci-fi with nonlinear story lines. When Jim had given her a video camera for her birthday three years ago, she didn't have to read the directions to use it. When they'd bought themselves a DVD player one Christmas, Katie had shown *them* how to use it. It was as if she'd been born knowing how to use the very technology that perplexed, fascinated, and ultimately had transformed the lives of her parents and their generation. Renie was convinced that Katie and her contemporaries had brains that were wired much differently.

Fifteen minutes later, she was in Jim's Hotmail mailbox, scrolling through the new messages. "Here it is," she exclaimed. "A response from someone named Sparky!" She clicked on the envelope.

Hi, Siamese.

I'm afraid I can't give you the name of the individual who posted the piece about the Everglades incident. They requested confidentiality. You said in your e-

mail that you had additional information about it. Our
message boards are open to the public, so feel free to
post there. Or, if you'd like, send me a confidential e-
mail concerning your information and I'll summarize
it, send it back to you for your approval, then work
it into my site newsletter.
    At this site, our concern is freedom of information.
                                    Best wishes,
                                      Sparky

    Renie jotted down Sparky's e-mail address, then told Katie to delete the note and to access her Yahoo e-mail account, which she used primarily when they traveled. "You're going to write her back?" Katie asked.

    "Absolutely."

    Moments later, Renie dictated a note to Sparky, and Katie typed it in.

    "That's it?" Katie asked.

    Renie read it over her daughter's shoulder. "Yeah, I think so."

    "You sure you want to send it?"

    "You don't think we should?"

    "Suppose this Sparky person is part of whatever happened to us?"

    "I think it's a risk we have to take. Right now, we don't have a whole lot of options, Katie."

    Her daughter pressed the SEND button.

16
INCREASE AND INNER TRUTH

The Downward Dog. The Crow. The Tree. Logan went through her yoga postures in the hopes that the routine would quiet her head. She did them outdoors in the midafternoon heat, next to the RV, with Jazzy perched at the inside window, seeming to watch her.

She and Abby were now in the Upper Keys, in an RV park where they had been ever since they'd fled the house. She could see the pale stretch of beach just beyond their site and hear the crashing waves in the ocean beyond it. The air smelled of salt and seaweed and deep summer, and every so often some atavistic part of her longed to immerse herself in the warm surf.

Only yesterday morning, she had watched Abby and her daughter and grandson swimming in the Atlantic waters and having the time of their lives. And she had envied them, envied their unity and closeness and obvious love for one another. She also had envied their visibility, that they could go swimming and she could not. Sometimes, she thought she would die of loneliness.

Her yoga routine tired her physically, but her thoughts continued to race along. She went back inside the RV and showered. She didn't bother looking in the mirror while she was wet. That sort of regret and nostalgia served no purpose. At the moment, Nash had her on the run, but it wouldn't last indefinitely. His resources weren't infinite and her greatest strength was her knowledge of what it was like to live as an Invisible, something even Nash couldn't claim. He had the science, but she and Tyler had the expertise. And one way or another, she would use that against Nash.

She put on invisible clothes and rubbed her hair with the towel, soaking up the excess water so that it would dry quickly on its own. In the little kitchen, she fixed herself a glass of cold herbal tea. The RV was large enough for two or three to travel comfortably, but not so large that it attracted attention. Abby's daughter and grandson had stayed with them a couple of nights, the only other people in the world who knew that Logan was an Invisible. The daughter, Chandra, always plied Logan with questions about what *it* was like. Dylan, Chandra's four-year-old son, believed that Logan was his invisible playmate. She liked having them around. They distracted her. And this afternoon they weren't here and maybe that was why she felt so restless, so unable to do anything constructive.

She often wondered what she would have done if Abby hadn't entered her life when she had. This was the what-if game: what if she and Tyler hadn't been recruited by Nash, what if he had gotten out of the hangar with her, what if this, what if that . . . Absurd, but sometimes this little game kept her sane.

Logan set up her computer on the kitchen table, connected it to her cell phone, and went on-line. She had her routine on-line: check on her stocks, her e-mail, read the news, her horoscope, her *I Ching* hexagram for the day. The Internet was her connection to the larger world, that world from which her invisibility isolated her. Here, everyone was invisible.

The stock market had had a bad day, Madonna was playing to sell-out crowds across the Northeast, the president's popularity was plunging, and a tropical storm churned through the Caribbean. Stephen King and John Grisham were vying for the top spot on the *Times* best-seller list and everyone was anticipating the release of the Harry Potter movie in late fall. Firestone and Ford were taking a beating, fires raged in the West, record heat waves had hit most of the country.

Seventeen new e-mails came up in her box—Abby's mailbox, actually—and as she scrolled through them, she felt a pang of disappointment that none of the e-mails came from Hacienda Manteles. All the e-mails appeared to be ads. Except for one. She clicked the exception.

> *Hi, Sparky,*
>
> *My friend sent the original e-mail for me. It's nice to know that confidentiality exists on the Web. My information about the recent events in the Everglades is up close and personal. I saw the village of wood and thatch fade from view. I saw it turn invisible. Since I was a witness, I am now being pursued by the individuals behind this abomination. I realize that I may sound like a nutcase, but it's a risk I'm willing to take. I need information and and I need help.*
> *hummingbird @yahoo.com*

Logan sat there a moment, staring at the screen, her heart beating fast, erratically. *This is it.* She felt it. This was the lead she and Abby had hoped for when they'd launched the weird&strange Web site several years ago. At the time, she'd known that if Tyler were still alive, he would find a site like this and had hoped that she might get a lead on Nash and his activities. The Web site, in fact, had led her to Homestead and now it had led her to another of Nash's victims.

She didn't know for sure if hummingbird was one of the Townsends—but it felt right. The e-mail trail didn't provide any information—like the name of a hospital or a real estate office—that gave a location. The author of the e-mail didn't mention whether he or she was invisible. But the Townsends *had* to be invisible. They had been in the village when the shrouding had occurred. Maybe the author of the note had decided that if he or she mentioned being invisible, Sparky would write them off as nutcases. Whatever the truth, she felt compelled to respond.

Yet, she hesitated. Caution had been her constant companion these last three years. This could easily be a trap set up by Nash or Colleen, who probably had figured out by now that she had stolen the hard drive from the control room at the base. She finally reached into a cabinet over the stove and brought out her worn copy of the *I Ching* and the cloth bag that held the three genuine Chinese coins that she and Abby had bought in Hong Kong a year ago, on one of their foreign trips where Abby was the paying passenger and Logan sat wherever there was a seat. The question she posed was simple: should she respond to arrange a meeting with hummingbird?

She tossed the coins six times and got hexagram forty-two, *Increase,* with a changing line to hexagram sixty-one, *Inner Truth. Favorable to have somewhere to go.* She felt this hexagram addressed her directly and that the changing hexagram, which concerned innermost sincerity, referred to whoever had written the e-mail. It didn't get much better than that. She clicked on the reply button:

> *Hummingbird, select a place where we can meet or let's meet in a private chat room on the weird&strange site. I understand your situation completely. The people behind the Tesla Project will stop at nothing to*

ensure the safety and secrecy of what they're doing. You are not the only victim. There are side effects from the process they used to shroud the village. If you were in the village at the time, then you already have an idea what some of those side effects are. But there are some things you may not realize yet. First, there's the sickness. It feels like the flu, only worse. Wheat grass will mitigate the symptoms. You can eat it raw or steep it as a tea. Seaweed, the kind you can get at the deli, does the same thing.

Massive doses of vitamin C work wonders. Take 20,000 milligrams by mouth in increments of 4,000, every two hours until the 20,000 mm ceiling is met. Continue this for three days. It will prevent any recurrence of the illness. Anything you eat will be visible for 6–8 hours, depending on how efficiently your body is metabolizing food. Your body temperature may fall about three degrees. Water—from rain, a shower, even mist—will make you visible to others.

The shrouding has very definite physiological effects and many of them won't be blatantly obvious to you. Your hearing will sharpen. Your night vision will improve immensely. The visible world, however, will look hazy to you and sometimes slightly out of focus. Your body will begin to use energy more efficiently and you won't have to eat more than one meal a day. You won't require as much sleep.

You'll feel the heat of the sun, it will provide you with the vitamin D you need, but it won't burn you. One of the things this means is that your skin won't age as quickly. Unfortunately, no one will know that but you.

There are many other subtleties that you will discover over time and that we can discuss in person. I hope I have provided enough information to ensure your trust and hope that we can meet very soon. Please

*give me a location and I will get back to you. I'll be
on-line for at least another hour, otherwise I'll check
my mail again tonight.*
Sparky

P.S. Click www.strange&weird.com/chat

As Logan pushed away from the table to make herself
another cup of tea, her computer jingled, signaling that she
had e-mail. She sat down again, clicked on the new envelope
from hummingbird.

Hi, Sparky. Let's meet in your chat room.
hummingbird

Logan clicked on the chat link.

<sparky is here>
<hummingbird> Hi, Sparky.
*<sparky> This should be very private. I'm glad you're
still on-line. How can I help you?*
*<hummingbird> You already have. How do u know
so much about what you call shrouding?*
<sparky> I used to work for the Tesla Project.
*<hummingbird> How do I know you don't still work
for them?*
*<sparky> How do I know you aren't one of their
computer techs?*
*<hummingbird> I guess we either trust each other or
sign off.*
*<sparky> It would seem so. I'm willing to trust. Are
you?*
*<hummingbird> Maybe I have more to lose than you
do. Why are you so willing to trust me?*
<sparky? Are you familiar with the I Ching?
<hummingbird> Sure. Which edition?
<sparky> Wilhelm. I also use the Huang edition.

<hummingbird> So u asked about this situation?
<sparky> Yes. I got hex 42 changing to 61.
<hummingbird> Increase to Inner Truth. Changing lines . . . ?
<sparky> The second line. About the ten tortoises that can't oppose it and how constant perseverance brings good fortune.
<hummingbird> Hold on. I'm looking it up.
<hummingbird> Still looking . . . Okay. Got it. I asked a question about whether we should meet. Hexagram 1, 5th line changing to hex 14. The Ching is saying okay. How about meeting us tonight @ 9the Cappuccino Express, 414 Green View Shores, Paradise?
<sparky> I'll be there, wearing a green Marlins baseball cap.

Meeting *us*. Logan hurried into Abby's room to wake her. They had an appointment to meet the Townsends. She was sure of it.

2

Nash gazed down at Andy Townsend, strapped to a platform in a pool of shallow water warmed to his body temperature. His head was slightly raised, so that he wouldn't drown, and his right arm lay outside the pool, in a specially designed polyurethane funnel that resembled a rain gutter. Electrodes ran from his arm, head, and temples to various machines that tracked his heartbeat, respiration, blood pressure, and brain waves. Of course, only the damp parts of his body were visible and even to Nash, who was seasoned to shrouding's disorientation, the effect was eerie.

He was seated on a stool because, despite the codeine, his leg felt as if jagged pieces of glass were being ground into it. The bike ride in Paradise had been foolish, a show for Colleen, he thought. It had exacerbated the pain. Even as he sat there, monitoring the machines and jotting down the figures on his clipboard, he popped another codeine into his mouth and chewed it.

The vital sign readings had changed significantly in the last thirty minutes. It appeared that Townsend was slowly shaking off the powerful tranks that had rendered him unconscious and would be rejoining the land of the living very shortly.

Nash stood and limped over to the counter. He picked up a bottle that contained distilled water and sprayed a fine mist across the seemingly empty space between the electrodes. Townsend's nose and cheeks came into view, then his mouth, his eyelids and ears. No rapid eye movement yet, so Townsend wasn't quite at the dream level.

Just to be sure that he remained visible once he was out of the pool and dry, Nash added a dark blue saline solution to the IV and watched, fascinated, as the stuff began its slow, colorful trek through Townsend's veins and arteries. It was like watching special effects in a movie, a dazzling spectacle that eventually would illuminate not only veins and arteries, but muscles and organs as well.

The first time they had done this to Dog, she was still shrouded and she had howled and snarled and struggled to escape her chain. He doubted that Townsend, who already knew he was invisible, would react in the same way, but until he knew for sure, the restraints at his chest and arms and legs would remain in place.

Renie and Katie Townsend had gotten away, but they'd brought in Townsend's brother. No matter how you looked at it, the Townsends would be problematic. When prominent citizens in a particular area disappeared, people noticed. Fortunately, Jim Townsend was self-employed, so his absence might not be noticed for a while. The only problem he anticipated on that score was if Jim or Andy had had any contact with his grandparents, who owned the house.

Nash's people had replaced the windows in the garage apartment and had cleaned up any trace of what had happened. The house itself had been uninhabited. Still, he worried.

Dobson poked his head into the room. "He come to yet?"

"He's coming around." Nash spoke softly. "What's going on out there?"

"Farris is eager to see what we caught."

"Keep him off my back for a while, Wayne."

"He's off." Dobson stepped into the room, but remained out of sight, in the shadows. "Colleen is talking to him."

Oh. "This may get ugly."

"It's always ugly," Dobson said softly. "And it could be otherwise. That's the tragedy."

"How could it be otherwise?" Nash asked, glancing back at Dobson.

"No Farris, no committee, no brass."

"Yeah, and all that equals no budget."

"I know, I know. This is the idealist in me speaking."

Townsend moaned softly and Nash glanced at the readouts again. Heartbeat accelerating, brain waves climbing now toward alpha, respiration and body temp increasing: he was definitely surfacing. Nash pulled a chair up to the edge of the pool and sat down. Dobson remained standing against the wall, so that Townsend wouldn't be able to see him.

Since Townsend's face had dried, Nash couldn't tell the precise moment when his eyes opened, but the electrodes moved as Townsend turned his head to the side.

"Welcome back, Doctor Townsend."

Silence.

"I know you're conscious and that you can hear me."

Silence.

Nash misted Townsend's face again. For seconds, no longer than that, the man's eyes were fully visible, glaring at Nash with a mix of contempt and shock. Then the water mingled with the natural moisture in his eyes and only spots here and there on his cheeks and forehead were visible.

"If you choose not to speak, that's fine," Nash went on in the same tone of voice. "But cooperation will get you much further than resistance. In fact, resistance is futile. We'll just keep you here in the pool, strapped down, and will feed you through IVs."

"Threats, then torture? Really, Mr. Nash. I expected something more dignified."

Nash leaned forward, his eyes following the stream of blue through the veins and capillaries in Townsend's face. "You misunderstand me. I make no threats and torture isn't what we do here."

"I suppose that depends on your definition of torture. From my vantage point, you've broken at least half a dozen laws, not the least of which is abduction. The last time I checked, that carried a minimum sentence of twenty-five years."

"We don't live by the same laws that you do."

Townsend laughed. "Right. Of course not. How naive of me. Okay, since I haven't been abducted or shot, since I'm not tied down and being held against my will, would you mind if I had a glass of water and something to eat?"

"Not at all. What would you like to eat? We have several excellent cooks."

"Two eggs over easy, with five or six strips of vegetarian bacon, half a cantaloupe, a glass of fresh squeezed OJ, a cup of Cuban coffee, and an arepa."

Good, Nash thought. They were making progress. He glanced back at Dobson and he nodded and slipped out the door.

"The food will be here shortly," Nash said as he hung up.

"How am I going to eat?"

"Under your own steam. In the event that you try to

escape once you're free of the platform, I'll have your brother killed, Doctor Townsend.''

With that, Nash slipped a remote control device from his shirt pocket and aimed it at the monitor mounted on the wall. He pressed a button and Jim Townsend appeared on the screen. He was locked in a small, windowless room that had only a toilet and a sink in the corner. He looked like a raving lunatic, shouting and banging his fists against the electronic door.

Nash pressed the intercom button and said, "Mr. Townsend, if you don't quiet down, I will instruct someone to come into the room and shut you up.''

Jim Townsend spun, seeking the origin of the voice, his eyes wild. *"Go fuck yourself!"* And he pounded his fists against the doors and continued to scream obscenities.

"Suit yourself," Nash said, and pressed another button on the remote control. "Panther, Jim Townsend is making too much noise. Please go in and shut him up.''

"You got it, boss.''

"Wait," said Andy. "Let me talk to him. I'll calm him down.''

Nash turned in his chair and shrugged, hands at his sides, palms turned upward. "Too late, Doc. You need to know we're serious.''

And then, on the screen, the electronic doors whispered open and Panther stepped into Jim Townsend's room, right fist grinding against his left palm. Jim jumped around him, fists balled in front of him, a parody of a boxer. He kept shouting, egging Panther on. Panther whirled once, kicked out, and his foot sank into Jim's stomach. He stumbled back, eyes wide, startled, arms clutched at his waist, and then Panther whirled again, moving with the speed and dexterity of an acrobat, and knocked Jim's legs out from under him. He went down and Panther now danced around him, kicking him in the ribs, the head, and Jim rolled up into a tight ball, moaning.

"Jesus, stop, please," Townsend gasped. "I'll do whatever you want."

Nash pressed the intercom button again. "That's enough, Panther. Put him out."

Panther slipped a hand into his pocket and brought out a hypodermic that he jabbed into Jim Townsend's neck. Seconds later, Jim went slack and Nash turned off the TV.

"Panther loves his work." *Loves it maybe a tad too much.* "He's totally without scruples."

Andy's respiration and heartbeat had shot up and Nash knew he was struggling with the reality of his situation. "What . . . what the hell do you want from me?"

"Cooperation, Doctor Townsend. That's all."

"Cooperation. Fine. You have my cooperation. But in return, I want your word that my brother won't be harmed. That he'll get the medical attention he needs and that . . . that homicidal maniac won't be allowed near him."

"Done."

The door opened and Colleen breezed in with a tray of food. She set it down on a nearby table, came over to Nash's side, and put a hand on his shoulder, a gesture that told Townsend she was important in the scheme of things. "How're you doing, Doctor Townsend?" she asked.

"Just ducky," he replied.

"Hmm. We're a little grumpy," she remarked. "That's what low blood sugar will do for you. Let's get him unhooked from the pool, George, so that he can eat. Then Ross would like to talk to him."

They disconnected Townsend from the medical equipment. He was still weak from the trank that had been in the dart, from lack of food and water, but thanks to the blue dye in the saline solution, it was easy to grasp his arms and help him over to the table. Nash actually let Colleen do most of the work so that he wouldn't have to limp in Townsend's presence.

But Townsend probably wouldn't have noticed. His focus

was the food. He didn't just eat; he attacked the food, shoveling it into his mouth with the rapacity of an animal that hadn't eaten in weeks. Nash and Colleen glanced at each other. Her brows lifted, indicating that she had questions. Nash didn't want to step out of the room and leave Townsend alone in here and the room wasn't large enough for them to speak without him overhearing them. So he handed Colleen a pad of paper and a pen. She scribbled something, passed the pad and pen back to him.

Where should we put him?

He wrote: *With Tyler. Then call in Ross.*

Committee people are here.

How many?

Three.

Nash squeezed the bridge of his nose. Tyler might refuse to talk to them, but he felt certain that Townsend would cooperate. And perhaps if Tyler saw Townsend cooperating, he would fall in line. Even if he didn't, though, would it matter? This would be the committee's first exposure to Invisibles and what a spectacle it would be—the splendid blue dye coursing through Townsend's veins, his food moving through his digestive system, the novelty of it all.

Colleen interpreted his hesitation as reluctance and quickly took the pad and pen from him and wrote: *We're in a strong position even if neither of them cooperates. And we also have the promise of two more Invisibles to come.*

"Where're my wife and daughter?" Townsend asked, talking around a mouthful of food.

As if reading their minds, Nash thought. "Still at large. But they'll be joining you shortly."

Even though he couldn't see Townsend's face, Nash knew the man was grinning, that he was silently cheering his wife and daughter for remaining out of their reach.

On the pad, Nash hastily scribbled: *Bring the committee to the apartment in one hour.*

17
ANDY AND TYLER

The food had revived Andy in a way that had seemed impossible thirty minutes ago, revived him despite the pepper he had poured on his eggs and the hot sauce he had slathered over the arepa. Right about now, his ulcer should be shrieking. Instead, he didn't have so much as the faint whisper of heartburn. He wouldn't break any records for strength, endurance, or even clarity of thought, but compared to how he'd felt when his eyes had opened in that miserable twilit room, this was pretty damn close to nirvana.

He could move his hands and legs again. He could turn his head without the presence of the goddamn electrodes. They had given him clothes to wear that hid his digesting food and most of the blue shit that coursed through his veins. But looking down at the clothes disoriented him because the clothes were visible and, therefore, just as hazy as everything else he looked at. The pool in which they had kept him had left his skin as puckered and withered as that of a prune, but he didn't care. Once he'd realized just what kind of power Nash wielded in this place, his priorities had snapped into utter clarity.

Cooperation? Fine, no problem, just leave his brother alone.

A human guinea pig? Hey, he was honored. *But please, God, keep Ren and Katie safe.*

He had no idea where they were taking him now, up and down halls in a golf cart, his hands and legs shackled, Colleen at the wheel, Nash on one side of him and the homicidal maniac, Panther, on the other. He found himself staring at Panther's massive hands. His fingers clenched and unclenched against his thighs, a vein throbbed at his temple, and twice the man looked at Andy and grinned as if to say, *Hey, fuckhead, you're next.*

He forced himself to notice other details—that Nash and Colleen seemed to have an intimate relationship and that Nash walked with a cane. He tried to hide his limp and minimize his use of the cane, perhaps for Colleen's benefit or perhaps so that Andy wouldn't perceive him as weak. But the physician in him had already accessed the problem as one of several things: a congenital abnormality or the result of disease or of a recent injury.

Even though Andy had no facts, no evidence, nothing solid to go on, *disease* resonated more strongly than any of the other possibilities. In fact, the longer he stared at Nash's bum leg, the greater his certainty that the problem with his leg was due to a childhood disease. Given Nash's age— late forties, early fifties—that narrowed the possibilities to diseases that had prevailed during the 1950s. Foremost among them was polio.

"Your leg, Mr. Nash. Was it due to polio?" Andy asked.

The shock on Nash's face told him he'd hit it squarely. Before Nash recovered enough to reply, Panther slammed his elbow into Andy's side. His ribs exploded with pain, he gasped and doubled over.

"His leg's none of your business, pal," hissed Panther.

For moments, no one said anything else and Andy remained doubled over, trying to catch his breath, and then the pain in his ribs just ebbed away. When he raised up, Nash was looking at him. "How . . . how did you know?"

"I work in ER," Andy replied, and let it go at that.

The cart finally stopped at another electronic door and a guard waved them through, into an apartment made almost entirely of glass, where the air felt blissfully cool, around sixty-five degrees, he guessed. Music played, a piece by Ottmar Liebart.

Nash stepped out of the cart first, leaning heavily on his cane. Colleen was right behind him. Panther snapped, "Get out nice and slow, Doc."

"Hey, Tyler," Nash called. "You've got company."

About thirty feet away, a man was sitting at a computer, his back to them. He wore a sweatshirt with a hood that covered his head, jeans and moccasins. But when he stood and turned, Andy realized the truth. *He's like me. An Invisible.*

The man—Tyler—stepped out of his moccasins and came toward them. Although Andy could see the guy's feet, he knew that Nash and his group could not. To them, it appeared that Tyler had no feet. Tyler drew the sweatshirt off over his head so that, to the others, he looked like nothing more than a pair of blue jeans moving toward them.

"Very funny, Tyler," said Colleen.

Yeah, it is, give me more, Andy thought, barely suppressing a laugh.

"Who's the blue man?" Tyler asked as he neared the cart. His voice sounded blunt.

"Tyler Griffin, Andy Townsend," said Nash.

"Another victim. Shame on you, George." Tyler winked at Andy, a conspiratorial wink that Andy knew the others couldn't see. "And just what the hell am I supposed to do with him? Instruct him on the ins and outs of life as an Invisible?" Tyler laughed. "Well, shit, fella, welcome to the new world,'' and he threw out his arms, a gesture that only Andy could see. ''. . . and to the glass cage. I would really appreciate it, George, if you would get that cart out of my living room. It's messing up the floor.''

''Panther, unshackle Doctor Townsend and then remove the cart,'' Nash said.

Panther unshackled Andy, told him to step out of the cart, then drove the cart out of the apartment. Nash limped his way toward the kitchen table. ''Let's sit over here.''

''Let's not,'' Tyler said.

''We need to talk,'' Nash replied. ''The four of us.''

''I'm really not in the mood to break bread, George,'' Tyler said, then went over to Andy and leaned close to him. ''The first law of life as an Invisible, Doc, is to realize that without us, none of this would exist. A heady concept, isn't it?'' Tyler brought his mouth so close to Andy's ear now that he could feel the heat of his breath. When he spoke, his voice was a whisper; Andy doubted that Nash and the others could hear it, especially with the music playing in the background. ''Play along. We're stronger as two. We'll get a chance to talk later.'' Now he raised his voice to a normal tone again. ''So let me guess. We're going to chat about the arrival of the committee.''

''That's right,'' Nash said, sinking into a chair across from Colleen.

The committee. It smacked of authority, Andy thought, the final arbiter, some Medieval church council that would decide whether he would be hung or pardoned for his sins. The committee was the physician's equivalence of the AMA or the local hospital board. It would attempt to impose order on the chaos that had corrupted man's ideas about what was possible. It would try to whip the fractals into some recognizable shape and would do this by laying down restrictions, law, dogma, and enforcing that dogma through threats. *Cooperate or we'll kill your brother.*

Tyler, as if confirming everything Andy was thinking,

leaned toward him again and whispered, "The committee has never seen an Invisible. If we answer their questions, we get more privileges, more freedoms, and then it will be easier to get the fuck out of here."

"What was that, Tyler?" Nash sat forward, frowning.

"I'm just explaining the facts of life as an Invisible," Tyler replied.

Colleen pushed away from the table and went over to a control panel on the wall. She turned down the music. "You can explain those facts to all of us, Tyler."

"Colleen, Colleen," Tyler said, clicking his tongue against his teeth. "You just don't cut it as a toughie."

"Shut up, Tyler," Nash snapped. "And cut the audio, Colleen, turn off the security cameras in here, and turn the music back on. What I have to say stays here, among the four of us."

She started to protest, but apparently thought better of it. She slipped a device out of the fanny pack at her waist that resembled a Pocket PC, but smaller. She entered several numbers on a keypad, then nodded. "All right. We're private. And here comes the music again."

Nash folded his hands on top of the table. "The committee got tired of waiting for you to decide when you wanted to speak to them, Tyler. So they're here and will be in shortly. Tyler and I have talked about this already, Doctor Townsend, but I'll recapitulate for your benefit. If you cooperate with the committee and answer their questions, our funding for this project will continue. That means that we can keep working to find a way to reverse the shrouding. If you don't answer their questions, the project will be shut down and you and Tyler will be transferred to a facility in D.C., where it's likely that your quality of life won't be much better than that of a lab animal. In such a scenario, I don't know what would happen to your brother."

"In such a scenario," said Tyler, "what would happen to you and Colleen? What makes you think either of you would be exempt from the same thing that would happen to Doctor Townsend's brother?''

Colleen, obviously exasperated with the conversation, rolled her eyes. ''My God, Tyler. You're making this sound like a Communist regime or something. All George is saying is that our funding is on the line and if we lose our funding, the project falls completely under the jurisdiction of the NSB.''

''Exactly. And we become their property,'' said Tyler. ''Whatever term you give it, it's still slavery. But it's been slavery for the last three years anyway.''

Colleen cast an angry look at Nash and stood up. ''I told you this wouldn't work. You can't wear both hats, George. I'll go get Ross and the committee.''

With that, Colleen hurried out of the apartment. Nash hesitated, then got up with apparent effort and pain, and limped after her. As soon as the electronic doors shut behind them, Tyler said, ''You're the guy from the Everglades. You were in the village when they zapped it.''

''Uh, yeah. But who the hell are you?'' Andy asked.

''That's a long story.'' He spoke quickly, urgently. ''My wife and I were Nash's first human guinea pigs three years ago. By choice. Something went wrong, Logan freaked, and took off. I've been here ever since.''

''For *three years?* In this place?''

''Most of it in this place.''

''Have you tried to escape?''

''In the beginning. But I guess what kept me here was the hope they would find a way to reverse the shrouding. But we'll talk about that later. There're things you need to know about being an Invisible. Like your hearing. Is it better than it used to be?''

''Better? Shit, I can hear a pin drop in another room.''

''Well, with time, it'll improve beyond that. You'll never see Visibles as completely clear. Up till now, the only other Invisible I've seen was Dog. She—''

"A black Lab?" Andy exclaimed.

"You've seen her?"

"She's been with us ever since we fled the village."

"She's not a typical dog. The repeated shroudings changed her in ways that Nash doesn't even suspect. And it's changed us, too, in ways Nash doesn't know about. The way you think, the way you perceive, your psychological makeup, your gut feelings . . . all that is changing. There are some things you simply *know*."

Like the polio, Andy thought.

"I guess it's Nature's compensation for invisibility. Something about the shrouding activates the ninety percent of the brain that we don't use. It won't be obvious all at once, but you'll notice it. You're not *ordinary* now, Doc."

Andy thought of the way his musings about chaos theory and fractals had come to him in the shower, shortly before the house was broken into. "Give me an example."

"Okay. Your body temperature is probably about three degrees lower than what's normal. Or it will be shortly. But you can raise or lower it simply by focusing your attention on doing so. That's just a simple example. There're other things we'll get into when we have more time. So far, though, I haven't been able to bust out of here by focusing on that." He grinned as he said it, but there was a resigned sadness about it that echoed years of isolation and loneliness.

"Did you get sick right after it happened?" Andy asked.

"Fuck, yeah. And until they got Dog, they didn't know how to treat it. Then one day they saw her eating grass—wheat grass . . ."

Renie was right, Andy thought.

"I think you get the sickness only once. I suspect it's like getting chicken pox or measles or something, except that it gives you an immunity to diseases that only Invisibles are susceptible to. And you'll find that you don't get sick very often as an Invisible. That's another side effect. Our immune systems are good. Really good. But as a doctor, you'd know more about that than I do.''

"Right now, I'm not medically certain about much of anything.''

"I hear Nash out in the hall. We don't have much time. Are your wife and kid here, too?''

"I don't think so. But my brother was in a windowless room where Panther beat him up.''

"He's an Invisible?''

"No, he's visible. He was helping us. Maybe they took him to medical. Nash threatened to kill him if I don't cooperate.''

"He'd do it. He has his humane moments, but basically he's as much a shit as Farris, the other prick you'll meet. But don't worry about your brother. We'll get him out. If it's up to Nash, they'll probably let you stay here. I think he's pretty convinced I'm not a security risk and there's no other place where they can keep an eye on us like this glass cage. But if it's up to Farris, we may get separated. If we do, I'll find you.''

Now Andy heard voices, too. "They're close.''

"Yeah. I'll set out food, let them think it's all very friendly. The more cooperative we are, the sooner they'll leave.''

Nash entered first, with another man in jeans and a blue work shirt. Colleen was behind them and behind her were other men, officious types, Andy thought, maybe military. Despite the obvious differences in body types—this one tall, that one muscular, this one balding, that one graying—he found it difficult to distinguish any of the four from each other. It was as if their mind-sets were so dangerously similar they had sculpted the way they looked. The internal made manifest, he thought.

No one bothered to introduce the members of the committee. This was right in keeping with the idea that they weren't separate beings, but were actually a collective entity, a *he*, rather like a biblical God that would mete out justice and punishment. The only people Nash introduced were Wayne Dobson—the guy in jeans—and Ross Farris, the man Tyler had mentioned.

Now that Andy got a closer look at him, his appearance was slightly different than the others. He wore beige chinos, for instance, while the other four wore suits. The vein that throbbed at his temple and the hard, determined set of his mouth told Andy that Farris was a likely candidate for a stroke or a massive coronary. He *knew* that Farris had high blood pressure and some secondary physical problems, some of them intestinal. Once again, he didn't know how he *knew* this. He simply did, just as he had known that polio was to blame for Nash's limp.

He looked to be somewhere between his mid-forties and his mid-fifties. As soon as he spoke, Andy felt an intense, visceral dislike for the man.

"Let's be seated, gentlemen. Food and drinks aren't necessary, Tyler."

"To me they are," Tyler replied, and finished what he was doing at the counter, then brought over a tray of goodies for the guests.

Raw veggies and dip, cheese and crackers, glasses and a large pitcher of lemonade. Everything made of plastic, Andy thought. No potential weapons. The food would keep him visible for hours, but so what? He wasn't going anywhere, that much was obvious.

"There," Tyler said when he'd finished laying out the platters. "Food makes things civil, don't you agree, *gentlemen?*"

They didn't react to his sarcasm. Their expressions remained immobile, paralyzed, like masks. As Tyler took a seat, Andy reminded himself that to others, Tyler was just a pair of free-floating jeans and he was a pair of shorts, a T-shirt, sandals, and tributaries of blue. Pretty weird, even if you were prepared for it. But the musketeers sifted through notes and files and typed on their skinny notebook computers like bored businessmen.

They took turns with their questions. What was their initial shrouding experience like? Was it painful? Pleasurable? Exactly how did it feel? What was the sickness like? What were the first symptoms? As a physician, did Dr. Townsend have any insights about this sickness? What was it like to be invisible to other people? Was there a sense of isolation? Had their taste in foods changed? What senses had been affected by the shrouding? And so on.

Tyler, because he had been invisible longer, answered many of the questions about daily life as an Invisible. He didn't hesitate to point out that his experience, however, had taken place in isolation, as a prisoner, so it hardly qualified as a template. "In fact, I have many unstable moments, gentlemen. My temper flares, my patience is short, I don't sleep well, and when I do sleep I have nightmares. I lack companionship, stability, and a sex life. I have no privacy to speak of, I'm not permitted to communicate with anyone in the outside world, and my former life was torn away from me. I had a wife three years ago. I had dreams. All of that is dead.''

"We don't need a polemic," said Farris. "Just answer the questions."

"That's what he's doing," said Dobson, who looked annoyed.

"I *am* answering your questions, Mr. Farris. And it takes a polemic to do it," Tyler shot back.

Member One spoke up. "Mr. Griffin, if you were coaching someone who was going to be shrouded, what advice would you give to that person?"

Andy saw that Tyler's expression shifted from anger to interest. "Advice in what sense?" Tyler asked. "What to be aware of? How to move around as an Invisible? Side effects? How to navigate daily life?"

"Anything that would enable that individual to adapt more quickly to being invisible."

"Well, if that person isn't held against his will, then invisibility is certainly a new level of freedom. But you have to change how you think. You have to remember that even though other people can't see you, they can hear you. Some can sense your presence. You can't walk through walls or stroll across water. When you're wet, you're visible to others. When you eat, the food is visible to others."

Member Two asked: "There's some evidence that your hearing is vastly improved, Mr. Griffin. Is that true?"

Tyler smiled, a slow, sly smile the others couldn't see. "If you say there's evidence, then it must be true."

Good, Andy thought. Tyler wasn't about to give away too much. The less these bozos knew about life as an Invisible, the more valuable he and Tyler became to them and their agenda. The more valuable they became, the longer they lived. It possessed the certainty of a mathematical axiom.

"What about you, Doctor Townsend?" asked Member Four. "You've been invisible for what, less than two weeks?"

"Yes."

"Is your hearing vastly improved?"

"I haven't noticed," Andy lied. "I've been too busy recuperating from the sickness that shrouding brings on."

The members huddled together—not whispering, Andy noticed, but passing notes back and forth. Nash, Colleen, and Farris exchanged meaningful—and anxious—looks. Dobson seemed to alternate between annoyance and disgust. Andy decided that under other circumstances, he might like Dobson.

A palpable tension built up in the silence. It felt the way the air did when a hurricane approached land, the air crackling with something powerful and savage. This was the point, Andy thought, where stasis met turbulence and erupted, full-blown, into a chaos that would destroy his chances of escaping this place. So he leaped in.

"My experience hasn't been ordinary or usual, either. Maybe the negative aspects of invisibility would be mitigated if individuals are trained in pairs. But they would have to meet stringent psychological and physical criteria."

He sounded like a physician now, presenting a report to the hospital board. And for the first time since the musketeers had entered the room, their expressions changed and he knew he was speaking their language. Jesus God, was this all it took? Talk like a bureaucrat and they eat out of the palm of your hand? Fine, he could play this game. He'd been playing it most of his adult life.

"In many ways, the shrouding process may be facilitating a quantum leap in man's evolution." The musketeers exchanged meaningful glances. Even Nash and Farris sat forward, listening closely. Andy rushed on, somehow finding the words that he needed to convince these assholes the funding should be extended and thereby buying time for himself. "The shrouding process may inadvertently break the ceiling of what we, as a species, have believed, is possible. After all, Tyler and I are now so intrinsically different from you that our very existence demands a new scientific paradigm. And once there are more of us, who knows?"

The musketeers looked at each other, at Nash and Farris and Colleen; then Member One said, "You and Mr. Griffin haven't been exactly forthcoming in explaining how you're different—other than the fact that you're invisible."

Andy looked at the man, really *looked* at him—his fleshy jowls, his dark button eyes, the way he combed his hair. "I'll give you an example. The intestinal distress you've been experiencing isn't due to an ulcer. It's diverticulitis."

Member One frowned and sat back. The committee passed notes back and forth again. "And do you have this ability, Mr. Griffin?"

Tyler laughed. "Nope. I'm not a doc."

"He has other abilities," Andy said. "It's the quantum leap, gentlemen. Doctor Nash's invention is the bridge to the next evolutionary step for mankind."

With that the musketeers looked at each other, then rose in unison and left. Nash, Colleen, and Farris followed them out of the apartment. Dobson lingered behind.

"Can you do that with anyone?" Dobson asked quietly, gazing in Andy's direction.

"I don't know." He paused, focused on Dobson, and several images filled his skull. "When you sleep on your left side, your arm goes numb. It worries you. It shouldn't. It's just due to aging. Sometimes at night you feel a burning in your chest and lie awake thinking about how ... how your father ... or maybe an uncle, I'm not sure ... died of a heart attack. It's not your heart. It's indigestion. Stay away from those peppers your wife cooks. Green peppers, right?"

The color had bled out of Dobson's face. He opened his mouth, but Andy wasn't finished yet.

"The heartburn gets worse when you're stressed and your stress level is pretty high now, Mr. Dobson. You don't like what you see happening here and—"

"Shut up," Dobson hissed, his teeth clenched. Then he turned and strode quickly from the apartment.

"Goddamn," Tyler breathed, looking over at Nash. "You rattled Dobson. You rattled all of them. Where'd that stuff come from?"

"My shower last night." *When I made love to my wife for the first time as an Invisible.* "I think I bought us some time."

"Fractals, new species ... Jesus, Doc, that was impressive."

Nash limped back into the apartment a while later, his relief so extreme that he couldn't contain it. His grin stretched across the entire lower half of his face. He groped for Andy's hand and pumped it with an almost religious fervor. "A new species. Quantum leaps in evolution. New paradigms. Sweet Jesus, Doctor Townsend. We've got carte blanche."

Not for long, shithead.

18
THE SECOND BODY

The game they played was an old one, part of the oral tradition of ghosting. Consuelo's version of hide-and-seek. It was intended to hone Luis's skills. He didn't think his skills needed honing, but Consuelo said his ghosting ability was desperately in need of fine-tuning.

At the moment, it was Luis's turn to hide and he chose the pasture just down the road from the hacienda. He looked around quickly, seeking the right spot. The correct location was as important as the correct state of mind. Three horses grazed in the moonlit field, their bodies partially hidden by the high, fragrant grass. Just beyond them rose the old barn, one wall leaning to the side. It was still used for farm equipment, tack for the horses, old cars. The barn, he thought, would present a challenge.

Luis darted through the open door and backed up to one of the damp wooden walls inside. Shadows closed around him. The cold nipped at his bare hands, his face. He shut his eyes, let them roll upward in their sockets, and moments later felt the distinctive shift deep inside himself.

He heard Consuelo now, calling to him, her singsong voice echoing through the darkness.

"Come out, come out, wherever you are."

As if they were six years old.

With every moment that passed, Luis found it difficult to hold the state of mind necessary for successful ghosting. The center of his palm was burning again, his heart raced, his coat felt weighted, too heavy for his body. Sweat rolled down the undersides of his arms. The burning in his palm escalated and a strange paralysis spread through his limbs. Suddenly, a terrible roaring filled his skull and he catapulted through the air and soared high above the barn, the hacienda, into the moonlit sky.

An ecstasy seized him, the kind of emotion he hadn't known since he was a young initiate at the brink of manhood, and it propelled him through the air. He moved so quickly now that everything around him blurred. Below him, the moonlit mountaintops seemed to melt together, then flattened out and rose again. He knew he was speeding across countries and peaks, islands and oceans. And he sensed where he was headed. The burning in the center of his palm was a kind of beacon, a pulsating energy that would lead him to her.

He saw the distant outline of the southeastern U.S., with Florida protruding like some strange appendage into the deep blue sea. The moment he identified the state, he began to slow. He couldn't feel the burning in his palm now—his body was back at the hacienda, in the barn—but he was aware that the pulsations guided him to Logan.

As soon as he thought her name, he felt an overwhelming pull in a particular direction. It was as if he were a sliver of iron pulled inexorably toward a powerful magnet. He recognized all these sensations from his early shamanic training when he was taught how to journey in his second body. But it hadn't happened spontaneously in so many years that he'd forgotten the rushing thrill of it, the profound adventure.

He embraced the pull and suddenly found himself on a curb in a parking lot, asphalt broken up by islands of green. He turned slowly in place, seeking the direction in which the pull was strongest, and was drawn to a vehicle that was turning into the lot. An RV.

He was instantly *there,* next to it, and immediately became aware of Consuelo's voice, calling to him, and of his body in the barn, on the hacienda grounds, in Ecuador. He felt a sudden pull backward as his body responded to where he had placed his attention and remembered that the trick to traveling in the second body was to stay focused, to block any stray thoughts or desires that entered his awareness. He concentrated on the hot pulsations in his palm, his connection to the woman, to Logan, and the pull strengthened again. He extended his hands to touch the side of the RV and his hands passed through it, into the painted metal, and then he simply stepped through it and emerged inside.

A sleeping area. But no one slept here at the moment. He heard the voices of two women coming from the front of the RV. He moved through the door of the sleeping area and a cat, crouched on a chair, hissed and sprang at him— and passed through him. He felt its passage like a cold nail drawn across his heart. Terror. The cat was terrified.

''What's wrong with Jazzy?'' one woman asked.

''I guess she's unsettled by all the changes,'' the other replied. ''Got your baseball cap, Abby?''

''Right here.''

The women looked like two pearls of light with shapes inside them. One light shone more brightly than the other. Logan, yes, that light was Logan. As Luis neared her, the pulsing sensation in his hand ceased. He was certain that back in Ecuador the terrible burning in the center of his hand also stopped.

''My God,'' Logan whispered. ''Do you feel that?''

''What? What am I supposed to be feeling?''

Luis paused behind them. The Ghosted One sensed him,

but apparently couldn't see him. Yet, he could see her more clearly than he could see the other woman, Abby.

"We're not alone," Logan said softly.

"You mean . . . another Invisible is in here?"

"No. Something else. I think it's what Jazzy sensed."

Logan turned and extended her arms. Her fingertips penetrated his second body but all he felt was warmth, a tingling. Then he felt a sharp tug that came from outside the RV. He resisted it, he wasn't ready to move on just yet. He desperately wanted to communicate something to Logan. But the tug became too powerful to fight and he abruptly found himself outside the RV again, in front of a shop and a patio partially hidden by a hedge and trees.

Even as he moved toward the tug, he heard Consuelo's voice once more, calling to him. He shut it out, unwilling to return just yet. He suddenly saw the source of what had pulled him out of the RV: two bright cocoons of energy. No, three cocoons. It shocked him to realize he was looking at three more Ghosted Ones, a woman, a girl, and a dog.

How can that be? Who are they?

2

Katie watched her mother head toward the black woman wearing the baseball cap. She and Lucky stayed behind, right where her mother told her to wait. But she didn't like it. If something happened to her mother, if this was a trick, what the hell was she going to do? She was fourteen years old, invisible, and didn't have a clue how she would ever find her dad on her own.

She suddenly felt something nearby. She didn't know what it was until she glanced around uneasily and saw a man. She couldn't tell at first whether he was visible or invisible; he seemed to be a little of both. That was clearly impossible, though. You were either one or the other. She looked to her right, at the Visibles sitting around an outside table, then looked at the man again, comparing him to the others. Okay, he wasn't a Visible, she could see through him. But he wasn't an Invisible, either, definitely not.,

She moved quickly toward him, Lucky hurrying alongside her. The dog sniffed at the man's feet, barked, and drew the attention of people who heard Lucky but couldn't see her. "Ssshhh," she whispered. "No barking." Then, the man, she said, "Who *are* you? You're not invisible, but you're not visible, either."

He touched the top of her head and she felt it. But it wasn't an ordinary touch. It seemed to ripple through her, like heat or an electric current. And with the contact, came a name.

"Louise? That's a girl's name," Katie whispered.

The man touched her head again and this time she got it. "Luis. That's Spanish. If you're not invisible, how can you see me? Were you zapped?" She kept her voice at a whisper, but continue to question him, to talk. "My mom and dad and I were zapped and then last night these men broke into the apartment where we were staying and I don't know where my dad is now. I think they got him. Then . . . then we got this e-mail from Sparky . . . I'm pretty sure that's her, the lady wearing the green baseball cap—"

Listen to me. His voice entered her, that was the only way she could describe it. She felt it all over inside, like a touch but not a physical touch. Like a presence, but not intrusive. *Logan will help you. Trust her. I will find you.*

And then, just like that, he was gone and her mother was gesturing at her, hurrying her forward, and Katie ran across the black asphalt, the dog at her heels.

3

The last thing Luis remembered before he opened his eyes was the tremendous roaring in his head and the sense of movement. Now Consuelo was leaning over him, rubbing her hands roughly over his cheeks. His hand seized her wrist.

"I'm back, *Vieja*. I'm back." His voice sounded as if he had swallowed tar.

She helped him sit up, his back resting against the cool wood. "And?"

"The burning is gone."

"You saw her? The gringa to whom you gave the stone?"

"The gringa and two other Ghosted Ones, including a dog."

Consuelo rocked back on her heels, eyes narrowed with puzzlement. "You could see them just as you are seeing me now?"

"Yes, but only the girl and the dog could see me."

Consuelo reached into one of the pockets in her voluminous clothes and brought out a small container of orange juice. "Sip this and then we'll take the horses into the hills and you must tell me everything, Luis."

So he sipped and gradually felt stronger, more grounded. They saddled two horses and wandered into the steep, high mountains behind the hacienda. He talked, she questioned. Pretty soon, they were so high that the valley shimmered like a mirage below them. A condor glided through the moonlight, its wingtips varnished in pale light. A good omen, Luis thought. The condor was rare, but it embodied freedom.

"How does your hand feel now?" Consuelo asked.

"It doesn't hurt." Luis held his palm faceup and Consuelo shone a flashlight on it. There were traces of red that looked raised, like a thin scar, but the pain was completely gone.

"While I journeyed, it pulsed and the pulses got stronger as I neared the woman."

"Did you see Tyler?" she asked.

Had he? Details of the journey already had faded. It seemed that something had happened related to Tyler or to Nash or to both of them, but he didn't know precisely what that *something* was. The more he thought about it, struggling to remember, the clearer was his sense that Tyler was being housed at the Ponce facility. The moment he felt this certainty, he recalled his entire conversation with the girl and suspected her father was being held at the Ponce complex, too.

"You must answer the woman's e-mail, Luis. I know you've hesitated about doing this, but it's clear from your journey that you must. And then you must go to the States and settle this once and for all."

"My intervention won't settle anything. Besides, my hand is fine now."

Consuelo stopped her horse, Luis stopped his. The horses whinnied in the silence and pawed at the ground. Even in the dark, Luis felt the moment when Consuelo turned her ancient eyes on him. Then she shocked him by laughing. "You're afraid. I can't believe it. You're actually afraid."

"I am not."

"You are. That's it. When your hand was on fire, your fear drove you out of the jungle. You have been hiding here in the mountains, Luis, hoping the situation would resolve itself. A situation that *you* helped bring about by passing on knowledge that should never have left our tribe."

His anger leaped out from some forbidden pocket deep inside him. "They already had the technology. All I gave them was the ingredient to stabilize the ghosting. And the money they paid me, Consuelo, bought supplies for the tribe—*your* tribe, my adopted family."

"I already know your relationship to my people," she said dryly. "What is your point, Luis?"

"The money bought food the tribe didn't have, paid for Western medicines that did what herbs and spells and incantations couldn't do for the children who were dying, for the couples who could not conceive. Because of that money, the tribe now has a future. Five years ago, the tribe numbered just eighty-four. We had seven children five and under. Seven, that's all. The tribe's future depended on *seven* children. Now the children are thriving and the tribe is—"

"One hundred and forty-two strong." Her voice sounded weary. "Yes, I know the statistics. And I stand here and tell you we cannot escape the greedy encroachment of civilization. Every day, our tribe's territory shrinks by twenty acres or more and we are driven deeper and deeper into the jungle. In a decade, maybe less, there will be no more jungle and those of us who remain will be living on government reservations, like mutant animals in a zoo. Perhaps our youth will be alcoholics. Perhaps they will turn their backs on our ways and seek their place in the western world. Perhaps they will know enough about ghosting to carry on our traditions, in some form. We don't know. Since the beginning, our shamans have foreseen this divergence. But none has seen the outcome."

"So what are you saying, *Vieja?* Just what are you saying? That we should stop struggling to survive?"

"I am saying that ghosting is an art that must be taught."

"Without children, there is no one to whom the art can be taught."

"Then the ability will die. It cannot be sold to the highest bidder."

She tapped her horse's sides, urging it forward. His horse followed. The trail narrowed to a ribbon of moss and dirt, and their horses picked their ways carefully across the precipitous terrain. With each step, with each moment of silence between them, his emotional battle escalated.

"Right now," she said, "you're thinking that I am an ignorant woman who has never been out of Ecuador and what can I possibly know about the larger world? Right now, you are justifying what you did. You saved the tribe, you gave the tribe a future . . .''

Luis said nothing. It was precisely what he was thinking.

''But when the Internet arrived in Quito, when all those Internet cafés sprang up overnight in the new city, Luis, I was there. I learned to navigate that weightless world. I paid my eighty cents an hour because I had to know what I was missing. And I came to one conclusion. Our people won't all die at the same time. So there will always be at least one of us who knows the ghosting. As long as there is one, then there can be two. If there are two, there can be four.

''But this knowledge cannot be sold or given away for some ephemeral greater good of the tribe. It must be taught, it must be shared, it must be lived. That is the correct and only thing to do. And if the knowledge is shared in the way it is intended, then perhaps in this strange new world there is a way that ghosting can be used to benefit others. But these gringos are not using it to benefit others. And since you have given them something of ours, you must take it back and correct what you set in motion.''

Luis had heard enough. He galloped ahead, the cold air biting his eyes until they teared. His anger and pride collapsed into shame and when the shame was used up, the only thing that remained was a naked fear that he would fail in what he must do.

4

Renie followed the visible woman into the RV, Katie and Lucky right behind her. The instant she saw the woman seated at the table—an *invisible* woman—she felt as if her life had unraveled completely. It was one thing to live what she had lived through these last weeks with her husband

and her daughter. But it was something else entirely to discover they weren't alone, that there were other invisible freaks out here in the universe. And hey, if there was one more, then there could be dozens, right? Christ, for all she knew, there might be an entire race of invisible people, sharing the air that she breathed, sharing the planet, sharing her living room and her bedroom, a species of voyeurs.

"Hummingbird?" said the woman, rising from the table, her mouth twitching into a quick, beautiful smile.

"Uh, yes. Sparky?"

"Sparky is actually Abby. I'm Logan," and her hand closed around Renie's, a live, flesh-and-blood hand, warm and dry.

Renie's knees felt as if they were hollow and she sank into the nearest chair. "I don't understand," she whispered.

"Hon," said the woman named Abby, "neither do I. You just can't worry about it, though. We'll explain what we can. But we need to make tracks." Everyone grab a seat. We're outta here."

19
POWER PLAYS

In the first week of its new incarnation, the project had changed in ways that Nash had expected, but that nonetheless made him uncomfortable. Numerous types of lab animals had been shipped in, rats and mice, birds and lizards and snakes, and Christ knew what else Colleen and Farris had ordered. Some of them had been shrouded already on a smaller and more refined version of the platform he'd used three years ago with Logan and Tyler. Farris had put Colleen in charge of the lab animals, but because Nash was still needed to oversee the actual shrouding, he'd seen more than he wanted to of the direction that part of the project seemed to be headed.

At the moment, he was in the apartment with Tyler and Andy Townsend, videotaping their chess game. He had to sit on a tall stool to do it because his leg now hurt constantly. At times, the pain was so bad that his cane seemed no more substantial than a twig and he was actually afraid that if he stood with his full weight on both legs, his right leg would buckle. At night when the pain often intensified, he had begun using a walker to get around, but only within the confines of his home and only when he was alone.

Both Andy and Tyler wore clothes, so they were visible, but since neither of them wore gloves their hands remained invisible. When a chess piece moved, it seemed to move of its own volition, exactly the kind of stuff the committee members loved to see on tape.

The time he spent here, with them, was his fieldwork. It was what made everything worthwhile, all the lies and the bullshit and the endless bureaucracy. Every hour here expanded his own knowledge and understanding of the effects of prolonged invisibility. He had thought a great deal during this last week about what this new incarnation of the project meant now and might mean in the future. He had reached a kind of peace about the whole thing and had made some important personal decisions about his role in the project.

Oddly, his decisions had coincided with images of the committee members sitting around a VCR, discussing the potential ramifications of the Invisibles. In his imaginings, they talked about the Invisibles in much the same way that Andy had in his impressive speech, as a new species, a prototype for some entirely new way of being. He intended to document as much evidence as he could to substantiate that idea.

Tyler had been playing chess for several years now, pitting himself against the electronic set that had taken up permanent residence on the coffee table or against any of the employees who would play him. He was alarmingly proficient at the game, but from the looks of it, so was Andy. Nash wondered how long Andy had been playing before he'd gotten here. Probably years, he thought, judging from the moves he made.

"How long have you been playing chess, Doctor Townsend?" Nash asked.

"Oh, about two hours."

Nash laughed. "I didn't mean this particular game."

"Until two hours ago, when Tyler explained the basics, I never played a game of chess."

Nash slowly lowered the camera. "That's impossible," he blurted out. "You just executed a strategy that Bobby Fisher used."

"I did?" Andy seemed genuinely surprised.

Tyler chuckled. "I keep telling you, George, shrouding affects everyone differently. Andy was a bright guy before he got zapped and the shrouding seems to have enhanced his intelligence."

Nash's thoughts raced through various types of intelligence tests he could administer to Andy. Of course, they wouldn't mean much without knowing what his IQ was before he was shrouded. With the committee—and thus, the NSB and the Pentagon—backing this project a hundred percent, however, he could get that information easily enough. Some distinct advantages had emerged as a result of this "merger."

"What other changes have you noticed in yourself, Andy?"

He unzipped his jacket and a moment later was invisible from the waist up. "You mean, besides the most obvious change?"

"I can see Tyler's influence in that move." But hey, it made good video and the brass always loved this stuff.

"C'mon, Tyler, it's your move," Andy said with a trace of impatience in his voice.

"So besides the obvious changes, Andy, what other changes have you noticed?" Nash asked again.

"We've already talked in depth about that, George. Let's talk about your leg instead. How badly it hurts these days. How you're eating painkillers like candy. Codeine, isn't it? Yeah, let's talk about that and about why the effects of a childhood polio should make your leg hurt *now*. As a physician, I frankly think there are some very serious underlying problems we should be looking at."

How does he know about the codeine? Nash didn't take codeine when he was with Andy and Tyler. He stopped the camera and rewound it to the point where Andy had started talking about his leg. He would tape over it and didn't even intend to respond to Andy's remarks about his leg.

"Are you less patient and more cynical?" Nash asked.

Andy laughed—not at what Nash had said, but because he completely ignored Andy's observations. "Sure. More cynical and less patient. But that's probably because I'm locked up, George. My dreams are more vivid, sometimes violent. But I think that's because no one has made good on that promise about my brother. Remember that promise, George? That I'd be able to see Jim?"

"He's been under the weather. We wanted to keep you from being exposed to whatever he's got."

"How considerate."

Nash ignored the thick sarcasm in Andy's voice. The camera was still running, recording all of this, exactly the sort of detail the committee wanted. "Tyler got sick once. It was real difficult to treat him. So we don't take chances."

"The only time I've been sick," Tyler said, "was right after the shrouding."

"What's Jim have?" Andy asked.

Bad lie, Nash thought. It sometimes slipped his mind that Andy was an ER doc. "The flu."

"This isn't flu season, George."

"Hey, that's what our doctors told me, so that's what I'm telling you."

"Your doctors. Tell me about *your* doctors, George. What's their background? What kind of medicine do they practice in the real world?"

"I'll drop their résumés off, Andy. Looks like it's your move." Nash turned off the video camera. "You boys want something from the kitchen for dinner tonight? Fresh tuna, baked potatoes . . ."

"Only if you have some pretty señoritas serving the

stuff,'' Tyler said. "Which reminds me. Whatever happened to *my* list of requests, George? So far, I haven't seen an increase in personal privacy, the restrictions on my use of the Internet haven't been lifted, and I sure as hell haven't seen any gorgeous woman walk through that door who's ready for a night of hot sex.''

"It won't all happen overnight. These things take time.''

Tyler laughed. "Shit, George. You'd make a great politician.''

"He *is* a politician,'' chirped Colleen as she strolled into the apartment carrying a lab tray. "Thanks to his political skills, you two are allowed to stay in the same apartment. So be grateful, Tyler. You at least have the company of another Invisible.'' She set the tray on the table next to the chess set. "Who's first?''

"Jesus,'' Tyler groaned. "The vampire lady is back.''

"This is the third time today you've drawn our blood,'' Andy said. "What gives?''

"We're just testing blood sugar levels at various times during the day.''

"The same thing can be done through urine samples.''

"Well, we're running other tests, too.''

"Such as?''

Nash smiled to himself. Apparently Colleen also had forgotten that Andy was a doc and now she was scrambling for answers. "Cholesterol levels, enzyme levels . . . a lot of stuff. So, who's first?'' And she flashed her most bewitching smile, as if that alone would compensate for her lies.

"Okay, me first,'' said Tyler.

Colleen handed Tyler the syringe and Nash turned on the video camera again and watched on the camera's screen. The only thing he saw—and that every other Visible would see—was the syringe rising up like some sort of poltergeist phenomenon. Then it moved to a diagonal position and began to fill with blood. The brass would love this, too.

Colleen waited until Tyler was through and had handed

her the spent syringe before she passed one to Nash. It was
just a security precaution, like the trank syringes in her fanny
pack and the trank gun in the pocket of his windbreaker and
the Glock he carried under his jacket. Only once in three
years had they ever used anything on Tyler and that had
been way back in the beginning, when he'd been placed in
the apartment. Nash suspected that Andy Townsend would
be as compliant. After all, both men knew their best hope
of regaining their visibility lay here.

What they didn't know—what no one knew, not even
Colleen—was that Nash had known for a long time how to
reverse the process. It wasn't always successful and he'd
never tried it on humans, but the theory was sound. He'd
kept it to himself because it enabled him to study the long-
term effects of shrouding on a human being, and how many
other researchers on the planet had that kind of opportunity?
This was his life's work, after all, not just a job or a whim,
and he deserved compensation for all the dedication and
passion he had poured into it. Yes, there were times when
guilt raised its hideous head and chided him for using Tyler
like this, for playing God with another man's life. But he
made up for it by providing Tyler with everything he desired,
except for his freedom.

Except for a woman with whom he could have sex.

Except for unlimited Internet use.

Now there was Andy, who would yield more information,
more knowledge.

Of course, he would have to do something about amending
the conditions in his contract with the NSB and the committee. They wanted reversibility in the shrouding by the end
of the year. But once they had that, he would be expendable
and they would do whatever they wanted with Tyler and
Andy. So, one way or another, he either would get an exten-
sion or he would free them.

"Excuse me, Doctor Nash." A soldier marched into the
apartment, one of Farris's good soldiers, a young, burly

brute of a man who wore more paraphernalia than a marine landing on the shores of enemy territory. "Mr. Farris needs to speak with you."

The interruption pissed Nash off. Farris was always trying to pull rank, to make it clear to Nash that he was no longer top dog. "Tell him I'll be there when I finish here."

"He needs to see you now, sir. I've got a cart waiting outside."

A cart, for Christ's sake. "I'll be along in a few minutes, Sergeant. Please wait outside."

The sergeant started to say something, but apparently thought better of it. He turned on a dime and left the apartment. "That turkey's got an orange up his ass," snickered Tyler, and he and Andy exploded with laughter.

Nash and Colleen exchanged a glance. Her brows lifted slightly, asking what was up. Nash shrugged. No telling what the hell was going on with Farris.

Andy finished drawing his vial of blood and Colleen capped it, put the vial and the spent syringe in their appropriate spots in the lab tray. "Thanks, guys. You make my life easier."

"C'mon," Tyler said. "We're the reason you're pulling in nearly two hundred grand a year."

Colleen laughed, but it was an uneasy laugh, Nash noticed, and wondered how Tyler knew anything at all about what Colleen made. "Let me know who wins the chess game," Nash said, and picked up his video camera case and left the apartment with Colleen.

Neither of them spoke until they had passed the control room. "Did I ever tell you about my nephew, George?"

"Your nephew?" Nash shook his head. She had told him about her two sisters, her alcoholic mother and philandering father, every sordid detail about her dysfunctional childhood, but he had never heard about her nephew. "Uh, no, I don't think I've heard about him."

"He's a smart-ass. You tell him the sky is blue, he insists

it's gray and argues with you about it until you're convinced the sky really *is* gray.''

''Sounds like a lawyer in the making.''

She smiled at that. ''Yeah, but he's a brat. He takes liberties that kids aren't supposed to take. He crosses the boundary between kid and adult on a daily basis. Tyler and Andy are like that. We've been too familiar with them, too . . .'' She paused, searching for the right word. ''Too chummy, I guess. We wanted so much for Tyler not to create waves that we catered to him. And now we're catering to Andy.''

''You bet your ass we are,'' Nash countered. ''Research goes a lot more smoothly when the subject of your research isn't hostile and doesn't have to be zonked out on Thorazine.''

''You're not hearing me, George.'' She turned to him, her black, shiny hair curling just so at the edges of her jaw, hair that his fingers ached to touch. ''*We're* in charge, but they mock us, poke fun at us, try to humiliate us, and they . . . they . . .''

''*We're* the enemy,'' Nash said, his voice quiet. ''What the hell do you expect?''

The sergeant marched over to them. ''Are you ready, Doctor Nash?''

Nash ignored the good little soldier and gave Colleen a look that said, *Do you get it?* Then he looked at the soldier. ''Sure, let's get going.''

2

''You're a convincing liar,'' Tyler said, laughing. ''He believes you never played chess before.''

''He can't see my face, that's why it's so convincing.''

''You think she's screwing him?'' Tyler asked, setting a tray filled with raw vegetables on the table.

"Probably," Andy agreed, even though he didn't give a shit what Colleen did or with whom. He pulled his jacket back on. The temperature in the apartment today stood about sixty-two degrees, a bit crisp for his tastes. The cooler the ambient air, the easier it was for the thermal-sensitive camera in the living room to detect them. The jacket made him more visible, but what the hell. Privacy in this place was a pipe dream.

"You think she's attractive?"

"Gimme me a break, Tyler. She's a knockout."

He nibbled at a piece of raw broccoli. "My wife is prettier. Classier. And shit, Logan's got scruples, something Colleen has never heard of."

"You don't talk much about her," Andy remarked.

"We weren't married more than a couple of months when we signed up for Nash's little project. He was offering thirty grand and assurance that the process was reversible and we passed the tests. We got fifteen, Logan freaked during the shrouding, and I'm here and who the hell knows where she is? There's not much to say beyond that. Nash says she's alive, though."

"How do you think she's fared all these years?"

"Logan's a survivor. I'm sure she's done just fine. What about your wife and kid? How do you think they're doing?"

He'd thought of little else this past week and not once had he doubted that Renie and Katie were getting along just fine and were trying to figure out where he was and how they could free him. "Good. I think they're doing really good. Both of them know how to cope with change."

For hours during the past week, Andy had lain awake at night, thinking about his life. Sometimes, the scenes unfolded with an exquisite slowness, almost as if they were happening right then, as if they were real and this were just some terrible nightmare. Other times, the scenes rushed through him, memories so fleeting that they seemed to have happened to someone else. Maybe someday he would be looking back at his time as an Invisible and these memories would be quick and elusive as well.

The memory that kept returning to him again and again was the night he'd awakened to find Renie lying beside him, her eyes wide open, staring at the ceiling.

What is it? he'd asked.

Andy, can you give Buddha an overdose of morphine?

It was the second time she'd asked and his answer had been the same. *That's murder.*

He has a feeding tube. He can't move. He can't swallow. And he's aware of it all. That's murder, Andy. The morphine would be humane.

Jesus, Ren, I could lose my license.

No one will know, except you and me and Buddha. It's what he wants.

It's out of the question.

And then he'd rolled over and gone back to sleep and they'd never discussed it again. Not long afterward, Buddha had passed away in his sleep and Andy always had wondered if Renie had helped him along. The law called it assisted suicide, but that was hardly the case if Buddha had been asleep. What was more likely, he thought, was that Renie had *delivered* him, a term favored by the Hemlock Society and the Right to Die groups, *delivered* him by covering his mouth and nose, *delivered* her father because he was suffering and her husband wouldn't order additional morphine that would have allowed him to pass on painlessly.

He'd thought a lot about that in the past week. "My wife's fine," he repeated, and wondered if he was trying too hard to convince himself.

"Let's get some fresh air," Tyler said, and nodded toward the sliding glass doors.

They stepped outside, walked past the small trampoline that Nash had brought them for exercise, and paused at a patch of dirt to the side of the patio. Andy glanced at the tall concrete wall to his right, hating it, then dropped his head back and peered up at the screen twenty feet overhead and wished he could see more stars.

"Okay, let's go through it again," Tyler said quietly.

Andy picked up a stick and sketched the layout of the facility: four rectangles, pairs that were side by side, facing north to south, connected by long passageways. Rectangles one and two, the easternmost complexes, held the front lobby and a number of offices that were a front, Tyler said, for what really went on here. Here were the cafeteria and dining area, staff rooms, and the general administrative offices. The medical area lay in the northeast rectangle.

During a code-three alarm—a breech of security in their apartment—steel panels immediately descended, sealing the apartment and all four buildings. Tyler wasn't sure whether the passages between buildings were also sealed off, but it made sense that they would be, Andy thought. Tyler also believed that the ceiling sprinklers in the hallways outside the apartment would come on during a code-three alarm, but couldn't be sure because he'd never attempted to escape.

Rectangles three and four, in the westernmost complex, housed the heart of the facility, security and private offices for the researchers and scientists, the psychologists, docs, and everyone else associated with the Tesla Project. Tyler was pretty sure that one or both of these buildings had rooftop helipads. Their apartment lay at the southern end of the southwest building. At the north end of the northwest building lay the research area. He believed that was where Jim was being held and Tyler felt certain there was a Tesla device in the research area that Nash's people used to shroud objects and small animals.

"So it should be a straight shot from us to research," Andy said.

"Yeah, but every few hundred feet are thermal sensors that will pick us up in a heartbeat. They're calibrated to pick up any temperature from ninety-four degrees and up. Right now, our body temps are about ninety-five point six.''

"So we need to lower our body temps a degree."

"Meditation and a cold shower beforehand can lower it about a half degree, but I'm still working on the other half degree. Even if we manage to get our body temps down the full degree, we're going to be moving around a lot, which will bring the temp right back up. I'm not sure about this part yet. The other thorn is buying ourselves enough time when we bust out of here so that we can get to the other end of the building without the alarm being triggered. That means we'll have to do this at night, when there's just a skeleton crew around here, and we'll have to do it on a night when Fatso is in the security room out there."

"Fatso?"

"He's a nice ole guy who should've retired ten years ago. But Nash keeps him on because he feels sorry for him. He falls asleep a lot out there in the security room or he sits in here and shoots the shit with me. We'll need him in that booth the night we bust out."

"What nights does he work?"

"Weekends."

"So how do we get out once we have Jim?"

Tyler picked up the stick and tapped the north end of the building, just outside the research area. "About the time they got the dog to use in shrouding experiments, they built a wall around the north end of the research area so the dog could go outside. It's similar to what we've got around our little play area, but not as secure. I think that's the best way out once we spring your brother and test the Tesla machine."

"Suppose the alarm sounds and the sprinklers come on? Then we're visible."

"We have to make sure the sprinklers don't come on."

"Does the computer in the security booth here control anything outside the apartment?"

"How far is it from here to the north end of the building?"

"The equivalence of three blocks. Long blocks."

" Then this place is huge."

"Yeah, but we're talking about four buildings, connected by long passageways. That's how they saved money, with those corridors. It's cheaper to build long corridors that connect buildings than it is to construct one huge building."

"Hey, it's still a long way and if the alarm goes off, we could be cut off at the pass anywhere along those three miles."

"And that's why we're taking the time to plan this."

Andy suddenly had grave misgivings about this plan. There had to be a better way to bust out without having to risk a three-mile trek past thermal sensors and ceiling sprinklers that could come on at any second. But what?

Embrace the chaos, he thought. Right. *And trust your hunches.*

"Dinner's coming. Hear it?"

Andy listened to the night noises, then he heard it, that clatter of wheels against the floor outside the apartment. "Let's get back inside."

3

The sergeant and his spiffy electric cart, one of the new editions that had arrived at the complex since the takeover, delivered Nash to the entrance of the research wing. "Mr. Farris is in the control room," the soldier said.

Nash limped out without acknowledging the young schmuck in any way. He leaned heavily on his cane as he made his way over to the door. Before he swiped his card through the security slot, he popped two more codeine pills and chewed them up. They would work for an hour or two and then the pain would shriek to life again.

The heavy metal doors clicked open and he limped into the hushed, rarefied air of the research department. Most of this department's employees had kept bankers' hours in the past to avoid overtime pay and other expenses that frayed at the budget. But now that the budget wasn't an issue, all of that would begin to change. Farris had announced as much only two days ago during a staff meeting. The new schedule would be implemented the first of the month, with researchers and scientists working in three shifts like hospital employees.

We need people on this day and night, Farris had said. By *this,* Farris had been referring to the training of four individuals for shrouding, finding a way to reverse the shrouding process on command rather than waiting for the process to reverse itself, which still hadn't happened with Tyler or with Andy, and collating the massive amounts of data that had been collected so far in the project. An ambitious undertaking, Nash thought, and Farris was tackling it as though it were a military operation.

At the moment, the department was deserted and Nash decided to look in on Jim Townsend before he went to see Farris. After Panther had beaten him up, he'd spent two days in medical, then was moved to a room in research. No, not a room, Nash thought, but a cell with a cot, a toilet, and a sink, where his movements were monitored. He had recovered from his injuries with no apparent ill effects, got his three squares a day, and was allowed to exercise in the department gym, under the supervision of one of the staff.

Bottom line? Jim Townsend was a wild card, kept here only as leverage to maintain Andy's cooperation. But the arrangement couldn't last indefinitely. Farris already had suggested shipping Jim to one of the covert psychiatric facilities, where the government's mistakes disappeared into the system. Nash had argued against it. He thought it best to let Andy see his brother at least once before they did anything. It was only a matter of time before Farris pressed the issue again.

When he turned the corner, he saw that the cell door at the end of the hall stood open. He hurried toward it, practically dragging his bum leg behind him. He found Farris stumbling to his feet, a hand pressed to the gash on his forehead, blood seeping through his fingers. Scattered around the area where Farris had lain were pieces of a wooden chair.

"Jesus, the bastard attacked me," Farris hissed, looking at the blood smeared across his palm. "And took my gun."

"Which way did he go?"

"Toward the exercise yard."

Nash moved out of the room as quickly as his bum leg would allow him, one hand clutching his gun, the other gripping the cane. His mind raced with the endless possibilities. If Jim made it over the fence, if he made it into the fields, if he made it into town, if he made it to a phone, if if if . . . No matter how he looked at it, if Jim Townsend got out, they were fucked.

The door to the yard stood wide open, a slight breeze blowing through. Nash limped to the doorway, silently cursing his leg for slowing him down, and hit the switch that turned on the yard security lights. There, impaled in the glare, was Jim Townsend, scrambling up the wire-mesh fence like some sort of giant spider. *"Townsend,"* Nash shouted. *"Stop right there!"*

But Jim didn't even hesitate. He just moved faster and faster, the fence rattling. Nash limped outside where he would have a better shot and shouted again for Townsend to stop. A small, niggling voice in the back of his head kept telling him something was very wrong with this whole scenario, but Townsend had reached the top of the fence.

Farris tore past Nash, shouting at Nash to shoot him, shoot him fast. *"He's going to tear through the overhead screen and drop over the side. Shoot the bastard!"*

And Nash still hesitated. It was one thing to play God with another man's life but another thing altogether to end it. He had played God for this project, had compromised his beliefs, but he had never killed anyone for the sake of this project. A moment later, Farris fired two shots, fired with a weapon he must have had hidden on his body, and Jim Townsend froze against the fence—then dropped back and struck the ground.

Nash stood there, paralyzed at the sight, and Farris rushed past him, one hand still pressed to his head, and ran over to the body. "He's dead," he called.

And still Nash didn't move. That voice in his head was louder now, hurling up scenes in a nonlinear order—the broken chair in the cell, Farris sending a sergeant to fetch Nash, Farris's head bleeding, the juice in the electrified fence not functioning, the cell door open. Then the scenes fitted together like pieces in a puzzle and Nash's rage propelled him forward.

Farris must have seen something in his face because he suddenly frowned and got to his feet. "We have to get the body—"

Nash fired at the ground inches from Farris's feet. Dirt and pebbles flew up.

"Jesus, George, what—"

He swung his cane and knocked Farris's gun out of his hand. He swung it again and slammed the cane across Farris's stomach, driving him to his knees. He fell forward onto his hands, gasping, and Nash jammed the barrel of his gun against the base of Farris's skull.

"If you *ever* pull a stunt like this again, Ross, I'll kill you and not blink twice."

Just in case Farris wasn't understanding English right then, Nash sank the end of his cane into Farris's ribs, pushing him over onto his side, then got real up-close and personal and jammed the barrel of the gun into his nuts. Farris's eyes bulged, sweat broke out on his face.

"And I'll shoot for your balls, Ross," he whispered. "That's a promise." He stepped back. "Get rid of Townsend's body."

Farris lay there in a fetal position, groaning and clutching his groin.

PART THREE

EMBRACING
CHAOS

JUNE 30—JULY 2

"Probability is the guiding force of everything
in the universe...."
—Scott Adams

20
VISITORS

The sun was barely visible above the trees when the RV pulled alongside the single rusted gas pump at Last Stop Quik Stop. To Logan, the place looked like a last stop she could do without—the parking lot filled with potholes, the windows and doors of the convenience store covered with several years of grime, and the trees at the sides of the property shrieking to be trimmed back.

Her cat peered down from her perch above the stove and mewed softly, asking Logan for a pat and maybe some dinner, thanks. Logan filled Jazzy's bowl and placed it on top of the fridge. Jazzy jumped up there, glanced once toward Lucky, as if to make sure the dog couldn't get to her chow, and proceeded to wolf down dinner.

Over the last two weeks, the visible cat and the invisible dog had reached a kind of truce, except when it came to food. Lucky was always trying to eat the cat food.

"I think this is a bad idea," Abby said. "We can't afford to trust anyone right now."

"We don't have to trust him," Renie replied. "When I

spoke to Sam on the phone, he remembered us. He'll rent us a boat. All you have to do is mention my name.''

''And what're we going to do with the RV when we're out in the swamp?''

''Park it somewhere.''

''Yeah? And where would that be, girl? In this here parking lot? If I leave the RV here, this guy's going to want to know where I'm going. I mean, that would make sense, right?''

''He won't ask questions,'' said Renie. ''We'll pay him not to ask, pay him to rent the boat, it'll be fine.''

''Let's do it,'' Logan said. ''We don't have any other options right now. I'll go in with you, Abby.''

''I'll wait out here with Katie until you're ready to look at the boat,'' Renie said.

For weeks, they had camped in various parts of the Keys, never more than a few miles from the spots that held memories for Logan of her first year as an Invisible. It had brought back all of the strangeness of that time, the terrible loneliness and the even deeper yearning for her life before Nash had entered it. Her life with Tyler. Her life with graduate school. Her life as a Visible. Even if she regained her visibility tomorrow, nothing could redeem the time she had lost, the years that Nash and his obsession and lies had taken from her.

But in all fairness to Nash, she and Tyler weren't without blame. They had seen themselves as adventurers, Nash had offered them thirty grand to indulge that fantasy, and they had accepted the offer. They had read the fine print and signed their names. Now she was three years older and a different species altogether from the woman who had sat on the platform that morning and confessed her misgivings. And Tyler. Surely during the last three years he'd had an opportunity to escape, to find her. So where the hell was he?

And her one possible lead, the Hacienda Manteles, had

gone nowhere. The only thing she'd heard was a standard reply with a description of the place, its rates, and the dates when they had vacancies.

Abby opened the door to the RV and stepped down. Logan followed her out into the humid night air and slipped in behind her when she pushed open the dirty glass door to the shop. An old man was crouched at the end of an aisle, restocking the shelves. "Evening, ma'am."

"Hi. I'm looking for Sam," said Abby.

He straightened, his knees cracking, and grinned. "Reckon you be lookin' at him."

"Hi, Sam." Abby extended her hand. "I'm Abby Sparks. A friend of Renie and Andy Townsend."

"Right, right." He shook her hand vigorously. "Mighty good talkin' to her yesterday. You pickin' up the boat?"

"Yes. I'm actually going to meet them at the Flamingo marina. Is the boat ready?"

"Got two boats you oughta look at. They're out back."

Logan fell into step behind Abby and Sam, close enough so she could get through the door without having to open it again, but far enough behind so her footsteps weren't audible. As soon as she stepped outside, Logan spotted Renie, Katie, and the dog off to the left, near the trees. The dog, tethered to a rope that Katie held, was sniffing through the grass. But she suddenly lifted her head and looked toward them, then started barking.

Sam glanced around, frowning, seeing nothing. "I'm hearin' a dog, but not seein' a dog."

"It's probably in the mangroves somewhere," Abby said.

"I swear I know that bark."

Sam scratched his head and continued to stare off in the direction where Renie and Katie were now trying to quiet Lucky. The dog lurched forward, Katie lost her hold on the rope, and Lucky loped toward them, the rope slapping the ground behind her. Renie and Katie raced after her, trying to grab the rope, step on it, something, but Lucky was swifter.

When Logan raced toward her, the dog simply veered away from her, tail wagging as if it were some kind of game. They couldn't shout at Lucky, not without revealing themselves, so the air rang out with frantic barks, punctuated now and then by a gasp or grunt.

Then Lucky leaped up, her sleek, dark body aimed straight at Sam. Her front paws struck him on the chest and he stumbled back, arms grappling with something he couldn't see. Sam fell against a patch of grass at the side of the building and lay there laughing as Lucky covered his old, withered face with sloppy kisses. His hands moved down her invisible back and he kept saying the same thing over and over, "Jesus God, it's you, Dog, it's you. I knew I recognized that bark. I knew it."

He pushed himself to a sitting position and Lucky sank to the ground, panting hard. Sam's hands followed the invisible rope to the end. "Feels like a rope." His hands patted their way to Lucky's head. "And this feels like a dog." He looked up at Abby. "So how come I can't see the rope or the dog?"

Abby stammered, "Well, it's, uh, complicated."

"It's my fault," Renie said, breathless from running, and dropped to the ground beside him and the dog. "It's me, Sam. Renie. Andy's wife."

"Holy shit." He spoke softly, his eyes wide and startled. "Give me your hand."

Renie put her hand in his. "You remember those sounds you told us about out in the Glades? And about how the birds and insects flee hours before you hear the noises? Well, we found out firsthand what it's from, Sam. They're doing invisibility experiments out there."

"Holy shit," he said again. "But the dog, how come you have the dog?"

"She was out there," Katie said. "They were using her for their experiments."

"The mother, the kid . . . where's the doc?"

"We think they have him," Katie replied. "Logan's here with us, too."

"Who's Logan?"

"Right here," Logan said, and touched his leathery hand.

"She's been an Invisible for three years," Katie told him.

"Holy shit," he whispered for the third time. Sam got slowly to his feet and glanced around uneasily. "Reckon it might be safer to move that RV into the garage out back, where the boats are. Under cover."

"Good idea," Abby agreed. "Thanks. I'll go bring it around."

"Let's go take a look at them boats." Sam glanced from one side to the other and shook his head again. "This'll take some getting used to. Talkin' to empty air."

"I'm on your right," Logan said. "Renie and Katie are on your left. And Lucky's in front of you."

"Makes me dizzy, jus' thinking 'bout it. Reckon the boat's not for any trip to Flamingo, huh?"

Logan and Renie exchanged a glance. "I think we could use a guide, don't you, Logan?"

"Absolutely. You know your way around the Glades pretty well, Sam?"

"Reckon so. Where you headed?"

"To a huge chickee. It's like a village, but without any people. It's where they do their experiments. I think it's close to where you heard the sounds that night you told me about."

"Ayuh. And when you get there, what're you goin' to do?"

"Destroy it," Logan replied.

2

Nash poured himself a second bourbon and limped back to the desk in his study. Papers were spread out on either side of his notebook computer, page after page from his personal files on Tyler, as well as psychiatric reports, observations, and suggestions. Andy Townsend also had a file, but it was considerably thinner. Still, he had yielded important information in the last couple of weeks.

From this massive amount of data, he intended to compile a psychological profile of the ideal candidate for shrouding, a template to present to the committee. If they were going to train four people during the first year of the project's new life, then he was going to be damn sure that no wild cards got into the program. No more Tylers or Logans, no more ordinary citizens like the Townsends.

He laced his fingers together behind his head and rocked back in his chair, staring at the photographs on the wall above his desk. Most of the photos were family stuff, of him and his wife and their kids during the earlier years of their marriage, when things were good. There was one picture of him with the old shaman taken at a Cuban restaurant in Little Havana. They were both laughing at something Colleen had said, and Luis was avoiding the camera, his face turned to one side. A memento of better days, Nash thought, when he and Luis were equals, exploring the vast mysteries of shrouding.

Their friendship had begun to fray when Nash had brought animals into the experiments. It didn't matter to Luis that those early animals were reprehensible creatures—rats, reptiles, roaches, spiders. To Luis, all living creatures were equal and had no place in scientific experiments. When Nash had opened the project to human volunteers, Luis had become less cooperative, angrier, more accusatory.

You cannot play God.

After the Logan and Tyler disaster, Luis had stuck around for another few months, long enough to see Tyler's transfer to the Ponce facility, and then he'd left without any warning, left as abruptly as he had entered Nash's life nearly two decades earlier. A week later, Nash had gotten a letter from Luis, postmarked from Miami, promising that he would be back and that if Nash hadn't corrected his "heinous errors," he would blow the project wide open.

At the time, the threat had seemed ludicrous: Luis versus the NSB. What the hell did he think he'd do? Go to the media? Hire a consultant who would get him booked on *Oprah*? On *Larry King Live*? On the evening news? But over the years, whenever Luis had been sighted by Nash's employees, he had locked down Tyler's apartment and turned the complex into an armored camp.

It had been eighteen months since that last sighting and, during that time, Nash actually found himself missing Luis's input, his ideas, and his knowledge of ghosting, the closest thing he had ever seen to shrouding. Even now, he often wondered if the two tapped into the same energy, but through different venues—one through technology and the other through some mental and spiritual discipline whose true nature eluded Nash.

Over the many years of their association, Nash had hoped that by observing Luis he might learn how to shroud using nothing more than the disciplines that Luis used, the intense focus of his consciousness to achieve what Luis referred to as the *shift.* But *observing* was not the same thing as *doing* and despite Nash's repeated requests, Luis had refused to instruct him in the ways of ghosting.

You would use it to play God.

And so here he was, still mystified by Luis's ability and strangely terrified that the Ecuadorian would return and somehow blow everything wide open. Nash had yet to figure out exactly *how* Luis might do that, but no longer doubted that he could. It seemed he'd spent the last three years braced against that possibility, always looking anxiously over his shoulder, expecting to see the old shaman unfolding from the woodwork.

He turned the photo around, so that it faced the wall. It depressed him to think about Luis for the same reason that it depressed him to think of Logan, of Renie and Katie Townsend. They were all glaring unknowns, wild cards, beyond his control, and therefore a threat to his project. At least Jim Townsend was out of the picture, buried in a pauper's grave somewhere out near Lake Okeechobee, Farris had told him, the only time they had spoken since the night of the shooting.

Dobson knew about it, of course, and even though he hadn't said anything when Nash had told him, his disgust was apparent in his eyes. No, not just disgust. Contempt, a bone-deep contempt for Farris and everything he represented. A few days later, Dobson had mentioned it. *How're we any different from Farris, boss?*

Of course they were different. They were . . .

Don't go there.

He drew his attention back to the computer screen, to the things that he *could* control. He had made a partial list of psychological attributes and read them over now, testing them against some internal gauge.

Self-containment. This was the ability to be so comfortable in your solitude that you didn't need other people. Neither Tyler nor Logan had had this trait three years ago. They'd had it in their marriage, as partners, but not as individuals. He suspected Tyler's isolation these last three years—at the complex, as an Invisible—had taught him how to *navigate* solitude, but that wasn't the same thing.

Strong sense of self. Farris's shrinks, he knew, would rip this one apart because his wording was wrong. But Nash grasped the essence. This was the ability to stick to what you believed even when consensus reality was screaming that you were wrong. If you saw the sky as green and authority—which represented consensus reality—kept telling you no, the sky is blue, you wouldn't change your mind simply because everyone else disagreed with you. This trait was essential for navigating areas that were invisible.

Belief in a higher authority. He fully expected Farris's shrinks to give their stamp of approval for this one. It covered everything from a belief in God or the government or some other icon as the final word, the final arbiter, the gigantic period at the end of a sentence. These were people who felt most comfortable when rules were spelled out and a moral code was delineated. They liked black-and-white worlds, no gray areas. In many ways, of course, this attribute was the direct opposite of the one before it. But the ideal candidate would be able to accommodate both traits.

"George, George. It won't work."

The voice, barely a flutter of softness somewhere behind him, paralyzed him. He couldn't move, couldn't draw or expel his breath, couldn't even blink.

"You're still playing God, my friend."

Nash's muscles suddenly released him and he turned slowly in his chair, noticing how it squeaked. His arms dropped away from his head and came to rest in his lap. The taste of bourbon clung to his tongue, the spit in his mouth dried up, he could barely swallow. He glanced toward the window, where the blinds were drawn against the darkness, then blinked against the dim light in the room. As his eyes became accustomed to it, he saw a shape unfolding from the shadows. It was him. The shaman. Here. In his home, his den, his sanctuary.

"Luis." His name felt sharp and foreign against Nash's tongue, as if he'd bitten into a bitter bark or inhaled a mouthful of dirt. "My God."

He looked unchanged, dressed in the same kind of clothes he'd been wearing the last time Nash had seen him, baggy blue pants and a cheap cotton shirt, the clothes of any com-

mon *campesino*. Even his sandals were humble, handwoven
apragatos.

"How . . . how di—did you get in here?" Nash asked,
already knowing that Luis would laugh at the question, that
the question, in fact, had no bearing in the reality this man
inhabited. "I mean, when did you get in town?"

Luis slapped his hand against his thigh and howled with
laughter. "Word games, George. I never really left." He
didn't just step out of the shadows—he *unfolded* from them
and moved into the dim light cast by the lamp on Nash's
desk. His hair looked grayer, but just as thick, and he had
grown a beard since Nash had last seen him. "You won't
win this battle, George. I gave you ample time to correct what
you did, but it's only gotten worse. You don't understand the
rules. You have never understood the rules."

"I make the rules."

"Really?"

The shadows swallowed him again and a moment later,
he stood less than a foot in front of Nash. Yet, Nash hadn't
seen him move. Before he could say anything, Luis touched
his cool, deft fingertips to Nash's forehead and images
exploded in his mind, images of the Tesla village burning,
of Colleen and Farris fucking, of soldiers in the Ponce facility
armed with M16s. Then the whole thing collapsed into a
rushing river of images and sensations and emotions that he
couldn't sort out because everything came at him too quickly.

"You are not God," Luis whispered, and pain burst in
the center of Nash's body and he gasped and doubled over.

When he could finally breathe again and could straighten
up in his chair, the old shaman was gone.

Nash shot to his feet so fast that his cane, resting against
the side of his chair, clattered to the floor and his right leg
buckled. He went down hard, knees striking the floor first,
and then fell forward onto his hands, gasping from the pain.
For long moments, he sucked air in between his clenched
teeth, struggling against the pain that sang through his leg.

When it subsided somewhat, he rocked back onto his heels and grabbed on to the corner of his desk with one hand and picked up his cane with the other.

He limped his way over to the walker near the window, hooked the cane over the handle, and now moved around the room, turning on lights. Nothing. No Luis. He pushed the walker through the rest of the house, checking closets, supply rooms, bathrooms, even under the beds. Luis was nowhere in sight.

Nash turned on the security lights outside and pushed the walker through the door and out into the yard, following the sidewalk that angled down toward the pool. Nothing. It was entirely possible he hadn't been here physically, that it had all been some sort of shamanic trick of consciousness. Yet, the experience had been too real for that. Luis had *touched* him. Even now, Nash felt the residue of those cool fingertips against his forehead.

He returned to his den and walked slowly around the room, lights glaring now so that every corner was illuminated, exposed. He checked the walls and the floor for some sign of Luis and found bits of dirt in the corner where he initially had seen him. He slid a piece of paper under it, scooping it up, and carried it over to his desk. He examined it under the glare of the florescent lamp, touched it, rubbed it between his fingers. Real, the stuff was real. It might have been there all along, but Nash doubted it. His cleaning lady had come earlier today and she was thorough.

But even more disturbing, he thought, were the images that had rushed through him when Luis had touched his forehead. *The Tesla village burning, Colleen in bed with Farris . . .* What the hell had all that meant? Had the old man simply touched all his surface fears or had those images been a warning?

Nash stood there near his desk, clutching the handles of the walker, his frustration and fear mounting inside him, his heart slamming against his ribs. He suddenly swept up his cane, swung it, and shrieked, *"Bastard, you bastard,"* and slammed the cane down on the framed photo of Luis.

It shattered, bits of glass and pieces of the frame flying off like miniature missiles. Nash kept swinging the cane and letting it fall, swing and smash, swing and smash, the rhythm so strangely soothing that he no longer felt any pain in his leg. He even moved through the room without his walker. *Swing and smash, swing and smash, swing and smash.*

And when the cane finally swung down to his side, he felt depleted, weak, used up, and backed into the nearest chair and sat down. He was breathing hard, as if he'd been sprinting, and sweat seeped from his pores. The mess in the room was pretty bad, but his leg didn't hurt, not even a whisper of pain.

"You can't defeat me, old man," he said softly. "You don't even know what the battle is about."

And then, to his utter horror, he began to cry, to *weep,* for Chrissakes, his fists pressed into his eyes, sobs shuddering through his body. *You did this to me, old man.* Of course he had. This was part of Luis's strategy, to put lies into his mind, to *infect* him.

He pushed out of the chair and actually made it across the room without having to use the cane. He called Panther's cell number and felt an enormous relief when Panther answered after the second ring. "Yeah, boss?"

"Where are you, Panther?"

"On the houseboat, at the marina. We're just getting ready to switch shifts out at the village. Why?"

"Get out there now. I want double the usual number of men out there on every shift."

"Not a problem. What's up?"

"I think Luis Manteles is back in town."

"I read you. We'll get out there right away."

"Stay in touch. My cell phone will be on."

"Will do."

As soon as they hung up, Nash called Dobson at home.

"Can you meet me at Homestead?" Nash asked.

"Sure. What's up?"

"I think Luis is in town."

"You think or you know?"

"He was, uh, here in my house."

"*Physically* there?"

"Yes."

"What do you want to do?"

"I'll meet you at Homestead, then we'll go out to the facility."

"I'm on my way."

When they disconnected, Nash rifled through his desk drawer, certain that he had saved that old letter from Luis. The threatening letter. The letter that promised repercussions. He went through mountains of papers, oceans of files and folders, but didn't find it. Frustration overwhelmed him. Maybe he had imagined that letter, maybe he had dreamed it up, maybe the goddamn thing didn't even exist. Was that possible?

No, no, he *remembered* the letter. But he needed to see it, to hold it, to read the words again. He needed to be *absolutely sure*. He jerked out one drawer and then another and another, and dumped the contents on the floor. Papers spilled from the files and lay strewn across the broken glass. Nash, on his knees now, clawed through papers, memos, copies of faxes, shocked that he couldn't find the stupid envelope.

He was sure he'd kept it. Of course he had kept it. He never would throw away something like that. He dumped out another drawer and there it was, the envelope with his name and address on the front in Luis's perfect script. *George Nash, PhD.* He tore it open, his fingers fumbling to unfold the single sheet of paper.

You have created an abomination. Your heinous errors will haunt you, but I don't know if that will be enough to change the course of events or to lighten the darkness in your heart. If you don't correct what you have done, then I will do it for you. This is not a threat, old friend. It's a promise, one warrior to another.

Luis

Nash read the words twice, three times, then crumpled the sheet of paper and shoved it down inside the pocket of his jeans.

21
SABOTAGE

Renie thought the airboat was perfect for what they needed. It was about half the height and size of a normal airboat, low enough so they could propel it with long paddles. It also had a smaller airplane engine and propeller that were standard on ordinary airboats. Sam had assured them the airboat could reach 100 miles an hour on the open water even if the water had saw grass growing in it. Airboats were noisy, but they were like hydrofoils—they skimmed the surface of shallow water where other powerboats couldn't go and got you where you were going very fast. But they weren't quiet. That worried her.

At the moment, Sam occupied the chair in the pilot's perch, which rose about five feet above the deck, and steered the airboat through a narrow channel. They were wearing earplugs to block the horrendous noise. Even though the plugs were visible, it was very dark out here. Sam and Abby swore the plugs were hardly visible at all.

Katie had settled in a spot at the front of the airboat, the dog beside her, and turned the powerful searchlight this way and that so Sam could see where he was steering. Renie, Logan, and Abby worked in the midsection, preparing what they would need to destroy the Tesla village.

Renie had no misgivings this time about venturing into the Glades. Even though she didn't like it any more than she had on June 8, she was doing what had to be done. She was, she thought, following Andy's advice: embracing chaos. Her deepest anxiety was of what would happen if, when all was said and done, when she had embraced chaos over and over again, they didn't regain their visibility.

Logan repeatedly had assured her this scenario was unlikely. The dog obviously had been shrouded before and regained her visibility and, according to the notes she'd found on the hard drive she'd stolen, the village usually regained visibility within twelve hours. It was more likely, Logan argued, that she and Tyler would spend the rest of their lives as Invisibles because they had been that way for so long. Years versus weeks, as if time made the vital difference.

Renie didn't find this argument particularly reassuring. After all, Lucky was still invisible and, so far, neither she nor Katie had experienced anything that gave them reason to hope the effects of the shrouding were wearing off.

Overall, Katie seemed to have adjusted to their situation far better than Renie. For her, this was just another adventure—more dangerous, certainly, than any other adventure she'd experienced—but an adventure nonetheless. Of course, she also believed the situation was temporary. In the event that it turned out to be permanent, it wouldn't take Katie long to get a sense of just how different her life would be.

Renie just wanted her life back the way it had been. She wanted to sleep next to Andy at night and to hear Katie chattering on the phone with her friends. She wanted to show and sell houses and property again. And most of all, she wanted to forget that she felt like the progenitor of a new species.

It had occurred to her numerous times that a couple of calls—to a colleague, to Iris with her numerous political contacts, to Andy's boss at the hospital—would split open Nash's secret. *Hey, Paul, it's Renie. We aren't missing. We're invisible and Andy is missing*. . . . But that wouldn't solve the problem of invisibility and might even make matters worse. Nash and his people had kept Tyler's existence a secret for three years and seemed to have taken extraordinary precautions to do so. No telling what other unscrupulous types might try to do. From time to time, she had visions of herself and her family living in huge cages, where they were periodically subjected to horrifying medical experiments.

Yeah, forget the media route. Too risky, too many unknowns. Their best option right now was to use their invisibility to their advantage.

At the end of the channel, moonlight spilled across the water in front of them, eliminating the need for the searchlight. Katie turned it off and Sam cut the engine back to idle. They all removed their earplugs.

"The place where I heard the noise that night was 'bout a quarter of a mile from here," Sam said, his voice hushed. "Reckon this village you tol' us 'bout can't be too far."

"It was in a lagoon," Renie said.

"A lagoon." From his backpack, Sam pulled out a hand-drawn map and a small flashlight. He smoothed the paper against his thigh, studying it, nodding to himself. "Yeah, okay, I know this place. Haven't been there since the wife passed on, but me and her . . . we used to fish in there. I—"

"I hear something," Katie whispered.

"Me, too," Logan agreed.

Abby cocked her head, listening. "Only thing I hear is insects."

"Boats," Renie said softly. "And they're headed this way."

"I don't hear nothin'," Sam said.

"Their hearing is better than ours, Sam," Abby reminded him. "Better kill the engine and that flashlight."

Renie moved up to the front of the airboat with Katie and slung an arm over Lucky's back. The dog whined softly, pawed at the floor of the airboat, and squirmed away from Renie. She found a spot in the midsection of the airboat and plopped down, her face hidden between her paws.

"She's remembering," Katie remarked.

Logan warned Abby and Sam that the dog was directly in front of them, and then an airboat flew past on the wider channel directly in front of them, its lights blazing in the darkness. Renie saw the pilot perched high in the pilot's seat and two passengers in back. The second airboat zoomed by seconds later, gaining on the first.

"Fool teenagers," Sam muttered.

As soon as the whine of the engines faded, Sam cranked up the outboard again and they edged out into the wider channel. "Lagoon's straight across this channel, on the other side of them line of trees." He pointed in the distance. "Let's just git there fast. Plugs back in."

The noise that exploded from the airboat engine set Renie's teeth on edge and vibrated in her bones. Invisible, she thought, but still susceptible to all the elements of the physical world.

As the airboat skimmed across the wide channel, water sprayed back inside, wetting them and turning them incompletely visible to Abby and Sam—a hand here, an ankle there, a nose, strands of hair, a forehead. The wind dried them nearly as fast the water wet them and by the time they made it to the other side of the channel, they were invisible again.

Sam cut back on the engine and they putted into the

narrower channels. Out came the plugs again. "It's not much farther," he said. "Logan, you'd best get that Zodiac ready."

He coughed suddenly, the first sign of that hacking, terrible cough that had racked his body the day Renie had met him. "You okay, Sam?" she asked when the fit had passed.

"Yeah, sure. That script your husband done give me helped a lot."

Andy and his kindness to strangers, she thought, and suddenly missed him so deeply that she felt the sting of tears at the backs of her eyes. *Andy, I'm embracing chaos and you'd better stay alive till I find you.* "What Zodiac are we talking about?"

"In here, girl," Abby said, patting a supply bag.

Logan untied one end, Abby grabbed the other, and they lifted and shook it until a compact package fell out. A package, Renie thought, that she could see with as much clarity as she could see her daughter and Logan. An *invisible* package.

"This was part of the load of stuff Nash insisted that Tyler and I pack during our first trip into the zone. Let's hope it doesn't have any holes in it."

They unfolded the Zodiac raft until it was as flat as a pancake; then Logan flicked a nozzle and it inflated. "Won't that there thing be visible when it hits the water?" Sam asked.

"Only the part that's wet," Logan replied. "I don't think it'll be a big problem, though, because it's dark."

"You got invisible paddles, too?" Sam asked.

"Yeah, actually I do." Logan reached into the supply bag and pulled out a pair of aluminum paddles with hinges in the middle that allowed them to be folded in half. "The problem isn't going to be the raft or the paddles. It's the stuff we'll be taking with us." She gestured toward the items in the boat's midsection, a gesture Sam and Abby couldn't see.

"That's not going to be a problem." Abby reached into her pack and withdrew a tarp.

The clarity with which Renie could see it told her it was as invisible as the Zodiac raft, yet Abby handled it as though she could see every inch of it. She shook it open and a slight breeze caught it and flapped it like a flag. Then it settled down over the visible items they would be taking with them on the raft. "I can't see them now," Abby said. "Can you, Sam?"

The beam of his flashlight passed over the area. "Nope."

"How'd you do that?" Logan exclaimed. "We've never been able to do that before. We've never been able to use an invisible object to cover something visible so that *it* becomes invisible."

"Well, after the hummingbird scarf turned visible," Abby said, "I started thinking about the effects of shrouding on different types of fabrics and textures. The scarf was the first thing to materialize in three years and I felt there had to be a reason for it. So I went through all the stuff that you had with you that day three years ago and just started experimenting. Cotton doesn't work as a cover because it's too porous. And most of the cottons we use are processed, like wool. Silk is organic, like rope and wood—two items that were the first to turn visible for Renie and her family. And that scarf is a hundred percent silk."

"So what's this tarp made of?" Renie asked, intrigued.

"Three different types of man-made, waterproof plastics. One part came from a large pocket on the inside of Logan's suitcase. Another piece lined the bottom of her suitcase. The rest of it came from a poncho she was carrying with her. If you look closely, you'll see the tiny stitches I used to connect them."

"You *sewed* this stuff together?" Katie exclaimed. "How'd you do that?"

Abby laughed. "With a lot of patience and a hose that was turned on and a big needle."

"Uh, ladies?" Sam interrupted, and gestured ahead of them.

There, through the trees, stood the village on stilts, a silhouette in the deeper shadows cast by the mangroves. "Wow," Katie breathed. "It's visible."

"Sure," Abby said. "It's wood."

"But we're as organic as the wood," Katie said. "So we should be visible by now."

"Yeah, we're organic," Logan said. "But we're a lot more complex than wood."

At the moment, Renie felt no more intelligent than a piece of wood. In fact, as she stared at the village—eerily visible out there in the lagoon—she wondered what the hell this whole thing was really about. Revenge? Making a point? Attacking Nash and his organization where they were weakest? All of the above? None of the above? Destroying the village wouldn't bring Andy back or return her to her former life. There were no guarantees that it would do anything except piss Nash off.

"I don't know about this," she said.

"What?" Logan balked.

"I don't know what the hell this is going to accomplish," she said.

"We're fighting back." Logan's passionate belief brought a hardness to her voice. "That's what it's about. And it's a little late to have second thoughts right now."

"But is it going to bring back Tyler and Andy, Logan?"

"It's going to weaken Nash's infrastructure. It's going to confuse them. These bastards are like terrorists. No, they aren't *like* terrorists. They *are* terrorists. We're declaring war. And if you don't want to go out there with me, Renie, I'll go alone."

In the end, Renie couldn't just sit here and watch. This wasn't a spectator sport. Either she was in or she was out. But more than that, she would go because she hated the village for what it had stolen from her.

They left their earplugs on the airboat and pushed away from it in the invisible Zodiac. The moon hadn't risen yet, but the stars cast sufficient light for Renie to see the details in the village and in the mangroves that embraced it. Weird, to see it visible now, she thought.

Even though the Zodiac and their paddles and their supplies were invisible, the raft left telltale ripples in the starlit water around them. That was the hell of it in this strange new world she inhabited. Visibles couldn't see them, but they could see the evidence of their presence.

A pit of dread opened in the bottom of her stomach.

2

Logan felt whole, invigorated, powerful. She felt better than she'd felt in three years. She was invading Nash's territory and doing it as an Invisible, as the mutant *he* had created, and Christ, she was going to leave a calling card that he wouldn't forget. That he deserved.

As the raft bumped up against the rear of the village, Logan passed the beam of her flashlight along the lower edges of the docks, looking for the Tesla coils. She didn't see anything that even resembled the coils she had seen three years ago. Yet, electricity had to be involved somehow. The experience that Renie and Katie had described fit her own experience too closely for there to be some other explanation.

Even though she believed there were other things involved in the shrouding process besides electricity, she didn't have a clue what the hell those things might be. There were many fringe theories—making an object or a person go ''out of phase'' in the space-time continuum, somehow altering the magnetic field around the object or person, even certain types of alchemical techniques. But in three years, she'd gotten no closer to the truth of the process, to the details, than she had been in the beginning. And if she didn't understand how the shrouding worked, then she certainly wouldn't discover how the process could be reversed. Only Nash, she thought, might have that knowledge. And if he had it and had never used it for Tyler, then he deserved whatever he got.

While Renie tied up the raft, Logan opened the bundle and removed the four cans of gasoline. She wrapped the tarp up again and put it in a dry spot in the raft. Once Renie was on the dock, Logan passed her the cans of gas, then scrambled up the ladder to join her.

"It's eerie to see the place visible," Renie whispered.

"And it's going to be so fucking gratifying to see it burn," Logan whispered back. "C'mon, let's hurry."

As they moved off in opposite directions, Logan glanced back and when Renie was about fifty feet away from her, she faded from view. *That* was really unsettling. She uncapped her can of gasoline and began splashing it across the dock, the huts, the thatch, even over the sides of the platform, so that the stilts and the gas on the surface of the water would burn. The stink of the gas filled her with a heady freedom, as if this single act might spell the beginning of her redemption, of the three years she had lost, that Nash had stolen from her. *A couple of matches, Georgie, and this place is history.* No more animal experiments, no more secrecy, no more human tragedies.

And maybe, just maybe, she would be one step closer to finding Tyler.

She dropped her empty can in the raft and seconds later Renie appeared again, hurrying toward her, grinning, her hair wild, exhilaration radiating from her like some sort of primal odor. "Revenge is sweet, isn't it?" Logan remarked.

"Bet your ass. This place is saturated."

They scrambled down the ladder again, into the raft. Renie untied the Zodiac, Logan readied the can of kerosene she would use to drench the torches, eight homemade babies, thick sticks wound tightly with cotton rags and twine. She brought out the box of kitchen matches and a backup lighter.

"Let's put some distance between us and the dock," Logan suggested.

"How much distance?"

"Fifty feet."

They lined the torches up against the side of the raft like little soldiers readied for battle, then paddled quickly away from the village.

3

Katie didn't like any of this.

She didn't like being separated from her mother, didn't like adults telling her what to do or not do, didn't like the adventure anymore. The adventure sucked. The adventure had collapsed into nightmare. If something happened to her mother out there and she never found her father, she would be an orphan. An invisible orphan. And just what the hell would she do then?

She couldn't even see her mother or the raft now. All she saw was the spooky village. Lucky began to growl, a soft, feral noise that raised goose bumps on Katie's arms. The skin at the back of her neck seemed to tighten, to pucker, as if someone had dropped an ice cube down between her shoulder blades. Then she heard what Lucky heard, the drone of an engine, a boat. "Abby, someone's coming."

"I don't hear nothin'," Sam said. "But yeah, yeah, I know you hear stuff before we do."

"Is your rifle loaded, Sam?" Abby asked.

"Loaded and ready." He grinned and reached between his legs and set the rifle across his thighs.

With that, Abby reached into her bag and brought out a gun.

Katie had seen plenty of guns on TV and in the movies, but she'd never seen one in real life. "You know how to shoot that?" she exclaimed.

"Girl, you never handle a gun unless you know how to shoot it and aren't afraid to shoot it to protect yourself or the people you love. Where's the sound coming from?"

Katie listened again. A part of her hearing seemed to be hurled out like a net over the lagoon and the surrounding mangroves and caught a variety of sounds—whistles, croaks, chirrs, splashes. But she was listening for what she'd heard moments ago, a pattern in these sounds, something akin to an *I Ching* hexagram, a repetition, a theme. Then she heard it, *chug chug click.*

"It's coming from behind us."

"Stay low, Katie. And hold on to the dog."

Katie felt like reminding Abby that *she* was invisible and already out of sight. But Abby had moved to the rear of the boat and Sam was scrambling down from the pilot's perch, his rifle cradled in the crook of one arm. They whispered urgently to each other, whispers that Katie heard clearly; then a powerful beam of light pierced the branches around them.

"You folks in trouble?" a voice called.

"No trouble," Sam called back. " 'Cept the fish that ain't runnin'."

The boat that came into view looked sleek enough to be on a magazine cover. Even though Katie didn't know squat about boats, she could tell this one was made for speed across wide-open spaces, not a snail's crawl through a narrow channel. The man who had called out to them wasn't wearing any sort of uniform that would identify him as a park ranger or a cop. But he was armed.

"Sorry to bother you," the guy said. "We've found some

people stranded out here in the last couple of days because of the drought.''

As the boat idled to a stop behind the airboat, a second man leaned forward from the shadows. ''We're going to ask you folks to move on. The park service is closing a huge section of the Glades for the next few days. Some sort of contamination in the water.''

A chill shot up Katie's spine. *I know that voice.* She raised her head a little, peering over the top of the large cooler, and got a good look at him. The black ponytail, the body of hard, rippling muscles, a cruel face: he was one of the men who had chased them at the Flamingo marina. Katie felt a growl coming up from someplace deep in Lucky's throat, felt her body tensing. She tightened her hold on Lucky, trying to silently communicate that she couldn't make a sound, and struggled to remember this guy's name.

Nash and Dobson and Panther, her mother had said. This guy was Panther. *Get outta here, Sam. These guys are bad news.*

Unless she released her hold on the dog, though, she couldn't get close enough to either Abby or Sam to whisper to them. But she was afraid that if she let go of Lucky, the dog would start barking or would lunge toward Panther.

''Contamination?'' Abby repeated. ''From what?''

''We're not sure at this time what it's from. We're just getting people out of the area.''

''That probably explains why them fish ain't runnin','' Sam muttered. ''Reckon we'll be on our way.''

''Sure thing,'' Panther replied, then turned a bright beam of light on the airboat and slipped on a pair of thermal-sensitive glasses.

In the space between that moment and the next, Panther pulled his gun. ''If you move, the invisible kid is dead. Drop the rifle, old man. *Now*. And you,'' he snapped at Abby. ''Get your arms up nice and high where I can see them.''

Abby's arms went up.

"Cover me," he told his companion.

As Panther stepped onto the airboat, Lucky suddenly wrenched away from Katie and launched herself at him. Katie screamed, *"No!"* and lunged for the dog, trying to grab her.

After that, everything happened so fast that it got mixed up in Katie's mind. Lucky sank her teeth into Panther's leg, the other guy fired his gun, and the bullet—*not a dart, a bullet*—pinged as it ricocheted off the railing. Panther flung Lucky away from him as though she were an annoying insect and Abby dropped to her knees and fired once, twice.

Katie felt the explosion in her teeth, her bones, an electrical sensation that sped through her, scorching her from the inside out. Panther's companion pitched over the side of the airboat and Panther stumbled back, clutching his shoulder, his expression seized by horror and astonishment that he'd been shot. Sam swung his rifle like a bat and slammed it across the backs of Panther's knees and Panther toppled over the front of the airboat and fell into the water.

Moments later, the airboat roared to life and lurched forward.

4

Renie's first torch arced through the air, burning with satisfying brilliance, and a heartbeat later Logan's torch followed. The torches hit the saturated village within seconds of each other and the entire north end of the dock ignited.

They hurled the second set of torches. One of them landed on the water. But the gas on the surface of the water caught fire and flames curled like passionate lovers around the wooden stilts that supported the village. The other torch hit one of the huts and the thatch burned as fast and brightly as money, and sent up great spiraling towers of smoke.

Just as they started to light the third pair of torches, gunshots echoed across the lagoon, and Renie's head snapped around. *Katie.* "Oh my God," she whispered, and grabbed one paddle and tossed the other to Logan.

They paddled hard, turning the raft slightly so that it was aimed at the channel where they'd left the airboat. A tremendous explosion suddenly rocked through the village and the sound of it struck Renie like a hammer. She gasped and doubled over, fists squeezed to her ears to block it, but Logan shouted, *"The coils, the fire hit the coils! Paddle, Renie, paddle!"*

Pieces of flaming debris and smoldering embers rained down on them. Chunks of burning wood landed in the raft. Renie paddled with her teeth clenched and her body hunkered forward. She saw the airboat now, racing across the lagoon in the spill of the firelight from the burning village. Its searchlight flashed off and on, off and on, a signal that plans had changed.

Renie remembered that neither Abby nor Sam could see them and that even Katie wouldn't be able to see them if they were farther than fifty feet away. She swept up an unlit torch, lit it, and waved it back and forth, directing the airboat toward them.

As the two vessels neared each other, Renie spotted Katie standing at the front of the airboat, getting ready to toss her and Logan a rope. *She's okay, Katie's not hurt,* she thought, and a nearly crippling wave of relief washed through her. The airboat slowed and Katie tossed the rope and Renie caught it and pulled the Zodiac closer to the airboat so they could board. Abby reached over the side and somehow knew exactly where to grab the invisible Zodiac to steady it. Renie and Logan scrambled on board, Abby hauled the raft up after them.

"Everyone on?" Sam shouted.

"Get moving," Abby shouted back.

Sam opened the engine up wide and the airboat flew across

the lagoon, the roar of the engine so brutal, so relentless, that Renie's entire body felt battered, bruised, beyond repair. She and Katie huddled together, hands pressed hard to their ears. Beyond them, clouds of smoke billowed upward, great, greasy plumes that stank of revenge.

Renie still didn't know what had happened on the airboat, who had fired the shots. Her first inkling that anything was wrong came moments after the airboat plunged into a channel and Sam cut the engine. The sagging branches closed over them, the softer night sounds enveloped them, and in the strange, abrupt quiet, Sam said, "Goddamn thugs got me in the thigh."

He was halfway down the ladder when he said it and then he fell the rest of the way.

"Shit, holy shit," Sam was muttering when they reached him.

"Lie still." Renie slid a towel under his head and nearly passed out when Logan shone the flashlight at his leg. Blood, so much blood. It spread like dark ink through the fabric of his shorts and ran in rivulets across the wet deck.

Logan pressed a towel against the wound as Abby crouched beside him with the first-aid kit. "Just keep pressure on it, Logan."

"You know anything about gunshot wounds?" Renie asked.

"Used to be an ER nurse. Yeah, I know a thing or two." She brought out a pair of scissors, squares of gauze, a bandage. "I'm going to cut away the fabric, Sam. Logan, maintain that pressure."

"We need to get him back to the RV," Renie said. "Can you work on him while the airboat's moving?"

"I'll do what I can."

"You know how to get us back?"

"I do," Katie said, and set clean towels and a bottle of distilled water next to Abby. "You may need that stuff."

"Thanks. Get up there in the perch with your mom."

Not long afterward, the noise of an approaching chopper cut through the din of the engine. The troops had arrived to check out the explosion, Renie thought. Nash's troops or the fire department or the cops or the rangers: no telling which troops. But the airboat was well hidden now in the mangroves and she was less worried about the chopper than she was about Sam.

Renie knew enough about ER medicine to realize that if the bullet was still in Sam's leg, he would have to go to a hospital. If he went to a hospital, there would be a police report because it was a gunshot wound. If there was a police report, then Nash and his people probably would hear about it and Sam would be in deeper shit than he was right now. And so would they.

She struggled to focus on driving the airboat and listening to her daughter's directions. Turn left, go right. But it was like trying to ignore a migraine. They didn't need just relief. They needed a miracle and they needed it yesterday.

22
REVELATIONS

The stink of Sam's blood was almost more than Logan could bear. She, Renie, and Abby lifted him out of the airboat and carried him into the garage, where the RV was parked. He was unconscious by then and the towel that Abby had secured to his leg was soaked with blood.

Logan worried about where they would put Sam, worried that if they moved him too many times he would lose so much blood that he would die. "Where can you work on him most easily, Ab?" Logan asked as they carried him up the steps into the RV.

"The kitchen table. Once I get the bleeding stopped, we'll move him into the bedroom. But first I need to determine if the bullet exited the thigh. I need to know if there are any broken bones or busted blood vessels. I think the bullet missed the arteries, there was no *pumping blood,* but that's all I could tell out there."

"What about infection?" Renie asked.

"We have plenty of antibiotics for infection. After all, if Logan gets sick, she can't go to a doctor."

"How do you get the prescriptions?" Renie asked.

As the wife of a physician, Logan thought, of course she would ask.

"My brother's an MD in Miami. Periodically, I call him up with a complaint and he phones in a prescription. Katie, hon, there's a plastic tablecloth in the cabinet above the stove. Can you get it and spread it out on the table?"

"Sure."

Moments later, they set Sam down on the kitchen table. Logan's cat peered down from a shelf above the table, watching what they were doing. Logan gently lifted her from the shelf and put her on the floor, where she promptly hissed at Lucky, then backed away and ran into the bedroom.

"Katie, in that floor freezer there are medical supplies, including sterile gloves. Get everything for us, will you? The stuff's labeled. From the cabinet in the bathroom, I need the Betadine, the blood pressure cuff, face masks, and all the clean towels you can find." As Katie hurried off to collect everything, Abby moved the bloody towel slightly away from Sam's thigh, examining the wound again. "I'm going to wash up. Then each of you do the same. I'm going to need help."

"Can you save him?" Logan asked.

Abby didn't answer. She simply turned away and went over to the kitchen sink and began to scrub her hands and arms.

Logan thought she heard something outside and her head snapped toward the window. "I heard it, too," Renie whispered.

"What'd it sound like to you?" Logan asked.

"A car, coming up the drive."

"Take the Glock," Abby said. "Just in case."

The Glock, of course, was visible, but if she had to step outside the garage, she could stash the gun someplace where she could get to it quickly. *Just in case.*

It was hot and dark in the mammoth garage and sounds

echoed strangely. The drip of a faucet, insects buzzing at the windows outside, the quickening beat of her heart: everything seemed preternaturally loud to her sensitive hearing. Yet, she heard nothing *human* in here, except for the noises coming from inside the RV. She moved swiftly toward the partially open door of the garage, set the Glock on a shelf just above eye level, and slipped outside.

A car was parked in the driveway and a man was getting out. It was too dark for Logan to see his face. He shut the door quietly, then paused, his head moving from left to right, left to . . . His head stopped moving and he faced her. "Logan?"

The sound of her own name shocked her and she remained very still, barely breathing, simply watching him. She noticed he had a backpack slung over his right shoulder and that he wore simple clothes, jeans, a cotton shirt.

"It's Luis Manteles," he said.

Jesus, is it him? Is it really him?

"On the day you were shrouded, I tossed you a stone, do you remember?"

My God. "Luis." Logan strode toward him and touched his arm. "How . . . how did you find me?"

He felt for her hand, grasped it in both of his. "That stone I gave you. It connects us. And I used to stop here, when I worked for the project. Is there someplace where we can talk?"

"Yes, of course. Inside the garage. In the RV. But Sam . . . the guy who owns this place . . . is hurt."

"Hurt how?"

On their way back through the garage, she retrieved the Glock from the shelf and told him briefly what had happened out in the Glades. "My friend, Abby, is a former nurse and she—"

"The black woman," he said.

"How do you know that?"

"That stone I gave you. Do you still have it?"

"I carry it with me everywhere." She reached into the pocket of her jeans and brought it out. He couldn't see it, so she took his hand and guided his fingers to the stone.

He picked it up and turned it over in his hands, his thumb sliding across the embedded fossil. "This has connected us all these years." He pressed it back into her palm, slipped a pen-shaped flashlight from his shirt pocket, and shone it on his right hand. "This mark on my palm. Can you see it?"

"Yes. It looks like a scar. A recent scar. It's still red."

"For weeks now, it has throbbed with pain and the mark has alternated between what you see now and a hot, pulsating mass. It's how I knew things here were not going well. Every time I tried to turn my back on my responsibilities, the pain got worse. Now, there's no pain. Even the redness is fading. It's been a kind of beacon. That was how I found you. The fossil and . . ." He shrugged. "Luck."

"What . . . what happened that day, Luis? I mean, after I got away, what did they do to Tyler?"

"Locked him up, threw away the key." He shook his head. "Many things happened that should not have happened. I know where your husband is, Logan. He and the other man are being kept at a facility in Ponce, Florida. We're going to get them out. But there're things we must do first, beginning with Sam."

Tears stung Logan's eyes and she gently put her arms around Luis, hugging him close. "Thank you," she whispered. "Thank you for finding us and coming here."

"I am the one who is thanking *you*. Now I have the opportunity to correct everything I did wrong before."

With that, he took her invisible hand and they hurried into the RV.

2

A dog started barking as soon as Luis and Logan entered the RV and he smiled and stooped down, opening his hands, and the dog fell silent. Now he sensed the invisible dog approaching him, sniffing his hands. "Another of Nash's victims," he said.

"We found him in the village," said a young voice.

"And you are . . . ?"

"Katie. Katie Townsend. Hey, I know you," she blurted. "I remember you from—"

"From somewhere," he said, his voice soft. From his journey in the second body.

"From where?" another woman asked.

"I don't know," the girl said.

"I'll explain later," Luis told the woman. "And you are . . . ?"

"Renie," the woman said. "Renie Townsend, Katie's mother."

"And that's Abby," Logan said. The only other Visible here."

The dark woman wore a surgical mask and stood over Sam, stretched out on the table. She was fixing an IV tube to an IV bottle. Even from where Luis stood, he could see that Sam's spirit was sliding away from him, rising like wisps of smoke from the center of his chest, the crown of his head.

"You're Luis," Abby said, not hiding her astonishment.

"Luis?" said the other Invisible, the woman called Renie. "Is this the shaman who—"

"Yes," Logan replied. "Can you help Sam, Luis?"

"I don't know." He didn't offer hope, but didn't deny it, either. It was the simple truth.

"The good news is that the bleeding appears to be

slowing,'' Abby said. ''And the bullet exited the thigh. But he's got a hole in his leg and just stitching it up isn't going to solve the problem.''

Luis moved over to the table, next to Abby. He held his hands inches above Sam's heart and as the spirit smoke touched it, Luis felt chilled. He breathed deeply, evenly, and shut his eyes. He let his eyeballs roll upward in his head, and focused on an imaginary spot between his eyebrows.

If the man's spirit accepted the healing, it would gradually warm to his hands.

After a few moments, that was exactly what happened and Luis brought his hands to the spirit smoke. It felt warm against his palms as he placed his hands gently against Sam's chest. Only then did he open his eyes and look down at his hands. The spirit smoke no longer rose from Sam's heart. He kept his left hand over Sam's heart and turned his attention to the spirit smoke drifting from the crown of Sam's head. He let his right hand move slowly toward the crown and rested it there, fingers spread.

The spirit smoke no longer escaped from here, either.

''Yes, I can help him,'' he said finally. *But I don't know if it will be enough. I can't tell.*

''Sam told me how you healed the gash on his forehead,'' Renie said. ''One day in the store.''

''He healed himself. I was just a facilitator. But this injury is more serious. His reserves are very low.''

''What can we do to help, Luis?'' asked Logan.

And just then, he heard Consuelo's voice, a soft buzzing in his right ear. *Energy, he needs their energy, Luis.*

He needs more than energy, he thought back at her.

But once he has the energy, you can do the rest. I am here with you. I am always with you. Use what you know.

What he needed was Consuelo's Sight, the same Sight with which he'd seen the spirit smoke. But he needed it to see more deeply that he had ever seen.

"I need the four of you to form a circle around the table and join hands. With your eyes shut, the three adults are to imagine soft green light surrounding and then penetrating the wound on his thigh. Hold the light there as long as you can. Katie, your energy is the strongest, so your job will be somewhat different. You will imagine your hands resting gently against Sam's chest and then his head. Your fingers should be splayed, as mine are. When you feel heat in your imaginary hands, imagine that they are lit from within, radiating a soft, golden light. Can you do that?"

"Sure. No problem."

"Then let us begin."

Luis removed his hands from Sam's chest and skull and shut his eyes. He regulated his breathing, rolled his eyes up in his head, until they were focused on that imaginary point between his eyes. Then he reached for that timeless space and felt the shift deep within.

3

Katie didn't have any problem imagining what Luis had asked her to imagine. All she had to do was pretend she was using her video camera. Movies were all about pretend. But she didn't like keeping her eyes shut and what would it hurt if she opened them? She could still concentrate with her eyes open, she did it all the time.

Besides, she was invisible, who would know if she opened her eyes just an itty-bitty bit? It wasn't really cheating, was it? It wouldn't take away the strength of her imagining. It might even help.

So she opened her eyes and the first thing she saw was Luis's face, his eyes wide open, his expression filled with emotion. But was it pain? Joy? Or something else? Sweat rolled down the sides of his face, sparkled against his fore-head, and formed a dotted line across his upper lip. Now and then, his lips moved, like he might be praying. Or talking to someone. Sweat stains formed two huge half-moons under his arms. Beads of sweat had caught in the fine, pale hairs on his arms and sparkled like tiny Christmas bulbs. And his hands, shit oh shit, something was happening to his hands.

They were moving slowly through the air just inches above Sam's body, but they looked massive. And there seemed to be some sort of light around them, although she thought it might be the haze that surrounded everything that was visible. Now Luis brought one hand to within inches of Sam's thigh while his other hand moved in wide, sweeping circles about a foot above the wound. For moments, his hands seemed to get even larger, they actually seemed to be *growing*, widening, the fingers lengthening. Then the haze, the light, whatever it was that illuminated his hands, got brighter, brighter, until they seemed to be *glowing*. A golden glow, then white, then gold again. It was like a scene out of *E.T.*, a special effect that had been in so many alien movies ever since *E.T.* Except that it was *happening* right in front of her, holy shit, really happening, she was *seeing it.*

And suddenly, she saw the wet mass on Sam's thigh drying up. No, not just drying up. It was *vanishing*, as if some sort of device she couldn't see or hear was sucking it up. And at the same moment, the denim at Luis's thigh turned wet, like some sort of weird transfer from Sam to Luis. Pain seized the old guy's face, he gasped, his hands shook, the light in them dimmed, and for seconds they looked almost normal. Then his body leaned forward just a tad too much and Katie thought he was about to topple onto Sam.

She squeezed her eyes shut and focused everything she had on those imaginary hands. But instead of touching Sam's chest and skull, those imaginary hands took hold of Luis's shoulders and held him up. They held on to him until his breathing evened out and the color returned to his face. And when she opened her eyes again, he was staring right at her, staring as though he could see her.

He held out his hands, his real hands, palms up, held his hands toward her, at the exact spot where she stood, and she realized that he *saw* her as he did any Visible and that he was asking her to touch his hands. She let go of her mother's hand, then Abby's, and brought her hands to Luis's, palm to palm, receiving whatever he was giving her. And his hands exploded with light and she felt that light, felt the heat, the light, and a magnificent *something* that leaped from him and into her. Then he stumbled back and sat down heavily in the nearest chair, his body crumpling into it as though he were no more substantial than a piece of Kleenex.

She kept staring at him, then at her hands, then at him again, and thought: If he could do this for Sam, if he could heal Sam, then surely he could heal them, too. Surely he could make them visible.

4

As Dobson brought the chopper down on the rooftop helipad of building two, Nash saw three military choppers on the rooftop pads of the other buildings. He didn't know what, exactly, that meant, but knew it couldn't be good. He found out just how *not good* it was when he and Dobson reached the bottom of the stairs that led to research and medical and were stopped by a pair of soldiers armed with M16s.

"IDs, please," said the taller of the two men.

Neither Nash nor Dobson challenged them. But the pain in Nash's leg woke up again and he suddenly wished he had his walker. Screw what Colleen or anyone else thought. He needed that walker so desperately that he wasn't entirely sure he was going to make it to medical under his own steam.

Once they were past the soldiers, Dobson said, "This smells bad to me, George. Maybe I should go check on Tyler and Andy."

"Not yet. The—"

He never finished his sentence because Colleen rounded the corner in an electric cart and pulled up next to them. "George." She sounded breathless, the way she often did when she lied. "I've been calling your cell phone for the last hour, but you must've been out of range. I just left a message for you at Homestead."

A lie, for sure, Nash thought. "What's going on?"

"It's Panther. Hurry up. Get in." The whole story tumbled out as the cart hummed up the hall—the attack on the village, the explosion, the fire, Panther wounded. "They brought him in twenty minutes ago. He needs surgery on his shoulder, but he refuses to let them operate until he talks to you."

He recalled the images that had flashed through his mind when Luis had touched his forehead—the village burning, Colleen screwing Farris . . . "Is that why armed soldiers are here?"

"Ross has put the complex on the highest alert because of the attack on the village."

Even as she said this, electric carts with soldiers inside went past them. City hall had arrived, Nash thought, but it wasn't just bureaucrats. This was a full-blown coup. Farris had used the attack on the village to seize control of the complex—and of the project.

"It looks as if he thinks the complex is going to be invaded," Dobson remarked.

"It's just a precaution." She looked as if she was about to say more, then changed her mind.

Colleen drove straight to medical and none of the soldiers along the way stopped to ask for ID. In this brave new world, Nash mused, she was obviously hot stuff. She parked the cart outside the doors to the medical building, flashed her ID to the soldiers standing guard, and the three of them went inside, Nash limping along, a cripple in their midst.

"He's in room two," Colleen said. "He's sort of dopey from whatever they gave him, but he can still talk."

Nash nodded and glanced at Dobson, who said he would wait in the lobby. He touched the cell phone clipped to his belt, meaning that Nash should call in the event that he needed backup for anything.

"Panther said there was an old man and a black woman on the airboat that he and the ranger came across," Colleen said, adjusting her stride to his as they went up the hall. "He also said Dog bit him in the leg."

"A dog or Dog?"

"*Dog.* He wouldn't tell me anything else."

"Maybe he thinks you've changed sides, Colleen."

"Is that what *you* think?"

Nash looked at her then, into her lovely, lying eyes. "It's crossed my mind." He threw his arms out, a gesture that included not just the hallway and medical, but the entire complex. "Just who the hell gave Farris the authorization to move soldiers into the complex?"

"The committee," she replied.

"The committee," Nash repeated. "They're here, too?"

"Uh, no." She patted her hands against the air, as if she were stroking an invisible bear. "Keep your voice down, George. Please. Look, I don't think this is a bad thing, okay? They blew up the village just to let us know they're alive and well and now they're going to come for Tyler and Andy. That's their deeper goal."

"Oh? You've talked to them? To Logan? To Renie Townsend?"

"Well, no, of course not." She emitted a small, nervous laugh. "But it makes sense. It—"

"Yeah, yeah, I know. It's what Ross says." Nash leaned close to her, right into her face. "And what else does he say, Colleen? That Tyler and Andy are government property? That he's entitled to do what he wants with them? That in a few hours he's going to transfer them to a more secure facility? That's why the soldiers are here, isn't it? So that Tyler and Andy can be moved without resistance from anyone else.''

Her expression went hard as bone, as if the skin, the animated eyes, all of the soft, female parts of her lovely face suddenly had calcified. ''It makes sense to move them to a more secure location. You couldn't be consulted about the decision because we couldn't get in touch with you.''

At some level, he had known what the soldiers meant. But now that Colleen actually had voiced it, he knew precisely what he had to do. ''Tell me this, Colleen. What did Ross tell you about Jim Townsend?''

''The same thing he told you.''

''Really? And what was that, exactly?''

''That he was transferred to a federal psychiatric facility in Virginia. The paperwork is in my office. It's all there, George.''

Jesus, he thought. Farris and his stupid committee could have been a bit more inventive. ''Ross engineered Jim Townsend's escape, then shot him in the back as he was trying to scale the fence outside research. I was there, okay? I saw it happen.''

Her genuinely horrified expression led him to think that she believed him. But as soon as she opened her mouth, he realized the horror was directed at him, that in her mind, his words smacked of treason. She had bought into Farris's machinations completely. A crushing sadness and despair seized him. He had spent years with this woman, working with her, sleeping with her, loving her, and destroying his marriage in the process. And for what? For *this?*

''That's a goddamn lie,'' she snapped. ''Why are you lying about something like that, George? *Why?* I saw the paperwork, I spoke to the doc at the other end.''

Nash took an involuntary step back, away from her, from those lying, beautiful eyes. "Ask Ross where he buried the body."

He turned away from her and limped his way toward Panther's room. To his great relief, Colleen didn't follow him.

He slipped inside Panther's room, into the cool twilight where machines hummed, and barely made it over to the bed. He leaned against the nightstand to support himself. Panther, connected to an IV, lay very still, his eyes shut, his breathing soft, shallow.

"Hey, amigo," Nash said.

Panther's eyes fluttered open. "Bosth." The word slurred. "Dog wath there. Heard her bark. Mutt bit me." He went on for a full minute in his truncated, slurred speech, telling Nash the sequence of events. He could see the whole thing in his mind, each scene unfolding with maddening slowness. Panther and the park ranger had come upon the airboat with two Visibles on it—an old man and a black woman. But Panther said he'd been bitten by Dog, who had been in the village when the Townsends stumbled into it. This meant Renie and Katie Townsend had been on the airboat.

But the fire had been set around the same time that Panther had come upon the airboat. None of Panther's men had seen anyone around the village, so that pointed to an Invisible. Since no mother in her right mind would send her kid off to set fire to a village, it made sense that Renie had done it.

Or Logan.

How could Logan and the Townsends have found each other?

"And I fig'erth out thomething elth."

"What?"

"I rec'nized the old man. 'Member Quikth Thop Lasth Thop, bawth? 'Member that plathe?"

What the hell was *that* supposed to mean? Then it hit

him. When they had started looking for a location in the Glades to build the village, they often stopped in at a convenience store—the last stop before the Everglades National Park. He recalled the old guy who had owned the place, Sam someone. He remembered that Luis used to stop in at the store for cigars, beer, water, snacks, when they were on their way into or out of the Glades. The big question, of course, was how Sam Someone had ended up on an airboat with Invisibles.

"You're sure it was the same guy?" Nash asked.

"Pothithive. Didn't remember him till later, bosth."

"You did fine, Panther. The docs are going to get your shoulder squared away."

"Watch your bath, bawth."

Watch your back, boss.

He left through the door that opened into the surgery observation area and limped into the service corridor before he called Dobson. "You still in the lobby, Wayne?"

"In the rest room, actually."

Even better. "What's the phone number for the Last Stop Quick Stop?"

"The what?"

"That shop at the edge of the Glades."

Dobson didn't ask why he wanted the number. He simply thought a moment and, because he was a numbers man, reeled off the number. "What's going on?"

"Meet me in the shrouding area. I'll come in through the fire exit. Maybe sure the room is secure until I get there."

"What're we doing, boss?"

"Making things right."

And I'm going to be a whole man again, without pain.

23
SNAKES

She wasn't a doctor. But Renie had been married to a doctor for sixteen years. She had watched Andy working in emergency rooms. She had seen the carnage that passed through the ER, victims of stabbings, car accidents, gunshots, strokes, hemorrhages. She had witnessed the miracles and the failings of modern medicine. But she had *never* seen anything like this.

Several hours ago, Sam had been dying. His blood pressure had been sixty over thirty, barely high enough to sustain life. He had lost so much blood that his toes and the tips of his fingers had been ice-cold. His lips were blue from shock, his organs were shutting down. He had looked like her own father had looked in the final hours before she had pinched Buddha's nostrils shut and covered his mouth with her hand. She knew how death looked as it neared. She knew.

Now Sam was sitting up on the couch, sipping at a hot brandy and nibbling like a fussy rabbit at the food Abby had made him. He had showered, so it was easy to see the tiny scar on his thigh where the bullet had gone in. On the back of his thigh was another small scar where the bullet had exited. The bullet, in its zigzag journey through Sam's thigh, apparently had missed bones and arteries. That in itself was probably miraculous, but the rest had shattered her beliefs about what was possible.

Luis looked drawn and pale, but reminded her of the ad for the Duracell battery. Relentless. He would just keep on going and would do it all despite the fact that he had identical scars on his thigh, the right thigh, just like Sam. This was like the therapist/patient transference, except that it was *physical.* The evidence was here, right in front of her, laughing at her, mocking her. *Oops, Renie, the world isn't quite like you thought, is it?* But shit, why should this shock her more than the fact of her own invisibility? That sure didn't fit into her worldview, so why should this?

If that wasn't enough, here they were, sitting around the table in Logan's RV, a map of Homestead Air Force base in front of them. In less than an hour, they would leave for the base.

Luis had drawn the map from memory. Even though they had no way of knowing whether the shrouding area was still there or still in the location Luis had pinpointed, Logan had gotten into the bunkers once already and felt sure it could be done again. They all agreed it would be safer to try Homestead rather than the Ponce facility, where security probably had been tightened because of the destruction of the village. Once they were visible, they would go to the FBI about Tyler and Andy and the Ponce facility.

The big unknown in this plan, Renie thought, was that even if they got into the shrouding area, only Luis had any idea how the reversal might be accomplished. He had admitted that his knowledge was skimpy and confined to a handful of experiments they had done on lower animal life before he had quit the project. Hardly what she wanted to hear at this point, but what the hell.

"Do you know how to run the equipment?" Abby asked.

"I know what to do, but have never understood how it works."

A slow, deep ache spread across the back of Renie's neck. She rubbed it and looked slowly around the table, trying to put the faces into a coherent order, into a sequence that made sense. But none of it made sense. There was Sam, the old geezer. There was Luis, shaman. And here, Logan, an Invisible for three years, and next to her, Abby, a Visible without whom Logan couldn't function well in the visible world, and way over there, sound asleep, an invisible dog, with a visible cat not too far away, and then, Katie, her flesh and blood, as invisible as Renie was. Christ oh Christ, she needed fresh air. She needed a glimpse of stars and sky, needed to feel the hard, durable ground beneath her feet.

She pushed back from the table, said she needed to get some air, and fled the RV, the garage. She didn't stop moving until she was outside, spine against the wall of the garage. There, she doubled over, gulping at the warm, humid air, arms clutched to her waist, and bit back the sobs that raced up her throat.

Can't deal with it. Doesn't compute.

Suddenly, the *two against one* axiom that had dominated her life as a mother and a wife seemed absurd. And so did a lot of other things she'd thought were important. Suddenly, her life seemed no more significant than that of a mosquito diving into a sweet, fleshy cheek in search of dinner.

She slid down to a crouch, pressed the heels of her hands into her eyes, and thought of her father. *Hey, Buddha, you there? You present? You in attendance? What's it like over there? You and Mom playing bridge? Planning that trip to China? Hey, is there anything after you die? Is it all just shit in the wind? Hello, anyone home?*

The only time in three years that she had felt Buddha around was the day in Paradise weeks ago, when he'd appeared to her and told her to eat the grass that Lucky was eating. Okay, so maybe she imagined it, maybe it was some sort of hallucination brought on by the invisibility sickness. But it had been damn real at the time and his advice had cured her of the sickness. Before that, though, there hadn't been anything that even smacked remotely of visitations from the dead—no items that fell inexplicably to the floor, no lights that blinked off and on, no keys that refused to work. And according to the mediums on Web sites, on *Oprah,* in books, these were signs that the dead were around, trying to make contact. Well, hello, it hadn't happened to her until that day in Paradise.

She heard the footsteps in the garage, soft, measured steps that held a certain weariness, a bone fatigue. She heard the garage door creak as it opened and heard the footsteps moving across the dry, worn grass. "Are you all right?" Luis asked.

Renie's hands dropped away from her face. The old shaman was crouched next to her, his spine against the wall. He couldn't see her, yet he had found her. She didn't want to go there, to speculate. The old guy spooked her.

"I needed fresh air."

"In Ecuador, in the jungle where my tribe lives, the air smells like this, but richer because there is more greenery. In the mountains, it smells like paradise." He gestured toward the sky. "But the stars have different placements. The Southern Cross is visible."

"How did you do that?" she asked.

She didn't have to explain, he knew what she referred to. "It's like ghosting. When you ghost, your molecules are changed. I changed his molecules."

"That's not possible."

He smiled at that. "Not in your world."

"So your world came to my world."

"Or yours to mine."

"Or our worlds collided," she said softly. "So if you can do this, then can't you do something similar to make us visible again?"

"I don't know. I actually tried with your daughter, after I'd finished working with Sam. But it didn't work. I don't know if I can do it or not. The technology rendered you invisible and it may be that only the technology can reverse the shrouding. I just don't know."

"Do you think Nash knows?"

"Yes. He probably denies any such thing, but yes, I'm sure he has tried it on objects, perhaps even on the small animals." He paused, then said: "Your daughter," he said. "She will have a choice."

"Christ, she's only fourteen. She'll have lots of choices in her life."

"Not those kinds of choices. You see, ghosting works differently for children than it does for adults. Children are still becoming who they are. Adults are already locked into this process. We're *un*-learning. But children are still *learning*. A child's consciousness is more flexible."

"You're speaking in riddles," Renie told him. "I flunked that course."

"Your daughter has a gift and the invisibility has awakened it."

"A gift for what?"

He ran his hand over his stubbled jaw and inhaled deeply. "That's for the two of you to uncover. Your role will be one of guidance." He paused. "Bob? No, Buddy. Or Buddha. Yes, Buddha. What does Buddha mean to you?"

The transition was so rapid that it took her a moment to realize what he'd said. One moment he'd been talking about Katie and now he'd mentioned Buddha. Shaken, she said, "It's what we used to call my father."

"You did what had to be done."

Renie felt her body drawing in as he spoke, her skin tightening over the bones. Her mind threw up the mental equivalent of hurricane shutters and spun them into place, locking out the rest of the world. But she still heard his voice. The shutters didn't keep out his voice.

"You did the right thing," he went on.

"You don't know shit about my father." She was so pissed she felt like slugging him. "You couldn't possibly know, so stop pretending that you do. Jesus, I hate that. I hate pretension. I'm awed by what you did in there, for Sam. I don't have a fucking clue how you did it and I don't think the *how* matters as much as the fact that he's on the mend. But you never met Buddha and I just met you, so you can't possibly know shit from shinola, Luis."

"Shit from shinola." He repeated the words and shook his head. "Shit is *mierda* in Spanish, but I don't know that shinola word. I don't know how to translate that."

"Fuck off, that's the translation."

"You squeezed his nostrils shut."

Renie didn't move.

"You honored his final wish. And you hold that secret to you, like shame. But there is no shame in what you did."

Tears rolled down her face, she didn't trust herself to speak. It seemed as if she had waited for years to hear someone say these words, that there was nothing to forgive, that she had done the right thing. "He couldn't move," she said softly. "He had a feeding tube in his stomach. He couldn't speak. Then . . . one day when . . . when his medicine gave him a little mobility, he . . . he scribbled four words on a piece of paper. *Begging. Help me. Please.* When he could still speak, he begged me to help him die, so I knew what the words meant. Two days later . . . while he slept . . ." Her voice cracked and she couldn't go on.

"There is nothing to forgive," Luis said, getting up. He held out his hand and she grasped it and he pulled her to her feet. "But those are empty words until you believe it."

She nodded and squeezed his hand once, thanking him. He walked off and Renie stayed where she was, listening to the night sounds that drifted through the mangroves.

2

The shrouding room in the research area was deserted at this hour and Dobson locked the doors so that it would remain that way. Nash pulled the blinds, then booted up the computer and took Dobson step by step through the process. Dobson had seen it before, but never in this capacity, where he would have to initiate the program and guide it through the shrouding.

"What about stabilization, boss? Don't you need that herb?"

"I don't keep it in here. This will keep me shrouded long enough to get to Andy and Tyler. But as soon as I'm shrouded, you'll have to override the controls for the thermal sensors along corridor two, in the apartment, and in the back stairwell that goes to the roof. This will create phony thermal images on the monitors. You'll also have to bring the chopper over there. And then we'll go to Homestead." The village had been destroyed and with the complex under Farris's control, he couldn't risk bringing Andy and Tyler in here. That left one option: the shrouding area at Homestead. He handed Dobson a Pocket PC identical to the one that Colleen had. "You know the code."

"If Farris overrode your fail-safe—"

"He doesn't even know about it. Colleen doesn't, either."

Dobson smiled. "You never really trusted her."

"I guess not." He didn't want to talk or think about Colleen. "If something goes wrong, there's a file in my safe at home that should be mailed to the *Miami Herald* and the *New York Times* detailing everything about Project Tesla. Use it as collateral for your own safety."

"Nothing's going to go wrong," Dobson said. "I've put

my own safeguards in place. The committee won't be able to touch me.''

Nash wondered what he meant by that, but didn't ask. Now wasn't the time. He was simply grateful that Dobson knew as much about the project as he did.

He gathered together papers, a laptop, clothing, and other items that might prove useful to him and stuffed everything in a battered backpack. His gun and ammunition would go with him into the zone, as would the clothes he was wearing, the trank gun, several trank syringes, a second Pocket PC on which he kept his notes. He would take the cane, too. He believed that Tyler had been telling him the truth about the healing properties of shrouding, but just in case he had been lying or the properties didn't kick in right away, the cane would be with him.

Dobson helped him load everything onto the small platform. Nash limped up the several steps and, with considerable effort, eased himself into the canvas chair.

"You can change your mind, boss."

Nash shook his head. "I can't let Farris seize control of Tyler and Andy." What he didn't say was that the shrouding would end the pain he'd lived with for most of his life and would make him whole again. "Let's go."

Dobson went back to the computer, shut the door of the soundproof booth, and suddenly Nash was all alone—and scared.

Moments later, the humming started. In the past, he'd been wearing headphones and had been sequestered inside a soundproof booth during the shrouding and had been spared the sound effects. This felt strange—not uncomfortable, not painful, just strange. But that quickly changed as the humming escalated in pitch and intensity. The overhead lights flickered as the electricity was ratcheted to the next level. Nash barely noticed. He was struggling against the painful sensations in his skull, in his ears, in the very foundations of his being.

The muscles in his bum leg started to twitch, to cramp, and then to tighten. An excruciating agony shot through his leg from toe to hip, hip to toe, over and over again. He snapped forward at the waist to grab on to his leg, to massage it, to speak to it, to hug it, love it, whatever it would take to end the pain. The humming collapsed into an outright shrieking inside his skull and his hands flew to the sides of his head as if to clutch the pain, to contain it. Then light exploded around him and the last thing he saw before he lost consciousness was his bum leg shaking uncontrollably, an entity separate from him with a will and life of its own.

He came to with Dobson leaning over him, his eyes large and dark behind the lenses of the thermal glasses he wore. "Boss, it worked! It fucking worked! But we need to get out of here now. The shrouding set off an alarm."

"I . . . I . . ." He couldn't form whole words. He was too immersed in sensations. Dobson, the room, everything beyond the platform looked hazy, as if he were seeing it through a dirty window. When he glanced down at himself, at his arms, his legs, his clothes, everything looked real and yet different. His ears rang, his body felt as if it were made of some malleable material. He was dizzy.

"I've turned off the sensors in corridor two and in the apartment. But you're going to have to move fast. Maybe we should take a cart. I can drop you off close to the apartment, then head up to the roof."

"Just take me as far as corridor two, Wayne."

Nash got unsteadily to his feet. His legs felt soft and spongy, as though they were made of wet clay. Only the barest whisper of pain remained, small points deep in the leg's bones. He grabbed his pack, picked up the cane, and moved slowly off the platform. He tested his leg first by not putting too much weight on it, letting the cane take the brunt. Then he gradually added a little more weight and a little more until he was hardly depending at all on the cane.

"My God," he whispered. "Tyler was telling the truth,

Wayne. My leg ... my leg ... it's like a new leg. The shrouding has some sort of healing property ... it—''

"C'mon, George. We've gotta move."

Nash heard the alarm now, a high-pitched, maddening sound beyond the room, and he suddenly understood how acute his hearing had become. His entire body, in fact, felt sensitized, as if a faint electrical current ran through his skin.

"Got to do one thing first," Nash said, and went into the soundproof booth.

He keyed in the sequence of numbers and letters that would not only erase the computer's hard drive, but render the equipment completely useless. Damned if he would let Farris or Colleen, the committee or the NSB or the Pentagon or anyone else claim what was his. Fuck them all.

When he finished, he threw his cane down and hurried out into the service corridor, Dobson close behind. They got into one of the carts parked near the door to the loading dock. His leg wasn't perfect yet, far from it, but compared to what he'd been living with for the last few months, this was paradise.

They sped past medical, past research, and turned out into the main corridor. The shriek of the alarm felt like nails being driven into his skull. He quickly fished out the earplugs he'd put in his pack and squeezed them into his ears. They helped, but didn't completely block out the noise. Dobson drove the equivalent of two long city blocks without being stopped; then a soldier waved him down.

Nash leaned close to Dobson so he could hear him over the shriek of the alarm. "He's not wearing thermals. I'll get out here and meet you on the roof."

"Good luck, boss."

As the cart came to a stop, Nash slipped off and hurried away, relishing his freedom of movement, of motion without pain. His gait wasn't totally free of the limp, but it was

already so slight that for the first time in decades he didn't
need his cane.

3

The apartment had gone into lockdown as soon as the alarm
had sounded. To Andy, that meant prison: no way out, the
security cameras providing a fresh, new view of the living
room every two or three seconds, audio at maximum capacity, able to pick up the drop of a pin. Anything that might
provide cover for their voices was also in automatic shutdown—the radio, TV, stereo, even the computer.

Even in lockdown, however, no one could require them
to wear visible clothes. But it wouldn't surprise him if Colleen or Nash or someone else showed up with syringes filled
with that blue saline that made them glow like radioactive
heaps. This time, though, he would be ready.

Andy went over to the control booth window and watched
the soldier on duty. He wasn't wearing thermal glasses.
Instead, he was alternately watching the monitor and something on the small TV to his left. Andy couldn't see the
monitor from where he stood, but he could see its reflection
in the glass and it sure didn't look right. The reddish yellow
blobs that represented body heat were moving around on
the far side of the room, roughly in what would be the TV
and computer area. But here stood Andy, at the window of
the control room, and Tyler was in the bathroom.

Even more intriguing was the fact that the soldier seemed
completely oblivious of the discrepancy. It occurred to Andy
that the soldier probably couldn't hear the alarm because it
was at the other end of the building and even if knew the
apartment had gone into lockdown, he might not know why.
So what the hell did *that* mean?

It means two against one.

The old math, but with a different application.

He picked up a pen and a pad of paper, darted across the living room, and ducked into the hall. He scribbled a note, tore off the sheet of paper, and slipped it under the door. Seconds later, the door flew open. Tyler took the pen and the pad and scribbled: *Plan 3. Let's do it.*

Plan one, plan two, plan three, plan four: over the weeks of their confinement together, they had devised a number of plans to fit any number of different scenarios. Andy liked this plan least of all because it entailed leaving the apartment and entering the booby-trapped complex. But opportunity wasn't just knocking; it was hammering its heavy fists against their door.

Tyler grabbed a visible jacket off a hook on the back of the bathroom door and slipped it on. Andy hurried into the living room and ducked down behind a chair closest to the door while Tyler went over to the control booth window and banged his fists against it. "Hey, you in there! Something's happened to the doc. He slipped in the bathroom. Hey, man, you hear me in there?"

Moments later, the apartment doors whispered open and the soldier tromped in, his heavy combat boots announcing his precise location. "What happened?" he asked Tyler.

"Shit, man, I don't know." Tyler sounded agitated, scared. "He was showering, I heard something, and when I went in, he was lying on the floor. He's out like a light. He's down there."

"You first," the soldier said.

And when he passed within a foot of the chair, Andy sprang to his feet, grabbed the M16, and swung it into the soldier's face, knocking him back. Tyler spun and his legs kicked out, one and then the other, again and again and again, moving at the speed of light and battering the poor fucker from the right and the left until he fell. Tyler threw off the jacket, so that he was invisible again, Andy swept up the rifle, and together they pulled the soldier into the bathroom and wrapped electrical tape around his hands and feet.

They relieved him of his radio, his cell phone, his trank gun. Tyler smashed the first two with the butt of the M16 and swept the pieces under the bathmat. He emptied the tranks into the toilet and tossed the empty gun into the shower. Andy unclipped the remote-control device from the soldier's belt and they ran back into the living room.

And there stood George Nash.

An invisible George Nash.

"You saved me step two," said Nash. "Hurry. We don't have much time. That alarm is from the shrouding area."

"Why the hell should we trust you?" Tyler snapped.

"Because he's one of us now," Andy said, and shoved Tyler forward.

Moments later, they were following Nash down a narrow corridor that appeared to be some sort of service artery that ran between this end of the building and the kitchen. Andy noticed that although Nash favored his bum leg, he didn't limp like before. He was no longer a *cripple.*

At a juncture in the service corridor, they went left, and stopped at a door with a security box next to it. He slid his ID card through the slot, the door clicked, and they hurried into a stairwell. "Two flights up and we're all home free," Nash said.

"Just hold on a goddamn minute," Tyler said, and grabbed Nash's arm. "What's going on? Why're you shrouded?"

Nash wrenched his arm free of Tyler's grasp. "Calm down, for Christ's sake. Farris seized control of the project and of the facility. He was going to have you two transferred tonight to some other facility. I couldn't allow that."

Tyler exploded with laughter. "Give me a fucking break, George. You don't have a benevolent bone in your body. You shrouded because of your leg and because you're scared shitless."

"Yeah, that, too." He tossed Andy a cell phone. "Call

five-five-five fourteen-twelve. It's the number for Last Stop Quick Stop. It's where your wife and daughter are, Doctor Townsend. And I have reason to believe Logan is also there, Tyler. Tell them to meet us at Homestead Air Force Base. I think I can reverse the shrouding there.''

With that, Nash started up the stairs. But Tyler, who had spent three years stifling his rage, lunged for Nash, caught the back of his shirt, and whipped him around. They both fell back and hit the landing, still clinging to each other, struggling against each other. Andy shouted, his voice ringing out in the stairwell, and somehow managed to separate them. Tyler stumbled back, blood oozing from a corner of his mouth, his eyes wild, his face bright red with rage, adrenaline still pumping through him. He shoved Nash up against the wall and Nash collapsed to the bottom step, clutching his stomach.

''Jesus, I'm gonna puke,'' he mumbled, and folded at the waist and vomited on the floor.

The sickness, Andy thought. Nash already had the shrouding sickness.

''Help me get him up the stairs.''

Tyler, still in a kind of enraged stupor, took Nash's other arm and, together, he and Andy half carried him up the first flight of stairs. ''Make the call, Andy,'' Tyler said. ''Make it now. Then we'll know if he's telling the truth.''

''Not much time.'' Nash slumped against the wall and wiped his shirt over his sweating face. ''When I slid my ID through the security box, it registered on the computer. They'll know where we are.''

Andy punched out the number. It rang and rang, five rings, eight, and then a hoarse, male voice said, ''Last Stop.''

Jesus God. It's him. The old guy with the hacking cough.
''Sam, this is Doctor Townsend. Do you remember me?''

Silence, then: ''Holy shit. Doc. Holy shit . . . Hey, Renie. It's him. It's Andy. . . .''

Andy squeezed his eyes shut, felt his knees turning to

butter, felt his spine scraping against the wall in the stairwell as he slid down it to the floor. "Is it him?" Tyler hissed. "Is it the guy who owns—"

"Andy?"

Never had Renie's voice sounded so beautiful to him, so musical, so utterly and completely perfect. It was a moment before he could speak, before he could even make his tongue move against the roof of his mouth to form her name. And as soon as he spoke, she started to cry, soft, muffled sounds that tore at his heart. And somewhere in the room with her, he heard Katie and then another voice came on the line. "This is Logan. Is Tyler with you?"

"Yes. Meet us at Homestead as soon as possible."

"Let me speak to Tyler."

Andy handed Tyler the phone. "It's your wife."

Tyler's fingers closed around the cell phone, but he didn't bring it to his ear. He just kept looking from it to Nash to Andy.

"Talk to her, for Christ's sake," Nash snapped. "We need to get moving."

Only then did Tyler bring the phone to his ear. "Logan."

She must have said something to him because his face suddenly caved in and he rubbed his hand over his face, hiding it from Nash and Andy, and his entire body started to tremble.

Andy helped Nash stand up straight and move toward the next flight of stairs. "Tell her the shrouding area is at the southeast corner of the base," Nash said. "They should go in through the back entrance. They'll have to cross an abandoned runway, a couple of trailers. There's a security box outside that back door. Punch in three eights, a four, the pound key, and spell out *snakes*. The dog will take them the rest of the way."

Tyler repeated this verbatim as he followed Nash and Andy up the stairs. At some point, he handed Andy the phone and he spoke to Renie again. The connection began to break up. She reeled off a cell number where he should call her back. They were now pulling out of the Last Stop. Abby said it would take them at least forty minutes to get to Homestead and that was only if they were moving like a bat out of hell.

"Who's Abby?" he asked.

But by then the connection was gone and Nash stumbled and threw up again and Tyler hissed that he heard them, heard the soldiers, running this way. Andy and Tyler grabbed Nash under either arm and dragged him up the last flight of stairs, his feet banging against each step, his body stinking of vomit and throwing off an intense heat that Andy knew was a raging fever. Had the sickness come over him that fast? He couldn't remember. It didn't matter. It had hit Nash that fast and if he sank into a coma, they were fucked. Wheat grass, he thought, they needed some of that wheat grass.

Just as they reached the top, he heard the door below them crash open. Farris shouted, *"You'll never make it outta here alive!"*

Andy threw his weight against the door. It sprang open and they stumbled out into the humid night air, the fresh air, the sweet smell of summer and freedom. But there was no chopper waiting for them, not on this roof. The only chopper he saw was lifting up from the roof on the next building and speeding toward them. He broke away from Nash and Tyler, shut the door, and looked frantically around for something to push against it. But there was nothing. No mop, no broomstick, no convenient movie prop that would keep the bad guys from pouring through this door in about ten seconds.

"The card," Nash muttered, and pressed it into Andy's hand. "Slide it in the slot, punch the star key. That locks it."

"Keep running," Andy shouted.

He dropped the card, scooped it up, slid it through the slot. His hand shook so badly he had to grab it and steady it to punch the star key. He heard the lock snap into place and then he ran, ran with his arms tucked in at his sides and his body hunkered over, ran in a zigzag to make himself a more difficult target.

Now the chopper swept in low, a rope ladder dangling from the open side door. He saw Tyler stumbling toward it, one arm clutching Nash's waist, supporting him. The chopper came in low, about a foot above the roof, and Tyler helped Nash grab on to it and he began to climb.

The rooftop door exploded open and soldiers poured out and opened fire. Bullets pinged against the rooftop. *Bullets*, not darts this time. Andy ran in a jagged line, reached the rope ladder, and grabbed on. The chopper lifted upward like some huge, prehistoric bird and the ladder swung.

Oh Jesus. I'm going to fall.

He didn't look down. He looked up, up to where Tyler was already inside the chopper and leaning over, pulling Nash inside. Andy kept climbing, hand over hand, right foot, left foot, and the ladder kept swinging in wider arcs and gathering momentum, and the fucks below him kept firing.

Then he was in, crawling the last few feet to safety, and Tyler slammed the door shut. The chopper lurched higher and tore away from the facility. Andy lay on the floor, sucking air into his lungs, his head spinning. "Everyone okay?" Dobson shouted.

"Okay," Andy gasped.

"Okay," Tyler echoed.

"Boss?" Dobson shouted.

Nash didn't say anything at all and Andy raised up on his arms and saw Tyler leaning over him. It was too dark to see Tyler's face but he didn't have to see it to know that Nash had been shot, that the man who held the secret to reversing the shrouding was badly injured.

"Boss?" Dobson said again.

"He's been shot," Tyler called back.

"Jesus God. You're a doctor, Townsend, do something."

Dobson's voice crackled with emotion. "There's a first-aid kit in the back."

Andy rocked back onto his heels, grabbed on to the edge of the seat, and pushed himself up to his knees. Nash lay on his back, his breathing ragged, a bloodstain spreading rapidly through the fabric of his shirt. Chest wound. Shit, Christ, shit. Andy tore open the front of Nash's shirt and pressed his hands over the blood that spurted from the wound. Artery, the bullet had hit an artery. And he was winging through the dark in the middle of fucking nowhere and a first-aid kit wasn't going to do squat to prolong Nash's life.

"Here." Tyler set the first-aid kit on the floor next to Andy and snapped it open.

He knew at a glance there was nothing in here that would help Nash. But he told Tyler to open the bandages, grabbed a towel on the backseat, and kept pressure over the wound. Nash's eyes fluttered open and locked on Andy's. His mouth moved, blood rolled across his lower lip. "Stay still, don't speak," Andy said.

But his mouth moved again and this time both Andy and Tyler leaned close, trying to hear what Nash said. "In my pocket. Letter. Give. To. Luis."

Andy dug his fingers into the pockets of Nash's jeans and pulled out a wadded sheet of paper. Before he could unfold it to read it, a soft shudder rippled through Nash's body and he died. With him went Andy's hope of regaining his visibility.

24
HOMESTEAD

The RV stopped deep inside a citrus grove across the road from Homestead Air Force Base. The scent of lemons and oranges and grapefruit wafted through the open windows, a richness of odors that, in any other situation, would have Renie salivating. But at the moment, all she wanted to do was get out of the RV and into the building. The faster they did that, the sooner she and Katie and Andy could reclaim their lives.

The math was simple, Renie thought. Including Lucky, they numbered four Invisibles and three Visibles, seven in all. They agreed that the only Visible who should accompany them was Luis, because he knew something about shrouding. Abby had cut a piece off the invisible tarp to hide the Glock and a cell phone, which were both visible. Logan carried the gun, and Renie had the cell phone. They put Lucky on an invisible rope and got out of the RV, a motley troop with just one visible member.

They made their way along the edge of the grove, moving parallel to the deserted road that ran past the base. The only light out here came from two dim street lamps. Beyond the lights, Renie could make out a wire-mesh fence, a couple of trailers, and the long concrete building that was their destination, but little else. Logan had told them that perimeter security would be practically nil, but suppose this was all a setup? Suppose the information Andy had given them was wrong? And where had he gotten his information? *Suppose this, suppose that, knock it off.*

When they were roughly parallel to the midway point of the building, Luis said, "I need a few minutes. We'll be safer if none of us is visible."

"You can ghost *here?*" Logan asked.

"I can do it almost anywhere."

"And you can stay ghosted while you move around?" Katie exclaimed.

"Yes."

"But how?" Renie asked.

He laughed. "That's taken me most of my life to understand. But basically, I become the element through which I move."

That said, his eyes rolled back in their sockets until only the whites showed. Renie, Katie, Logan, even the dog just watched him, saying nothing, none of them moving. There was a perceptible change in Luis's breathing pattern and his eyeballs flicked back and forth under his eyelids, as though he were in REM sleep. Other than that, though, Renie didn't see anything unusual. After three or four minutes, the haze that surrounded Luis—that surrounded any Visible she looked at—began to fade away and she realized she could see him as clearly as she saw Katie and Logan. That clarity flickered for a few seconds, as if it were trying to stabilize, then it stopped and his eyes opened.

Lucky whined and pulled at her leash, sniffing at Luis's shoes.

"You're like us," Katie whispered. "I can see you clearly."

"And I can see you. All of you. But I can't hold this indefinitely."

"Let's go," Logan said, and darted out of the trees.

No traffic passed through here at this time of night. A slight breeze skipped across the fields and the warm summer air swelled with the scents of night-blooming jasmine, citrus, and the black, rich soil that made this area so perfect for crops. They reached the other side of the road, hurried down a shallow incline of grass, and stopped at the wire-mesh fence. It looked old and rusted and wouldn't be standing, Renie thought, when the next hurricane roared through here.

Renie and Logan took hold of the bottom of the fence and pulled it upward, bending the wire so they could all crawl under. They brushed the dust and dirt from their clothes, then moved quickly forward, across an abandoned runway, a pile of rubble that looked as if it had been a hangar, and past a tractor. The warm breeze was at their backs now, stirring up dust and bits of papers and carrying a whiff of smoke.

Cigarette smoke, Renie thought, and it was coming from the pair of trailers just in front of them. They slowed. Renie took Lucky's leash from Katie and held on to it. Voices reached them, two men talking at the front of the trailers. Logan cut to the left to make a wide berth around the end of the trailer to the right and Renie saw a pair of guards, smoking, goofing off on the job. They walked within twenty feet of the men and neither of them had any inkling that they weren't alone.

When they were well beyond the men, they started moving fast again. They cut through a dark parking lot with eight or nine cars in it, and now she could see the building that was their destination. It was illuminated by a single security light bright enough to reveal that there were no windows on this side of the concrete building and only one door, probably a fire exit. It looked to be two stories high, with a glow coming from the roof.

As they neared it, two things happened almost simultaneously. The fire exit door swung open and a guard with a rottweiller on a chain leash stepped out. Lucky growled and the rottweiller either heard it or smelled Lucky or maybe even saw her, saw all of them. It broke into a fierce, frenzied barking and lunged toward them.

The guard jerked back on the leash. "It's just a goddamn rabbit, you fool dog," he snapped, and turned on his flashlight.

The beam struck them and the dog really went nuts. Renie swept Lucky up into her arms and ran, flat-out ran, Katie racing alongside her, Logan just ahead of them, and Luis lagging slightly behind.

As they rounded the corner of the building, the dog's howls and barks echoing behind them, Renie heard an approaching chopper. It was coming in fast and low, but she couldn't tell what direction it was coming from. They moved along the back of the building and found a door with a security box outside it. Logan keyed in the code that Andy had given them and nothing happened.

"Jesus, I must've keyed it in wrong."

"Do it again. Fast."

Lucky squirmed in Renie's arms, the rottweiller's barks sounded closer, and the chopper swept into sight now, lights blazing from its belly and spilling across the back of the building. Renie and Katie hugged the wall, watching the chopper as it passed overhead. Then the heavy metal door clicked and Luis shoved it open.

They piled into a dark hallway. Katie turned on her penlight and shone it at the floor so they could see where they were going. Luis leaned into the door, shutting it, pressed down on the handle to lock it, then slammed a dead bolt into place. Moments later, Renie heard shouts and the rottweiller's barks outside the door. It sounded as if the dog attacked the door, leaping up against it, clawing it, trying to dig its way inside. Lucky squirmed out of Renie's arms and leaped to the floor. Instead of doing what a normal dog

would do—instead of attacking the door from the inside—
Lucky took off up the hallway, the rope slapping the floor.
She knew where she was going, Renie thought, and the four
of them followed her.

About two hundred yards later, the hall dead-ended. "It's
a trap," Logan whispered. "Christ, it's just a trap. How
could I be so stupid, so—"

"We were told to follow the dog," Luis snapped.

Lucky sniffed along the edge of the wall, her tail wagging,
and then she stopped and glanced at Katie, at Renie, and
barked. Renie and Katie crouched down and patted the wall,
looking for a handle, a knob, a control panel, anything. All
that stood between them and the guard and his lunatic dog
was the steel vault door—and the gun that Logan carried.
But if they got through the door and Logan shot the dog,
she would also have to shoot the guard and whoever else
he had recruited on his way over here. Not acceptable, Renie
thought, and moved her hands faster, with more pressure.

Suddenly, a section of the wall slid open, revealing an
open elevator. Renie looked at the others. "Well?"

The dog sniffed her way into the elevator. "Lucky thinks
it's safe," Katie said. "That's good enough for me."

The control panel in the elevator had only two buttons,
one green, the other red. "What the hell," Logan muttered,
and punched the green button.

The door slid shut and the elevator rose quickly, effort-
lessly. Fifteen seconds later, it opened into a comfortable
family room, replete with soft, recessed lighting, chairs and
couches and bookcases, a large-screen TV. "Is this the right
place, Luis?" Renie whispered.

"I've never seen this room."

"Great," Logan muttered. "That's just great."

"Hello," Katie called.

Her voice echoed strangely, bouncing off the windowless
walls, the high ceiling. They stood there, the four of them
and the dog, listening to those echoes, chilled by the empty

silence of the room. Then a loft area lit up and a voice called, "Ren? Katie?"

Sweet Christ. "Andy?"

He emerged into sight as he scrambled down the loft ladder. Behind him was another Invisible—Tyler, it had to be Tyler—and then a Visible appeared, a man Renie recognized from the marina, the man called Dobson, Nash's right hand. She didn't know what the hell was going on, what Dobson was doing here, but it no longer mattered. Andy's arms went around her, around Katie, the three of them pressed together so tightly that old mathematical axiom, *two against one,* ceased to exist.

2

The gun slipped out of her hand and clattered against the floor. Logan stared at Tyler, he stared at her, neither of them moved. She couldn't define the moment, it didn't fit anywhere in her template of experience for the last three years. It didn't fit, period.

He looked almost the same as he had looked the last time she'd seen him, thinner, perhaps, his body more compact and muscular, but otherwise physically unchanged. He seemed as uncertain as she was, just standing there, one more soul lost in the machinations of Nash's obsession and now struggling to find his way out.

"I . . . You . . ." he stammered.

"Ditto," she whispered, the last word she'd said to him that day three years ago.

"Logan."

When he said her name, she came undone inside. All of the walls she'd erected for the last three years came tumbling down, no more important than what she would eat tomorrow. Her body twitched, her feet uprooted themselves from the floor, and she moved toward him, biting at her lower lip, her heart opening and embracing him long before they actually reached each other.

3

Luis shut his eyes, sought the special place within himself, and felt a distinctive shift as he became fully visible again. Wayne Dobson, standing in front of him, just shook his head and smiled.

"I can't say that I'm surprised you're here, Luis."

"And since you're here without George, that means it's time to make things right."

"I couldn't agree more."

"Where is he?"

Dobson's smile shrank. "Dead. He died on the chopper, as an Invisible." From the pocket of his flight jacket, he brought out a crumpled sheet of paper. "The doc found this on him."

Luis took the sheet of paper, smoothed it open. He remembered writing this note, remembered mailing it. *One warrior to another* . . . He folded the sheet of paper, slipped it into his wallet. "Did he shroud willingly?"

Dobson nodded. "For reasons both selfish and altruistic. Farris called in the military and basically took over the complex. Invisibility was the only way we could get Andy and Tyler out. He also couldn't live with the pain in his leg anymore."

"Then he died as a warrior."

"Absolutely."

"And you, my friend? What will you do?"

"What I do best. Clean up the mess and get on with my life. We need to move fast. A chopper from the facility was following us. This room is secure, but we can't stay here indefinitely.''

So Luis got right to the point. "How do we reverse the shrouding?''

''I've never done it before and never saw George do it. But I know he experimented with small objects—pencils, a lighter, a pack of smokes, like that. He ran the shrouding process in reverse and had some successes, but not with anything living. He knew something was missing and more than once said he wished you were around to guide him.''

''So we can't guarantee them anything.''

''There were never any guarantees, Luis.''

A crushing despair clamped down over him. He couldn't do it, couldn't reverse what technology had done, couldn't because he didn't know how. The people whom he had adopted, the ones who had mastered ghosting, had never factored technology into the equation. Technology had nothing to do with any of it—how they lived, who they were, their ability to ghost. Technology belonged to the brightness in the cities, to the Internet cafés in Quito, to the TVs and radios in the mountain towns and villages where people dreamed of joining the Western world. Technology had never made it into the Oriente. It had never penetrated the jungle.

Once, years ago, when he was just a young initiate, a man from the city had been brought into the village by a twelve-year-old boy. The man was dying, he was in a coma, he had been bitten by a venomous snake, and the boy begged Consuelo to heal him.

Why? she had asked. Why should I heal him?

Because he saved my life, the boy had replied. Because some months before, the boy had gotten sick and wandered away from the village and ended up at the edge of a mining camp where the man had been working. The man had taken the boy in and nursed him back to health.

I owe him, the boy had told Consuelo, and so she healed him.

She had healed him without drugs, without technology, without so much as a doctor within several hundred miles. And the man had healed and after two or three years of living with the tribe, had returned to the Western world and had written a book about his experiences. He had revealed a lot about the tribe, but he'd refused to reveal its location, refused despite tremendous pressure from his publisher, from the press, from the Western anthropologists who wanted to study and dissect the tribe.

In many ways, George Nash had been Luis's equivalent of that man dying of the snakebite. And like that man, he had redeemed himself. Surely this deserved some effort on his part, no matter how futile or ridiculous.

"Where's the shrouding area?"

"We're standing in it."

"The entire room?"

"Except for the loft, where the control area is located. It's well shielded."

"And if it works, can we get them out through the roof? That's how you came in, right?"

"Yes, but it won't be safe now." Even as he said this, Luis heard shouts from the rooftop just above them. The other chopper had landed and Farris and his troops were looking for a way into the building. "There's another way out. George believed in redundancy, Luis. Good thing, too, otherwise the Invisibles wouldn't have a chance."

"And this whole project will be just one more cover-up?"

"I don't know. I think it depends on how we handle what we're doing right now."

But what do I *do?* Faced with the imponderable riddle of technology versus the indigenous ways, Luis scrambled through his memories, seeking something to bridge the two. Both shrouding and ghosting drew on the same electromagnetic energy to obtain the same results. But their methods differed. The shrouding process *changed* a person's electromagnetic field through a violent assault of electricity and sound. Ghosting molded and shaped that field so it merged with the qualities of the dominant element—air, water, metal, earth, even fire. Ghosting was more gentle—and therefore not permanent.

But the energy is the same. It always came back to that.

"When the equipment generates the electromagnetic field, is it possible to adjust the size of the field?" Luis asked.

"Sure. We did that all the time with the village out in the Glades. How large a field do you want?"

"I want it just large enough to accommodate myself and the Invisibles. If we move the chairs and couch into the middle of the room, the field should extend no more than six inches beyond the area where we are."

"Okay, what else?"

"Run the program for the shrouding, not for a reversal. The power should be about thirty percent of what you normally use." Luis hoped that would create an electromagnetic field powerful enough to enhance his own energy but not powerful enough to overwhelm him. "And you should increase it in increments of ten percent. We may have to go as high as fifty percent, but only if I tell you to and then only in the ten percent increments."

"You sure about this, Luis?"

"I'm not sure of anything," he replied.

Dobson and the others helped him move the chairs and the couch into the center of the room. Luis drew a circle on the floor with a pen that extended about six inches beyond the area, a sacred circle, that was how he thought of it, a symbol that both contained and protected. He and the others moved well away from the area while Dobson spent several minutes in the loft, testing the software and the equipment and experimenting with the parameters of the field.

When they were ready, the Invisibles took their places

within the circle Luis had drawn on the floor. Luis stepped into the circle with them, then ghosted.

4

Katie gritted her teeth against the humming and held on tightly to the dog. She could see Luis clearly now, standing in front of them, at the inner edge of the circle, his hands moving in large, sweeping arcs through the air, as though he were running his palms over the back of a large horse. His hands began to glow, a soft, pale glow at first, and then he moved them closer to the edge of the circle—closer to the *field*—and the air around them crackled and spat blue sparks.

The humming got a little louder, more intense. She felt it in her teeth now, in the back of her throat, deep inside her ears. Her mother tightened her grip on Katie's arm and her father, sitting on the other side of her, held on tightly to her hand. Now Luis turned and Katie saw that the crackling and the blue sparks were racing up his arms, around his head, down either side of his body, reaching clear to his feet and then under them. He looked as if he were inside a cocoon of crackling blue light and his body flickered between visibility and invisibility, one and then the other, faster and faster until she couldn't tell whether he was visible or not.

He moved toward the couch where she and the dog sat with her parents. His hands kept moving in those wide, sweeping circles, sometimes in one direction, sometimes in another, and sometimes they moved in opposite directions, one up and the other down. His body kept flickering. The humming leaped into a fever pitch and that drove spikes of pain through her skull. The scream that clawed at her throat never reached the air because he brought those crackling blue hands down close to her and her parents and something surged through her, something so powerful and strange that she would never have words for it.

The hair on her head stood straight up, pulling at the roots. Her skin seemed to come unfastened from her muscles and tendons and bones. Her heart hammered against her ribs, her nails felt as if they were being torn from her fingers and toes, and then the entire world burst with light.

5

The light. Renie was folded up inside the light, within an immense silence, a desert whiteness. Now a shape appeared in the whiteness and as it got closer, she saw that it was Buddha. Her father looked whole and healthy, his hair dark again, his eyes a vivid blue. She threw her arms around him, inhaled the scent of him, the faint aroma of cigars and the outdoors. She pulled back to look at him.

Am I dead, Dad?

He laughed and hooked his arm through hers. *Not at all. I'm always as close to you as this.*

The shrouding, he said, had changed them in fundamental ways and even when they became visible again, it might not hold all the time. There would be periods when they faded out, and during those times they would have tremendous freedom to explore areas of reality like the one they were in right now. Before the fades, there would be signs that, with practice, they would come to recognize.

So this place isn't real.

Of course it's real. Buddha stooped over and pulled out a handful of grass. There was grass everywhere, a continent of tall, emerald-colored grass that extended as far as she could see in every direction. He rubbed the blades between his fingers, let them fall, and Renie caught them. They felt real, smelled real. *Everything is real, Ren. Your world is right there. . . .* He opened his right arm and touched the air. *Another dimension is to my left. And just above our heads is yet another dimension. Invisibility has given you the ability to see these worlds, if you allow it. Embrace it.*

He touched his cool mouth to her forehead and she sprang to her feet in the room, air exploding from her mouth, and looked down at herself. Her body was solidifying, gathering greater clarity and dimension. *It worked, it worked, dear God, it worked. . . .* She spun and saw her daughter on her knees next to the dog, both of them gradually gaining in visibility. And there, slumped on the couch, was Andy, his body completely visible. Off to her left lay Luis, his body turning, and she realized that Logan and Tyler were still invisible and that one or both of them were turning Luis over.

When Renie ran over to him, to Luis, the air around Logan crackled and the hairs on Renie's arms stood up, as if from static electricity. "He's still alive. Let's loosen his clothes."

Luis's face was ashen, his clothes were soaked with sweat. His pulse, though weak, was steady. He coughed as Renie lifted his head and set it down gently on her thigh. His eyes opened slowly, as if the lids were weighted. And suddenly, Logan's body flickered into visibility and Renie saw her smooth, beautiful face, her short blond hair, and her large, dark eyes. Seconds, that was all it lasted before she flickered again and Renie could no longer see her.

"You're still materializing," Renie said.

"I don't think so." Tyler's voice came from her left, where a bottle of water seemed to be moving on its own through the air. "I think three years of invisibility is a lot to reverse."

"We can try again," Luis said softly, sitting up.

"Not now." Dobson hurried over to them, a cell phone in his hand. "We have to get out of here now. Can you walk, Luis?"

"Yes." He took a long drink from the bottle of water,

wiped his arm across his face, and they helped him to his feet. "I think so." He looked at Katie and the dog, at Andy. "It worked for them, so with time and practice, it can work for both of you as well."

"We'll see," said Logan. "Hold on to my arm, Luis."

Moments later, they followed Dobson out of the room.

5

For the first few minutes, Andy had trouble moving. His legs seemed to be out of synch with his brain. His ears rang. His stomach rumbled with hunger. He kept drinking in the sight of his wife, his daughter, and the dog that had started it all for them. He felt dizzy and exhausted, but not sick.

Once they were in the elevator, all of them crowded together, he could feel the crackling in the air around Logan and Tyler. Now and then, they turned visible, their bodies struck through with a crackling blue light, but once they were off the elevator and in a corridor, their moments of visibility had diminished considerably.

At the end of the corridor, they reached another vaultlike door that required the swipe of Dobson's ID card. They went inside, the door shut, and the space they were in began to move. Andy realized they were in yet another elevator.

"This will take us to the roof of another building," Dobson said. "The helicopter there will take you and your family, Andy, to a landing strip in the western part of the county. Your car is waiting there. Tomorrow, a statement will be issued that you weren't missing at all. You all rented a houseboat."

"The story's already in place?" Andy exclaimed.

"It will be by tomorrow." He handed Andy a business card. "I'll be in touch."

"Wait a goddamn minute," Tyler snapped. "You're Nash's lackey. You don't have the clout to do any of this."

"I covered my ass, made contacts, did what I had to do to make sure there was a way out if it came to this." He paused, looked at Andy. "That night you ... read me or whatever the hell it was you were doing ... all of it was right. That was when I made sure everything was in place."

"It wasn't soon enough to save my brother."

An expression of genuine sadness and pain seized Dobson's face. "Farris will pay for it, Doctor Townsend. I can promise you that much."

"What about us?" Logan asked.

"You're coming to Ecuador with me," Luis said.

"Take these, Luis." Dobson handed him a box of CDs that he slipped out of his jacket pocket. "I found this in the loft. The entire computer program and directions on how to build the coils and whatever else is needed. You can do whatever you want with it, Luis."

The old man slipped the box of CDs in his pocket.

"The chopper will let you, Tyler, and Logan off wherever you want."

Luis extended his hand and Dobson took it. "In the Quechua language, my friend, you are *Ali Shungu.* Good heart."

"Can you please open the door?" Katie asked, and reached over and picked up the dog. "It's kind of claustrophobic in here."

Dobson smiled then, a quick, genuine smile, a glimpse, Andy felt, of the inner man. "Sure thing."

With that, he pressed a button on the panel and the doors opened to the rooftop of the building. The warm night air rushed over him, around him, and Andy breathed it in and hurried toward the waiting chopper with the others. He settled in the backseat with his family and their new dog; then Dobson shut the chopper door, stepped back, and signaled for the pilot to take off.

When Andy glanced down, Dobson was still standing there, small and alone on the rooftop. Andy put one arm around Renie, the other around Katie, and rested his head against the seat and shut his eyes. The chopper flew on through the darkness.